P9-AQX-450

House of Mist

AND

The Shrouded Woman

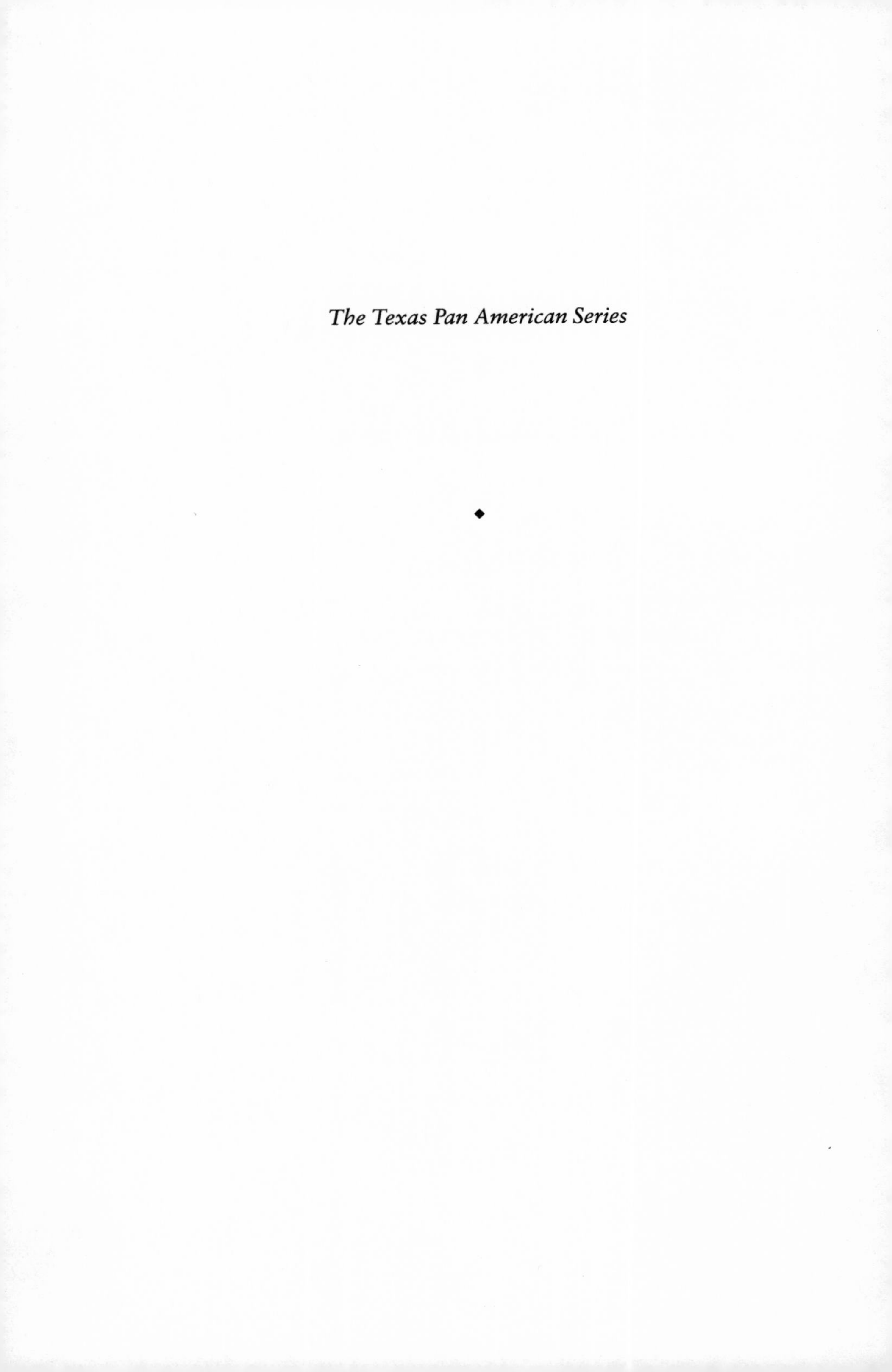

The Texas Pan American Series

◆

House of Mist

AND

The Shrouded Woman

◆

Two Novels by

MARÍA LUISA BOMBAL

Translated by the author

Foreword by Naomi Lindstrom

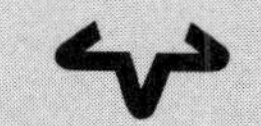

University of Texas Press
Austin

Printed in the United States of America

First University of Texas Press edition, 1995
Published by arrangement with Farrar, Straus & Giroux, Inc.

♾ The paper used in this publication meets the minimum requirements
of American National Standard for Information Sciences—
Permanence of Paper for Printed Library Materials, ANSI Z39.48-1984.

◆

LIBRARY OF CONGRESS CATALOGING-IN-PUBLICATION DATA

Bombal, María Luisa, 1910–
[Ultima niebla. English]
House of mist; and, The shrouded woman / by María Luisa Bombal ; translated by the author ; foreword by Naomi Lindstrom. — 1st ed.
p. cm. — (The Texas Pan American series)
Includes bibliographical references.
ISBN 0-292-70836-X (alk. paper) ISBN 0-292-70830-0 (pbk. : alk. paper)
1. Bombal, María Luisa, 1910– —Translations into English. I. Bombal, María Luisa, 1910–. Amortajada. English. II. Title. III. Title: House of mist. IV. Title: Shrouded woman. V. Series.
PQ8097.B67A22 1995
863 — dc20 94-27110

◆

CONTENTS

FOREWORD BY NAOMI LINDSTROM

The work of the Chilean novelist and short-story writer María Luisa Bombal (b. June 8, 1910; d. May 6, 1980) has been coming in for fresh attention and new readings. Successfully fusing fantastic elements and innovative construction with a critical vision of society, her fiction of the 1930s anticipated the magical realism that, in later decades, would fascinate an international public. Carlos Fuentes, one of the writers who won worldwide attention with a blend of the fantastic and a novelistic critique of society, has said, "María Luisa Bombal is the mother of us all."[1] At the same time that Bombal is receiving recognition as an early example of the great wave of innovation in the twentieth-century Spanish American novel, readers concerned with women's experience and status are also turning to her fiction.

Bombal spent her teen years in France, returning to Chile in 1931 after pursuing studies in French literature at the Sorbonne. In 1933 she moved to Buenos Aires, where she became part of the elite group of writers associated with the magazine *Sur* and its publishing house. The move to Argentina suited Bombal. The more conservative Chilean public tended to prefer realism. Buenos Aires readers, who had long had a taste for the fantastic, appreciated writers whose work summoned up fantastic, magic, and mythic forces. A number of authors in this experimental, antimimetic mode, such as Jorge Luis Borges, Pablo Neruda, and Bombal, were published and promoted by the literary matriarch who founded and presided over *Sur,* Victoria Ocampo.

In 1935, Bombal published the short lyrical novel *La última niebla.* It is a curious footnote to literary history that Bombal wrote this novel while sharing an apartment with Pablo Neruda and his wife; Neruda was also in a period of intense literary experimentation, composing portions of his poetic cycle *Residence on Earth.* Lucía Guerra Cunningham reports the two authors, simultaneously engaged in groundbreakingly original writing projects, "sharing the kitchen table."[2]

La última niebla is the basis of the lengthier work that Farrar, Straus published in 1947 as *House of Mist,* the text reprinted here. However, in the course of producing her own English version of her novel, Bombal felt free to make significant revisions and add entirely new segments. Readers of the English version may care to know that in the Spanish original the protagonist and her husband never achieve the belated rapprochement they enjoy in *House of Mist*. In *La última niebla,* the heroine, her lover, and her husband's dead wife are all anonymous; little is known of the latter two, and the lover may never have existed. The heroine's lengthy retrospective narration, filling the reader in on her birth and childhood and her husband's first marriage, occurs only in the English version. The allusions to folktales and the fairy-tale atmosphere are also unique to *House of Mist*.

The 1935 publication won the new author the respect of some important taste-setters. The influential Amado Alonso, in the opening and closing words of his 1936 essay "Emergence of a Novelist," emphasizes that *House of Mist* is an important work and that it and its author deserve widespread attention.[3] "Alone," the Chilean critic who long exercised the power to confer literary fame, drew attention to Bombal's work. In a 1982 retrospective summary, Borges noted critics' esteem for Bombal: "Today, in Santiago, Chile, or Buenos Aires, in Caracas or Lima, when they name the best names, María Luisa Bombal is never missing from the list."[4]

House of Mist is characteristic of Bombal's fiction in its focus on the intimate experience of a woman of the landowning class. Bombal's heroine is gifted—or burdened—with an extraordinary imagination and an empathetic bond with the natural world. At the same time, she is acutely conscious of the repression she endures in her social role. This combination of attributes allows the novel to be both a highly subjective, first-person account of intensely lived emotional experiences and an often bitter novelistic assessment of the situation of women in the Chilean landed aristocracy.

Bombal's well-to-do heroines have little necessary work to perform. They are the ladies of households where domestic work is left to servants, although the male landowners are often outdoors, actively engaged in the running of their haciendas. While the women are expected to provide their husbands with offspring, maids raise their children and, at times, treat their mistresses like children. The protagonist of *The Shrouded Woman* mentally reproaches her maid: "That Zoila, why had she brought her up to be so helpless? Why hadn't she even taught her how to do her own hair?" In *House of Mist,* the heroine's husband objects even to her passing time with the decorative art of embroidery. These women's idleness enhances their value as luxury possessions that help maintain the prestige of their fathers and husbands. The concept of dowry is still alive. The heroine of *The Shrouded Woman* may have been separated from her first love by his sisters' belief "that she, Ana Maria, would not have brought enough money to him, in fact only that small piece of land from her father's hacienda."

While well-married daughters and well-bred wives bring men status and wealth, a persistently unmarried woman or one whose husband is absent has no status. Helga's husband offers several unsubtle reminders of this circumstance. He often tells Helga that she is indebted to him for rescuing her from spinsterhood; to the Countess he says, "What do I care about your signature? It's of no use whatsoever on the contract. It's your husband's signature that's required."

Helga, the protagonist-narrator of *House of Mist,* typifies Bombal's heroines. She has a powerfully imaginative inner life and is able to decipher messages from the natural world. Still, her specialness is disregarded by most of those around her. Until the novel's closing pages, she is underappreciated by the man who controls her lot in life, and who prides himself on assessing matters by objective standards. The Bombal heroine preserves, into the rationalistic twentieth century, some of the qualities of the sorceress, divining woman, or nature goddess. She enjoys an exceptional attunement to the natural world, which often provides her with clues as to the course her life is taking. She finds in water and associated entities, as well as trees and earth, a plenitude of significance well beyond the objectively observable.

An example is the ominous opening scene of *House of Mist.* An uneasy bride arriving at her marital home, Helga finds that a winter mist has surrounded the house and befogged its windows—a realistically likely occurrence. But Helga's perceptions go further; she is certain that a tenacious humidity is pursuing her and turning on her in an actively hostile spirit: "It was at that moment that every evening the mist, knowing me to be at last defenseless, would begin the silent, perfidious siege of my being."

Bombal's *La amortajada*, published in 1938 by Sur, was awarded the Premio Municipal de Novela in Santiago de Chile. It appeared in 1948 as *The Shrouded Woman*, again in the author's own translation. In this case, the English version does not represent a drastic departure from the Spanish original.

The Shrouded Woman is known, above all, for its innovative treatment of narrative voice and point of view. It is principally dedicated to relaying the thoughts and memories of the protagonist, Ana Maria, as she spends the night at her own wake, is carried to the family crypt in the morning, and releases her individual personality to enter into the rhythms of the cosmos. Though lying dead at her wake, she is able to open her eyes enough to see the people who appear at her side to pay their respects. As significant figures from her past come into her field of vision, each unleashes a rush of memories. A third-person narrator often ushers in the heroine's discourse and narrates entire passages, though from Ana Maria's point of view. Yet the novel is most memorable for the shrouded woman's first-person reminiscences and comments.

Other voices make themselves heard in the novel. From time to time, a spirit calls to Ana Maria. This voice is that of a guide in the passage from life to death, encouraging her to release her hold on her living self. Fernando, a family friend who for years remained at the beck and call of the disdainful, already-married Ana Maria, also registers his inner voice in the narrative. His is an ambivalent discourse in which reproaches for Ana Maria's selfishness toward him commingle with expressions of continuing attachment. Near the end, a different voice, that of Ana Maria's longtime father confessor, offers a meditation on her life. The novel's closing passages narrate Ana Maria's experiences in her encrypted coffin. Seeking immersion in "the death of the dead," she allows herself to become part of a fluid, undifferentiated realm. Esther W. Nelson, inquiring "Who speaks in *The Shrouded Woman*?," raises the possibility that all the voices in the novel may be projections of Ana Maria's consciousness, and that she is intuiting the thoughts of others.[5]

Ana Maria retrospectively views her life almost exclusively as a set of personal ties. Her focus reflects the fact that, as a woman of the landed class, she had virtually nothing else to occupy her attention. During the scenes she remembers, Ana Maria appears doing no work more necessary than knitting and embroidery. In a posthumous insight, communicated by the narrator, Ana Maria considers the situation of men, "directing their passion to other things," while "The fate of so many women seems to be to turn over and over in their heart some love sorrow while sitting in a neatly ordered house, facing an unfinished tapestry."

Ana Maria draws some often bitter, reproachful, and remorseful conclusions about the way those in her circle have behaved toward her and one another. She perceives in the connections between them a general failure to benefit from the possibilities of true intimacy. Friendships, family bonds, and amorous relations are all marred by selfishness, oneupmanship, jealousy, and a self-defeating unwillingness to establish strong ties with others. Though perceiving flaws clearly, Ana Maria must also forgive them as part of letting go of life.

The heroine's ambiguous suspension between life and death is not the only element of myth and magic running through *The Shrouded Woman.* While Bombal often assigns empathetic powers to female protagonists, here the heroine's son, Fred, is gifted with a "sixth sense which linked him to the earth and to that which is secret." Fred, who appears to possess a language all his own, is able to receive communications from nature. The child's special powers come to the fore in the nightmarish scene of the disorienting carriage ride. The riders and horses, suddenly unable to recognize the countryside around them, panic. Fred saves them by reading a warning in a giant flower of ill omen.

The Shrouded Woman was the last new piece of long fiction from Bombal, who experienced enormous difficulty disciplining herself to write. Up to the end of the 1930s, she continued her career as a creative writer, authoring both filmscripts and short stories. In 1939, she published in *Sur* "Las islas nuevas" ("New Islands") and "El árbol" ("The Tree"), two stories to which critics have frequently returned. A less-noted piece of short fiction, "Trenzas" ("Braids"), appeared in *Saber Vivir* in 1940. "Lo secreto" ("The Unknown") appeared in a 1941 edition of *House of Mist.* All these stories appear, translated by Richard Cunningham and Lucía [Guerra] Cunningham, in the 1982 *New Islands and Other Stories.* "La historia de María Griselda" appeared without attracting much attention in 1946, and was rediscovered and republished in 1976. Readers who approach this story hoping for more of Bombal are disappointed to find that it repeats a considerable amount of material already utilized in *The Shrouded Woman.*

During the 1940s, 1950s, and 1960s, while married to Count Raphaël de Saint Phalle, Bombal lived in the United States. Her U.S. residence helps explain a curious circumstance. Bombal virtually ceased publishing new material and concentrated upon reworking her great successes in English. During her last years, many of her followers heard that she was struggling to finish a novel, said to be entitled *El embrujo* ("The magic spell"). She was also reported to have written English-language plays, short stories in Spanish, and essays. There is no reliable, complete inventory of her unpublished work. According to Isabel Velasco, Bombal left an unfinished novel and many other unpublished works in various stages of completion; they are in a bank vault, and access to them is controlled by her daughter.[6]

Bombal's fame is that of a writer exceptionally able to convey an empathy with magic and mythic forces. Followers of fantastic writing and literary critics with an archetypal approach have always been drawn to her writing. Since the mid-1970s, she has also won an audience concerned with her representation of the haute-bourgeoise woman and her circumstances. Bombal's narrative also extends its appeal to readers who enjoy absorption in stories filled with mysterious symbols, inexplicable happenings, and a general air of myth and magic.

Notes

1. Carlos Fuentes, cited in Lucía Guerra Cunningham, "María Luisa Bombal," in Diane E. Marting, ed., *Spanish American Women Writers: A Bio-Bibliographical Source Book* (Westport, Ct.: Greenwood Press, 1990), p. 42.

2. Ibid., p. 42.

3. Amado Alonso, "Aparición de una novelista," *Nosotros* (Buenos Aires), No. 3 (June 1936), 241–256.

4. Jorge Luis Borges, "Preface," María Luisa Bombal, *New Islands and Other Stories*, trans. Richard and Lucía Cunningham (New York: Farrar, Straus, Giroux, 1982), unpaginated.

5. Esther W. Nelson, "Un viaje fantástico: ¿Quién habla en *La amortajada*?," in Marjorie Agosín et al., eds., *María Luisa Bombal: Apreciaciones críticas* (Tempe, Az.: Bilingual Press/Editorial Bilingüe, 1987), p. 185. Nelson, p. 198, concludes that the narrator of *The Shrouded Woman* can never be unambiguously identified.

6. Isabel Velasco, "Algo sobre María Luisa Bombal," in Agosín et al., eds., *María Luisa Bombal*, p. 21.

◆

House of Mist

To my husband, who has helped me
to write this book in English

◆

◆

PROLOGUE

I wish to inform the reader that even though this is a mystery, it is a mystery without murder.

He will not find here any corpse, any detective; he will not even find a murder trial, for the simple reason that there will be no murderer.

There will be no murderer and no murder, yet there will be . . . crime.

And there will be fear.

Those for whom fear has an attraction; those who are interested in the mysterious life people live in their dreams during sleep; those who believe that the dead are not really dead; those who are afraid of the fog and of their own hearts . . . they will perhaps enjoy going back to the early days of this century and entering into the strange house of mist that a young woman, very much like all other women, built for herself at the southern end of South America.

◆

PART

One

◆

ONE

The story I am about to tell is the story of my life. It begins where other stories usually end; I mean, it begins with a wedding, a really strange wedding, my own.

I shall never forget that dark, empty church in the early morning, the vacillating light of the oil lamps on the altar and myself in a pathetic black dress. Only the little bunch of artificial orange blossoms pinned to the bodice of my dress by the good nurse who had brought me up, made me look like a bride. The sacred rites of the marriage ceremony were pronounced so hastily by a priest seemingly so indifferent that Daniel and I found ourselves made man and wife without having even realized just at what moment we had said the word yes. Then came our exit through a side door with our two witnesses: the judge and his clerk, in place of an escort.

I remember, once we were outside the church, how the sight of my miserable little trunk laid on the front of the carriage which was to take us to the railroad station had suddenly made me feel quite ashamed. I remember that long train, moving heavily, always and ever toward the South, across plains and between hills; then finally that other solitary station, lost there in the desolate countryside, where we were the only ones to get off.

A little peasant, hardly more than a child, was waiting for us with horses and carriage. For an instant amazement seemed to nail him to the ground as Daniel ordered stiffly:

"Open the door and help your new lady, Andrés!"

The last stage of our journey to the hacienda was made in an awkward carriage both luxurious and old-fashioned. Hours seemed to pass until at last I heard Daniel say:

"We are arriving. Here comes the mist."

From the end of the horizon, where the big forests were beginning to spread out and across the dreary brown plain where giant brambles stood motionless, crouched in the shadows like huge, frightened beasts, the mist was actually pushing forward to meet the carriage.

At first its early clouds seemed to float lazily around, dimming the windowpanes; then the horses entered knee-deep into the soft flaky waves it was unfurling in front of them as if out of the ground itself. Finally, horses and carriage plunged entirely into a silent world where the mist stood still, suspended in space, in rows of impalpable curtains.

I hid my face on my husband's shoulder.

"I'm so happy!" I said.

But Daniel remained unmoved, distant, indifferent to the weight of my loving head on his heart, while the carriage went forward into the mist. And as I lay close to this tall, taciturn, handsome young man who was now my husband, all at once came back to me the strange past by which we were now bound together to share the same house and the same destiny . . .

◆

TWO

"What are you doing in my garden?"

I could see myself leaning over the curbstone of an abandoned well looking up amazed to find standing before me a boy with rough, curly, brown hair and eyes of an intense chestnut color: Daniel at the age of twelve. He was so big and so strong that all of a sudden I felt very small, much smaller than I actually was for my seven years.

"Your garden!" I repeated, astounded.

To my mind the vast, abandoned, bramble-filled garden which extended all around us was a forest. The word "garden" I thought could be applied only to the carefully tended lawns like those around the house next door, my uncle's house where I was living.

"Which way did you come in?" the boy asked.

I pointed broadly at the widely spaced bars of the gate, covered with growing vines, which separated the two estates, but I was unable to explain that ever since I could remember I had been coming through those bars without ever having found a living soul in the forest.

"And what were you doing there leaning over this well?" he continued harshly.

Terrified—that strange boy looked exactly like the enchanted Bear in my fairy tales—I answered shyly:

"I was looking for the Prince."

"What Prince?"

"Prince Toad. The one who has a small golden crown on top

of his head. Help me pull up this pail! Maybe he's inside of it," I added hurriedly, thinking in my fright that if I found the Prince there, he might protect me from the anger of the Bear.

But the Bear now looked astonished and quite friendly.

"Tell me, little idiot, how do you know that kind of a toad exists?"

"Because I read about him in my books."

"In what books?"

"In the storybooks my mother left me."

"Is your mother dead?" he asked brutally, as if he were enjoying it.

"Yes, and my father is too. I'm an orphan," I explained in a low voice, almost ashamed.

"So am I," the boy said simply.

I looked at him, surprised and relieved.

"You're not the Bear then?"

"What Bear?"

"The one in the stories, the one who is Master of the Forest."

"How silly! Of course I'm not a Bear," he said crossly, "and besides this is not a forest, it's my garden, the garden of the house my parents left me. They left books to you, didn't they? Well to me they left this house and this garden. Do you understand?"

"Yes . . . so you're an orphan too!" I exclaimed delighted, suddenly realizing there could be other orphans in the world besides myself.

"That's it. That's it! Now let's look for . . . that Prince," he interrupted, cutting short abruptly the flow of my joy.

The chain of the old well was rusty, and we had to work a long time before we succeeded in pulling up a pail filled with mud.

"Here he is!" my companion cried, plunging his fingers inside the pail. "Here he is! I have him, your Prince!"

Alas, it was only a frog.

"Tell me, little idiot, I don't see any golden crown on his head . . ."

"Because it isn't the Prince . . . but still, that little frog looks very pretty. . . . See, it doesn't have a gold crown, but has eyes with gold on them, look at it."

"You're making fun of me!" Daniel cried, throwing the poor beast savagely into the brambles.

"Oh . . . you're mean!" I stammered, my eyes filled with tears.

"Of course I'm mean!" he replied violently. "Didn't you say I was a Bear?" He hurled himself upon me. And in no time, I found myself lifted from the ground and swept away in a wild race around the trees. Scared and unsteady on the shoulders of the Bear, I held on to his hair. He dropped me to the ground, with a cry of pain.

"You nasty brat!" he moved away angrily.

"Come back, Bear, come back, don't be angry, let's play again," I pleaded.

"No, I won't. You're afraid, just like all other girls."

"I won't be any more, not any more, I promise. Be the Bear again, just once, it's fun!"

"Well, perhaps tomorrow. Now it's time for me to go to school."

"Don't go."

"You're crazy, I must go. It's only because I have to go to school that I came to live in this house. Otherwise I'd have stayed at the hacienda with my uncle."

"So you have an uncle too!"

"Of course. My Uncle Manuel. He is my uncle, my godfather and guardian all at the same time, and he says that he will leave all his haciendas to me when he dies. Then I will supervise the mills and ride horseback all day, hop! hop! hop! And you," he suddenly spoke out again, cutting short his own effervescence, "don't you go to school too?"

"No."

"I see, you're too small."

"I'm almost eight," I retorted, smarting.

"Then if you don't go, it's because you're lazy."

"No, I can't go because I'm an orphan," I declared gravely.

"Well, that's funny! My sister, who is an orphan just like you, has been going to school for a long time. Uncle Manuel sent her to school in Europe. Tell me, little idiot, I'll bet you don't even know where Europe is . . ."

◆

THREE

"Aunt Mercedes, I'd like to go to school with Teresa."

Teresa was my cousin and the only daughter of Aunt Mercedes and Uncle Arturo, my guardians.

"Don't you know that little girls who are orphans never go to school?"

"But why?"

"Because . . . that's the way things are. Please don't sit on my lap. You interfere with my knitting."

"But, Aunt Mercedes, the sister of the big boy next door is an orphan like me, and she goes to school. The boy himself told me that their Uncle Manuel sends her to school far away in Europe."

"Arturo, do you hear what the child is saying? It seems that Manuel Viana has decided after all to spend a few pennies on the education of his niece."

"Why yes, he sends the girl to school abroad and the boy to school here," I yelled at the top of my voice. "And if they go to school and are orphans like me, why can't I go to school too, Aunt Mercedes?"

"Because in your case it's different."

"But why is it different?"

"You'll know all about it some day when you're grown-up. But, for the present, I must ask you to go look for Mamita and tell her never to let you come in the drawing room when you're just back from playing in the garden next door. Look at your shoes all covered with mud, and my poor carpet . . ."

You'll know all about it when you're grown-up. Those words, coming back at me in almost everything that concerned me, appeared to be the most serious drawback to being an orphan.

"I'd like to take piano lessons like Teresa."

"It's not possible."

"Why?"

"You'll know some day when you're grown-up."

"I'd like to go to the fancy dress party with Teresa."

"You're not invited."

"Why?"

"Because that's the way it is. You'll understand later when you're grown-up."

"I'd like to have a picture of my mother."

"Doesn't your father's picture satisfy you?"

"Why yes, Aunt Mercedes, of course I like the picture of my father! I'm glad to know my father was so handsome, so blond, and that his eyes had such a kind look, but . . . I should also very much like to know how my mother looked."

"She was a brunette like you, and she had very dark eyes, just like yours."

"Did you know her, Aunt Mercedes?"

"Good gracious, no! But everybody says that was the way she looked."

"Would you let me see her picture, Aunt Mercedes?"

"Impossible! We haven't got a single picture of her in the family."

"But why?"

"Well, it will be explained to you when you're grown-up."

My Aunt's frivolous, reproachful, and always hostile attitude towards me did not make me particularly unhappy; nor did the selfishness of my little cousin who was never willing to play with me; nor even the lack of affection shown me by Uncle Arturo who ignored me completely, except when once in a while he gave me a slightly embarrassed look as if he felt ashamed to have under his roof the orphan daughter of his own brother.

To compensate for all this indifference, however, I had the steady and tender love of Mamita, the good nurse in whose care I was placed when, as an orphan five years old, I was brought from the capital to this house in a far-off southern town. I also had the storybooks left me by my mother from which a teacher, coming especially for me, had taught me to read. Then there were the linen room, the laundry, the kitchen, the hothouses and the stables to amuse myself in; all very exciting places where something always seemed to be happening.

But above all, above all, from the day when the recollection of my sad childhood begins, in the bushy garden at the house next door I had the intermittent, capricious friendship of a big chestnut-colored bear.

◆

FOUR

"Helga! So your name is Helga! What a funny name!"

"It's the name of the daughter of the Marsh King and of an Egyptian Princess."

"Not really!"

"Yes, and their story is in my books. Imagine! One day the Princess was sitting on the shore of a kind of lake in the middle of the bog when suddenly she saw a stump turn around and stretch out its long miry branches like arms. It was the Marsh King himself who lives in the bog . . ."

"Oh, no!"

"Terrified, the poor Princess sprang away into the shaking quagmire and she sank at once and the alder stump after her; it was dragging her down . . . Isn't it frightening?"

"Yes, very frightening. But tell me, didn't you make up all those silly tales yourself?"

"Of course not. That story's from one of my books and it isn't a silly tale. Every one of the things that is told in my storybooks happened once upon a time."

"Well, then why don't they happen any more? Why haven't we ever found your Prince Toad, for instance?"

"We will find him after a while, if we are patient."

"But I'm tired of running after him and tired of waiting for the appearance of that famous Fairy with hair as blond as wheat and eyes as blue as sapphires . . . Listen, do you hear? Somebody is playing the piano at your house."

"That's my cousin. She began taking her lessons at home yesterday. If you want to come into our garden, we'll look at her through the windows of the veranda and we'll watch her doing her practicing."

"Let's," Daniel magnanimously acquiesced, and . . .

"Look, look," he exclaimed five minutes later, his forehead glued to the windowpane of the veranda. "It's the Fairy!"

"Who?"

"Your cousin! She's the Fairy, she has hair as blond as wheat and eyes as blue as sapphires. How beautiful she is, oh my, how beautiful!"

Yes, little Teresa was indeed beautiful. And she became more and more beautiful as she grew up. Her deep blue eyes livened up with gold spangles; her light blond hair turned into molten gold and her delicate complexion acquired a warm golden hue. So thus resplendent in the midst of others she seemed always enfolded and held in a ray of sunlight.

Teresa! Her parents were infatuated with her, people on the street stopped to watch her go by, and, as for me, I became almost silly with excitement whenever she condescended to ask me to turn the pages of her music while she was playing the piano.

There was nothing indeed that Teresa could do except play the piano and look beautiful. Yet somehow I felt that to be so beautiful might be the one task assigned by God to certain people; their beauty some kind of a message or mission from Him that they must carry. And thus to me, Teresa, so slim, harmonious, and golden, was like a spring, a cool, babbling spring close to which one felt a great contentment and a great desire to be good.

◆

FIVE

From the moment he saw her through the windows of the veranda, Teresa became the object of Daniel's admiration and purest passion.

I did not feel jealous of her, no, quite the contrary! Daniel's love for Teresa made my friendship absolutely indispensable to him for I was the only one who could from day to day give him an accurate report of everything concerning her. Thus that love became the big secret shared between us and it was to unite us for many years in lengthy conversations and in plans elaborately prepared, even though they always seemed to go amiss through Daniel's cowardice.

So many times it happened that on the day Teresa was to carry her big dictionaries to school, Daniel as he saw her coming would quickly vanish instead of offering her his help, as I had suggested he should do! Once he stupidly remained hidden behind the big rhododendron where I had succeeded in dragging my cousin that he might unexpectedly appear and throw himself at her feet to present to her as a gift the pearl cuff link he had stolen from Uncle Manuel.

"But, Daniel, why? After this had all been arranged, why didn't you do it?"

"Because . . . I don't know what happened to me. Because maybe I'm just a wild country boy. And I'll always be wild . . . like Uncle Manuel . . . That's what he tells me himself . . . That's what the principal at school tells me. . . ."

And as it turned out both Uncle Manuel and the principal were quite right in their expectations.

◆

SIX

"Poor Judge Rivas! Manuel Viana did him a very poor turn when he gave him the guardianship of his nephew and niece," I can still hear Aunt Mercedes a few years later saying in her high-pitched voice. "Imagine, Arturo, Señora Rivas was telling me that the boy did not want to go back to college after the death of his uncle. That he's living at the hacienda wearing spurs or sandals like a peasant; that he is a hard worker but a miser as exacting as his uncle was, the only difference being that Manuel Viana was saving his money so that he could waste it on his famous collection of books and rugs now rotting away in the mist at the hacienda, whereas the boy only saves to buy more and more land. They say that his woods, his lands, are like a mania with him. It seems he has even bought from his sister a large part of the lands she inherited under the will. And, by the way, Arturo, do you know that they do not get along at all even though they're twins? Señora Rivas told me that the Judge tried in vain to make him go to Europe to attend the wedding of his sister who married a count. It seems that the boy refused to go because, he said, the man was marrying his sister for her money. Just as if a real count could ever marry the little Viana girl for anything but her money!"

"But, Aunt Mercedes, she's very pretty, she dresses well and dances beautifully. Daniel himself told me so . . ."

"Well, that's fantastic! Anyway what do you think of a boy of seventeen whose best friend is a child of twelve like Helga? Wouldn't you say, Arturo, that the boy is slightly backward?"

At that point Uncle Arturo, instead of answering, gave her one of those frigid glances that automatically made her stop the flow of her commentaries and turn upon anyone unfortunate enough to be close to her.

"Go to bed, Helga! Who gave you permission to stay up so late these last few days?"

"But Auntie, you know I prefer to go up at the same time as Teresa. I like so much to help her fix her hair for the night. Don't you want me to help you brush your hair and make up your braids, Teresa?"

"Certainly," Teresa answered mechanically, with her usual adorable and distant smile . . .

◆

SEVEN

"Daniel, do you know that last night Teresa let me help her brush her hair again? If you could only see her hair when it's undone! Oh Daniel, it's like a golden shower! And soft, soft to the touch as if it were made of silk!"

"Really!" Daniel whispered.

"Besides, you know, when it has been carefully brushed, it's made up into two long braids. And they are heavy and slippery, like two beautiful snakes. I'm sure that if they were cut off, they would still keep alive by themselves."

"That's it!" Daniel cried so unexpectedly that it startled me. "Helga," he added, and he took hold of my wrist, "Helga, tell me, do you love me?"

"Of course! But don't hold my arm so tightly, you're hurting me."

"Helga, if it's true that you love me, tonight you will take the big scissors that are kept in your aunt's workbox, the ones you were forbidden to use to cut out your pictures, do you remember? And with them you will cut off Teresa's braids."

"Cut off Teresa's braids!" I exclaimed, horrified, in the same tone as I might have said: "Cut off Teresa's head!"

"Yes, and you'll bring them here to me. Then I'll be able to touch them and hold them as you do and it will be almost as if I had Teresa with me always, everywhere, all the time! Helga, would you do that for me?"

"Oh no! I never could! Oh, Daniel, I . . ."

"Listen to me. It's very easy. First, you steal the scissors during the day. Then, at night while Teresa is asleep, you quickly cut off one braid with a big sweep of the scissors. After all, one is enough for me! Then you run to your room, hide it under your pillow, pretend to be asleep and bring it to me here next morning, hidden under your apron. Now, do you understand? You see, it's really quite easy."

"Yes, but when Teresa wakes up and sees . . ."

"She won't know who did it."

"And if she wakes up while I . . ."

"Just do it quickly. One stroke of the scissors, and you run! In the dark she won't be able to notice who did it."

"Oh, Daniel! I never could!" I said to him the next day. "I went as far as to steal the scissors, and here they are. But never, never, will I dare to cut Teresa's beautiful hair. Oh Daniel, couldn't you take my braids instead? I will cut them off right here for you, if you like."

Daniel gave a short contemptuous laugh.

"*Your* braids! What would I do with your braids? I don't like black hair anyway. Besides, you're not the one I'm in love with, it's Teresa."

"I know. But, Daniel," I continued imploringly, "you know I could never do that, it's not right!"

"You will do it for me, if you love me."

"I do love you, but . . ."

"No, you don't love me. The very first time I ask you to do something for me, you're not willing to do it. After all, a friendship with a girl is never any use. I'm disgusted with you, that's all. Goodbye."

"No, no!" I moaned, trying to hold him back through the bars of the gate, where most of our meetings took place.

"Let me go. I don't want ever to see you again."

"No, no! I'll do what you want but don't get angry, don't leave me, please, Daniel."

"You'll do it this evening then, will you? This very evening, so that I can take the braid with me to the hacienda. I'm going there tomorrow. It's promised then, is it?"

With dry throat, and eyes filled with tears, I nodded in panic. Then leaning over to my cheek, across the bars, Daniel kissed me for the first time.

"You're brave, Helga," he said, "as brave as a boy."

◆

EIGHT

It was both that kiss and that declaration which held up my faltering steps as I went to Teresa's room that evening. They gave my trembling hands the strength to accomplish the act which was to change the course of my life . . .

Teresa was asleep. With one breath, I blew out the night lamp on her side table. Then, leaning over the bed, I searched with my hand among the pillows and, finally taking hold of one of her braids, I slipped the scissors close to the roots of the hair.

But alas, I was very soon to realize that it was quite impossible to cut a thick braid with a single quick stroke of the scissors. The hair kept slipping between the blades and the work was progressing very slowly. Teresa began to toss about. I stopped cutting. My heart was throbbing. When I forced myself to go on, I did it so clumsily that I pricked her in the neck with the point of the scissors. She came half awake then and drawing herself up, stretched out her hands in the dark.

At that moment I lost my head. Wildly I made up my mind to complete the job all at once, and throwing myself on Teresa, I began to cut as best I could while she, now fully awake, started to scream loudly enough to awaken an entire city.

I was lost! I knew it immediately and did not even attempt to escape. And thus it was, they found me standing in my long nightgown at the head of Teresa's bed, shaking like a leaf. My right hand was still clutching the big scissors, and from my left hand, tightly held, hung long tufts of blond hair while my cousin, dishevelled, cheek bleeding, was screaming like Mateo and Tadeo, our favorite little pigs we had once heard being killed . . .

◆

NINE

"A monster! Jealousy! Depraved mentality! Bad natural instincts! Later she'll want not only to disfigure her cousin but perhaps also to kill her! It might be necessary to send her away forever! Oh God, what can be done with this unfortunate child? She's too young to be locked up! But in any case, we must get in touch with Adelaida. After all, she's your older sister, Arturo. And the child is as much her niece as yours. She certainly should look after her now. Besides, Adelaida lives alone, she's no longer a young girl and should not forever dodge her responsibilities . . ."

Those were the comments I overheard from my room where I was kept locked up like a dangerous beast.

"The reason, unfortunate child! Tell us the reason that made you do such a thing! Please answer! Say something! Did you really hate your little cousin without saying a word about it . . . just because she is prettier than you are? Why don't you answer? Won't you please answer? Really, it's enough to drive one mad. She won't answer! She keeps silent all the time, Doctor. And she doesn't even cry, Doctor, just like a criminal, like the most hardened criminal."

Yes, I remained heroically silent regarding the motive of my offense. I did not even confess it to Mamita, for I was afraid that in order to exonerate me, she might repeat everything to my aunt.

But whenever I found myself alone, I would run to the window to take a look through the trees at Daniel's window. Any kind of a sign from him would have been all I needed to make me understand that he knew I had tried to fulfill my promise to him.

But his window remained closed and dark and I never found out whether or not he understood. For one morning at dawn a carriage drove Mamita and me to the railroad station. From there Uncle Arturo shipped us away to the big city where I was born and where Aunt Adelaida was henceforth to assume full charge of my troublesome little person.

◆

TEN

Yes, Aunt Adelaida, the only sister of my father and Uncle Arturo, was no longer a young girl, as Aunt Mercedes had so loudly proclaimed. She was, and probably had been for a long time, just an old maid.

It was now from Aunt Adelaida that I learned Aunt Mercedes was no more than a silly, plebeian, provincial girl whom Uncle Arturo had been foolish enough to marry for her good looks, long since vanished, and for her fortune, which he had thrown away at the gaming tables. Nevertheless, he had remained a prisoner of that marriage to a person of a lower class. For Aunt Adelaida emphasized that he *had* married a person of a lower class. Yes, she, Adelaida, had suffered a great deal on account of her brothers. And in order that I might appreciate the full extent of her kindness to me, I should know that it was on account of them that she had remained a spinster. For when she was a young girl, of an aristocratic and wealthy family, she could at the time she made her debut have married anyone she wanted. But her parents had died very soon afterwards, and later on her two brothers had ruined her: Uncle Arturo financially by squandering all the family fortune at gambling; and my father socially by the terrible scandal of which I would be told "when you are grown-up" . . .

"The poor dear lady!" Mamita would sigh. "It is indeed fortunate that God gave her so many excuses to deceive herself. If it had not been for her brothers' folly, no doubt by looking at herself in the mirror she might have understood why nobody ever wanted to marry her."

Bursts of laughter from the two servants resounded, followed by an abrupt silence when the steps of the "poor dear lady" were heard.

"Quiet! Be careful! She is making her daily round," they warned. "When she is not walking around with a broom in her hand, she is flying seated on top of it," they added, chuckling like two schoolgirls.

And even though it seemed terrible, one had to admit that poor Aunt Adelaida, so very long and thin, with her big colorless eyes staring into space, with her profile like a bird of prey, was indeed the striking image of one of the witches in my books.

Happily, she made use of her time in a manner entirely different from a witch.

Aunt Adelaida spent her mornings in church and her afternoons in bed, suffering from the same heart ailment which had been fatal to my father. Her unsatisfactory state of health, however, did not prevent her from receiving a large company of people who talked, intrigued, and gossiped while they drank tea around the large silver brazier standing close to her bed.

Only when everybody else had gone and her two oldest friends remained with her, was I called in and allowed to take my place near the brazier with my embroidery. For my aunt had made up her mind that I should learn to sew and to embroider as a means of earning my living later on. "Considering that this child cannot possibly ever think of getting married," she would say, "Mother Maria de los Angeles has promised me to take her in the linen room of the convent."

One day, however, I ventured to mention that I would like so much to be able to play the piano. A horrified response from my aunt cut short my suggestion.

"Well, that would be the last straw! You, an artist!"

And so it happened that learning to sew and to embroider became very soon the main object of my course of studies at the convent, where, to my keen disappointment, I was never allowed to join with other children in the classes but instead was given only private instruction.

This strange isolation, the reason for which was to be explained . . . "later when you are grown-up," did not in any way hinder the flight of my imagination nor my passionate love of life.

I enjoyed my embroidery very much and I liked having people go into ecstasies over the perfection and the elegance of my work. But since Mamita, who was suffering from rheumatism, had to go back to her province, and I had to sleep alone in one of the wings of the enormous old house, it was with the people of my fairy tales and in their world that I found shelter during the night.

What a glorious achievement it would be for humanity to understand that each one of us has within himself a well into which he can descend during sleep and by means of which he can escape into infinity! For was not God himself standing at the top of the holy ladder of light with angels moving up and down when Jacob reached the bottom of it during his sleep?

Actually it was deep down in the magic countries of my storybooks that my own well descended and far into them that it led me:

Soon after I had fallen asleep, I usually found myself in a dark forest where I never failed to take the lost path that came out at the grotto where the good Princess Eliza was knitting with her poor bruised hands the twelve tunics of nettle which were to give back their human forms to the twelve swans, her brothers.

Or else I was among the five little sirens, sisters of the one who fell in love with a young prince of the earth and gave up her palace of pearls, her beautiful algae-colored tail, and her enchanting voice, so as to be able to live with him. During the night when all in her earthly palace was at rest, the poor little mermaid would come walking down the marble steps to cool her tiny burning feet in the deep waters of the sea. Her sisters would then swim up to the spot in order to sing for her. And I was there singing with them.

At other times, the moment I fell asleep I would find myself among a great throng of people gathered on the principal street in a city of the Middle Ages, looking in wonderment at the retinue of the Princess Cruel as she went by. Twelve fair young girls, each clad in a white silk robe and bearing a golden tulip in her hand, rode on coal-black steeds before or beside her; the Princess herself had a snow-white palfrey, the gold crown that pressed her rich dark tresses seemed made of stars, and the light gauzelike mantle that robed her shoulders was composed of many thousand various-hued butterfly wings. And she was so beautiful that forgetting how cruel she was, the crowd cheered her wildly as she passed by, and I would cheer with the crowd.

Quite often I found myself gliding over vast steppes in the great white sleigh of the terrible Snow Queen, with Kay, the handsome young man whom she had stolen from his fiancée, sitting by my side. And it happened that Kay resembled Daniel in a striking manner. And, because Kay was so much like Daniel, that silent and frozen world in which the Snow Queen took us driving was the world into which I preferred to descend during my sleep.

For the memory of Daniel was growing in me day after day instead of receding. At first it brought me regret, then it was my haven in loneliness. Gradually it changed into my dream of every day, becoming later my only source of happiness.

From that time on, my unconscious sentiment for him grew into conscious and passionate love. Daniel was now my own sweet secret. It was his name I wrote on the windowpanes that the early winter frosts tarnished; his name I silently called three times whenever I saw a shooting star fall in the star-swarming skies at summertime. And no longer did I feel afraid of the future, for suddenly I decided that sooner or later Daniel must come to take me away, no matter what might be the mystery overshadowing my life.

That mystery, as a matter of fact, was going to be unexpectedly cleared up long before the time when I was "grown-up."

◆

ELEVEN

It happened late one afternoon, as the rain was falling hard upon the roofs of the town.

I was sewing in my aunt's room while she dozed, very much disappointed at not having had a single visitor all day, when the doorbell sounded downstairs.

My aunt straightened herself up on her pillows and tried to figure out who could be brave enough to call on her in the rain so late in the afternoon.

Suddenly we heard a frightened cry from the maid who had gone down to open the front door and someone coming up the stairs in a great hurry. Almost immediately a woman was there standing motionless and haughty on the threshold.

She was a tall, very slender woman dressed all in black. From behind a thin veil her cold gray eyes were staring hard at me.

"Good evening, Elena," I heard my aunt say at last in a halting voice.

Without even condescending to answer her, the tall woman walked up to me, the picture of a beautiful, threatening archangel, and I felt her long, gloved hand coming down with crushing force on my shoulder.

"So you are Enrique's daughter?" she asked in a voice hoarse and trembling. I remained silent while she turned to my aunt.

"So, Adelaida, what I was told, yet could not believe was true! You have actually taken the illegitimate daughter of your brother into your home and were hiding it from me!"

"Go away, Helga," my aunt commanded me.

But I was not able to obey her, for the hand of the stranger was pressing more and more heavily on my shoulder.

"You are making a fool of me and everybody knows it, Adelaida. You are deceiving me with the same cruelty with which your brother deceived me all through his life! You—"

"We have had enough of drama, Elena!" interrupted my aunt. "I did everything I could in order not to hurt your feelings. But I was wrong. I should have said in the first place that this child is the daughter of my brother and that I owe her a minimum of protection."

"And to me! To me, the legitimate wife of your brother. To me, your sister-in-law and your childhood friend, don't you owe a minimum of respect?" the stranger suddenly burst out. "Do you think you should have done me the indignity of taking under your roof the daughter of the woman for whom my husband publicly ridiculed and forsook me . . ."

And as her hand at last loosened its grip on my shoulder, my father's wife almost collapsed on the carpet, sobbing hysterically.

Her smart little hat slipped back on her head. I noticed then that she had gray hair and a faded complexion, and that notwithstanding her delicate profile and slender waist, she was almost an old woman.

"Helga, go away, go away, I tell you!" Aunt Adelaida shouted at me, finally making up her mind to jump out of bed in order to assist her sister-in-law . . .

However, when she called me back to her room a few hours later, she was once more in bed looking so pale and tired that I realized at last her heart disease was quite real and not a comedy as most people were saying behind her back.

"Sit down, Helga. God only knows how many times I have put off this moment, always fearful that you might be too young to learn the circumstances of your birth. But, considering what you have heard this afternoon, I feel it is my duty to tell you now, this very evening, the sad story of your parents."

However, the story of my parents was not sad.

It was the love story of a young bride, the wife of a Danish shipowner on a visit to this country, and of a young man, like many others, sentimental and socially prominent.

They met at a ball and fell madly in love with each other.

The husband went back to Europe, but, to the great scandal of the entire city, his young wife remained here in a lovely secluded house enclosed in a big park, waiting by night and by day for the visits, always too brief, of the man she adored and who shared her love, yet had not separated from his wife.

For Elena, it seems, had tried to poison herself when my father told her he wanted to leave her. Then never having fully recovered, she had almost lost her mind. And that is how my father had come to pledge to himself that he would never forsake her.

In the meantime, a little girl was born to the young foreigner and she was given the name of Helga. Afterwards only for a few short years was the young woman able to drag on her fragile charm and broken health.

One morning having been called posthaste by the servants of the beautiful villa, my father arrived just in time to be informed that the young woman had died alone in the middle of the night.

And it so happened that when the hour came to lay her in her coffin and when for the last time he was kissing her lips, he suddenly collapsed on her dead bosom, as if struck by lightning.

"He died of love," I cried.

"No, of a heart attack," corrected Aunt Adelaida, obviously shocked by the keen interest with which, without sorrow and without shame, I was learning at last the secret of my birth.

For it happened that as she was speaking, I understood quite clearly that to live a great love, with its joys and its pains, and to die from it, might well be a destiny assigned by God to certain people. And that, contrary to what Aunt Adelaida was telling me, my parents had not committed a crime but bravely fulfilled their mission in life.

This truth, which my mind had so clearly grasped, the awkward language of my fifteen years, however, could only express by:

"Oh, Aunt Adelaida, how marvelous! How marvelous it is they died in that way! Wouldn't you wish also that you had lived such a great love?"

Aunt Adelaida jumped as if bitten by a snake.

"No!" she threw violently in my face. "No, I never would have wanted to bring into the world a girl for whom my guilty love would always be a bar to happiness."

With that outburst she killed my simple joy. Her argument seemed to me unanswerable and it broke my heart. Speechless, overcome, I sprang to my feet, ran to my room, closed the door and threw myself on the bed.

For a long time I cried. I cried until finally I fell asleep, exhausted. Then a gentle breath of Spring came to me out of the depth of my slumber, and in my dream suddenly I found myself under a tree in bloom, laden with bees. The subtle perfume emanating from its golden branches, together with the melodious humming of the bees, started gradually to soothe my sorrow, and to fill me with an indefinable well-being, a soft deep joy such as I had never known in all my brief existence.

"That is happiness!" I said ecstatically.

"Yes, and that happiness will be yours," I heard a woman's voice whispering close to me.

"Under this tree and in my dreams, perhaps, but not up there in life, for Aunt Adelaida told me so."

"Yet you will find this tree in your own life, Helga."

As I turned around to see who was talking to me, I found myself facing a frail, adorable young girl dressed all in white. Her long hair was flowing over her shoulders and her large dark eyes were as soft as those of a deer.

"You will find your happiness under this tree some day, I promise you," she repeated with a smile, and that smile carried such tenderness that I woke up in great joy and peace.

Aunt Adelaida, already dressed for church, was standing at the foot of my bed. She looked embarrassed and did not appear to notice that I had not taken my clothes off all night.

"Helga," she said to me, "I remember that once you asked me for a picture of your mother. Here is the only one we ever had. It was taken when she was already very ill, but nevertheless you will see that she was very pretty and that you have the same eyes she had."

And leaving me utterly amazed, Aunt Adelaida hastily went out of the room, after having dropped the portrait in my hands.

I looked at it and could not help a cry of surprise. A frail, adorable young girl dressed all in white with long hair flowing over her shoulders, and dark soft eyes like those of a deer, was looking at me from the portrait with the same tenderness she had shown in my dream.

For it was indeed my mother who had promised me happiness under the blossoming tree.

And there, as in her picture, it was her extreme youth which appealed to me most. Deeply moved, I told myself that I would grow up and become old, but that my mother would remain forever slender and frail waiting for me under the tree. And I was almost grateful to her for having died so young, so pretty . . .

◆

TWELVE

My seventeenth year brought an event never to be forgotten: Teresa's first ball.

When in order to display the star just appearing on the family horizon, Aunt Adelaida decided to invite her beautiful niece from the provinces and to reopen the drawing rooms of her house, she did not realize to what extent this ball given for Teresa was going to change the course of her life . . . and of mine.

My first meeting with my cousin after those five years did not precipitate the painful scene I had imagined, and I did not have to ask her forgiveness for the past, as Aunt Adelaida had suggested I should do.

Standing in the middle of the room which had been prepared for her and which I had decorated myself with large bunches of blue iris, Teresa ran to meet me and kissed me warmly as soon as she saw me appear bashfully on the threshold.

"Helga, how nice of you! Aunt Adelaida was just telling me you were the one who arranged this room for me. And I notice that you didn't forget I adore blue!"

I looked at her unable to answer, not even able to return her kiss. For what I had forgotten was how extraordinarily beautiful Teresa was. Yes, she would always be more beautiful than the most idealized memory one could retain of her! In order to describe her, comparisons and images, even those most worn out, most excessive, would come to one's lips; yet, when applied to her, all those hackneyed phrases seemed to regain their strength, their full meaning.

And thus it was possible effectively to say of Teresa that she was as exquisite and pink as the dawn, as glamorous as a radiant noon, as slender and haughty as Diana the huntress; and that her hair (the hair I had mangled in those days long ago, and which I helped on the evening of the ball to put up on her forehead in a crown of tresses) flowed through the fingers like a miraculous cascade of fluid gold.

How happy I was when Teresa allowed me to be her attendant on the evening of the big ball!

It was I who helped her put on the hyacinth-blue dress that Aunt Adelaida had ordered from Paris for her. I who put on her feet the tiniest little golden slippers with the highest heels I had ever seen, I who clasped around her neck the famous necklace of fine pearls which as little girls we had so much admired in the jewel case Aunt Mercedes only opened on special occasions. And it was still I who handed her at the last minute the little handkerchief perfumed with Chypre she had forgotten on her dressing table.

How grateful I was for the kiss she threw me as she went by, ready to descend the main staircase to the first strains of the orchestra!

I have never known a success equal to that won by Teresa on the night of her first ball. Leaning over the ramp on the landing, I saw her waltzing to the strains of the violins under the ecstatic gaze of the whole assemblage. And there I remained almost the entire night, dancing too . . . in my thoughts . . . but only with one, just one dancer—Daniel. And he was so tall and I so small that my cheek rested on his heart while he held me in close embrace . . .

No, nothing could be compared to Teresa's success. She was instantly acclaimed queen of the season.

Consequently, the spacious drawing rooms of our house remained open in anticipation of the brilliant marriage Teresa was to make, a match worthy of Aunt Adelaida's ambitions. And it was in vain that from her distant province Aunt Mercedes dispatched one letter after another asking for the return of her daughter. Her jealousy, because a sister-in-law whom she hated was giving her daughter the social position and the entertainments she herself was unable to give her, did not, however, find any echo in Uncle Arturo who was secretly encouraging his sister's course of action.

In the meantime, very naturally, and to my complete satisfaction, I became the companion and private maid of my cousin. Every morning it was my custom to awaken her by placing on her pillow the flowers sent by her admirers. I dressed her three times a day, and sewed and pressed for her all afternoon.

But it was in the evening when I brushed her beautiful hair before putting her to bed that we had a chance to talk and that she would tell me of her successes while looking at herself in the mirror, humming a tune from a waltz dedicated to her by its composer.

It was in such an atmosphere of joy and confidence that she suddenly asked me one day:

"Helga! Why did you try to cut off my braids that time long ago? Was it because you hated me?"

"No! Oh, no!" I protested and the brush almost slipped out of my fingers. "No, Teresa, I never hated you! I swear."

"But then, why did you . . . ?"

A wild desire took hold of me to pronounce that name which for so many years was burning my heart night and day.

"To carry them to Daniel," I heard myself saying.

"To Daniel? You mean to your friend Daniel Viana, our neighbor?"

"Yes, that's it. Daniel was madly in love with you, and since I was his confidante, he asked me to cut off one of your braids, because . . . well, because he did not dare go near you, and then . . . well, because he could not live without you, so that . . ."

"Oh, Helga, Helga, that's really funny! That wild boy, that bear, in love with me and asking you, a child, to . . . Oh, Helga, I can't get over it, it's really too amusing, it's . . . !"

And her beautiful, pearly laughter echoed in the silence of the great house.

"Hush!" I exclaimed, looking toward the door, afraid that Aunt Adelaida might suddenly appear in her dressing gown and send me scampering to bed.

Teresa stopped laughing, then with voice playful and increasing curiosity:

"But you, Helga, you, why did you listen to that boy and why did you let yourself be accused later?"

"Oh, I don't know . . . perhaps I was afraid of him. After all I was only a child and he was . . . by the way, how is he now, Teresa?"

"Exactly the same, I suppose. I meet him sometimes but I never look at him. However, from now on, I will look at him, you may be sure, now that I know that . . ."

And her laughter rocketed once more, and not daring to reveal my love, I laughed with her, in a cowardly way, at the handsome boy whom I adored . . .

However, the social season was drawing to a close, and much to the annoyance of Aunt Adelaida, Teresa was turning down one after the other all proposals of marriage. Until suddenly one evening on her return from a ball where she had been a sensation in a lovely dress of moonlight blue, she announced that she wanted to go back to her mother for a while.

She left. A few weeks later, Aunt Mercedes informed Aunt Adelaida by letter of the coming engagement of her daughter to a young man of their acquaintance, handsome, rich, and of good family.

"So much the better for her!" concluded Aunt Adelaida as she told me of the event. "After all, Mercedes' daughter could only marry someone of her own station."

Then after she had read to me a postscript in which Aunt Mercedes asked that I come to help prepare with my "fairy's hands" my cousin's trousseau:

"You will go," she said to me. "I don't wish to be accused of the slightest lack of courtesy towards this woman and her unfortunate daughter."

She tore the letter into small pieces, threw them away in the brazier, and went down to close forever the shutters of her drawing rooms. After that, putting her hand to her heart, she once again remembered that she was a very sick person.

But I could not even pretend to feel any compassion for her, so stunned was I in my heart by the sound of a big bell pealing full blast: *Daniel! Daniel! Daniel!* Surely he will be invited to Teresa's wedding! You will surely see him again! *Daniel! Daniel! Daniel!*

◆

THIRTEEN

"Helga, I want you to meet my fiancé."

A silence, then again the laughing voice of Teresa:

"Don't you recognize him, Helga?"

Yes, I recognized him only too well, this tall young man with chestnut hair and taciturn mien.

"You know, Helga," Aunt Mercedes was saying in her high-pitched voice, "your cousin asked me not to name him in my letter to Adelaida so that she could surprise you herself. Now tell me, what do you think of your childhood friend, don't you think he has grown taller, more attractive?"

Indeed, Daniel had become as tall and handsome as I had pictured him in my imagination, but never could my head rest upon his heart should we ever dance together, for he was going to be Teresa's husband!

I could hardly hear his first words, however, so great was the joy with which his voice filled my being.

"May I give Helga a kiss, Teresa?"

"Why yes, of course," cried Aunt Mercedes. "I give you permission in any case since it is to this child you owe your happiness! Oh, Helga, why didn't you tell us five years ago the reason you tried to cut off your cousin's braids? She might have then cast on Daniel that same little glance she gave him only two weeks ago, and for four years now I would have been a grandmother!"

Leaning down, Daniel kissed me on the cheek. Through my memory suddenly flowed the recollection of that hurried kiss given me five years earlier across a garden gate. And with pride I could not help thinking that it was through an act of mine, which I had at the time thought of no consequence, that five years later love had come to Daniel. Yes, his happiness was of my own doing. And all of a sudden I felt a great bliss, as if it were me in a way he was marrying too.

◆

FOURTEEN

How short seemed to me the time of Teresa's engagement! And how I created the illusion for myself of prolonging it by expanding the designs I was embroidering on the linen of her trousseau during the long evenings of Daniel's courtship!

Every afternoon at five o'clock exactly, Aunt Mercedes would open the doors that separated the drawing room from the veranda where I was busy with my handwork.

"Daniel will be here in a few minutes. You may entertain him, Helga, until Teresa comes down."

A few moments later Daniel would appear on the veranda, carrying a little box of sweets and a large bunch of flowers. He always gave me the sweets, but kept the flowers in his hand, as the bouquet was intended for Teresa, and he liked to offer it to her himself the minute she made her appearance.

And each time I was afraid that Teresa might make fun of this ceremonial which was the same every day. But each time, however, Teresa took the flowers, and thanked him with her most tender smile.

And whenever that happened, I could not help thinking of her uncontrollable laughter on the night I had told her of Daniel's passion for her. Could anyone possibly have passed from scorn to love in such a short time? How and why had her heart changed? I kept asking myself continually, not daring to speak to her about it.

For there no longer existed any intimacy between Teresa and myself, and soon I discovered that the idea of having me come had originated entirely with Aunt Mercedes. From the time of my arrival, on the contrary, Teresa barely spoke to me, and by her coolness, discouraged all advances on my part.

And yet, how much I actually enjoyed those long afternoons when she was playing the piano for Daniel in the big drawing room.

Under strict orders from Aunt Mercedes, the door of the drawing room was always left open on the veranda where I was doing my embroidery . . . a little chaperon, discreet and so grateful to be allowed to keep watch over love.

And that is how, bending over my needlework, I enjoyed the presence of Daniel kept busy turning the pages of the music Teresa played.

Teresa used to play for hours, seemingly forgetful that she had a fiancé seated by her side on the edge of the bench.

She played, and at her touch everything she played assumed a melancholy and distant tone, was like a long sigh, serene and sad.

And I enjoyed that music which sounded like a plaint in the moonlight, so completely was it in accord with the sweet agony of my heart and with the twilight slowly tinging blue the windowpanes of the veranda until I found myself, with my work and my dream, entirely submerged in the darkness.

Behind me the piano almost always stopped playing at that moment, and listening attentively, with heart beating and eyes closed, I would delay the time of lighting the lamps, so as to receive in thought on my lips the kiss I knew Daniel was giving Teresa in the shadow of the drawing room.

Daniel! Daniel! In order to get used to his happiness, he too might have liked perhaps to prolong the brief period of his betrothal. For when he was with Teresa, he always seemed lost in an awkward, admiring silence, giving the impression that he did not fully realize or even believe that his dream had come true.

His shyness, his stiffness, his forgetfulness reached a point which could hardly be imagined. One hour before leaving for the church, he suddenly discovered that he had forgotten to have the names engraved inside the wedding rings.

And so it was with the point of my needle that Teresa, already draped in her wedding veil, had the charming idea of herself engraving hurriedly the name inside the gold ring which he was to place on her finger at the altar . . . that gold ring fated to remain buried in the mud at the bottom of the lagoon where she was to be drowned only one month later!

◆

FIFTEEN

For we had not yet fully realized that Teresa was married when already she was gone, taken away by Daniel.

And we were only just beginning to get accustomed to the idea that Teresa had gone out of the daily routine of our lives, when already she was back, lying dead on her maiden's bed, her two emaciated hands crossed on her bosom. Her closed eyelids were resting heavily on two bluish, livid circles. And with nose pinched and mouth fallen, her entire face had an expression so sad that all those who had known her before stood dumfounded, overcome by a strange terror.

That expression—no one had ever seen it on her while she was alive! Nor could anyone, except possibly me, ever have associated it with her or reconciled it with her pearly laughter and her carefree joyousness.

Her tragic death, likewise, was so entirely out of relation with the happy, commonplace life which should have been hers that it became necessary for everyone to relate and repeat over and over again all the circumstances of the accident: "She was drowned, yes. She was rowing all by herself towards the middle of the lagoon. Merely for amusement, of course. One does not find much entertainment on an estate lost in the middle of the woods while the husband is busy at the mills! Her foot must have slipped; she did not know how to swim and she was drowned, yes. When they found out that she had disappeared, the rowboat had been adrift on the waters a long time . . ."

And people raised their hands to heaven uttering suppressed sighs while they surrounded Daniel with hypocritical curiosity. But standing still and staring hard at the dead woman, Daniel's attitude was such that nobody dared distract him with the slightest word of condolence from his terrifying contemplation. . . .

◆

SIXTEEN

As soon as her daughter had been carried away, Aunt Mercedes retired to her own quarters, closed the shutters, and went to bed. Thereafter she refused to leave her room where she remained all day long in the dark, inert. For her sorrow was one of those that the light of the sun might turn into violent despair. And it was while waiting for Time, Doctor, and Priest to bring her back to normal life, that my uncle decided to turn over to me the management of the house and the care of the linen.

From the moment when I saw him walking out, his shoulder helping to support his wife's coffin, I should have considered Daniel gone forever out of my life together with the dead woman. But somehow, an expectation of something, I did not know what, accompanied by an absurd premonition of happiness, made me continue, without any feeling of bitterness, to mend all the old linen on the veranda where, only a month before, I had been embroidering the fine trousseau of Teresa.

Until one day that thing happened which I had been waiting for without knowing it.

A distant ring of the front doorbell, steps in the hall, and the door of the main drawing room opening with a great clatter. Then Daniel standing very close to the chair where I was sewing.

"Helga! I've come . . . I had to see you, Helga . . . to see all this . . ."

Suddenly his voice died away.

"Sit down, Daniel. Uncle Arturo has been expecting you for a long time," I heard myself saying in the most natural manner.

And from that day on, Daniel came back every week. . . .

Every Saturday he would arrive at the same hour he had been in the habit of coming during his courtship of Teresa. He would come through the drawing room, open the door to the veranda, and sit down without saying a word.

The evening would go by slowly, and all the time I kept on sewing, filled with the happiness of his presence, while he stayed there smoking by my side, lost in grim reverie.

"Speak, tell me something . . ." he said at last, as the darkness enfolded his silence and mine.

And I would talk to him of our common childhood, of our games of long ago, and of all those years of my life I had lived away from him; I told him stories out of my fairy books and of the magic countries where I used to travel at night.

By and by, I came to speak to him about Teresa. At that moment I felt his attention sharpening in the dark.

But when with memory and imagination exhausted I stopped talking, he remained silent as though unable to find words to repay my fervor.

Yet I could feel his silence bringing me closer to him, as close, perhaps, as his most intimate confidences would have brought me.

In this way the entire summer went by. The first Saturday of autumn brought Uncle Arturo a letter from Aunt Adelaida: "It is most astonishing, really, that after I practically brought up the child, I should be deprived of her at the time when I need her most. . . ."

The same day, at five o'clock exactly, Daniel's ring at the front door found me busy packing my trunk. The moment I heard him, I stopped my work and there I stood, expecting against my better judgment the impossible miracle to happen of which I had been dreaming all morning: Daniel in a commanding tone telling me, "You will not go away, Helga. You are my child, my friend, my sister, I'm taking you under my roof. . . ."

In the silence of the first floor, I suddenly heard some kind of precipitous running, then a voice:

"Helga! Helga! Helga!"

For a moment I did not realize that it was Daniel calling me. Never had anybody needed me enough to call me with such an anxious voice.

Again I heard precipitous steps, this time on the stairway, and almost immediately Daniel appeared on the threshold of my room.

I looked at him, astounded, while he was catching his breath, little by little, like someone who has just been badly frightened.

"You were there? Why didn't you answer me?"

I kept silent, bewildered at seeing him in my room, only two feet away from Aunt Mercedes lying in her bed.

"You were not on the veranda . . . nor your sewing things either . . . I thought you were gone . . ."

"I'm going away this evening. Didn't the maid tell you when she opened the door?"

Daniel shook his head and stared at me.

"That's because she is new and . . ." I began to explain when he interrupted dryly.

"Why are you leaving?"

"Aunt Adelaida is feeling very ill, so . . ."

"So she is in need of a nurse, while here they no longer require a seamstress," he concluded, cutting me short again.

"It isn't my fault!" I murmured after a silence, not realizing actually what I was saying.

It was then he came close to me, and, putting his hand on my shoulder, almost knocked me over with happiness, as with a great blow.

"Helga," I heard him say in an angry voice, "will you marry me?"

I was looking at him, stunned, feeling the room whirling around, when suddenly, Aunt Mercedes was there standing in front of us.

"What did you say, Daniel?" she cried hysterically.

"I was asking Helga to marry me," Daniel replied quietly. And I noticed then that there was hatred in the look he gave her.

"But your wife, Daniel! have you forgotten her so soon? Didn't you ever love her, that unfortunate daughter of mine?"

"God is my witness that I have never loved anyone but Teresa and I still love her with all the strength of my soul," Daniel declared in a solemn heavy voice.

"There, you see, Helga, you see, you little schemer, this boy does not love you!" Aunt Mercedes said, turning quickly toward me with such an expression of joy in her eyes and in her voice that it frightened me.

"Excuse me, Señora," Daniel interposed, "it is true that I do not love Helga, but I will give her a home where she won't have to sew. And I . . . I won't be alone any more there at the hacienda, in all that mist . . . Helga," he repeated, taking me forcefully in his arms, "Helga, will you marry me?"

As my only answer, I let my head drop on his heart, as I had so often done in my dreams.

Whilst in the throes of the most violent fit of rage I ever witnessed, Aunt Mercedes cried out: "Out of my house, you ingrate, you intriguer. I throw you out! Both of you! Out of here! Out of here! Both of you!"

◆

PART

Two

◆

ONE

No, happiness in coming to me had not taken the road happiness usually takes, I thought to myself, nestling against Daniel's shoulder, as the coach carried us deeper and deeper into the fog.

Nor does the love which has come to me as my share have the usual appearance of love, I reflected later with sadness as I saw Daniel draw from me in silent irritation.

From the day he had asked me to marry him, Daniel had in every way discouraged all sentimental demonstrations on my part. And a grim look had always frozen on my lips the passionate words ever ready to rise from the very depths of my heart.

"Be patient, child, be patient!" Mamita had so wisely said to me in that room where Aunt Mercedes' anger had held me until the moment of my marriage. "You have your entire life before you to tell this boy you love him. The important thing is to tell it to him at the right moment. And for that moment you must learn to wait; you must learn to win that moment . . ."

I recall how the echo of those words had once more made me lift my head defiantly. Yes, I will win the right to tell Daniel I love him, as I have already won the right to go forward with him in this carriage towards the same house and the same destiny . . .

Just then the coach gave a violent jolt and the horses stamped their feet, neighing low.

"Andrés, hey Andrés," Daniel called impatiently.

"The same thing happens every time, don Daniel. This is where the horses refuse to go on, they're afraid to go around the lagoon at night," our young coachman said, turning around on his seat.

"Nonsense! Can't you tell it's already dark and that they don't see a thing? Besides, have you forgotten that carriages have lights?"

The carriage then came to a complete stop, and little Andrés jumped down, noticeably wounded in his dignity.

I leaned over the side of the door. An acrid and humid smell of woods, of ferns and of stagnant waters was rising out of the mist now thick enough to blot out the entire landscape. A halo of whitish vapor formed around the two lamps as the boy was lighting them.

In the meantime, Daniel had taken his place on the driver's seat.

"Get in the back," he ordered, as the boy attempted to take hold of the reins again. "Try to be the gentleman, since you're not able to be the coachman."

He whipped the horses, and they jumped up, their hoofs splashing furiously in the mud. The carriage creaked and swayed, throwing me from side to side, and while the young boy was trying to steady me by the arm, it started forward brutally.

Daniel's whip was snapping continuously in the dark, and the horses were rushing through the mist in a wild, blind race which frightened me badly.

"Oh my God, what is it?" I cried.

"The horses," answered Andrés in the midst of the uproar. "They're afraid to go close by the lagoon at night. They run wild, if they're forced to do it."

"But why?"

"Because of doña Teresa. She haunts the waters in the night."

"Teresa!"

"Yes, she goes looking for her ring left buried in the mud at the bottom of the lagoon when she was drowned . . ."

"Oh, keep quiet, Andrés! And you, Daniel, for God's sake, stop!"

The trees of an avenue obliterated by the mist were now whipping with invisible branches the windowpanes of the carriage which finally came to a sudden stop as abruptly as it had started.

"Here we are," Daniel said to me. "Step out, while I help that little idiot with the horses."

I pushed the coach door open and plunged ankle-deep into a carpet of damp leaves. Then, as I took a few steps through the fog, straining my eyes to place things, my foot struck upon a stone step. Groping about in the dark, I crept up a stairway leading to an enormous silent mass crouched there in the fog like a huge recumbent beast. It was the house. My house!

I stretched out my hand and tenderly felt its heavy door studded with iron nails. All of a sudden, with a grating sound the door began to open by itself.

Badly frightened, I turned around to call Daniel. But at the bottom of the steps the carriage was no longer to be seen, as if it had sunk in that sea of mist spread out at my feet.

Once again I turned around to face the house. The door now lay wide open in front of me, and out of the depth of darkness the light of a solitary lamp was beckoning me to come in.

Don't you see, it's the magic castle, the castle of the Bear! My imagination always immersed in the world of my fairy tales suggested to me.

Of course, that's it, I acquiesced, all my fears already dispelled as I crossed the threshold of the "castle" going towards the mysterious light.

My steps resounded on the stones of a hall with vaulted ceiling as high as that of a church. A lamp was burning at the foot of a broad staircase whose flight was stopped by a sumptuous garnet-colored velvet curtain. I went up the steps and lifted the curtain. Before me a long, a very long gallery, with huge tapestries hanging on its walls, was beckoning me towards the light of another lamp. I entered the gallery, the sound of my footsteps now muffled by soft rugs. Beyond the light, another hall, then a winding staircase and again a long corridor with stained glass windows, leading to one more lamp.

And forgetful of all I had heard about this extravagant palace built in the heart of the forest through the folly of Uncle Manuel, I kept on following with passionate curiosity that endless trail of lamps . . .

Until finally I reached a door beyond which the last lamp seemed to be burning:

A huge room with heavy draperies, with impressive furniture, and a large canopied bed. And lighted from head to foot in the reflection of the last lamp a young girl with large, slightly haggard dark eyes and rumpled hair.

I looked at her and she looked at me. Shyly I smiled at her but her face seemed to contract painfully. Suddenly, I noticed she was carrying a small bunch of orange blossoms pinned to a dress as poor as mine. And then I realized that this pitiful creature looking at me from the depths of a mirror was myself.

Oh God! What Prince would ever want to stretch out his loving arms to such a miserable little bride with her wrinkled dress and dusty tresses?

I can still see myself in that room, running frantically to the closet in search of the beautiful dressing gown which had belonged to Teresa—the dressing gown which I had myself cut and sewed.

"That dressing gown belongs to you by rights, and so does the entire trousseau," Mamita had said to me as she helped me with her half-paralyzed hands to pack my own poor linen. "By the work of your hands and with your tears you have earned the right to that trousseau and you should use it without remorse."

I remember the thrill with which I took off my dress and muddy boots and put on Teresa's turquoise-blue dressing gown and golden slippers. I remember how I came back then to sit before the mirror and how I took down my tresses and started to brush my long dark hair with the same silver brush with which she must have brushed hers.

And it was out of the depths of the same looking glass which on her wedding night had reflected her image that I saw Daniel appear, dragging after him my shameful little trunk.

No, never shall I forget the start he gave when he saw me nor the intense wild look with which he held me as he stood there very pale, silent and motionless on the threshold.

I can still remember the strange uneasiness which made me put down Teresa's brush on the dressing table and turn halfway around on the seat, while with a fierce look he started moving towards me.

Perhaps I shouldn't have done it, I thought in a panic. How did I dare? . . . And why did Mamita advise me to? . . .

But, to my complete surprise, once he was near me, Daniel closed his eyes and with hands taut slowly started to caress my flowing hair, the lace on the dressing gown . . . Big silent tears were rolling down his cheeks.

Frantic, shivering, I was calling on my love for the words that should be spoken, when brutally he raised me by the shoulders and drew me to his breast.

"Teresa!" he murmured, crushing his lips against mine . . .

What took place after that was unquestionably the most tragic experience any woman in love could have had to endure in all her life.

No, I do not wish to describe that strange wedding night in which I came to know passion through the striving of a husband who sought in me the memory of another woman.

I do not care to tell of my torture as I felt him embracing through me the fleeting ghost of a dead woman. The torture of feeling him there against me, longing for the warmth, for the scent of another flesh, forever gone! The torture of hearing his anguished voice speaking in my ear the words his tenderness meant for Teresa. No! I could not!

All I can say is that the dawn following that night of so long ago found me lying close to Daniel, my eyes wide open, motionless, shattered, indifferent to the weight of his forehead that sleep had made so heavy on my shoulder.

◆

TWO

"Good morning, Señora!"

I awakened with a start, out of a deadening torpor. Daniel was no longer by my side in the bed.

"I beg your pardon, Señora! Don Daniel left instructions for us to call you."

"Daniel! Where is he?"

"But . . . at the mills, of course . . . and he will not be back until late in the evening . . . He asked us to tell you that also."

"Thank you . . ."

"Amanda, Señora. My name is Amanda."

"And me, my name is Clara, Señora."

Clara! Amanda! I couldn't realize at that moment what a part they were going to play in my life.

I looked at them, noticing their supple waists, their long black braids, their half-slanting greenish eyes, so typical of the peasants from the extreme South, and I smiled pleasantly at them, while both were talking at the same time.

"We are Daniel's foster sisters. We live on the other side of the lagoon . . . and for the last three years we've been servants in the house."

"Serena, our younger sister, also was . . ."

"But as she's going to get married this winter, she isn't working here any longer."

"So Serena is engaged?" I inquired, just for the pleasure of repeating their sister's lovely name. My question, however, seemed to open up between us a flow of confidence and friendliness.

"Yes, Serena is engaged. She even expects to get married this winter. She is to marry someone from the city, a carpenter, both good-looking and wealthy . . . he has a workshop of his own . . ."

"Yes, he asked her to marry him the very first day he met her."

"The very moment he heard her play the guitar and sing!"

"Because, you know, Serena sings and plays the guitar better than anyone in the neighborhood!"

"Why, people even take long trips just to hear her, Señora."

"Well, I would certainly like to hear her too," I suggested cheerfully, much to the young girls' satisfaction.

"We'll tell her to come and sing for you, Señora."

"Wonderful! Splendid! Do you think she might come today?"

"Yes, Señora, but you know she is now working on her trousseau . . ."

"However as she probably isn't as clever with her needle as she is with her guitar, tell her that if she sings for me, I will sew for her. Yes, that's what we'll do! . . . Certainly I can sew, in fact very nicely. Clara, Amanda, ask Serena immediately, today! And we will all sew for her while she sings for us."

And it all happened exactly as in my fairy tales. I became the lady of the manor, faithful wife of the absent warrior, doing her embroidery in the great hall of the castle, surrounded by her attendants; a solitary young noblewoman fighting her anguish and the long winter with the rhythm of a ballad and the devotion poured out on the roses her needle is shaping.

Amanda, Clara, and Serena; Serena's guitar! And those long afternoons given over to the work done on Serena's trousseau became the citadel in which I managed to live most of the day, safe from sorrow and . . . from the mist.

The mist! It stuck like ivy to the house. It spread lazily over the neglected lawns of the vast park opened up by Uncle Manuel in the very heart of the forest. It invaded the forest with its wandering smoke and spread a large ring of vapor over the lagoon where Teresa was drowned. That mist! I can still see it closing in between the reeds, floating over the stagnant gray waters, to the edge of which some mysterious force had drawn my steps on the very first morning of my arrival.

"Andrés, is that you?" I cried, as I saw a rowboat slip by in front of me.

"Yes, Señora." With a quick swing of the oars, the young boy brought the boat to a stop at my feet.

"Wouldn't you like to come with me to the islands?" he asked shyly.

"What islands?"

"They can't be seen from here on account of the fog, but there are two of them in the middle of the lagoon. They're full of ducks' nests. You can see flamingoes there often, too."

There were, it is true, small islands right in the middle of the lagoon, but also in the mire at the bottom was buried the gold ring for which Teresa was haunting the waters like a moon-struck undine.

"Don't be afraid, Señora," the boy said to me as if he could read my thoughts. "It is only when night falls that 'She' comes, in search of the ring. You can ask my sisters. It is only at night that they're afraid to go around the lagoon." And the eyes of Andrés—greenish, slanting eyes, like those of Amanda, Clara, and Serena—pleaded with me so effectively that I jumped into the boat, not having the heart to disappoint him in his longing for companionship.

That lagoon! Fear seemed to float over it as heavily as the mist. An intolerable feeling of uneasiness was sweeping over me, more and more, as the boat went through waters as dense and silent as lava.

"Let's go back," I was about to say to Andrés, when suddenly out of the mist, very close to us, gushed a sort of wild, plaintive cry.

For a moment the boy and I faced each other, motionless, as if petrified with terror.

"It was a sea gull!" he whispered at last.

"A sea gull, so far from the ocean!" I mumbled.

Just a second the boy kept looking at me, then, bending over the oars, he started to row frantically towards the shore.

◆

THREE

Little Andrés was right. His sisters did not seem to be afraid to come around the lagoon in the morning. And it was lightheartedly that they did their sewing with me all afternoon on the trousseau of the betrothed girl.

But an hour or so before dark, Clara would get up to set on the table the cold supper Daniel and I were to eat by ourselves later on. Amanda would go upstairs to turn down the beds and light all those lamps that had guided me on the night of my arrival. In the meantime, Serena would put away her guitar and all the sewing things strewn on the big table while waiting for her two sisters to come to fetch her so that they could get back home on the other side of the lagoon before nightfall.

For it was indeed only at night that Teresa would begin to haunt the waters in search of her ring and that they were afraid to meet her frantic ghost!

Amanda, Clara, Serena, many times it happened I tried to induce them to talk about their unfortunate mistress! But everytime I mentioned her name, their heads would go down on their work and they would remain stubbornly silent.

One afternoon, however, as Serena was getting ready to put away her guitar, she casually drew out of her instrument two or three last chords which sounded so entrancing that I exclaimed in delight:

"Oh Serena, what was that?"

"A song doña Teresa liked," the young girl answered pensively, speaking for the first time of her own volition my cousin's name.

"Sing it for me!"

"It's too sad."

"But I love sad songs."

"I will sing for you only the first stanza," Serena suddenly acquiesced, while casting an anxious look towards the door and the big stairway as if afraid to see her sisters appear. Then after she had again drawn from her guitar the somber chords I had so much liked, her voice began to warble in a sort of plaint:

Aguas abajo,
Boga una niña
Boga diciendo:
Se va mi amor!

Adios, Adios! se fué su amor!
Adios, Adios! se fué su amor!

Down the river
A girl is rowing,
Rowing and singing:
Farewell my love!

Farewell, farewell! she said to love!
Farewell, farewell! she said to love!

Her voice lingered on the refrain.

"The second one now, Serena!"

It wasn't I, it was Clara, standing very pale on the threshold, who was calling for the second stanza! And Serena eagerly obeyed her:

Aguas abajo,
Boga una niña
Boga gimiendo:
Adios vivir.

Adios, Adios! dice al vivir.
Adios, Adios! dice al vivir.

Down the river
A girl is rowing,
Rowing and moaning:
Farewell to life.

Farewell, farewell! she said to life!
Farewell, farewell! she said to life!

Serena lingered, this time very briefly; then looking me suddenly straight in the eye, she said in a whisper: "And now begins the third stanza. Listen, carefully, Señora!"

Aguas abajo . . .

she began, when a great frightened cry interrupted her:

"No! No! No!" Amanda was coming in a rush down the stairway. "Stop, Serena! I told you you shouldn't. And you, Clara, how dare you! God would punish you! God would punish all of us, I tell you!" Amanda cried out.

"But what's the matter, but why?" I exclaimed.

Obviously trying to control herself, Amanda answered with strange unsteady voice.

"This song is too sad, Señora, and besides it's high time for us to be going. Come, Clara, Serena, . . ." she ordered. And thus, bowing their heads, the two younger sisters timidly followed their elder without even daring to turn around to wish me goodnight.

They left, and again, as on every other evening, I remained shivering and distraught in the middle of the big hall, the high vaults of which were already beginning to fill with darkness . . .

It was at that moment that every evening the mist, knowing me to be at last defenseless, would begin the silent, perfidious siege of my being. Vainly would I try then to forget that outside it was becoming more and more dense until eventually it would fill the night with its essence as impalpable as air, as fleeting as water, and yet as capable of swallowing up sounds and images as death.

And it was in vain that I kept walking up and down the stone floor of the big hall in order to stir the vaulted ceiling with the echo of my footsteps; and in vain that I tried to revive the bluish flame licking with a whistling sound the logs, always damp, in the enormous chimney.

The mist! I could feel its sly pressure encircling, shutting in the house more completely every moment and smothering me too, until at last I found myself compelled to break the silence with a great hysterical cry.

But as I opened my mouth, that call, ever ready to rise from my heart, invariably would flow to my throat.

"Daniel! Daniel!" I would cry.

Many times as it happened, would come the immediate answer to my call: the tinkling of the silver rings of his heavy peasant spurs on the steps of the outer staircase.

I would then rush to open the massive door, closing it again swiftly behind him in the face of the mist. And raising myself on tiptoe, I would lovingly reach up with my lips to my husband's indifferent cheek.

I felt happy. The presence of the Bear was all I needed . . . and that look in his chestnut eyes, caressing in spite of himself, as well as the absent smile that lit his face at times when I was helping him out of his poncho or waiting on him at table, as if he had been one of those dazzling knights spoken of in my fairy tales, filled me with delight.

"Why were you calling to me a little while ago?"

"Because I wanted you to come back."

"Yet calling out my name as you were doing would not have made me come back had I been far away."

"But fortunately, you were not far away."

"Come now. Admit you're still scared at night as when you were a child. Admit that all your life you'll be nothing more than a faint-hearted little idiot."

"It's not true! As a child I was never scared, but now, right now, yes, I'll admit, I'm terribly scared."

"What about?"

"About all this mist . . . and all this silence everywhere."

"What silence? There is no silence. If you'd only take the trouble to listen carefully, you'd hear all kinds of things in that silence. Here, give me your hand, close your eyes and try to listen with me . . ."

"No, Daniel, no, let go my hand, you're hurting me . . ."

"Listen, I tell you! I insist that you listen with me. Do you hear? Do you hear that clock going tic-tac, tic-tac, tic-tac?"

"There are no clocks in the house, Daniel. The bronze one in the green drawing room is broken, you know that!"

"Yes, there's a clock in this house, Helga. There's a clock everywhere in the world going tic-tac, tic-tac, tic-tac. And everything changes, everything moves away, everything disintegrates a little bit more on each one of those tic-tacs . . . Tic-tac, listen to this house crumbling away on each tic-tac, a little more. Listen to it, Helga, listen! Tic-tac, tic-tac . . ."

And it happened that in spite of myself, I was beginning to hear the precise working of this destructive rhythm hidden at the very center of life.

Tic-tac! I could hear, out there in the abandoned tower, the books in the enormous library shriveling up, turning yellow, being blotted out, collapsing in rows . . .

Tic-tac! I could hear the sumptuous tapestries, eaten up by mold giving in a little bit more. I could hear the worms crawling inside the wood of the furniture and of the gold carved panels.

Tic-tac, I could hear the old bricks of the tired walls loosening up. I could hear their paint flaking and peeling . . .

Yes, tic-tac, tic-tac, I could hear all this somber, fantastic palace, built through the folly of Uncle Manuel, decaying, crumbling, slowly going back into the slime of the earth and of the past . . .

"No, no, Daniel. This house Uncle Manuel loved so well, we must not let it be destroyed. You must bring men to . . ."

"What does this house matter to me, Helga? There is only one place in the world where I would like to stop the work of the clock—and that is at the bottom of the crypt where Teresa is buried. Tic-tac! Do you hear it beating against her coffin? Do you hear her bones moldering away a little more still?"

"Oh Daniel, my poor Daniel!"

"Tic-tac! Can you hear her disintegrating fingers rolling into the hollow of her chest now reduced to ashes? . . . Tic-tac! . . . No, no! Stop, clock, stop! Leave me at least that little handful of ashes, that very small earthly proof that I once had a wife whom I adored! . . ."

Dear God! I cannot find words to explain clearly the terror and the pity Daniel's madness awakened in me. All I can say is that during those long dreadful evenings I shared his suffering until ready at last to fall as exhausted as he on our bed of sorrow.

However, while he was lying in a pit of darkness, his spirit gathering strength to start suffering again, slowly from the bottom of the well through which I used to escape in my dreams, a giant impalpable snake seemed to be unfolding rings of smoke towards me. The mist! The mist now settled in the very core of my nature, like the clock in the heart of Daniel's nature.

I could feel it puffing and rising up in me and projecting itself beyond me, I could see it creeping inside the house, dampening the mirrors, extinguishing all color, obliterating every object, filling all the rooms one after the other . . .

Then I would wake up by the side of Daniel asleep, and the entire night I would stay there, lying close to him, tired, cold, destitute of all desire—of the desire to live as well as of the desire to be dead . . .

◆

FOUR

It happened one morning, one morning I shall never forget!

Voices and laughter and sounds of some unusual activity were tearing holes in my slumber long before I awakened with the joyous feeling that the sun was at last coming through the mist.

The skies outside were as gray as usual but I could detect a note of gaiety in Amanda's voice.

"Do wake up, Señora, get up quickly!"

"What is it? What's happening?"

"The Countess is downstairs, Señora. You must get out quickly on the balcony if you want to see her . . ."

"No, come out on the big terrace, everything can be seen better from there . . ." Clara blurted out, as she rushed into the room. "She has a big retinue with her—beautiful carriages filled with attendants, hunting dogs, coachmen, lackeys—really she travels like a queen! Come, come quickly!"

I can still see myself running barefoot through the corridors, preceded by the breathless Clara and followed by Amanda helping me as best she could to get into a dressing gown.

The Countess! Daniel's sister was there! I was at last to see her, I was to see this gay, capricious girl whom he had forbidden us even to name and whose picture I had tried in vain to find in some other place than in the memory of her three foster sisters.

Drawing herself up on the balustrade of the big terrace where she was already on watch, Serena explained to us in great excitement:

"Don Daniel is actually refusing the Countess permission to pass through the hacienda on the way to her hunting lodge."

I looked down greedily at the spectacle unfolding itself before the main entrance of the house.

The beautiful carriages full of people, and the dogs and lackeys of whom Clara had spoken, were all stationed at the foot of the central staircase in a turmoil of barking, trampling of feet, and shouts. In the middle of the staircase, standing very straight in front of Daniel who looked as if he wanted to overwhelm her with his great stature and obvious wrath, was a graceful young woman very slim in her long riding skirt, the train of which she was spreading over the steps with a majesty unbelievable in one so small.

Daniel's sister! I lost my heart completely to her the moment I saw her and heard her there in the middle of the stairway, the true picture of a merry squirrel holding off a lumbering, ill-tempered big bear.

". . . Then, it's your last word?"

"Exactly. And I would suggest you open a new road across the woods if you want to take your circus outfit to the lodge because over my roads you'll never be allowed to travel, my dear Maria . . ."

"Mariana, if you please!"

"I've always known you by the simple name of Maria. It was your mother's name, don't forget!"

"I've added to that name the even more simple one of Ana, which was the name of your grandmother, and don't you forget that!"

"You're getting to be pretty sophisticated since you've become the Countess of . . . I don't know what!"

". . . de Nevers. The Countess Guy de Nevers. I imagine it's a difficult name for a country bumpkin like you to remember, my dear brother, even though you've seen it written often enough on the papers you asked my husband to sign when you stole my lands."

"You mean when I paid you an amount three times their value; that money you're now wasting in nonsense and folly."

"I prefer to spend money on what you call nonsense and folly rather than save it to live among bats and sequestered women."

"What! Will you repeat what you've just said!"

"I've already forgotten it. And now, let's get through with it, Daniel! Are you going to lend me the keys of your *tranqueras,* or force me to make a detour on roads that would break down my carriages and my nerves?"

"Must I repeat to you for the hundredth time not to depend on ever again using anything that belongs to me."

"Listen, Daniel. If I told you that this is the last time I expect to trample on your damn roads, would you lend me the keys?"

"And why should it be the last time?"

"Because I believe I'll get rid of the lodge . . . sell it . . . to you . . ."

"Do you really mean that?" Daniel exclaimed, burning covetousness at once evident in his harsh, trembling voice.

"And why not? Are you going to lend me the keys now?"

"Maybe, if you'll promise to come back tomorrow so we can agree on terms for a contract of sale," he said, dangling the keys under the nose of the young amazon who caught them on the fly.

"I'll be back tomorrow . . ." she promised, rushing to the bottom of the steps where a groom immediately helped her mount a beautiful chestnut horse.

". . . unless I should change my mind!" she concluded, lifting her head to her brother still standing at the top of the staircase.

I could then distinctly see her eyes full of mischief, her pretty turned-up nose and her reddish-brown curls fluttering under a black velvet three-cornered hat.

And then I heard her laugh, a laugh that seemed to scatter little jingle bells in the air as she disappeared in the mist, closely followed by her mad, joyous retinue.

◆

FIVE

Somehow she must have changed her mind, my lovely sister-in-law; for, to my great disappointment, she did not come back the next day, nor the day after that, nor . . .

But the recollection of her bewildering passage, as well as the knowledge that she was there, so close, carrying on that dazzling mad life Daniel reproached her for, filled me with a strange happiness.

And while Amanda, Clara and Serena were doing their sewing with me, our conversation had now become more animated, on account of this new and thrilling topic—the Countess de Nevers.

"She has changed a lot! Little Maria was never as pretty as that when we were playing together here at the hacienda."

"And imagine our foster sister now a countess! Why, she would never speak to us if she saw us again!"

"Why not? She was never proud."

"Yes, that's true. She was too gay, she liked having fun too much to be proud."

"It seems, in that respect, she hasn't changed. They say there's a lot of fun going on at the lodge. In the evening all the lights are ablaze, and dancing keeps up till very late. One of the guests or else the Countess herself plays the piano . . ."

"Why do you stop talking when I come in?"

"But we were not talking, Daniel, we were just sewing."

"Yes, you were talking. What were you talking about?"

"Well . . . We were talking about someone whom you have forbidden us to mention."

Daniel blushed.

"I thought so," he muttered, "I thought so . . ."

Whereupon the rage he had been unable to unburden himself of on his sister suddenly fell upon our innocent heads in an avalanche of abuse followed by a strict warning never to dare try to get in touch with that undignified woman who had come to the lodge to amuse herself without her husband.

Yet, as I was listening to him swearing and threatening, I realized with great satisfaction that his shouts no longer brought me fear. The laughter of Mariana seemed to be still ringing its gay jingle bells in my heart, and I felt light as if in expectation of some unforeseen happiness.

◆

SIX

Mariana! I was so eager somehow to see her again, even from far off, that one afternoon I went out into the forest as far as the woods belonging to the lodge.

The mist was rolling its smoke around the trees, catching in the brambles and dragging itself close to the ground over the dead leaves. And through the mist I walked; I walked until I heard a stamping of horses' hoofs and the echo of a laughter I would have recognized anywhere.

I was trying to hide behind a cluster of ferns in order to see without being seen, when I heard a crackling of branches and a couple of greyhounds were suddenly springing at me.

I'll never know how I managed to jump out and disappear as light as a deer through the trees and the fog.

And just as if I had been a deer, the dogs started on my trail, urged on by the horsemen who evidently thought they were chasing some wild beast.

And I was running away, I was running through the woods, panic-stricken, breathless, wanting to scream, wanting to stop, but unable to overcome the senseless terror that was forcing me to this mad flight.

The huge trunk of a fallen tree was obstructing my way. I climbed over it and as in my fright I attempted to jump to the ground on the opposite side, I crumpled down on a bed of brambles.

Two, three, four greyhounds were immediately upon me. I felt their noses in my hair and on my clothes and terrified, I shut my eyes. But somehow, to my great surprise, they seemed to press all around me, solicitous and friendly. Timidly, I started to stretch out my hand to caress them when I heard the horsemen coming to a stop on the other side of the big tree. I heard one of them dismount and climb over it. Then I saw him lean over my bed of brambles.

He was a tall young man, slender and dark. He looked at me silently for a few moments. I must have seemed queer lying there, pale, disheveled, covered with mud, with the dogs jumping all over me.

"What is it, Landa, tell me!" cried an impatient voice from the other side of the tree.

"But . . . it's a deer, of course!" the young man answered, turning around to assist his questioner in climbing up to where he stood.

And then suddenly Mariana was there in front of me. She too looked at me silently.

"A deer, yes," she said at last, and I could hear the little jingle bells of her laughter fluttering pleasantly over my head.

She was making fun of me as she had made fun of Daniel. And it hurt my feelings so much that, swallowing my tears and raising my head, I flung out at her:

"No, I'm not a deer. My name is Helga and I happen to be the wife of your brother."

Still another silence, then all of a sudden came a great cry of joyous surprise, and there was Mariana on the ground by my side.

"Helga, Helga! Why, of course, you couldn't be anyone but Helga! It's wonderful, Landa, wonderful! I now introduce you to my sister-in-law, that sister-in-law of whom we spoke the other day . . . you know, the daughter of the Danish woman and of the handsome Del Rio, who died of love. You are familiar with the story of course, Landa?"

"Yes, Mariana, but . . . I believe this child is hurt . . ."

"I'm afraid I've sprained my ankle," I murmured, ashamed, after I had tried to stand up.

"Oh Lord, poor darling! But why did you run away like that? We were urging the dogs on, believing they were after some kind of an animal."

"I was really frightened," I whispered, looking admiringly at Mariana.

My gracious, how great was her charm! And how happy and proud it made me to be treated by her as a friend!

"And also what beautiful eyes as of a deer at bay you had! For you know you really look a lot like a deer. She has the same softness, the same gracefulness, don't you think, Landa? But what I cannot understand is how such an exquisite creature ever could have married a man like Daniel . . ."

"Daniel, oh my God! He has forbidden me . . . and how will I ever be able to get back home by myself?" I sighed, suddenly overcome.

"He had forbidden you to see me!" cried Mariana catching my thought on the wing. "Well it will give me great pleasure to take you back to your house, and my dear brother had better be careful! Landa, you're going to take Helga in front of you on your saddle and you'll follow me to the Tower where Bluebeard lives. Don't you be afraid, Helga."

Indeed, I was not afraid. I would have followed to the end of the world this fascinating, frolicsome creature who, after she had called her dogs together, was now leading us through the forest.

The arm of the stranger was holding me tightly at the waist, while the movement of the horse kept throwing me rhythmically onto his chest. A soft warmth seemed to radiate from him.

From time to time I would look back over my shoulder to catch a glimpse of his face with its fine strong features. And his cold gray eyes shining like stars under the brown eyelashes, enfolded me each time in a glance as soft as a caress.

A strange well-being was gradually taking possession of me, and with it a desire to remain forever nestled on this breast, forever held in those arms which could hold without hurting. . . . It was only after we reached the house and he had left me at the bottom of the staircase that I understood this well-being was called happiness.

Yes, I had been happy in the arms of a stranger!

That discovery surprised me so much that the arrival of Daniel and the rudeness with which he greeted Mariana affected me only slightly.

"What are you doing here?"

"Waiting for you to thank me and to thank Mr. Landa here for having brought back your wife whom we found almost dying in the forest."

"I would rather thank you to leave my house as soon as possible, you and your friend."

I gave a start, somewhat embarrassed. However, the young man seemed to be quite as much amused as Mariana by Daniel's complete lack of manners.

"Could that mean you do not wish to have us stay for dinner?" Mariana inquired laughingly.

"Exactly," Daniel replied unmoved.

"In that case I invite you to come to dinner tomorrow at the lodge with your charming wife."

"I will never take my wife to the house of a married woman when her husband is away."

"Well, bring her to me in town then . . . I am giving a big ball two weeks from today . . . it will be a wonderful chance to show the world the lovely sister-in-law you have so graciously presented to me."

"Your sister-in-law does not have any ball dress, and I don't even know how to dance," jeered Daniel.

"I will have my most beautiful gown ready for her, and she will dance with other men and not with her husband, as is customary at balls."

"And would you mind telling me what is customary at balls for husbands to do while their wives are dancing with other men?"

"I wouldn't know," Mariana said, and her eyes sparkled with a disturbingly mischievous look, "but what you can do while your wife is dancing is to arrange with my husband all the particulars regarding the sale of the lodge."

Daniel gave a start. Then, obviously affected:

"Tell me, Maria, why must I go to a ball to close that deal?"

"Because I have decided this very moment not to sell the lodge to you unless you bring Helga to my ball."

"Which means you will keep your lodge, my dear Maria," Daniel retorted angrily.

"Very well then, but I warn you that in the future I intend to use your roads to go in and out with my dogs, my friends, and my carriages as much and as long as I please."

"And I warn you I intend from now on to use a shotgun on anyone I find on my lands without my permission . . ."

"Tell me, Daniel, don't you think that it might be more pleasant for you to go to a ball rather than spend the rest of your days in jail?"

"Get out, Maria, get out, before I make up my mind to throw you out!"

"Goodbye then. But remember, it will give me the greatest pleasure to have you stop at my house at the time of the ball . . . which will be exactly two weeks from today, don't forget . . . I'll be waiting for you!"

"And you'll find yourself waiting until hell freezes . . ."

◆

SEVEN

Two weeks later towards nine o'clock in the evening, the valet who answered the doorbell at the main entrance of the stately home of the Count and Countess de Nevers glanced haughtily at the two women and a man in traveling clothes who were asking for the lady of the house.

"The Countess can see no one at this hour. The Countess is giving a large ball this evening . . ."

Amanda and I looked at each other with ecstatic delight while Daniel, in a fit of rage, pushed the side of the door into the face of the dumfounded servant.

"Will you please inform the Countess that Mr. and Mrs. Viana, her brother and sister-in-law, are downstairs . . . Step inside, Helga! And you, Amanda, instead of gaping at the white gloves of that young idiot, make him take in the bags!"

Indifferent to the increasing vulgarity behind which Daniel was hiding his spitefulness for having had to give in to the demand of his sister, I at last crossed the threshold of that house which had been the object of all my thoughts and dreams for the last two weeks.

No, never could I describe the whimsical luxury, the charm, the simple refinement of that house, blossoming with flowers and already lighted up for the ball which was to begin exactly one hour before midnight.

All I can say is that, motionless, wonderstruck, there I stood at the entrance of a huge white and mauve hall opening through archways in the rear into a drawing room as pink as the dawn with French windows in the back facing a garden made bluish by an unexpectedly intense moonlight.

However, I barely had time to delight in the enchantment into which that delicate mauve pink, and blue perspective had plunged my mind and my senses, when . . .

"Helga, darling, so you have come! And I who dared not believe that husband of yours would relent!" Mariana was rushing down the big stairway, drawing behind her the lace train of a long smoke-colored negligee which brought out wonderfully the tawny shades of her hair and the unusual splendor of her snowy white complexion.

"And you, my dear brother, since you made up your mind to come, why couldn't you have done things the right way?"

"What do you mean by that?"

"In the first place, you should have let me know the exact time of your arrival so that I could have sent for you at the station. Then you should have come twenty-four hours earlier. Do you realize that there are only two hours left to dress your wife and to get myself ready?"

"Strange! And I was thinking that what you have on now is a ball dress."

"Have your fun! But after all let me tell you that I'm not in the habit of wearing rags when I'm at home . . . Anyway, why should I waste my time answering you? Come, Helga, let's go upstairs to your room. And by the way, who is this girl?"

"It's Amanda. Don't you recognize her, Mariana?"

"Yes, of course I do. How could I ever forget all the fun we had together? But now let's go upstairs. Come on, Bluebeard, this way. This way Helga, Amanda."

"I brought Amanda so she might help me to get dressed," I said timidly, as we followed Mariana to the first floor.

"And also that she might see me at first hand, get acquainted with the house and watch the ball . . . isn't that right, Amanda?"

"Yes, it is!" acquiesced Amanda, and we all laughed while Mariana led us down a corridor towards the back of the house.

"Look, I've prepared a real lovers' nest for you," Mariana finally said as she pushed open the door.

I cried out in amazement.

The room assigned to us by Mariana opened on that garden I had admired at a distance from the ground floor, and as the curtains had not been drawn, the room appeared entirely bathed in blue moonlight. The mirrors seemed filled with blue water, the walls covered in satin gave out a blue light, and the large bed was draped in a spread of soft tulle, vaporous and blue.

And while Mariana was lighting the lamps, and their white light was dispelling the blue enchantment, I ran to the window and pressed my forehead against the windowpane so that I might see at close range that magic garden.

But, to my great surprise, I observed that what I had thought to be a large garden was no more than a square lawn caught between high walls covered with ivy. Almost hidden under the ivy, a little grated iron gate in the center wall seemed to open on a passageway. In the middle of the lawn stood a small marble fountain. And as a frame for this fountain, four cypress trees were shooting their compact somber jets toward heaven.

"Quite a setting for romance, isn't it?" Mariana suggested in a pleasantly mocking tone. "However, I would advise you to keep that entranced look for a more worthy spectacle, the one for instance you will see in the mirror when I have you all dressed up and with your hair done for the ball. Come . . ." she added, leading me by the hand.

"Good!" Daniel agreed. "Good, Maria, and while you're getting this extraordinary spectacle ready I will present the contract to your husband, for I wish to see him right away, if you don't mind."

"Unfortunately, the man you're going to see right away is his valet who's going to supervise your change of clothes. For just between ourselves, Daniel, it would put me to shame to have you appear in the middle of the stairway with your spurs on."

Daniel gave a forced smile which, however, broadened when he heard his sister add in a kindly tone:

"Nevertheless, I promise you that not later than tomorrow at noon you will have succeeded in depriving me of that little bit of land that until now you have failed to steal from me. Is that clear?"

I will always remember the thrill with which I followed Mariana to her apartment and into that pleasantly warm boudoir with rich soft carpets where the chief feature appeared to be a large mirror with three separate panels. This she immediately ordered folded up.

"You mustn't look at yourself until everything is finished . . . Ginette, bring us the gown, you know the one I mean. Amanda, help your mistress to take off her things and pull down this dreadful lump of hair . . ."

And that is how, standing motionless in the middle of the boudoir of the Countess de Nevers, and as passive as a doll, I let myself be dressed by her.

"You know, Helga, I've never worn this dress . . . not because I don't like it, but because it was made to suit someone slimmer, younger and more romantic-looking than myself . . . You see, it was really for you that I had this dress made, before I even knew you . . . Don't you think it strange, Helga? Perhaps, after all, there is something of a witch in me!"

In spite of myself, I gave a start. A witch, she had said! The disturbing joy that emanated from her mocking laughter and from her graceful squirrel-like gestures, the expression of her eyes, as reddish brown as her hair, were indeed exercising over me the same kind of fascination that, in my fairy tales, the dangerous witches, those who looked like the good fairies, used to exercise over human beings.

And all those pleasing falsehoods she was whispering in my ears! How could I be more slender or look younger than she, and what was there in me that could make me appear so romantic?

"Your eyes, your eyes so dark, so soft, and ever seeming a little afraid. And this pale complexion of yours and that long narrow neck, and that hair, Helga, that hair as dark as your eyes yet not quite black, thank God . . . for black hair never could have that silken quality yours has. Hand me my tortoise-shell brush, Ginette, that I may show Amanda how to brush and dress this beautiful hair! . . . You know, Helga, I really believe you have the most beautiful hair in the world!"

"Oh no!"

"Hasn't Daniel ever told you so?"

"Daniel only likes blond hair," I answered, trying to dismiss the memory of Teresa's tresses.

"There you are, and that's why one should never depend on a husband for admiration! Hasn't he ever told you that you have a most unusual type of beauty?"

"But, Mariana, Daniel does not see beauty of any kind in me."

"And yet, if another man this very evening found you attractive, that would be enough to make him discover suddenly that you are bewitching!"

"Oh really, Mariana, is it possible?"

"More than possible. But, poor darling, don't you by any chance ever feel a desire to be admired by someone else than that bear of a husband of yours? Beauty is something so rare, so short-lived. Just think, Helga, from the moment we are born, old age works upon us all the time. Today, for instance, our bodies are already less supple than they were yesterday, and tomorrow our skin will be not quite as soft as it is today. Tell me, Helga, would you want to become ugly, to have lines in your face, to grow old, and be lost forever on that awful hacienda all the time full of mist, by the side of a husband always indifferent and not be able to say to yourself that at least one night your beauty was recognized, admired . . . desired . . . ?"

And as she was talking in that caressing tone, Mariana was running her tortoise-shell comb through my hair over and over again, and behold little by little I could feel the memory of my childhood and of my love for Daniel gradually slipping away from me. I could feel that burning desire to make him love me becoming weaker and weaker in my heart. And in my mind Daniel himself was getting smaller and smaller . . . until finally he was no more than a sulking, brutal boy to whom, for no reason at all, I was sacrificing my youth and my beauty, day after day . . .

All of a sudden, vividly, came to my mind the vision of an episode in one of my fairy tales:

"Then the lady took Gerda by the hand and they went together into the cottage. The windows were very high, and their panes of different colored glass, red, blue and yellow, so that when the bright daylight streamed through them, various and beautiful were the hues reflected into the room. Upon a table in the center was placed a plate of very fine cherries, and of these Gerda was allowed to eat as many as she liked: and whilst she was eating them, the lady combed her hair with a golden comb. And as the lady combed little Gerda's hair the child thought less and less of her foster brother Kay, for the lady was an enchantress. She did not however practice magic for the sake of mischief but merely for her own amusement . . ."

Yes, Mariana was a witch, and life tonight exactly as in my fairy tales, I thought, giving myself up entirely to this marvelous present in which I was being dressed for a big ball. And suddenly I felt a longing to be beautiful, admired—desired.

"Now, look at yourself! Open the mirror, Ginette!"

As the three panes of the mirror were unfolded, I could see in front of me and on either side a fascinating, very slender young girl draped in a tunic all of white, with a long train of floating gauze. A knot of black tresses interlaced with pearls rested on the nape of her neck, bringing out a dainty swanlike effect. Her dark soft eyes were looking at me fixedly.

Overwhelmed with joy, I stretched out my hands towards that living image of my mother that the magic fingers of Mariana had made to spring up from the depth of my being, like an undine out of the depths of the waters!

"Splendid! I see you're beginning to become conscious of your own beauty and really to appreciate it!" chuckled the kindly witch. "And now, Ginette, bring me my little fan, the one embroidered with pearls. It will fit in beautifully with the dress. Thanks. Take it, Helga, and try to learn to use it while I go and get myself dressed."

And it felt as heavy and cold as a jewel that little white fan all embroidered with pearls. I unfolded it with awe under the admiring glance of Amanda.

Just at that moment, someone angrily turned the knob of the door from the outside.

Ginette ran forward and set the door ajar.

"The Countess does not want anyone to come into her boudoir."

"I don't care to go in, if only she will come out and speak to me in the corridor," the voice of Daniel answered.

Mariana obeyed, while Amanda drew closer to me, obviously sharing my fear that something might come at the last moment to shatter my wonderful dream.

Soon the sound of a discussion reached us from the other side of the door.

". . . and it had to be from the valet that I found out accidentally while he was dressing me up like a monkey that your husband had left for Europe two weeks ago!"

"But, Daniel, why are you so angry? What does it matter to you if my husband has left for Europe? It wasn't with him that you expected to dance, was it?"

"It was with him that I expected to close the contract."

"But after all, what does it matter! Didn't I promise you I would sign it tomorrow?"

"What do I care about your signature! It's of no use whatever on the contract. It's your husband's signature that's required. You know it and yet you made me come from the other end of the world to take part in your carnival, you damn cheat! Besides, I was a fool to believe you. You've always been a cheat—even as a child, you cheated at games."

"It's not true. You're the one who's always been a tyrant—and still are."

"Certainly, and I will prove it by taking my wife back with me right now to the hacienda. Let me get by."

"No, I won't let you deprive the poor girl of her happiness . . ."

"Let me get by, or I will strangle you right here!"

"You might strangle me, but I'll never let you get by!"

"We'll see!"

And as Daniel and Mariana were thus struggling at the door, once more the naughty children of not so long ago, I could see myself again in my traveling clothes, going back into the mist at the hacienda, my only chance to see life gone forever.

A groan of helplessness was heard, then pushing the door open, Daniel appeared suddenly on the threshold, dishevelled, his necktie to one side. Yet as he entered the room and caught sight of me, he stopped abruptly and stood there, as if petrified.

I realized at that moment that the amazing transformation in my appearance, which had given me so much joy as I faced the mirror, had now struck him, and thrown him into a stupor that was paralyzing his anger.

"You . . ." he began. "The dress is pretty," he added dryly.

"Doesn't it suit her perfectly?" Mariana thoughtlessly interposed as she came back into the room.

Anger once again flashed in Daniel's eyes.

But before he had a chance to speak, something in me, a kind of desperate force, took control of my two hands and compelled them to join together and to reach out to my husband in a passionate gesture of prayer.

A silence followed during which we remained standing, facing each other, I with tears rolling down my cheeks, he staring at me looking more and more angry.

Then, suddenly, he turned his back on us wildly and rushed out of the room, slamming the door behind him.

A few minutes later the valet appeared to inform us that Mr. Viana wished to say to Mrs. Viana that he expected her to go to the ball without him. "And then he threw me out and locked himself in his room where he intends to sleep all night!" concluded the servant, finally losing his self-control and dropping his formality.

Mariana burst out laughing in a way that Ginette probably thought highly undignified in a countess. For she suggested quietly:

"It seems to me that Madame la Comtesse should now be thinking about getting dressed herself."

"Certainly, certainly, Ginette, I'm at your disposal. As for you, Helga, stay with me and don't make such a face. Don't you know, you little fool, that there is nothing more amusing than a ball when husbands are away? If they were there, we would never be able to carry out the really original entrance I've planned for you. Listen to me carefully. When all the guests have arrived and as the orchestra strikes the first waltz, I will give you a little sign from downstairs and only then you will come down in all your beauty and majesty . . . Oh Lord, how amusing it will be! . . . Now listen, you must come downstairs very slowly and . . ."

And that is exactly what took place one hour later, when at the signal given by the Countess de Nevers, who looked unusually striking in a black velvet dress spangled with thousands of little golden stars that scintillated at every movement of her body, I came down the main stairway, walking very slowly, to the strain of the first waltz.

My heart was beating violently and as I came down, every head was lifted up to me. Even those couples who had already started to dance seemed to slacken the rhythm of their step in order to be able to look at me. A murmur was running through the hall when all of a sudden a frightening thought took possession of my mind:

"Dear God I had forgotten and everyone else likewise seems to have forgotten that to go to a ball one must know how to dance, and that I . . . oh my God . . . I don't know how to dance!"

◆

EIGHT

Here begins the account of one of the most extraordinary experiences any woman has ever lived through.

Everything I have written up to now which may have seemed trivial and unimportant to the reader was nevertheless a necessary foundation for the episodes that are to follow.

If the simple story I am relating now had been written as a novel, and if I had had to choose a title for every one of the chapters, I would have named this one THE BALL, further trying in a subtle way to warn my reader of the importance of each one of the details, even those which in themselves seem altogether insignificant . . .

At the foot of the stairs, Mariana was waiting for me, ready to present me to her guests.

"My sister-in-law, I want you to meet my sister-in-law . . . Here is her dance card." The women offered me their hands, staring at me with the most intense curiosity. And the men rushed forward to seize the little dance card Mariana handed them with a smile.

"But, Mariana, listen, I don't know how to dance . . ." I whispered to her between two introductions, expecting to see the house explode and vanish the moment this horrible confession was made.

"Nonsense! Beautiful women always know how to dance. Isn't that right, Landa?"

"Most decidedly. Would your sister-in-law do me the honor of dancing this first waltz with me?"

Landa! Landa! My emotion as I saw him standing there before me was so great that I could feel myself growing pale, and for a moment I lost the notion of all meaning behind acts and words.

He bowed and so great was the joy that filled my being when I found myself once more in his arms that I understood suddenly I had been waiting longingly for that moment.

I did not know how to dance . . . but, to my great surprise, I found myself actually dancing. All I had to do was to give myself up to the will of this handsome young man and to the rhythmic sway of the violins.

Yes, I was dancing, gliding, barely touching the floor with my little silver sandals, just as in my room at Aunt Adelaida's I used to dance in my imagination and more often still in my dreams.

And just as in the castles of my dreams, thousands of mirrors seemed to expand a thousand times the light of a thousand chandeliers with their myriads of crystal drops. And it was as if I and all those elegant, dazzling youths—for there was not a man at this ball with a white beard nor a single woman with glasses or gray hair, as there had been at Teresa's ball—were dancing in the very heart of a great diamond cut into a thousand glittering iridescent facets.

I have never been so happy in all my life! I thought, enraptured.

The arm encircling my waist seemed to hold me closer, and the beautiful, cold gray eyes of my dancing partner made themselves caressing.

"Nor I either!" he said in an ironical voice.

I realized then that, inadvertently, I had spoken the words aloud.

I felt myself blushing. And there I was stumbling, getting caught in the gauze of my long train which I had not picked up and thrown over my bended arm, as I now observed all the women were doing.

"I beg your pardon . . . oh my God, I don't know . . . I have forgotten how to dance," I admitted piteously.

"Why, not at all!" Landa replied, bending over to help me disentangle my train. "Not at all! Don't you know that elves never could dance in dresses from Paris?"

His voice was laughing at me while his eyes were holding mine tenderly.

"Come . . ." he said to me all of a sudden. "Come! Let's have some champagne." And he led me by the arm out of the circle formed by the dancers.

Five minutes later he was pressing a heavy crystal cup filled with champagne to the one I was holding in my hand.

"To the sadness, to the poetry, to the frailty of your beauty, I drink, Ebba Hansen," he said, looking straight into my eyes.

"Ebba Hansen, but that was the name of my mother!" I exclaimed.

"And you, you are her living image!"

"Did you ever know her?" I asked, deeply affected.

"I saw her once at this very place where you are now. She was standing with her back to the fireplace exactly as you are this moment."

As I looked at him with amazement, he explained:

"You see, this house, which has been completely done over by your sister-in-law, was the home of doña Angelica Portal, an adorable old lady who up to the time of her death was a very faithful friend of your parents. And as doña Angelica happens to be my godmother, I used to come every Sunday to have lunch with her. . . . It was many years ago and I was only about fourteen. The first time I saw your mother I fell madly in love with her—like all the rest of an entire generation. Her life to us stood for the most beautiful love legend of the time . . ."

"My mother! My mother was in this house!"

"Yes, in fact she lived only a few steps from here. I remember that as soon as I found it out I came over quite often to my godmother's, hoping to escape through the back door to her villa and there I would climb the high wall of the park only to look at her from a distance through the trees."

"What was she like?"

"Young, adorably young . . . and frail, too frail to carry so great a love."

I felt tears coming into my eyes and, as I tried hurriedly to conceal them, I put down the crystal cup on a small table and opened my fan.

"What a lovely fan you have there!"

"It's not mine, it's Mariana's," I answered ingenuously.

Landa looked at me again with that tender, mocking expression that disturbed me and appealed to me all at once. Then, as the violins were striking a new waltz, he drew me again to his arms and we started to glide away.

How long, in violation of all social customs, did we dance together forgetting that I had a dance card? I do not know.

All I know is that at length a strange weariness seemed to come over me, filling my bosom with sighs and all my being with a burning desire to be carried away by a great love. A great love! To live it and to die from it . . . like Ebba Hansen.

I was looking at Landa. His gray eyes were now shining like stars under his black lashes, his breath was on my cheek, his arm was holding me close . . .

Just at that moment, suddenly, the entire room flared up in a livid bluish flame, and all at once every light in the house went out.

The orchestra stopped playing.

There was a moment of deep silence immediately followed by an uproar in which laughs, exclamations, questions, and answers crossed each other . . .

"What was it? Some new trick of Mariana's? No, there must have been too many lights. The moonlight in the garden! It was artificial! The gas lines must have blown up!"

The orchestra began to play again, and then the miracle happened—the couples resumed their dance, falling in with the daring attempt of the musicians to get the ball going again in the dark.

Standing still in the center of the room, Landa and I could feel the dancers gliding by all around us and now and then the women brushing us lightly with their veils and their perfume.

"Shall we dance?" I was about to ask my partner when suddenly I felt his lips pressing down on mine.

My heart seemed to come to a stop in my breast, as well as all sense of time in my brain, and I stood there, motionless, receiving that kiss like someone hearing pure crystalline water falling drop by drop on a dry, thirsty part of his being.

The flames from a few candelabra, though still uncertain, were beginning to appear here and there opening gaps of light in the darkness while drawing large, ghostlike shadows across the ceiling. And my heart and my reason suddenly reawakened from the spell that had kept me helpless in the arms of that man who was not my husband.

I still don't know where I ever found the strength to tear myself away from his lips, to withdraw from his embrace, and to run across the drawing rooms, overwhelmed by the same panic which had made me two weeks before attempt to escape from his pack of hounds in the forest.

Through a darkness torn by gleams of light and by voices I fled holding with one hand the train of my dress and pushing away with the other an excited, joyous crowd which was delaying my escape towards the staircase.

That staircase I reached at last and up I went hurriedly, clinging to the railing whenever I stumbled or got caught in the gauze of that horrible train.

Breathless, I felt my way gropingly down the corridor that led to the back of the house.

When finally I found myself in front of the last door—the one which I knew to be the door of our room—I stopped for a moment, rearranged my hair, picked up my train and, beginning then to feel more confident, I turned the knob. The door refused to open. It was locked from the inside.

Remembering the story told by the valet, I made up my mind to knock several times in order to awaken Daniel.

I knocked gently at first, then more firmly, but nobody answered from the inside.

"Daniel," I called. But still there was no answer and the door remained closed.

"Daniel, open the door!" I implored. But Daniel remained implacably silent.

A great lassitude came over me then, and with it a longing to lie down, to close my eyes, to let my imagination rest to the sound of the music I could hear coming up from the floor below.

Retracing my steps as far back as the staircase, I leaned over the railing. The ball had now resumed its sway in the light of the candelabra Mariana had ordered placed in every corner of the hall. And on the ceiling and along the walls could be seen a fantastic dance of shadows, strange counterpart of the ball of the Countess de Nevers.

That wonderful Mariana! I could catch a glimpse of her dress glittering here and there and could hear that laugh of hers sounding almost continuously as she was cleverly turning a disaster into a most original and attractive entertainment.

Over at the very end of the hall the pink drawing room, now deserted, was plunged in darkness. Into my mind came the picture of that large deep sofa I had seen there when the swing of the dance had brought us back and forth under the arches with their heavy raised curtains.

I do not yet understand how I ever found the courage to go once more down those stairs and to walk across the hall as far as the sofa into which I finally dropped down, exhausted.

No one can see me here! I thought, my eyes half-closed. With its back to the big hall, the sofa faced the French windows which had been left wide open. And from the garden, where the moonlight had faded away, came floating a night scent of damp ivy.

The violins were now playing a melancholy tune. And the long journey from the hacienda, the dance, the champagne, and the intensity of my feelings had left me with only one desire, and that was to remain there, comfortably settled, unseen by anyone, enjoying the soft music and the cool perfumed night air.

Something, however, was weighing heavily on the wrist of my right hand—Mariana's fan dangling there at the end of its velvet cord. And I remember how I was wearily delaying making the effort required to take it off, when I heard quick steps on the carpet in front of me.

Reopening my eyes with a start, I peered through the darkness.

It was then that the grating sound of a door turning on its hinges made me jump up from the sofa. And before I had time to become aware of what I was doing, I found myself standing on the sill of one of the French windows and calling to the man on the other side of the fountain who was getting ready to go out through the small iron gate.

"Landa, are you leaving?" I heard myself exclaiming.

Landa, for it was he, turned around, his hand still on the knob of the door.

"No, I'm not leaving . . . I'm running away," he answered.

A moment of silence followed, during which I found time to notice that some kind of a subtle mist was actually, little by little, spreading through the garden.

"Does it mean I shall never see you again?" I heard myself asking.

"You're the one who has wished it that way. So goodbye."

"No, no, stay, Landa . . . I want you to stay!"

"But why?"

"Why? Because I love you," I heard myself blandly confessing.

There was a sound of laughter.

"You mean to say you love me this evening?"

"Yes, that's it, only this evening. But this evening, however, I do love you passionately."

"Why? Is it because your husband has forsaken you?"

"Oh Landa, Landa," I moaned.

The mist was now obliterating the cypress trees and weaving its curtain of smoke between us.

"Then prove to me that you love me!"

"But how?"

"Come with me tonight."

"What are you saying?"

"I will bring you back before dawn. Nobody will notice your absence. Certainly not your husband!"

"But that's sheer madness!"

"Come. Then you will hold the memory of what real love is. It will help you to bear life at the side of a man who doesn't love you."

"He will love me."

"He will never love you. Besides, he's not worthy of you . . . and everybody knows the reason why he married you."

"Oh, you're cruel!"

"You've been more cruel to me many times. You made me lose my head, you lied to me . . ."

"I!"

"Yes, with your eyes and in your manner you lied to me . . . ever since that first day. And still you believe yourself honest!"

"Stop it!"

"Very well then, not another word . . . I'm going . . ."

The mist was already blotting out his tall silhouette. Half a second more and he would be forever out of my life . . .

"Goodbye."

"No, no, I'm going with you . . . until daybreak . . . my love!"

And walking down a stone step, I plunged into the mist now filling the garden, until on the other side of the fountain, I reached the hand he was stretching out to me.

The little iron gate once again gave its noisy grating sound as he closed it behind us. And shoulders bare, the long gauze train of my dress floating behind me, I found myself moving up a narrow alley, drawn by that strong-willed hand from which mine had no desire whatsoever to withdraw.

"Where are we going?" I sighed.

He pressed my hand harder but made no answer.

But he might just as easily have led me to the end of the world! All my lassitude was gone, and I felt light, happy, confident.

The mist covered the sound of our steps, enfolding us in a warm, peaceful atmosphere. Straight up the narrow street we went until we found ourselves in a small square.

The lights of a few street lamps were shining feebly through a halo of mist. Sumptuous mansions several stories high enclosed the square. In front of an old iron gate, gracefully balancing the heavy mass of houses on the square, my companion stopped.

Behind the gate lay a garden where the mist was floating between the tall slender columns of birch trees above an abandoned lawn. Beyond the birches one could see a one-story house almost falling down under the weight of honeysuckle.

And it was towards that lovely house that my companion guided my steps after he had pushed open the gate with his shoulder.

I can still remember how as we reached the entrance door, he let go my hand for a moment to pull out of his pocket a little key which he slipped into the keyhole. The door opened. Then taking my hand again, he drew me at last inside the house.

Inside the house the darkness was complete. And it was into that darkness he led me through a suite of rooms up to a last door which he threw open.

For a while I remained on the threshold lost in contemplation of what was there before my eyes.

In a high chimney, a big fire was lighting up with its joyous, warm gleam a room all done in chintz of faded colors. Graceful, old-fashioned furniture, a bed with a small canopy from the top of which a vaporous, white curtain dropped down to the carpet, first caught my attention.

Then, coming back to the mantelpiece, my eyes beheld a transparent glass case under which a little golden clock was eagerly pushing its arrow-shaped pendulum.

My heart missed a beat. I took several steps towards the mantelpiece.

That glass case, that delightful little golden clock standing there on top of the mantel, close to a mirror time had tarnished—I was sure I had seen them before!

And the gesture I was now making, as I raised myself on tiptoe to observe more closely the rapid coming and going of the little arrow studded with rubies—I had also a definite impression that somehow I had made it once before.

Perhaps does it happen that way when a place or a deed is written in advance in our destiny! I thought to myself. Perhaps this night and this handsome young man . . .

But I hardly had time to do any more thinking. Landa was at my side, taking my hand, kissing it, releasing from my wrist Mariana's heavy fan and laying it down on the mantel there beside the clock.

Then I found myself in his arms.

And that night I knew love . . . that love of which I had had only a glimpse through Daniel's taciturn passion, the love that gives and receives . . . the love that is knowledge, exaltation, tenderness . . .

How long did I remain afterwards close to the side of my lover asleep in the big bed? I do not know. But the little golden clock kept relentlessly counting, recording with its light tic-tac every sound of that well-being in which I remained lazily submerged . . .

while in the fireplace, the flame was gradually receding, turning bluish, the logs one by one falling to ashes.

Then all of a sudden a silvery tinkling, a sort of angelic note, a dripping as of a crystal bead was heard . . . it was the little clock sounding a half-hour.

I raised myself on the bed to look at my lover sleeping so peacefully at my side. How handsome he was, how very pale, his head sunk on the pillows! His long black lashes almost touched his cheekbones, and his breathing was so light that I had to bend over close to his lips to be able to hear it.

As quietly as I could, I got out of the bed, dressed, rearranged my half-undone tresses on the nape of my neck. And all the while I felt beautiful, happy, contented.

I walked back to the bed and, leaning over once more, gave my lover a lingering kiss on the forehead. For I did not awaken him, no. All had been too wonderful to risk bringing him back for a parting that might be commonplace. By myself, surely, I would be able to find the way to Mariana's garden, the way to my dreary past . . .

So I slipped out of the room and, feeling my way in the dark, I reached the front door of the house.

Outside, the silvery light of dawn was already piercing through the mist as I walked once more across the lawn where the birches stood. I pushed the gate open, went around the square and found the alley down which I ran.

I turned the handle of the little iron gate which again made a grating sound as it opened. I went by the fountain, and up the stone step . . .

And when I found myself back at the foot of that sofa which I had left a few hours earlier to follow my lover, the dawn had at last succeeded in completely clearing away the mist.

No one seemed to have taken any notice of my absence. The ball was now drawing to a close, and as I made my escape through the hall and up the stairs, I could still hear the inexhaustible laughter of Mariana sounding and resounding as she was taking leave of her guests.

When at last I found myself ready to knock at the door of my room, I discovered it was no longer locked from the inside.

An unexpected thought came over me which filled me with horror—Daniel had gotten up, had gone downstairs . . . our windows were facing the garden . . . he must have heard my conversation with Landa . . . seen me following him through the little iron gate . . .

But all my fears vanished when I went in, for Daniel was there fast asleep in the big bed and the windows of the room were hermetically closed behind the heavy curtains the valet must have drawn earlier in the evening . . .

Feeling somewhat ashamed, Daniel undoubtedly had opened the door after I had in despair gone down again to the pink drawing room—I thought, feeling easier in my mind—then, glad to know I was not enjoying myself, delighted to have succeeded in making me uncomfortable for the rest of the evening, and convinced that he had acted quite as he should, he must have gone back to bed and fallen asleep, this time leaving the door unlocked.

All this was so much like him that I could not help smiling as I got myself undressed and quickly and silently slipped into the big bed by his side. Then all at once I dropped into a deep sleep.

◆

NINE

It must have been high noon when I was called by Daniel, already up and dressed in his traveling clothes.

"Now, Helga, it seems to me you have had plenty of rest. And you, Amanda, will you please hurry with those awful bags? Trains are not in the habit of waiting for their passengers, you know! So hurry up!" And as usual, we obeyed his orders quickly and without discussion.

But when everything was ready, with hands suddenly unsteady, I picked up the beautiful gown my sister-in-law had lent me for the ball and announced firmly:

"I'm going to return it to Mariana. It will give me an opportunity to say goodbye to her."

"Very well . . . for, after all, it's quite probable you'll never see that cheat again! And you, Amanda, for the last time I tell you get busy. Oh, Lord, what a burden women are!"

"The Countess is asleep. I cannot disturb her so early. She never would forgive me, and you may be sure she would never forgive you either, Madame Viana. The Countess is going to the opera tonight and you can imagine how she would look, if she did not have her rest after being up all night at the ball! Of course, Madame Viana, you may leave the dress with me! Why, certainly I will be glad to say goodbye to her for you. . . . A pleasant journey, Madame Viana . . ."

And saying this, Ginette almost pushed me out of the boudoir.

But as I was walking back across the hall ready to join Daniel who looked very impatient standing by the wide-open entrance door, she called to me again from the top of the stairs:

"Madame Viana," she cried, and her voice resounded across the hall. "Madame has forgotten to give back the fan!"

"The fan!" I repeated, and all of a sudden everything went in a whirl.

"Yes, the fan Madame la Comtesse lent to Madame because it matched her dress so perfectly, the fan . . ."

The fan, yes the little fan embroidered with pearls my lover had detached from my wrist a few hours earlier and had placed on top of the mantelpiece, near the little golden clock . . . where I had forgotten it, yes, forgotten it!

"I must have . . . I think . . ." I stammered stupidly, "forgotten it . . . during the ball . . . somewhere . . ."

"And all you have to do is to look for it, my dear girl. It will keep you busy!" Daniel insolently hurled at the elegant Ginette.

A thousand times I have blessed him for the bluntness with which he thereupon grabbed me by the arm and pulled me away and into the carriage.

◆

PART

Three

◆

ONE

The train once more carried us towards the South as far as that small, deserted station where Uncle Manuel's coupé, driven by little Andrés, took us back again to the hacienda.

And the mist once more came out to meet us as it had on the night of our wedding, and we again entered into the mist, and the mist once more closed in upon us. And when we reached the lagoon, the horses were neighing and rearing so that Daniel was again compelled to take hold of the reins. And little Andrés related to me how, the previous night, two boys from the village who had come to fish by moonlight had seen a lady dressed all in white, sitting under the willow trees, sobbing. It seems, however, that it was only when they noticed that her hair was floating over her shoulders and that the train of her dress went so far as to disappear under the surface of the waters that they realized she must have been a ghost, and, uttering great cries, had run away to the Santa Ana mill where brandy had to be given to them.

However, greatly to my surprise, I noticed that it was entirely without any apprehension that I heard of Teresa's ghost, and without any feeling of despair that I found myself back again in the dull, dreary existence which was to be mine from now on.

And it was in fact, with a feeling of great calm, all very astonishing to me, that I went back to my old dresses, to my customary ways, and that I once more found myself face to face with the mist and its eternal silence . . .

A soft, penetrating inner voice seemed to be speaking to me at all times: "The years can go by now," the voice would say, "and lines can spread out over your face, and gray hair intermingle with your dark hair, your flesh become dry and your body emaciated by old age. . . . What does it all matter to you now? What does it matter to you if your body withers away, since it has known love? With this wonderful memory in your heart you will be able to bear cheerfully a long dreary existence, and even repeat day after day, without weariness all the small gestures that make up your daily life."

And in vain I found myself replying to that voice: "No, no, that night of love you call a wonderful memory was in fact only madness. A madness that leaves me amazed and stunned; a madness for which I want to pay with an entire life of devotion to Daniel . . ."

For the voice skeptically and smilingly kept answering me: "What's the use of imagining a remorse you never felt! Go on, Helga, enjoy the only moment in your life when you felt yourself loved. Enjoy it in your memory and in your dreams, and in that way you will find happiness."

"Happiness! happiness, in madness and in sin! Never, never," I protested.

But while I was getting dressed, walking, eating, talking to Daniel, and quietly carrying on a peaceful, empty existence, my imagination, all the time, in spite of myself, was every moment re-enacting over and over again all the details of my night of love.

And as it happened what the voice had said to me was actually becoming true: the memory of that unforgettable night was filling me with a mysterious sense of well-being, greatly resembling happiness.

In the evening after dinner, the luminous gray eyes of Landa would never fail to appear like two stars in the midst of the burning coals my hand was stirring in the fireplace. And I could not make up my mind to rise and thus break the silent ecstasy into which I was thrown by the sight of those eyes shining for me in the depths of the flame and lasting as long as the flame itself.

"What are you staring at in the fireplace all the time?" Daniel asked me one evening.

"Why, at nothing at all!"

"Then is it to the logs that you're sending all those tender smiles?"

I gave no answer but I could feel my heart throbbing.

"Be careful, Helga, if you keep on living like that in your dreams, next thing you know, you'll be talking to yourself."

And as I did not answer, he put on his spurs and his poncho and went out into the night, looking very angry.

◆

TWO

Certain mornings without any apparent reason I would awaken with a feeling that in the course of the next twenty-four hours some unexpected joy was about to enter my life. This made it possible for me to go through the day in a hopeful mood and almost with a sense of exaltation.

All afternoon while Serena was playing on her guitar one romance after another, while Clara was busy threading my needles, and Amanda was relating over again her impressions of the ball, I could not help expecting every moment that unaccountable event which was to change the course of my destiny.

And in spite of the sullen and persistent blame my conscience all afternoon was forcing upon me, I still could not help waiting for that miracle which never would seem to happen.

Until one day, however, right in the middle of a romance, Daniel suddenly burst into the big hall, looking very aggressive.

"I would certainly like to know when this much-talked-about trousseau can be expected to be finished," he said.

Serena stopped playing and Clara and Amanda looked at each other in surprise. For it was indeed quite unusual for Daniel to come back as early as this from the mills.

"The trousseau is practically finished now, Daniel, but I don't see any reason why our sewing should upset you so," I heard myself answering calmly.

"Upset me! You're the one who's upset . . . upset in the head! You spend your days dreaming and chatting over your embroidery and listening to those silly, stupid songs."

"They're not stupid, and Serena has a lot of talent," I answered stiffly, in fear he might have offended the young girl.

"As far as I'm concerned, I don't think she has any at all . . . and that is why I want her to leave immediately with her guitar. And as for you, Amanda, be good enough to light a fire; it's freezing in here! You, Clara, clear the tables and chairs of all that linen and thread and everything else."

"And what about me? What do you want me to do?" I asked Daniel, while the three young girls followed his instructions, trying to conceal their laughter.

He looked at me very coldly:

"You, you will take off my spurs," he said at last, intending clearly to humiliate me for my innocent mockery.

"With pleasure!" I exclaimed. And kneeling down swiftly on the stone floor, I began to undo the straps of those beautiful spurs with silver buckles that tinkled so prettily as he walked.

"Listen, Helga, you seem to be rather gay since that famous ball! Did you really enjoy it as much as all that?"

"Oh, yes," I sighed, thankful for the task that prevented me from lifting up to him my blushing face.

"So then it is about the ball that you are chatting all the time with those three young fools?"

"No, certainly not all the time!"

". . . And so presumably it is about the ball that you keep on dreaming day and night with your mouth wide open?"

"Oh but Daniel, never with my mouth open!"

"Why, yes! Ever since we came back, you never listen to me any more when I talk. And you don't even see me when I'm here. . . . By the way, have you finished putting away those spurs? Now stand up and look at me. There is something I would like to tell you."

"All right, I'm getting up. . . . Here I am, looking at you," I said, able at last to control my emotion. "What is it you want to tell me?"

"Nothing," he snapped back, after he had stared at me silently for a while. "Nothing except to remind you that I married you for the privilege of not seeing you do any more sewing."

"That's right!" I cried, as the words he had spoken to Aunt Mercedes when he proposed to me came back to my mind.

I do not love Helga but I will give her a home where she won't have to sew and I, I won't be alone any more there at the hacienda in all that mist . . .

I won't be alone any more in all that mist . . .

"Daniel!" I cried, suddenly realizing the meaning of his unexpected return and of his complaints. But he was already gone, slamming the door behind him.

◆

THREE

It was in the course of my long wanderings through the woods that the voice of temptation would speak to me with the greatest persuasiveness.

And I could not help listening to it and following it in all its crazy elaborations, as I went walking, enfolded, isolated, and protected by the mist now no longer my enemy but my silent accomplice.

"You were quite right to come as far as this!" the voice said to me. "Do you remember this tree trunk? This is the spot where you fell down while you were running away pursued by the greyhounds. Do you remember? It is here he took you in his arms and brought you back seated in front of him on his horse. . . . The traces of this never-to-be-forgotten return journey should still be on the damp earth there under the fallen leaves. Look for them. . . . Walk, walk farther still, go over every inch of that road he followed pressing you close to his heart. . . . He fell in love with you then, yes, he fell in love with you madly. That is what he told you once and a thousand times all through that marvelous night, do you remember?" *I am in love with you, madly! But you, you, Helga, do you love me a little? I? I, oh yes of course I love you, I love you! I love you!*

"Helga, didn't I tell you that some day you would be talking to yourself!"

Oh my God! I had spoken aloud, and there was Daniel standing in front of me as if sprung up by magic from behind the high ferns. What was this obsession that was making him follow me around?

"Is it me you love . . . that much?" he inquired.

"No, of course not!" I retorted angrily, the shame of having thus been trapped by him making me answer him in anger for the first time in my life.

And for the first time in his life, an answer of mine having probably wounded him in his pride, I heard him asking me in a voice which pretended to be calm:

"If it is not me, then it must be some imaginary being, a Prince perhaps, from one of your stories, maybe?"

"That's it!" I answered, accepting with much relief the suggestion he offered, for the fear of having betrayed my secret already had taken the place of my anger.

"Well, so much the better for you!" he said again after a pause. "So much the better for you, for only an imaginary being could respond to the love of a girl as skinny and silly as you are." And thereupon, insolently turning his back on me, he disappeared through the high ferns.

That same evening, little Andrés delivered to me a message from him: he would sleep at the mills from now on. That was the message he had sent.

"At the mills? But where, on sawdust?" I commented laughingly, ready to face what appeared to be a definite though unjust punishment for my behavior of the morning.

"There are beds there for the use of the night watchmen," Andrés was explaining, when Amanda interrupted him:

"Let him sleep where he wants to, that's his business after all, but I shall not let you spend the night all alone in this big house. I will sleep here tonight," she concluded heroically.

"Why, of course not. Thank you, Amanda. I assure you, you don't have to. I'm not afraid of ghosts, you know . . ."

◆

FOUR

It was true, I was not afraid of ghosts, yet that night I happened to be very much frightened by the terrific storm which woke me up suddenly in the middle of the night.

"Oh my God, my God!" I implored, trembling at each roll of the thunder and hiding my head childishly under the covers.

"Don't be afraid, don't be afraid, Helga . . ." the evil voice was beginning again to whisper in my ear. "Think of Landa, think of him and you will no longer be afraid of the storm. . . . Think of him . . . perhaps the same thunderstorm that awakened you here awakened him too out there in that lovely room with the faded chintz, so well known to you. . . . Look, now he is getting up, getting dressed, now he is walking through the house and through the garden where the birch trees are bending over, hustled by the same wind that is howling here down the corridors. . . . Look, look, here he comes now driving at top speed with two black horses and a carriage pushed by the wind with a great stir. Listen, it is here towards the South that he is being driven, it is to you that he is coming. . . . Your lover, yes, your lover! He is coming. Do you hear the gallop of his horses on the highway? He is coming, he is getting near; yes, now he is reaching the outer limits of the hacienda, now he is going around the lagoon, and through the grounds; now he is pulling up his carriage in front of the main entrance. . . . And here he is, entering the front door which as usual has been left unlocked . . .

and now, now, do you hear his steps sounding on the stones of the big hall? Do you hear them as he is coming up the stairs, coming through the corridors, do you hear them, Helga . . .?"

Yes, I was hearing them. I was actually hearing footsteps coming through the corridors and towards my room. I could hear them getting nearer every second.

And swayed by a sickening fear, quickly I raised myself on my pillows, but my trembling hand had not yet finished lighting the lamp at the side of the bed when the door of the room was pushed open brutally from the outside.

"Daniel!" I cried. "You frightened me," I added with a sigh.

"Oh! I frightened you! I who had come back because I thought that the storm might frighten you!"

He said it so pleasantly that I looked at him, not quite sure I could believe I had heard him right. There he was, soaked with rain, his curly hair sticking to his temples and his boots all splattered with mud.

"It was nice of you to come back in this weather . . ." I said at last, foolishly.

There was a silence.

"You're glad that I came back then?" he asked, and he started to walk towards the bed with a smile on his lips.

"Of course, Daniel. I'm glad . . ."

"But . . . are you glad that I came back only because you were afraid of the storm?"

"Oh, but you know I wasn't really afraid of the storm!" I heard myself answering timidly.

"Then . . . you're glad that I came back because . . . perhaps you miss me a little . . . do you, Helga?"

I was looking at him, overwhelmed by the sweetness in his voice. There he was, standing at the foot of the big bed. He looked handsome, he looked kind, and was almost asking me if I was in love with him!

That was just the way it was to be. This was the moment for which I had been waiting ever since the day of our engagement, the moment when I was to tell him of my love for him.

A great emotion swept over me and I fell back on the pillows, suddenly overcome by a strange weakness.

And all at once he was leaning over me there at the head of the bed. I felt his strong arms lifting me by the shoulders.

My face was almost against his and my lips close to his lips when suddenly I noticed the expression in his eyes and felt his breath.

His eyes were shining with a queer uncanny light and his breath was heavy with alcohol.

I tore myself away violently from his arms, and as he was reaching out to take hold of me again, I slapped him hard in the face, screaming:

"Get out!"

He remained standing there before me, his fists clenched, his face very pale.

"I hate you! Get out!" I cried again and fell back sobbing on the pillows.

When I lifted up my head dejectedly, he was no longer before me.

The wind rushing through the door he had left open as he went out was rustling all the draperies in the room and causing the light in the lamp to flicker. Oh God, a whole night still to face, with that storm outside and that other storm in my heart! Would there ever be any rest or happiness for me on earth?

Yes, there would be.

For when, completely exhausted, I finally dropped into sleep, I suddenly found myself under a big tree blossoming with golden flowers, swarming with humming bees. And the song and the fragrance that emanated from this wonderful tree filled me instantly with great contentment, deep calm, and profound joy. And marveling, I realized that once more I was finding myself in the world of my dreams, under the Tree of Happiness that my mother so long ago had promised me I would find on earth.

Ebba Hansen! Smiling, frail, and tender, there she was again, making the same promise to me . . . as the light of dawn forced me once more to return to my sad life.

◆

FIVE

It was because of that promise that eagerly and almost joyously, I found myself facing a day which was in fact to be so decisive in my destiny.

The wind was still rushing right and left, tearing into the mist and chasing after it, blowing it relentlessly out of the forest which I could see far off throwing up smoke on all sides, like a great castle on fire.

My curiosity stirred by this unusual sight, I wandered aimlessly for a long time through the countryside until I found myself all of a sudden at the edge of the lagoon.

The wind was beating furiously against the reeds and sweeping away from the top of the water the mist which seemed to be escaping towards the sky. Out in the middle of the lagoon I could now distinctly see the small islands with the giant ferns where, as little Andrés had so often told me, the wild ducks had their abode.

"If he were here now," I thought, "I'd be the one this time to suggest going to the islands." For that atmosphere of dread which heretofore had weighed on the lagoon seemed to have been swept away with the mist.

No, little Andrés was not anywhere to be seen, yet his rowboat was there before me lying in the mud close to the bank.

I pushed it on the water, jumped in, and found myself rowing clumsily towards the islands before I had time to think that I had never done any rowing in my life.

The water felt heavy, and I soon had to realize that the islands were farther than I had imagined. My arms were getting tired and I was out of breath. So I let go the oars and relaxed.

It was then the thought came over me that at this very moment the rowboat was resting over the spot where . . .

I shall always remember the sudden morbid curiosity which induced me to lean over the side of the boat to look down into the waters towards that muddy bottom where death had been waiting to drag down Teresa's beautiful body.

And never, never shall I forget the panic that overwhelmed me when there in the depths, I saw something like a hand stirring a crazy whirl of air bubbles. From the murky bottom of the lagoon a human body was now rising fast to the surface. With tight throat and taut muscles, I was just about ready to die of fright when the head and the smiling face of little Andrés bounded out of the water in front of me.

"Andrés, my goodness, what are you doing there?"

"Quiet!" the child murmured as he gripped the side of the boat with one hand. "It's a secret!"

"A secret?"

"Yes, I'm looking for the gold ring of doña Teresa. I have been looking for it for months. . . . There is nothing don Daniel would not give to have that ring. He told me so himself. As I am a good diver, I will surely find it some day . . . and then I will exchange it for his beautiful silver spurs. But it's a secret. . . . My sisters must not under any circumstances hear about it. They would be much afraid . . ."

No longer was I listening to the boy, for all my attention had now become fixed on a carriage I had just seen appear at the edge of the lagoon.

"Andrés, look, do you see anything over there?" I cried.

"I see a carriage, Señora, a town carriage drawn by two black horses . . ." he answered, stretching his neck with much difficulty above the aquatic plants. "If don Daniel could see it, he would surely take a shot at it. You know, he has forbidden strangers to go across the hacienda," he added, while, to my amazement, I realized that the carriage, which, in my fanciful imagining of the night before, my lover had taken to come to me, was there at the edge of the lagoon under a cluster of willow trees.

And now, oh my God, it seemed my lover was actually there too. Yes, there he was, looking out of the window of the carriage! I could see him plainly, even that far away my eyes could recognize with joy his handsome profile. And as I started to call to him: "Landa! Landa!" I could see him waving his hand at me gaily.

So he had come! He had come as I had secretly desired him to do! . . . He had come. He was there! He loved me! He loved me!

A report, the report of a gun, was suddenly heard over the lagoon and flocks of wild ducks rising from all sides blinded me for a long while with their frightened wings.

"It is don Daniel," murmured little Andrés, vanishing under the water as quickly as he had appeared.

I took hold of the oars again. But as I rowed back I soon observed that my friend's carriage no longer could be seen under the willows . . .

The silhouette of Daniel, however, stood out there motionless, at the very edge of the bank. Carrying a shotgun on his shoulder, he seemed to be waiting for me, threateningly.

"Well done! Well done!" I heard him a little later sneering as I struggled through the reeds with my rowboat.

And his sneering turned into noisy, sarcastic laughter when as I attempted to jump ashore, I fell awkwardly face down in the mud. I can still see him firmly set on his feet right in front of me, laughing and not making the slightest move to help me.

"Coward!" I heard myself crying out at him, almost in tears from rage and humiliation.

"Ha! ha! I can see you were not lying last night when you said that you hate me."

I kept silent as I picked myself up and tried as best I could to shake the mud out of my clothes. Then, angrily, I started to walk towards the path leading to the house.

But there he suddenly came at me again.

"Tell me, Helga, it must make you suffer a lot to live in the same house with someone you do not love?"

"And what about you, does it make you suffer?" I answered bitterly and, much to my surprise, my remark seemed to turn his irony to heavy silence.

My triumph, however, was short-lived. I can still see him with his long, quiet stride catching up with my little hurried nervous steps as I walked towards the house.

"Listen, Helga, to be frank it does hurt my feelings to have constantly before my eyes a girl as ugly and thin as you are. So, after all, considering you don't love me either, why shouldn't we separate?"

"But where would I go?" That exclamation for which Daniel was waiting, never reached my lips, however, for no sooner had it presented itself to my mind than the evil voice of temptation was already singing in me:

"Where? But just two steps from here, Helga. At the hunting lodge of the Nevers where Landa surely at this very moment is waiting for you. Why shouldn't you ask him to take you away with him? . . . He would take you away and you would live hidden in his old house behind the beautiful abandoned garden. And your love would be his whole life, his own secret. And in his arms your nights would be one long, perfect night of happiness . . ."

"Separate, yes, after all, why not?" I declared pensively.

And my answer seemed to nail him down to the ground for the second time.

"May I inquire if it is of your Aunt Mercedes that you would ask for shelter when you leave me?" he asked, however, a few seconds later, again drawing close to my side.

"You know quite well that she has rejected me and told me to leave her house," I answered calmly.

"That is too bad, for I do not think that your Aunt Adelaida would receive in her house a woman estranged from her husband."

"I don't think so either, Daniel."

He laughed again. "So perhaps it is to the linen room of the convent that you expect to offer your talents? But you know, my poor Helga, I'm very much afraid that you would be turned down there also for the same reason Aunt Adelaida would not take you in her house. So after all, in any case, I would have you back again on my hands!"

"Certainly not, Daniel. For if I left you, I would be going away with someone who under no circumstances would want to send me back to you . . ."

"Not really!"

"Yes, a man who's in love with me! Do you hear!" and as I stopped I looked Daniel straight in the face.

He stared at me silently for a while and then burst out with that same laugh which had humiliated me so greatly when I fell down on the bank.

"Very well, Helga," he said, "but I think it would be better for you to wash your face before you go out to meet your loving ghost."

"It's not a ghost!" I snapped back, this time seized with a rage such as I had never experienced in my life. "It's not a ghost! His name is Landa!"

"Landa!"

"Yes, Landa! And he is handsome, intelligent, and kind . . . a hundred times more so than you are!"

"Landa—why of course, isn't he my sister's friend, I mean the one who once before picked you up in the mud a little while ago in the forest?"

"Yes!" I cried, completely outraged. "Yes, but it did not prevent him from finding me prettier than all the beautiful women he has ever met in his life. . . . Yes, you can laugh, if you will, and tell me again that I am thin and ugly, I don't care now, for to him I am slender, beautiful, attractive, and my hair smells of jasmine and my skin is soft to the touch, and . . ."

"Don't be ridiculous, Helga," interrupted Daniel. "You speak of this man as if he had been your lover."

"He has been my lover!" I declared forcefully.

"And when was that? In your dreams?"

"No, not in my dreams! The night of the ball, he was my lover!" I said, and, standing near Daniel now motionless, I waited for the cataclysm such a confession must inevitably bring forth.

But no, nothing at all happened.

There was a silence, and then:

"The night of the ball! But how? At what time? Tell me," Daniel finally inquired calmly as he resumed his walk.

And I had to follow him, astounded, actually speechless with astonishment, in the face of his failure to react.

"All right then, go ahead, tell us about your night at the ball, my dear Cinderella! So when the great clock at the palace sounded the twelve strokes of midnight, what did you do?"

However, at that moment my indignation, once more reawakened by Daniel's everlasting mockery, gave me back the use of my voice:

". . . When the great clock sounded midnight," I continued, "all the lights went out in the house of Mariana, and I went with Landa through the little iron gate in the garden . . ."

"Outside the nightingales were singing and you kissed in the moonlight!" Daniel sneered.

"No, there was a heavy mist," I continued, trembling with controlled rage, "and we walked until we reached a house . . ."

"A house of mist, of course."

"No, a real house! His house! It was very near. Just walking up an alley and crossing a square . . . and I was in his home, in his room, in his arms . . . until daybreak!"

"Wonderful! But, tell me, at daybreak how did you manage to get back?"

"How? It's very simple! Once more I went across the square, walked down the alley, and came in again through the little iron gate, the same way I had left."

"And nobody noticed anything?"

"Nobody. Outside there was the mist and inside that uncertain gleam of the candelabra. So I came in and walked upstairs, went to our room, got myself undressed, slipped into bed, and fell asleep."

"And woke up, you should say!"

"Why?" I answered, stamping the ground with my foot.

"Because, I imagine, that is the way all dreams come to an end."

I could not help shrugging my shoulders with a sort of superior contempt.

"My dear Helga, even if all you have just told me was not a dream, still your whole story could not stand up because of one insignificant detail."

"Which one?"

"Me."

"You? How? What do you mean?"

"I want to remind you that even though I do not love you, yet I'm not the kind of a husband that would let his wife run up and down the streets with a lover."

"But you were asleep!" I answered, with a nervous laugh.

"I was asleep, me!" And for the first time since this scene had begun, I saw Daniel react. Taking hold of my wrists, he compelled me to look at him while he spoke with a harsh thrust on each word:

"Perhaps you have forgotten that when the lights went out, you came upstairs and knocked at my door before you departed with your imaginary lover?"

"Yes, I remember it well and I also remember that you failed to open the door and kept on sleeping," I added spitefully, now vaguely conscious that I had at last found the spring that could shake him in his self-confidence.

I had made the right guess.

"I did not keep on sleeping!" Daniel cried in a sharp voice, pushing me back violently.

I stumbled on the pathway, and my head struck the trunk of a tree.

"And what did you do then?" I shouted, unable any longer to stand his brutal manners. "What did you do, my dear husband? Open the door to me? Watch me go to bed and make sure that I did not go walking the streets with a lover?"

"Exactly!" he cried out like a madman.

"I don't remember that!" I laughed.

"How could you remember it since you had had too much champagne?"

It was my turn to protest frantically:

"That's not true!"

And in the face of my anger, the anger of Daniel seemed to vanish as if by magic.

"You certainly don't deny that you had champagne to drink?"

he asked in a bland voice, looking as though he was enjoying my indignation.

"Not enough to lose my memory," I answered, trying to recover my self-control.

"That's what you think. When one has never taken any champagne before and then one takes . . . a little too much, even if it's done in a casual way, Helga, it's quite possible to lose the memory of anything done later . . ."

"But certainly that was not my case!"

"It may have been more your case than you think, Helga, considering that you took champagne when you were already tired out by a long journey and in a state of excitement brought on by that silly ball."

"But what are you trying to prove to me?"

"Nothing, except to make you realize that when you came to knock at my door . . . you were absolutely drunk," he concluded rudely.

"Liar!"

"Didn't Amanda ever tell you?"

"Tell me what?"

"That the champagne you took had gone to your head to such an extent that you did not even see her when she helped you to come up the stairs and she walked with you up to my door."

"Amanda!" I was looking at him trying to figure out what he was aiming at.

"Yes, Amanda. Wasn't she watching the ball from the top of the main staircase?"

"Yes, but she went to bed as soon as the lights went out. She told me so herself."

"She went to bed as soon as the lights went out, but only after she had helped you upstairs and brought you to my door."

"It's not possible, she would have told me."

"She probably has more decency than you who seem to think it perfectly natural to drink too much champagne, to lose all notion of what you are doing, and then to dream that you are running away with a lover."

I did not answer, feeling suddenly a strange tightening in my heart. And silently we resumed our walk towards the house.

Amanda! When she was telling her sisters the story of the ball or commenting on it to me, she had never ceased repeating how very lovely I had looked and how happy I seemed when over and over again I went by dancing under the banister of the stairway where she stood watching. Then she would tell how, when all the lights went out, she had gone to bed in order to keep forever clear in her memory the picture of the superb, brilliant spectacle the ball had been up to that moment. If she had helped me to go upstairs and had walked with me to the door of my room, she had never said one word to me about it, no, never . . . I was reflecting.

I noticed now that Daniel was observing me stealthily with a sort of strange curiosity. Instantly a new light entered my mind.

"You're lying!" I said to him. "You're making a mockery of me and of my love. Any falsehood you can think of is good enough for you so long as you know that it will offend me in what is dearest to my heart."

"My poor girl," Daniel answered, "we are at the house now, just call Amanda and ask her about the whole thing. You will find out soon enough that I'm not lying to you."

He laughed, and again I kept silent, feeling once more in my heart the same strange uneasiness I had already felt a little while before.

Then, as I entered the house and hurried to the first floor in search of Amanda, my thoughts made my uneasiness grow into real anguish . . .

If it was true that, on the night of the ball, Amanda had helped me go upstairs, then Daniel was right in asserting that the champagne had really made me unconscious for, actually, I had never seen Amanda. And if I had lost consciousness sufficiently to be unable to see her, or even to know or remember that she had helped me on the stairway and along the corridors up to the door of our room, then Daniel might possibly be right also when he claimed that he had opened the door . . . and that it was in my bed and in my dreams that I had lived my beautiful adventure with Landa . . .

"Amanda, here you are, at last!"

"My goodness, Señora, what have you been up to? You have mud right up to the end of your nose."

"Yes, I fell down."

"Please come and let me take off your clothes and your shoes! What a shame! How did you ever get yourself into such a mess?"

"At the edge of the lagoon. Listen, Amanda, why didn't you ever tell me that you helped me go upstairs the night of the ball and that the champagne had affected me?"

"Well, it seems that don Daniel now wants to spoil the pleasant memory you have of your only ball. Don't let him annoy you that way, Señora . . . You are much too nice to him! It's a shame!"

"But, Amanda, tell me, is it true that you helped me to go upstairs?"

"Why, of course it's true. And what of it! What difference can it possibly make to you? Nobody noticed it in all the excitement and in the darkness, and you had been perfect up to that point. A real queen of beauty! What's happening to you? Oh my God, Señora, you're not going to make yourself unhappy over that foolishness, I hope."

"No, no . . ." I protested, trying to conceal my misery. "But why didn't you ever mention all this to me?"

"That's the point exactly, because I did not want to spoil your recollection of the ball as don Daniel is doing right now! . . . Here, here, let me put your blue dress on now . . . The cold weather is over, you know . . . and the mist seems to be clearing up for good! Spring is here . . ."

"Yes, spring is here," I repeated in a dull voice, not finding enough strength to help her get me dressed!

"Now, now, Señora, turn around so I can button you up in the back . . . That's it, thanks . . . Besides, you should have no regrets on account of leaving the ball at the time you did . . . for in the light of the candelabra, it seems, things didn't go so well . . . About half the guests left as soon as the lights went out . . . Yes, from the top of my attic I watched so many carriages going off! I even stayed at the window more than one hour before going to bed as I wanted to get a good idea of what the big city is like . . . so many roofs, so many roofs there under me . . . so many gaslights!"

"But, Amanda, how could you see all that through the mist?"

"What mist?"

"Don't you remember the heavy mist that night?"

"Mist? There wasn't any mist, Señora. Besides, I am told that there practically never is any mist at all up there . . . You must have been dreaming about the mist here, most likely . . . But now, Clara is calling you downstairs . . . Remember, this is Saturday and don Daniel is lunching at home, Señora. You'd better go right down before he starts to get impatient," Amanda concluded.

And I obeyed her mechanically, unable to articulate a single word.

"The mist? You must have been dreaming about the mist here!" No! No! That wasn't possible! I couldn't have been dreaming! That terrible, marvelous adventure, the guilty memory of which I had never been able to put aside; that night of love, every detail of which remained more vivid in my memory than the most important events in all my life . . . it couldn't have been a dream! That wasn't possible. Someone must be mistaken. There must be some kind of monstrous error somewhere . . . I was saying to myself as I sat down at the end of the long dining room table facing Daniel.

"What a face!" he cried, giving me an insolent look. "The very mask of tragedy! I need not ask you the result of your inquiries upstairs . . ."

Then, all at once my power of resistance collapsed.

"Daniel," I pleaded in a low voice, at last setting aside all my pride. "Daniel, tell me, is it really true that you opened the door to me when I came up and knocked after all the lights had gone out?"

"Yes, of course, I opened the door to you."

"Well then, is it really true that I slept all night in our room by your side? Is it true, Daniel? Tell me, I beg of you! Can it be that Landa never was my lover?"

"Of course he never was! For in that case he surely wouldn't be alive today! Who do you think I am anyway, Helga?"

"Then it was all a dream! It's not possible, it's not possible . . ."

"On the contrary, it's more than possible. All your life you have lived in dreams rather than in reality . . . And wasn't it exactly what took place at the beginning of our friendship? Do you remember Prince Toad, the one with a little golden crown on his head, the one you always made me look for in the garden, like an idiot? . . . do you remember . . .?"

"Oh my God, my God!" I moaned, entirely crushed by his arguments, and then burst into tears.

For a few moments Daniel, amazed, watched me crying loudly, then:

"Stop it!" he exclaimed, hitting the table with both fists. Frightened by the violence of his outburst, I stopped crying.

A silence followed during which we both endeavored to regain our self-control.

"By the way, Helga, this seems to be the first time you care whether one of your dreams is real or not," he said at last, very coldly.

"Yes, I do care, I really do care . . ." I murmured, holding back my tears with great difficulty.

"You do care, you do care . . . !" Daniel repeated, staring at me with irritation. Then, suddenly, striking his forehead, he remarked in a voice once more wide-awake and mocking:

"Why certainly, of course you care, for after all—how could I have forgotten it?—a little while ago you wanted to leave me to join that gentleman! Dear me, what a surprise the poor fellow would have had seeing you suddenly arrive, throwing yourself in his arms, and . . ."

But now, it was my turn to interrupt Daniel in his sarcastic vein with a great joyous outburst. For—dear God—how could I have forgotten it? Landa had actually come, he had called to me from his carriage near the lagoon a little while earlier, and was surely waiting for me right now at the hunting lodge of the Nevers. Would he have come and would he have dared call to me if there had not been that night between us? Daniel was lying. Since he was not willing to admit a thing which wounded his pride, he must be lying. Where his lies began, where they ended, I could not say. For it was obviously true, according to Amanda, that the champagne had to some extent made me lose control of my actions. But he was lying when he insisted that my night of love was nothing but a dream . . . and I was going to prove it to him at once.

I got up from the table.

"Where are you going now?"

"To order the carriage."

"What for?"

"What for? To go to Landa, of course, and throw myself in his arms as you suggested!"

He looked at me for a moment without saying a word, then roaring with laughter:

"Do you expect to go all the way to the capital with my horses and carriage?"

"No, only as far as the hunting lodge of the Nevers, right here, next door."

"To the lodge?"

"Yes, to the lodge, where Landa arrived in that carriage at which you fired a few shots this morning at the edge of the lagoon . . .

Why do you look at me like that? Are you going to try to convince me now that I've been dreaming again?"

"Dreaming what?"

"That there was a carriage under the willows and that you took a shot at it!"

Another silence followed during which Daniel continued to look at me without making any answer.

"Well, what's the matter now? What's happening?" I inquired, moved in spite of myself by his attitude.

"It so happens that I did not shoot at any carriage this morning," he answered at last.

"What were you shooting at then?"

"At the flamingoes. They arrived here a few days ago. For a long time I've made up my mind to get one of them mounted for the house."

"Then, according to you, there wasn't any carriage under the willows and it was just another dream of mine, is that what you mean?" I inquired insolently.

"No, this time it wasn't a dream, it was just a vision you had," he answered calmly, "because, as a matter of fact, it is quite impossible for a carriage to have been there under the willows."

"And why is that, if you please?"

"Because . . . I'm going back to the lagoon right now to catch those flamingoes. If you'll come with me, I'll show you why . . ."

◆

SIX

How can I explain the confusion, the anguish that overwhelmed me while I was following Daniel to the lagoon?

And that feeling I had, of carrying on a cruel game begun by him when we were children. Yes, it was just the same then as it was now when I had to defend my dreams against the skeptical and destructive spirit of little Daniel.

"Listen, Helga, you were telling me that there was a toad with a little golden crown on his head, right under this stone?"

"Yes, of course."

"Well look, I have just lifted the stone and there isn't anything there."

"Then it must be somewhere else, on a visit to the fairies, perhaps."

"It isn't true, he is not at the fairies or anywhere else because there is no such toad anywhere . . ."

"Listen, Helga, you were telling me that under the big white sea shells, one could always find some little siren with green hair."

"Yes, surely."

"Well, all this month I spent at the seashore with Uncle Manuel, every time I went down to the beach, I turned over all the white sea shells I saw, but never found any little siren under them."

"Perhaps they weren't the right sea shells you turned over."

"It isn't so. What happened was that no little sirens ever existed except in your imagination! . . ."

"Listen, Helga, you were telling me that you had seen a carriage under the trees," he was saying to me now.

"Yes."

"Well now, look at those willow trees over there and tell me if a carriage could ever have stopped under them!"

For a certain length of time—I do not know how long—I stood there silent and motionless at Daniel's side, unwilling to believe what my eyes actually saw. The willows! Only their heads could be seen! Their trunks were almost entirely under the water of the lagoon greatly swollen by winter thaws.

And it was, in fact, practically impossible for a carriage not only to have stopped under the trees but even to have gotten near the spot where the willows stood, without having been stuck in the mud.

"Now are you convinced that the carriage never existed and that you only had a vision?"

I did not answer.

I was overcome.

"Look, someone is moving about in Andrés' rowboat," Daniel exclaimed.

"Andrés! Andrés! Andrés!" I cried, all my hopes suddenly bursting out once more in a great flash . . . "Andrés has seen the carriage too, Daniel. It couldn't have been a vision, for he has seen it too!"

"Was Andrés with you?"

"Yes and no. He was swimming over there by the islands when . . ."

"He was swimming by the islands!" interrupted Daniel. "Why? What was he doing there?"

"He was looking for Teresa's ring," I explained, thoughtlessly betraying Andrés in my anxiety to get quickly to the bottom of things.

But Daniel was no longer listening to me:

"Hey! You! Who gave you permission to go through by the lagoon?" he cried to a peasant who suddenly appeared before us. "I have forbidden all of you people from the lodge to enter my grounds. If you want to be in the service of my sister, that's your business. But I order you not to use my roads or go across my hacienda!"

"Well, well, of course you must be right, don Daniel," the peasant answered in a dignified manner. "However, you might consider that it is very hard for us to travel that long roundabout way . . ."

"That's no reason to break down the locks of my *tranqueras* and to come over to shoot at my ducks!"

"Oh no, don Daniel, sometimes we may jump over your *tranqueras,* but nobody has ever thought of going after your ducks!"

"Well then, tell me what are those men doing out there in Andrés' rowboat?"

"When we were going by on our way to the village, we saw the boy swimming over there . . . And then when we got back on our way to the lodge, we saw this!" the peasant concluded, showing us the vest, the linen trousers, and the sandals of little Andrés, all scattered on the ground among the reeds.

There was a silence.

"Then," continued the peasant, "we came to the conclusion that it wasn't natural he should be in the water so long and, besides, we couldn't see him anywhere. So my two friends decided to take the boat to go and see what was happening at the spot where we had seen him swimming . . ."

"But surely he must be on one of the islands. That's where he was resting between one dive and the next!" I exclaimed.

"Well then, why didn't he answer when we called him?" replied the peasant.

"But still, I . . ."

"Oh, shut up, Helga!" Daniel nervously interrupted, stamping the ground with his foot. "And yet I had absolutely forbidden him to do any more diving! Once already he almost drowned himself, and now he wants to start it all over again!"

"But why . . ." I was saying, when Daniel impatiently explained:

"Don't you know, there is a maze of aquatic plants with long roots there, there where . . . where you know!" he concluded, and then suddenly he walked away towards the bank of the lagoon.

I remained alone with the peasant who, visibly embarrassed, was watching from the corner of his eye his two companions in the rowboat near the islands.

"You are from the lodge?" I heard myself inquiring, my heart beating hard.

"Yes, Señora."

"There are people staying there now, aren't there?"

"No, Señora."

"Didn't Mr. Landa arrive there this morning?"

"No, Señora. Nobody arrived. Besides, the Countess has just written, asking us to close the house entirely."

"Are you sure, are you sure nobody arrived there this morning?"

"Well, I should certainly know, Señora, for I'm the steward at the house . . ."

"See here, Lisandro!" Daniel was crying out to the man while retracing his steps. "It looks as though your companions are making signs to us from over there . . . over there, where the boy was swimming . . ."

"Yes, of course, and they seem to be leaning over . . . as though they had discovered something . . . Oh dear Lord, dear Lord, I hope that little brat of an Andrés has not done the trick and gotten himself drowned . . ."

Yes, that little brat of an Andrés, as the peasant had said, had done the trick and gotten himself drowned! . . . And it was in his own rowboat that his poor little body, half-naked, his hair heavy with mud, was brought back.

"Andrés! Andrés! Andrés!"

I knelt down. I dared to touch his icy forehead, I dared to touch his hand with its strangely tightened fist, and I was still calling to him:

"Andrés! Andrés! Andrés!"

But he did not answer. Forever silenced was the only voice that could have said: "Of course not. The Señora did not have a vision, I too have seen the carriage."

And now, that he had been carried away, by Daniel, now that all of them were gone, lying there among the reeds, I understood at last that that night of love which my conscience had rejected had nevertheless been my only source of patience, that it was because of its burning memory that I had accepted to live, and to grow old without any hope of happiness, in that deserted spot forever surrounded by the mist.

For now, now that I knew all was but a dream, life to me seemed no more than a long, dull, purposeless road along which in time I would become old and die without having known love . . . Daniel had gone away without casting a single look of mercy on me and on my despair. Yes, through my pitiful confession I had even destroyed all possibility of a future between us . . . Only shame, sadness and emptiness of life were to be my future.

What was the use then for me to live? It would be a hundred times better to die, yes to die, rather than become one of those derelicts the stream of life carries away.

After all, it would be so easy! Just to go back to the lagoon, walk into the water until I should lose my footing, then . . . nothing. Nobody would come to stop me, to rescue me from those muddy waters, haunted by sorrow . . .

But somehow, I was mistaken.

Many years have passed since those events I am now relating, and yet distinctly in my memory I can still hear the great heartrending cry which reached me at the very moment I was letting myself go under the water, after I had lost my footing.

"Helga! No! Stop!" the voice of Daniel was crying out . . . just a second too late.

◆

SEVEN

And now, in order to obtain a clue to future events still to be unfolded in this story, my reader will have to take leave of me and go back one hour to Daniel as he was carrying the dead body of little Andrés into the house.

Poor child! It was on the stone table in the main hall that they laid his body so thin and cold. And there he remained, stretched out, his eyelids half-open on pupils death was beginning to dim.

It was when Daniel was getting ready to close those eyelids, that the footsteps of the three sisters were heard coming all at once on a wild run.

For a long while a terrifying silence held sway around the table.

"Andresito!" one of them said at last softly.

And Daniel saw them bustling around the body of the drowned boy, as if he were a sick child or one asleep.

"Andrés, poor Andresito!"

"Oh my God, it isn't possible!"

"Andrés, what have you done!"

And as one of them closed his eyes, and another pushed back a muddy lock of hair and kissed him on the forehead, the third (it was Clara) was taking the right hand of her little brother in her own so that she might loosen its fingers still strangely held in a tight grip.

Then something dropped out of his partly opened fist and rolled down on the stone floor. A ring!

"Teresa's gold ring!" Clara cried out in a strident voice, after Daniel had picked it up and showed it to them in his outstretched palm.

"A curse on it! A curse on it!" she kept repeating hysterically. "It was she who killed him! It was she who lured him to the bottom of the lagoon to kill him . . . while all the time we were loyal to her! We were keeping her frightful secret! We were protecting her with our silence and our prayers, protecting her soul already damned! . . ."

"No, no, Clara!" interrupted Serena, in a sort of agonized exaltation. "You are wrong, Clara! It was not Teresa who killed Andresito. It was God Himself! It was God punishing us for having kept the secret of her crime, for actually protecting wickedness against innocence! God . . ."

"Calm yourself, Serena," Amanda put in. "Both of you, keep quiet!"

"No, Amanda, God wants us to speak. . . . Look how He has used Andrés' hand to bring out the truth . . . 'Speak, you must speak,' He was just telling us when He made the ring fall down at our feet. Why did you keep silent?"

"Because we love Daniel, that is why we kept silent," Amanda suddenly put in impetuously. "And not to keep the secret of that unworthy woman. God knows it, therefore He could not have wanted to punish us for attempting to save Daniel so much suffering . . ."

"Yes, but also we kept silent because we were afraid!" Clara once more interposed in that same strident voice, as if possessed. "We were afraid of the ghost of Teresa, afraid of her vengeance, afraid that she might show herself to us as she shows herself at night on the lagoon! We were afraid of her tormented soul, admit it now, Amanda!"

"No, no!"

"I dare you to say no again! I dare you to swear it here before the dead body of your own brother!"

Then, after casting a distracted look on the body of little Andrés, Amanda burst into tears and ran out of the room . . . while Daniel followed her, almost screaming:

"What do you know that could have made me suffer, speak . . . what has Teresa done? Tell me!"

Amanda had dropped on one of the benches in the anteroom and was now sobbing heavily.

"We have always loved you as a brother, Daniel, even though you are now the master!" she moaned, taking Daniel's hand and speaking to him suddenly in the old familiar way, as they used to do when they were children playing together.

"I am your brother!" Daniel exclaimed, deeply moved. "I've always loved you, in spite of my disagreeable manners . . . and little Andrés whom I often treated so badly—I really loved him very much . . ."

"It was Teresa who killed him," spoke again the inexorable voice of Clara, just then appearing on the threshold accompanied by Serena. "You are the eldest and it is by right your privilege to tell Daniel the truth about Teresa, but if you don't do it, then Serena and I will tell him!"

"But speak, all of you!" burst out Daniel. "Teresa, my poor Teresa, what is this terrible thing they are accusing you of?"

"Of never having loved you," Amanda said then in a solemn trembling voice.

"Of never having loved me?" Daniel repeated.

"Yes, she said to us over and over again a thousand times that she did not love you and she was always sobbing when she said it. She used to cry all day long when you were not in the house . . ."

"She was in love with someone else, that's what she told us, Daniel!"

"Yes, someone else who did not want to marry her, and that's why she married you, on account of spite and also because you were so rich. She's the one who told us, Daniel!"

"It's not true! It's not possible!" Daniel said, struggling not to believe them. "You're mistaken. Or else you're insane! Why are you making all this up?"

"We're not making anything up. She told all of this to us herself."

"It's not true. If it were true . . . it's not to you she would have told all this. She would have been crazy to do it. Just as crazy as you all are, this very moment!"

"Crazy, yes she was crazy. So crazy that she went out to kill herself!"

"Kill herself? Kill herself, you say! And of course, she also told you that she was going to kill herself!" Daniel shouted now like a man out of his mind.

"No," Serena snapped back, "she did not tell us, but the morning of the day she was drowned, she asked me to sing the plaint of the young girl adrift on the waters, sobbing because of an unhappy love.

Aguas abajo
Boga una niña
Boga diciendo
Se va mi amor!

Down the river
A girl was rowing,
Rowing and singing:
Farewell my love!

"That's what the first stanza said, but it was the third, the third stanza that she asked me to sing to her that morning. To sing it again and again! And do you remember of the third stanza of that song, Daniel?"

"No, no, no, I don't remember anything. You're crazy; go away, I don't want to hear any more . . ."

"You must, you have to know, for your own good, Daniel . . . and for the sake of Helga. Listen, this is what the third stanza says:

Aguas abajo
La hallaron muerta
Ahogada y fria
Quiso morir!

Down the river
They found her dead,
Drowned and cold
She wished to die!

"She wished to die! Do you hear, Daniel? She wished to die!"

Yes, Daniel was hearing. From the depth of his memory the cry of the plaint was now coming up within himself and also the memory of many other things on which he could not help passing judgment with a clearness such as he had never known before.

Adios, adios! Quiso morir!
Adios, adios! Quiso morir!

Farewell, farewell! She wished to die!
Farewell, farewell! She wished to die!

Teresa! Her silences, her lack of confidence and her haughtiness towards him, he had accepted as proof of discretion, reserve, and natural pride in a being so prodigiously beautiful . . . perhaps after all, they were only a threefold manifestation of her profound indifference to him . . . And that terror, which came over her at night as he was caressing her which he had thought to be bashfulness might have been the denial of all her being . . . And, who knows, perhaps, it was sorrow which in less than a month of marriage had made her lose weight to such an extent that all her clothes became loose at the waist, and her rings fell from her fingers; even her wedding ring . . . her wedding ring, that ring which was different from all other wedding rings because the name of the betrothed had been inscribed inside by the bride herself . . . Ah, that smile with which she had taken hold of the needle on the morning of the wedding and had carried out that daring, charming gesture . . . !

And suddenly possessed by this latest recollection:

"You're lying, you're lying, all three of you!" Daniel said, as he raised to his lips the hand in which he was holding tightly the precious ring. "Teresa loved me! And the proof of it is inside this ring."

"Yes, it is inside the ring! It is inside the ring, the proof that she did not love you! Daniel, look at the name she inscribed inside the ring."

"Yes, look inside the ring, Daniel."

"She did not love you, look inside the ring, Daniel."

They were moving up on him all three of them, like three gloomy archangels sent forward by the inexorable God of Justice. "Look inside the ring!"

Daniel moved close to the high windows, raised the ring to the light and started to decipher the name which had been hastily inscribed on the inside with the point of my needle.

D . . . a . . . he began to spell, then suddenly he felt as if struck by a bolt of lightning . . . v . . . i . . . d . . . he concluded, reading only by a superhuman effort.

David! That was the name Teresa had inscribed inside the ring which he was to place on her finger in front of the altar! That was the name she carried in her heart when she married him . . . The name she must have had on her lips when she killed herself . . .

He ran to the door, opened it, fitfully drew a deep breath of air as if to save himself from choking and finally let himself drop down on the stone steps of the outer staircase.

"She did not love me!" he murmured . . .

"She did not love me!" he kept repeating in a dead voice, until Amanda found at last the courage to go to him.

"She did not love you, but Helga loves you!" she said.

He shook his head with an absent-minded look.

"Yes, Helga loves you! She has always loved you, to the point of self-denial and self-sacrifice. She kept silent as we did, and hid the truth from you, as she thought she was hiding it from us, the truth in regard to that woman for whom you spurned her so cruelly." Abruptly Daniel seemed to come back to life:

"Helga knew it?" he asked, lifting his head.

"Yes, Daniel, she knew it. And it was Teresa herself who told us she knew it . . ."

◆

EIGHT

Yes, I knew.

But God is my witness that never, never even the shadow of a thought that I might tell Daniel what I knew, came to my mind.

I knew, but I had even forgotten what I knew, so great was the conviction anchored in me that the revelation of the scene I had witnessed would break Daniel's heart forever.

And now, after so many years have passed, I cannot even recall without a feeling of anguish that dreadful scene in which I can see Teresa back from church in her magnificent wedding gown . . .

"Now you should make a brief appearance in the reception room, then come back upstairs as soon as you can and put on your traveling dress," Aunt Mercedes feverishly was instructing her daughter, who stood motionless in front of the mirror in her own room. "Even though it is disappointing to the guests, Daniel told me he wanted you to be ready to leave early. Now, Helga, hurry and pick up your cousin's train, and go downstairs with her. In the meantime I will get the bags ready. Oh my goodness, Teresa, how beautiful you look! Do you know that when you made your entrance in the church on your father's arm, people were moved to tears? And did you notice that outside the church there was a mob scene as you came out? I imagine that never happened to the little Viana girl, even though she had become a countess! That little upstart, who did not even take the trouble to come to her brother's wedding!"

"Leave me alone, Helga!" cried out Teresa in an altered voice as, obeying Aunt Mercedes, I was bending over to pick up her train.

Very pale, her eyes blazing, she was shaking from head to foot.

"My little girl, what is it?" Aunt Mercedes asked, coming forward eagerly.

"And you too, leave me alone! Both of you, leave me alone!" Teresa cried out once more, as she burst into heavy sobs.

"My poor darling, what's the matter? Dear Lord, she must be all tired out. Perhaps her nerves have gone back on her. Helga, go quickly and fetch me the orange flower water you'll find on my dressing table. After that go downstairs and call Daniel."

"Daniel! What for?" Teresa cried out with a start.

"But . . . he's your husband!"

"No, he's not my husband! And what's more I don't want to go away with him!"

"See here, Teresa, see here my little girl," stammered Aunt Mercedes, "why do you say that?"

"Why! Why! Because you know as well as I do that I do not love him!"

"Now, look here," Aunt Mercedes said, throwing a sidelong glance of deep anxiety in my direction. "If you had not been in love with that young man, you certainly would never have married him. The trouble with you is you're overtired. To have to sit for all those photographs has . . . Now go on, Helga! Go and do what I asked you to do!"

"No, stay here, Helga, I want you to stay! If you go downstairs to call Daniel, I will throw myself out of the window!" Teresa moaned. Whereupon she threw herself on the bed and started to weep loudly.

"Lock the door, Helga, someone is coming!" Aunt Mercedes commanded.

"And you, Mother, go away, I beg of you, go away! I want to be alone with Helga, oh please go away!"

"As you wish, my dear," Aunt Mercedes replied dryly, recovering her self-control as if by magic. "Anyway, I was rather anticipating all this! One should never expect any gratitude from one's children. Of course, that's the way life is. However, I beg of you, think of your poor father, Teresa! On account of him, you cannot go on acting this way, you might kill him . . ."

"All right, all right, Mother! I promise I'll try to get over it. But please let me cry all I want now, by myself. Oh please leave me alone, please!"

Lying in the folds of her long veil, her beautiful hair entwined with orange blossoms half-undone on the pillow, Teresa prostrate on her own maiden's bed was sobbing violently as I came over to sit down by her side.

"Is it true that you do not love Daniel?" I asked her sorrowfully.

"I do not love him, Helga. I love someone else! I love a man who did not want to marry me!"

And there, in the agony of her despair and in her need of someone to talk to, Teresa revealed her sad secret to me.

She did not love Daniel. She loved someone else. A man,

worldly, handsome, rich, attractive, intelligent, with whom she had danced that entire season of her triumph in town. No, I did not know him. She never had spoken to me about him because she never talked to anyone about anything that really mattered to her. Yes, she had met him at some other ball, not at Aunt Adelaida's. For he never would have bothered to go to Aunt Adelaida's. He was a foreigner, a man much sought after, too brilliant to waste his time with old maids or with . . . young girls. Yes, he really hated young girls. They said of him that he was a born bachelor. Yet, with her, he was different. He had shown his interest in her publicly and had courted her and this had caused as great a sensation as her beauty. In fact, all the women were jealous of her. If she had married him, she would have become a social queen not only in the smart set in this country but also in all the capitals of Europe where he surely would have taken her after their wedding. But that was not all. If she had married him, she would at the same time have been the happiest woman in the world, for she had fallen madly in love with him from the very moment when he had bowed to her asking for her first waltz . . . But the social season was waning, and her admirer still was not making his proposal. What seemed worse, he even carefully avoided the smallest gesture, the slightest word that might involve him either in a formal or in a personal way. Never any flowers, any letters, or any invitation other than a conventional one, never any private aside except in full view of many people. Women were beginning to smile unkindly behind their fans when they saw her waltzing with him. Yet he was in love with her. Yes, she was quite sure of it. She could see it in his eyes when he came running up to her in the lobby at the theater, at the races, or out walking. She felt it in the trembling of his arm when they were dancing together.

"My dear girl," Aunt Adelaida had said to her one morning, "many times I have told you that you should not keep all your smiles for that foreigner. Here he is going back to Europe next week. Someone just told me, no doubt with the intention of being unpleasant, as you may readily imagine. You know, I have always very much disliked having your name coupled so often with the name of a man who has no principles and no religion. That was my answer. And so good riddance to him! I'm tired of seeing him all the time around you! It's on account of him that you're losing all your opportunities for a brilliant marriage . . . everybody can see you have eyes only for him . . ."

"Is it true that you're going back to Europe next week?" Teresa had asked her admirer that very evening while they were dancing.

"How could I ever leave a city where you are?" was his answer and then, looking into her eyes: "And you, tell me, would you ever become resigned to not dancing with me any more?"

"I'm going home tomorrow to my family in the province," she answered quickly, not realizing exactly what had made her tell him this lie.

"It's not possible!" he exclaimed.

And seeing him for the first time about to lose his self-control, Teresa knew her woman's instinct had made her strike in the right place.

"Yet nothing could be nearer the truth!" she said, laughing.

For a while he remained silent as they glided in close embrace to the rhythm of the music.

"Well then, I will have to go to your province too, Teresa."

"There are no dances there, David."

"But there's you, Teresa darling!"

She almost fainted with happiness. He had said: "Teresa darling!"

"However, I do hope you will change your mind and decide not to go," he added, once more in a frivolous mood, as the waltz was coming to an end.

She did not change her mind. And it was the reason for that sudden departure which had alienated Aunt Adelaida's friendship forever.

She went back to her province feeling quite sure that the handsome foreigner, unable to live without seeing her, would not fail to come to ask for her hand.

But the days went by and he did not come. It is true, he wrote to her clever, amusing letters that she read anxiously and tore up in a temper without answering them. In the meantime Daniel was there, Daniel, whose love for her I myself had revealed to her only a few weeks earlier. Daniel, always silent but still in love, Daniel, not quite so shy and now the overlord of a vast domain . . .

". . . the best match in all the South! What do you expect, after all, Teresa? Really, this girl is quite mad!" Aunt Mercedes kept lamenting. "She is as crazy as a March hare! There at Adelaida's she was turning down one marriage proposal after another, and here . . . No, Arturo, the situation is becoming serious. I feel sure she will eventually be an old maid. And what selfishness! Just think, by making that little sacrifice of marrying a young man, handsome, intelligent, serious and well-brought-up like Daniel, she could save us from such a dreary existence and help us out of poverty. Yes, poverty, Teresa, do you hear, your father finds himself unable to pay the mortgage . . ."

"Very well, Mother, I will marry Daniel Viana," Teresa, under the spell of some strange desperate idea, suddenly announced one day.

Made to realize on hearing of her engagement that he was running the risk of losing her forever, the handsome foreigner surely would come to break up everything and take her back for his own. That was her idea.

And that is how she had decided to become engaged.

The engagement was announced in all the newspapers of the capital. Yet he did not come. Even though she received no more letters from him, Teresa felt sure he had heard the news. But the time which had been set for her engagement was running out, and still he did not come.

And so the day of her wedding arrived and . . . still he wasn't there! Actually, however, and up to the last minute, desperately, stupidly, against all the laws of reason, she still expected him to come. Even in church when the priest was saying the words, however useless: "If anyone knows of any reason why these two should not be joined together . . ." She had foolishly hoped to see him suddenly appear before the altar and say: "Yes, I know one reason, this woman loves me and I love her! . . ."

"Oh what madness, what madness it was! He never loved me, Helga, never!" Teresa lamented.

Yes, what madness was hers! She had wanted to play with life, and life, to punish her, was now playing with her.

". . . And I have to go away with a man who is nothing to me and yet is my husband, while . . ."

Crushed, terrified, annihilated, I was listening to the outrageous confession of this young girl who, in her folly, had not hesitated to sacrifice the life and the heart of the man I adored.

". . . While I still love David desperately, desperately . . ."

I got up at last and leaning over the bed, I placed a firm hand on my cousin's shoulder:

"Daniel must never know, Teresa, never!" I said to her with all the strength I could muster and those were the last words I spoke to her in my life, for Aunt Mercedes was already knocking at the door.

I shall never forget the look Teresa gave me then, and how with her eyes she kept following me from that moment on.

"He will never know. Nobody will ever know, Helga. I promise you!" she said in a low voice as she kissed me just before she left . . .

And many a time afterwards I asked myself if my heart's outcry had not made her become aware at that moment of my love for Daniel.

◆

NINE

Indeed, my intuition had been right. Teresa had known I was in love with Daniel, yet not having been able to fulfil more than a part of the promise she had made to me, she had confided in the three young girls who had just told everything to Daniel. And so Daniel knew now that I had always loved him and that, even though I knew Teresa's secret, still I had kept silent.

And a great pity came over him which filled his entire being. Looking back now, he could see me as a pathetic little girl, ill-treated and despised, building up a dream world of her own as a shelter into which she had generously invited him to enter. He recalled how, as a big boy, rough and spoiled, he had taken advantage of my affection and abused it. How he had forced me to cut Teresa's braids and how, even then, I had been able to keep this secret for his protection. He saw me later working silently on the embroidery for Teresa's trousseau while he was kissing her close by in the shadow of the drawing room. And again, more vividly, he remembered our wedding night and the long winter of our marriage, in which I had once more, as always, kept silent while he was treating me cruelly and hurting me, covering me with ridicule and destroying my dreams . . . whereas with one word I might have broken up his own dream forever . . .

And he felt pain. He had to put his hand to his heart because he felt physical pain when he thought of all the harm he had done to me . . . to me whose only crime had been to be the woman who loved him. And thus an irresistible desire came over him to run to me, to throw himself at my feet, to beg my pardon, to take me in his arms and to tell me that he loved me—yes, that he loved me. For the miracle had happened, and suddenly he saw clearly within himself and with amazement realized that, without knowing it, he had been in love with me for a long time. Free at last from the grief of Teresa's tragic death, no longer able to think of her except as one whom he had never known, whose frivolous and dark soul filled him with repulsion and sadness, he could at last understand that I was the one he loved.

Yes, he was in love with me, and as he walked towards the lagoon looking for me, he was forced to admit to himself that the desperation with which he had fought me and tried to humiliate me ever since the night of the ball had actually been caused by spite, by anguish, and by jealousy.

Spite, because he felt that I had changed and had become indifferent to him. Anguish, because he no longer could feel burning at his side that silent, faithful love to which I had made him accustomed. And jealousy of all those men who might have come near me that evening; for since the moment he had seen me so beautiful in my ball dress, he had desired me intensely.

And all this he at last understood, as he reached the edge of the lagoon and saw me out there in the act of . . .

He then uttered a great cry and threw himself in the water, and as he was struggling to save me, he knew that I had become the most precious thing in all the world to him and that life without me would no longer have any meaning for him.

However, as I recovered consciousness, I did not realize immediately that it was in the arms of the most loving husband that I had come back to life.

"Why did you save me?" I said softly, reproachfully.

"And you, why did you keep silent so long about Teresa and the man she loved?" Daniel rejoined.

"Because I did not want to hurt you as you have hurt me; because I did not want to kill in you all desire to live."

"Do you really love me as much as that?"

"Yes, I loved you as much as that before I even knew the meaning of the word love."

And marveling, I realized that in making that acknowledgment of my love, I had spoken the words he had so desperately longed to hear since the night of the ball.

"Helga, Helga, you're so good, so frail, so lovely; when I think I have neglected you so long for someone who was never true to me, you who have always loved me, who have never understood what it means to be untrue, except in your dreams!" he exclaimed, covering me with kisses.

Thus what I had thought to be the greatest misfortune in my life had, in fact, become the cause of the great happiness which had finally come to me. For it was only because my adventure had not been anything more than a dream and I had not known or loved any man but my husband, that I had at last found Daniel's love.

◆

TEN

Spring had now arrived and with it all that remained of the mist disappeared. On the lagoon, no longer haunted by Teresa, the frogs could be heard in the evening spreading out their crystal chant. In the woods, the fountains also were singing, and likewise the blades of the big saws at work in the mills.

And yet Daniel and I, in all the long walks we took through the woods, happy, in love, hand in hand, never did we find the tree that could sing, the Tree of Happiness!

And because of that, in spite of myself, a lingering fear came quite often to interrupt my laughter and darken my thoughts.

◆

PART

Four

◆

ONE

"Now that we have found happiness, why is it so necessary we should find the tree in which it was nesting?" Daniel said to me laughingly. For he did not seem to have quite lost the habit of making fun of me once in a while.

"But, Daniel, you don't seem to understand! Since we haven't been able to find the tree, it means there is still some trial we have to face."

"Do you mean to say that what we have now is not true happiness?"

"No, I don't mean that, but . . ."

"Well then, as far as I'm concerned, I would be perfectly content to live all my life with that happiness which you say is not 'true happiness'!"

"Yes, I would too, Daniel, but . . ."

"But we have to find the tree! Helga, Helga, as long as you won't give up being a little girl . . ." he was starting to say with a mean look which made me lift my head in dread . . . "I'll always be in love with you!" he added, leaning over to kiss me.

And I laughed too . . . but all the time I felt a shadow spreading over my happiness . . . Besides, it was not the only one. The memory of little Andrés still alive everywhere in the house and on the hacienda constantly brought a touch of sadness into our daily lives.

That poor little ghost so pathetic, so benevolent! We could not help recalling often that it was through his sad death that our own happiness had come into being.

Had we forgotten it, the sight of Amanda would very soon have made us recall it. She moved about, pale and silent, only a shadow of the gay, bright young girl who had been more a friend than a servant to me.

Clara had left the house. The shock of her little brother's death having affected her mind, her family decided to send her away from the hacienda for a while. Serena, now married, had gone to live in some other part of the country with her good-looking carpenter.

Yes, without the sound of Serena's guitar, the house filled as it was with too many agonizing memories, was sad indeed.

"Perhaps we should go away for a while and spend some time in town, Helga. I think it would be pleasant for a change," Daniel suggested one day.

"Oh Daniel, I would love it!"

Yes, that same trip we had made when we were so far apart, so unhappy, we could make it now, hand in hand . . .

"Only I warn you in advance that I will under no circumstances see the Countess de Nevers or set foot in her house."

"Oh Daniel, I . . ."

"Absolutely not, Helga! It's not because I love you that I will stop hating Maria. Anyway I think it's a good thing for me to hate somebody . . . otherwise being all the time with you I might easily turn into a chunk of honey . . ."

◆

TWO

"It would be nice also on this trip to pay a little call on Aunt Adelaida," I suggested to Daniel on the train a few days later.

He jumped up and faced me with a strange look:

"Helga, I didn't want to tell you because . . . well, we've had too many tragedies . . . but your Aunt Adelaida died a few weeks ago."

"She was kind to me, in her way," I sighed after a long silence.

"Her attorney wrote me asking me to call at his office whenever I should come to town . . . Perhaps the dear old lady has left you something in her will!"

"Oh, I hope it's a letter or some word of farewell . . . poor Aunt Adelaida!"

Daniel gave me one of those looks in which the desire to make fun of me was tempered by some kind of tenderness.

"We shall soon know all about it, Helga. I promise to go there very soon after we arrive . . . if ever that miserable train makes up its mind to get to its destination . . . Look, we're already more than one hour late."

Mariana was waiting for us at the station.

I can still see her as she suddenly appeared before us pressing through the crowd, neat, smiling, prettier than ever under a mauve sunshade of gauze whirling over her shoulder.

Her charm, her fawn-colored eyes, that happy magnetism which radiated from her personality, instantly made me forget my pledge to Daniel.

"How glad I am to see you, Mariana!" I exclaimed, throwing myself in her arms.

"And yet not a word from you since the night of the ball, Helga!"

"Didn't you ever receive the letter of thanks I sent you?" I protested.

"Daniel must have intercepted it. Isn't that so, Daniel?" Mariana asked good-naturedly.

"Of course," Daniel answered with great simplicity.

And as I was staring at him, somewhat dazed:

"There's no reason to be so surprised, Helga," Mariana resumed. "He has always used that kind of tactics. And you, Bluebeard, give me a kiss anyway. Aren't you glad to see me again?"

"Not at all, my dear Maria. And besides, I'm trying to figure out how you discovered that we were coming to town and what the devil you're doing here anyhow!"

"The chief steward at the lodge wrote me, among other things, that you were coming . . . and I'm here to welcome you and to look after your luggage. I don't know if you've noticed that my coachman has already taken your bags."

"Good for you, Maria!" Daniel acquiesced. "It will save us the price of a cab. Last time, it cost me plenty of money!"

"Oh, Daniel!" I exclaimed, greatly shocked.

"Leave him alone, Helga, it doesn't matter. Let everyone play his part. His is that of Brother Miser and mine that of Sister Prodigal."

"Home, José!" Mariana ordered the coachman after we had seated ourselves in the elegant coupé.

"Nothing of the kind! To the Hotel Astoria!" Daniel cried.

"One moment, José. Do you mean to say, Daniel, that you don't intend to stop at my house?" my sister-in-law remarked, looking greatly surprised.

"We'll never set foot in your house again, my dear Maria," was Daniel's answer.

"But you can't do that! Helga, I have gotten everything ready for your visit. And besides . . . it isn't done. You cannot go to a hotel when my house is at your disposal with several guest rooms. What would people say, Daniel?"

"Perhaps they would say that since your famous ball Daniel Viana and his wife do not care to visit the Countess de Nevers, that's all."

"That's it exactly, Daniel! You cannot imagine how much gossip there has been already about my ball! People are likely to say . . . And, you know, when people are envious there's no limit to what they might say! They're likely to say . . ."

"For instance, that while your husband was away you led a life that your brother did not approve of."

"Exactly, Daniel. People are always so mean! Why should we give them another opportunity to gossip?"

"Well, you see, my dear, I don't think people are always so mean, as you say. And anyway, one does not have to worry about gossip when one has a clear conscience. To the Hotel Astoria, José!"

"No José, drive home, please!"

"Do what I ask or I'll take the reins myself!" Daniel cried. And as the carriage started to move at last he turned to his sister and added:

"Furthermore, I regret to inform you that neither my wife nor I will do you the honor of setting foot inside of your house during our stay in town, Madame la Comtesse."

A silence followed during which was heard the rumbling of the wheels over heavy pavement. And then suddenly the gay, insolent, proud Countess de Nevers, her eyes full of tears, sighed:

"But what you're doing to me, Daniel, is mean, it's really very mean!"

"I've always been mean and you know it, just as you've always been a liar."

"Why do you say that?"

"Because . . . I have a premonition!" Daniel answered.

"Well then, I must confess, it's true. I lied to you, if you call that lying!" suddenly exclaimed Mariana, now weeping copiously. "If I'm so anxious to have you stay with me, it is not on account of what people might say! No, it's on account of my husband who is now back from Europe and who has been told dreadful things about my ball. People have talked about it as if it had been some sort of terrible scandal, an orgy in the dark. They say that the blowing up of the gaslight had been planned in advance, and that the confusion which followed was so great that my sister-in-law felt outraged and decided to go upstairs to her apartment."

"That's ridiculous!" I cried.

"Yes, it's ridiculous and a terrible shame and everything else you might want to call it, yet my husband now hardly speaks to me and he has even threatened to get our marriage annulled in Rome. And I'm told that it might possibly be done because I've never been able to have a child . . . Oh my God . . . And now you're coming to town and going to live at a hotel. He will hear about it and it will be proof to him that all those monstrous stories and those anonymous letters which are poisoning his mind against me are true! Surely after that he will ask for an annulment!"

"Well, that might be the best thing for you. Then at least you will be left with a little money," Daniel retorted.

"Money, money! That's all you have in mind when you talk about me! Do you think because my husband is a foreigner and has a title that is any reason why I can't be in love with him? You yourself, didn't you twice marry for love, girls much poorer than he ever was? Well, I too have a heart and adore my husband! I was the one who ran after him to make him marry me. And if I play around now and spend money it is simply that I want to forget, yes, to forget my sorrow because I've never succeeded in making him love me the way I wanted him to . . . and . . . I will die . . . I will die if he ever leaves me!"

Poor Mariana! In order to cry her heart out, she had pulled back her small veil, and her pretty little turned-up nose which she was patting with a tiny embroidered handkerchief was actually as shiny as the nose of a kitten.

The tears were running over her face powder. And lying back on the cushions of the carriage, no longer trying for effect, she looked like the little red-headed girl she must have been only a few years ago on that hacienda lost in the mist.

"Drive to the Countess's house, José!" Daniel suddenly ordered the coachman. "Oh women, what a nuisance they are anyway!" he growled, leaning over the edge of the window to hide his emotion.

◆

And that is how it happened that on that very morning we made our entrance into Mariana's beautiful house in far more impressive style, I must say, than we had done on the evening of the ball.

I almost failed to recognize the big hall of so many memories in the well-proportioned square vestibule with soft carpets, its view of the pink drawing room now cut off by heavy curtains closely drawn.

Up the stairway we went. The landings were decorated with natural plants, and I noticed that filled with those enormous green ferns obviously brought down from the woods around the lodge, the house seemed to be—like them—pervaded by spring.

As soon as Mariana had led us into the same blue bedroom we had occupied on the night of the ball, I could not resist drawing open the silk curtains of one of the windows in order to take a look at the little garden.

The little garden was still just like a setting for romance: its four cypress trees casting straight to heaven their somber jet of green, the tiny fountain spreading out its endless watery pearl necklace, and the ivy on the far wall still partly covering the sinister little iron gate opening into the alley . . .

With a sudden uncomfortable shiver I turned back to give a kiss to Daniel busy placing the suitcases on the little stools Mariana pointed out to him.

"Good for you!" she cried. "I don't know what has happened to both of you, but this time you really look like a newlywed couple. Well, now that you have everything you need," she added, taking a last look of inspection around the vast room, "I will leave you with the request that you come down to the pink drawing room just before noon. That's the time set for luncheon. My husband is the very soul of punctuality. Please don't forget it, Daniel. As for you, Helga, I think it would be well if you made yourself lovely for him . . . he has heard a lot about you, about your beautiful eyes . . ."

And with that in mind I had gotten myself seated in front of the mirror, when a knock was heard at the door.

"Come in," I said.

The door opened. It was Ginette.

"Good morning, Madame Viana."

I smiled at her, feeling, nevertheless, impressed by her smart appearance and the slightly amused look she always put on when talking to me, then:

"How do you like this dress, Ginette? You know, I made it myself. . . . Don't you think it looks a bit . . . a bit . . ."

My candor seemed to disarm her, and she came to my assistance:

"A little bit too severe for Madame, who is so very young, of course. Besides, Madame looks well in any dress. She has such a pretty waist and is naturally smart. But now that Madame is in town, she should take advantage of the opportunity and make the rounds of the shops with Madame la Comtesse. . . . Considering that Madame Viana can well afford to do it, she should take better advantage of her figure and of her personality," she concluded, giving Daniel an oblique glance which made him red with anger.

"I'm much obliged to you for your good advice," he said to her curtly.

"Don't mention it, Monsieur," Ginette remarked, unmoved, after which she turned to me again while Daniel disappeared into the bathroom, banging the door after him.

"I had come to ask Madame if she had not by mistake taken away the fan of Madame la Comtesse in her suitcase when she left for the country the day after the ball . . . Madame no doubt remembers the little fan embroidered with pearls which was lent to her by Madame la Comtesse on the evening of the ball?"

"Oh yes! but I didn't take it away, I'm sure of that," I exclaimed.

"We have never been able to find it anywhere after Madame left. Several times I suggested to Madame la Comtesse that she should write to Madame about it but Madame la Comtesse does not like to write letters. That is a fact! So I beg your pardon for insisting, but wouldn't Madame possibly have some idea what she could have done with the fan during the ball . . ."

A picture, terrifying in its clearness and precision, all of a sudden entered my mind: a high mantelpiece, an ancient golden clock under a glass case. And Landa putting down next to it the little fan embroidered with pearls.

". . . For wherever Madame put the little fan down that is certainly where it must have been forgotten . . ."

Yes, in fact it was alongside the little, diligent, arrow-shaped balance wheel that so lightly registered every second of my guilt, that I had forgotten the fan . . . But no, no, that could not be!

I shook my head, trying to overcome the uneasiness now spreading its shadow over me.

No, it could only be in my dream that I had forgotten the fan there! In reality, I must have dropped it at the time Landa's kiss had made me lose my head or when I was escaping across the drawing rooms and up the stairs to this room I was now again sharing with Daniel.

". . . We have been looking for it in all the drawing rooms, in the stairway, and even in the corridors . . ." Ginette was still explaining, "but we did not find it anywhere."

"Oh, Ginette, it's dreadful, dreadful!" I murmured, looking fearfully towards the door of the bathroom on the threshold of which Daniel suddenly reappeared, half-naked, dripping with water.

"May I come in, Ginette?"

"Of course, Monsieur is at home. I'm the one who should be going!" Ginette answered, hurrying out as she cast an outraged look on the state of undress of Monsieur.

"Well, well! What did that pest want of you?" he inquired laughingly.

"Oh . . . nothing very special . . ."

"Just giving you suggestions as to how to make me spend my money, eh?" he joked, going back to dressing himself.

"That's it!" I laughed, pleased with the way the conversation was turning.

"You know, Helga, after all, she may not be entirely wrong, that hussy. Why shouldn't you ask Maria to help you order a few dresses for yourself."

"Oh Daniel, Daniel, how nice you are, how very nice! For such a long time I've been dreaming about a tailored suit of very light green, like the grass in the spring . . ."

"Well, order it, then!"

"And also about an afternoon dress of very dark blue like the sky when it's cold. . . ."

"Very well, if you can find one that color."

"And then I also want a pink dress, and another one pearl gray, but most of all, most of all, I want a very beautiful ball dress like the one Mariana lent me, but I want it yellow, of such bright yellow color that I could wear it with a little bunch of goldenrods in my hand and . . ."

"And so that all dressed up that way, you could again sleep all night on a sofa instead of dancing!"

A brief silence followed, then:

"Daniel, why did you say that to me?" I inquired, greatly surprised.

"Because that's exactly what happened to you *in* Mariana's beautiful dress in the pink drawing room on the night of your first ball."

There came another silence during which Daniel engaged in an angry battle with his collar button, then:

"Listen, Daniel," I said calmly, trying hard to understand, "you're telling me now in effect that I slept on the sofa in the pink drawing room the entire night of the ball. At the hacienda, however, you assured me that when I came up to knock at your door just after the lights went out, you opened the door and I slept by your side all night."

"I never said you slept by my side all night. All I said was that I opened the door to you when you came up."

"Well then . . ."

"Then . . . listen, Helga, I'm willing to confess that I led you on, or rather that I let you get yourself involved during our famous discussion at the hacienda. It amused me very much to watch you getting all mixed up with your own words and reasonings."

"I don't understand."

"Well, you see, Helga, it's quite true I opened the door to you as I said, but a little later than I had said."

"I still don't understand . . ."

"Now I'm ready!" Daniel announced, this time appearing on the threshold of the bathroom, neatly dressed, his hair carefully groomed. "Do I look beautiful?"

"Very . . ."

"And what's even better, I'm on time . . . it's not yet twelve o'clock."

"Listen, Daniel, I would like you to explain one thing to me. . . ."

"Certainly, come and I'll explain it all to you, while we go down to the pink drawing room. Give me your hand. By the way, you look very lovely in that dress which was said to be so severe. Come along . . . and now listen to me carefully. On the night of the ball—that door you see right here where we're now standing, only when I felt that your punishment had lasted long enough and after you had stopped knocking, did I make up my mind to open it . . . Do you follow me?"

"Yes," I nodded. For I could readily picture him, standing at that very spot where we were then, with a devilish smile on his lips, cruelly delaying the moment when he would open the door while, already discouraged, I had actually ceased knocking.

". . . but it so happened that when I did open the door . . . as I am doing now . . ."

And making the deed fit in with the word, Daniel opened the door, still holding me back by the hand.

". . . you had disappeared! You were not anywhere to be seen! And so, trying to catch up with you, I walked as far as . . ."

And continuing to make the deed fit the word, Daniel pulled me across the same corridors I had traveled on that unfortunate night of the ball when, together with the train of Mariana's beautiful dress, I was miserably dragging the humiliation and the anguish of having been literally locked out by my husband.

". . . I walked as far as this staircase," Daniel concluded as we reached the stairway where he stopped close to the banister . . . "it was here that I found Amanda."

"Amanda!"

"Yes, you'll recall that she had helped you to go up the stairs without your seeing her, when the champagne had affected you so much that . . . however, let's not go into that again. So Amanda, who had remained here watching in a motherly way all your comings and goings . . ."

"Why did she let me go downstairs again?"

"That's what I've never quite understood. However, like every other woman she placed the responsibility on someone else. In this case on me! 'You should have opened the door to the Señora,' she said to me. 'The Señora is acting in a very strange way. She did not even see me when I helped her go upstairs. And look at her now . . .' Then, standing next to her, I leaned over the banister to . . . my Lord, Helga, I must say this is all very beautiful!" suddenly exclaimed Daniel, still illustrating his story by deed, and leaning over the banister as he had done on the night of the ball.

"Placing those enormous ferns in the recesses of the wall, and everywhere else . . . was really a very good idea. Look, Helga, when seen from here the house is just like a winter garden, don't you think so?"

"Yes," I answered, without looking.

"You know, Helga, it seems quite extraordinary but this house is exactly the type of house that that little devil of a Maria wanted to own when she was not any higher than my knee. When I'm grown up, she used to say to me, I shall have a house entirely different from that of Uncle Manuel. My house will be gay like a garden; it will have walls covered with light-colored silks, soft carpets like lawns, it will have many lamps, orchids in beautiful vases. . . . A swamp on the third floor and a tower at the bottom of the cellar, I used to say just to annoy her. And I can assure you that every time I said it she went into a frightful rage."

"Very interesting, Daniel, very amusing, but would you mind explaining to me . . ."

"Explaining what? Oh yes, of course! Where was I in this exciting story?"

"At the point where, after Amanda had scolded you, you were standing next to her, leaning over the banister."

"That's it . . . So I was leaning over the banister, as I am doing even now when . . . Oh, but look, Helga! I hadn't noticed this before . . . that beautiful green carpet spread over the stairway, doesn't it look exactly like a strip of real lawn? . . . Come, let's tread upon its beauty before my dear sister forbids me to set my big peasant shoes upon it."

And as he was talking, as quick as a flash Daniel lifted me on his shoulders and started to run like a fool down the stairs, in no way disturbed by my frightened cries.

"There! Here you are safe and sound, Madame!" he said at last, dropping me down in the middle of the hall. "Now, I must locate the orchids . . . yes, after the carpet, the orchids. . . . Come, Helga, let's play at finding them."

"All right, all right, but first tell me . . ." I grumbled, imploringly and haltingly . . . "When you were leaning up there over the banister alongside of Amanda what did you . . ."

"Well, I saw you going down this hall, exactly as we are doing now," resumed Daniel, pulling me by the hand behind him. "But as those curtains I'm now drawing open were not closed then, as you undoubtedly remember, I could clearly see you from up there entering into that good old pink drawing room right at this spot and disappearing in this comfortable sofa in which you find yourself seated right now," he concluded, pushing me into that sofa, only too well known, facing the French windows.

Notwithstanding my increasing apprehension, I could not help casting an inquiring look all around me. The pink drawing room! How beautiful it was and how very pink, even in broad daylight.

"Look, Helga, here they are!" Daniel suddenly exclaimed, drawing my attention with a triumphant finger to a vase filled with orchids decorating the low table placed just in front of the much-talked-of sofa upon which I had collapsed.

"Yes, yes, but afterwards, Daniel, tell me. . . ."

"Afterwards, what?"

"What happened after you saw me disappearing into this sofa?"

"Well, that's simple. A few minutes later," he continued, "considering that you were not showing any sign of life, Amanda and I, still perched up there on the staircase, came to the conclusion that you had fallen asleep. The dear girl wanted to go downstairs to wake you up and bring you back . . . but, enraged by the ridiculousness of the situation, I spoke sharply to her and sent her right to bed. Then I walked back to our room with the intention of getting dressed and going downstairs myself . . . But it is then, that . . . Well, then I suddenly said to myself that after all it made no difference at all to me whether you slept down there on the sofa or in bed by my side . . . and . . ." Daniel hesitated, suddenly embarrassed.

"And leaving the door of the room unlocked so that I could come in whenever I should wake up, you went to bed and fell asleep," I concluded.

"It doesn't seem possible to hide anything from you," he said jokingly, his good humor quickly restored.

A silence followed during which I remained absolutely still, with throat tight, while he walking from one end of the drawing room to the other, looked more and more pleased with himself.

"But my dear, it's wonderful . . . here is an entire collection of jade fish and white china all over the place . . . Uncle Manuel this time surely would be green with envy if only he could see it!"

"But tell me, Daniel," I suddenly said to him, cutting short his exuberance, "why then did you tell me so positively at the hacienda that you had opened the door to me when I knocked? And why did you with your silences and your half-truths let me believe that I had slept all night by your side?"

"Well, as I told you before, in a way it amused me to see how you were taken in even more than I had hoped, and also how you got mixed up in your own stories and dreams . . . and above all . . . because it made me angry to have you say over and over again that I had gone to sleep without caring whether my wife was or was not walking the streets with a lover."

"Yet that's exactly what you did!"

"Excuse me, Helga, I went to sleep, it is true, but only after I had found out that you were comfortably settled here on this sofa, sheltered from the excitement of the ball . . . and now, whether you dreamed that you were going away with Landa from this sofa or from our bed upstairs doesn't really make any difference, does it?"

"Why, of course it does!" I answered, trying to laugh, while my heart was pounding to the breaking point, "because now what proof have we got that I did not in fact go out with Landa?"

"But what proof have we got that you did go out with Landa?" Daniel replied jestingly after a brief pause.

The fan! The fan! a voice was screaming inside of me! If it cannot be found here in the house, that fan becomes then the definite proof that I went out with Landa!

"Well now, Helga, you'll admit that my argument, in fact quite worthy of a lawyer, has successfully brought your little game to an end. And since we're talking about lawyers, in order not to lose the habit of being late at meals, I will now run over to call on your Aunt Adelaida's lawyer, I have at least twenty minutes, and . . ."

"Daniel," I interrupted abruptly, "if it turns out that my going out with Landa was not a dream and I really went out with him, what would you do then?"

A brief silence followed.

"Helga, darling, you would not be the woman you are, if you had gone out with Landa!" Daniel said at last, taking me in his arms. And I closed my eyes and kept silent while he kissed me murmuring:

"I will be back in a little while."

◆

He went out. How long did I remain there, motionless, under the spell of the strangest anguish? I do not know.

All I know is that, as that very anguish was pushing me unconsciously towards the French windows now wide open, presently, I found myself facing again the four cypress trees, the fountain, and the little iron gate hidden there under the ivy on the wall.

And it so happened that, spurred by the same subtle anguish, I walked down the steps and, sinking ankle-deep in the grass, went around the fountain and opened the iron gate which made a dreadful grating sound as it turned on its hinges, exactly as it had on the night of my dream.

And just as it had happened in my dream, the gate opened on a narrow sloping alley . . . and up the narrow street I went like one walking in her sleep.

And once more it happened that the alley led to a square into which I entered without hesitation. There the massive line of buildings enclosing the square was broken by a tall rusty iron gate, beyond which lay an abandoned garden, high birch trees, their airy leaves alive in the spring air! And behind the birches, closed, silent, looking as though it would fall down under the weight of honeysuckle and clematis, was the old colonial house of my dream.

It was now broad daylight. There was no mist. I had not taken any champagne and I did not have any feelings or desires except for my husband . . . yet unquestionably the house was there.

There it was, and my fan had been left inside of it together with my purity and my sworn allegiance to my husband.

There it was, and now I knew my night of love had not been a dream and I was not the woman Daniel thought I was . . .

I recall it was the surprised expression of some passersby that finally induced me to tear myself away from that gate, to let go of its bars I was holding tightly gripped, as if with my own two hands I wanted to feel its cold, its rust, all of its overwhelming reality . . .

Coming back now across the square, I walked down the alley, pushed open the little iron gate, went around the fountain.

Standing on the threshold of the French windows, a man was there, apparently waiting for me.

"Ah! Someone is coming at last! I say, how do you do, Helga!"

Puzzled, I stared at him for a moment.

". . . as I'm quite sure you can be no one but Helga! So much I've heard about those beautiful dark eyes!" he added, kissing the hand I held out to him.

And all at once, I realized that this slim man with grayish hair and a smile full of charm was the Comte de Nevers.

◆

FIVE

Guy de Nevers! How different he was from what I had imagined, this man, so simple, with such exquisite manners, at whose right hand I found myself seated at the table.

Looking at his lovely silvery hair, his delicate eagle profile, his smart-looking shoulders, his long well-groomed hands, I wondered, in the innocence of my eighteen years, how a man of forty could look so young and attractive. And I could not help noticing that even though he was unquestionably well-bred, Daniel alongside of him looked like a very handsome but rather heavy giant.

"Several times I intended to pay you a visit at the hacienda," the Count was saying. "For in addition to the pleasure of meeting you both, I also want very much to see that unusual house you're living in."

"Just a piece of bric-a-brac!" Mariana exclaimed.

"Oh no," I protested, "a real castle out of a fairy tale!"

"Neither one nor the other," Daniel broke in, with a look of contempt for both of us, and then, turning to his brother-in-law:

"Our Uncle Manuel," he explained, "a highly cultured man who in the latter part of his life became tired of people—for which we can hardly blame him—decided to build at the hacienda where he was spending his days a house that would be an adequate setting for all the beautiful things he had purchased in the course of his travels."

"Very interesting," the Count murmured.

"I'm willing to admit," Daniel continued, "that that kind of a palace, in the middle of the forest, surrounded by mist, might appear to be the creation of an unbalanced mind . . ."

"I beg your pardon, of an artist!" the Count objected.

"Do you think so?" Daniel asked, his eyes alight with pleasure. "Well, that's just what I was about to say. Our uncle, who also was our guardian and to whom Maria and I owe practically everything we have, may have been a bit queer but at the same time he was a very good man and a real artist."

"I knew it but still I'm glad to hear you say so," the Count said, obviously won over by the words and the simple manner of Daniel. "I have known about your uncle a long time. For I too appreciate beautiful things. And in particular I know that he owned some beautiful tapestries and a very important library."

"Oh, yes! There are all kinds of illustrated editions, some of them very rare, and a lot of old manuscripts, worth a fortune. This library is one of the most interesting I have ever known, a professor from some foreign country whose name I have forgotten, once said to my uncle . . . he looked like a German with a little goatee . . . And you see, he made the trip to the hacienda just for one purpose, to do research work day and night in the library. . . . And imagine," concluded Daniel with childish vanity, "it is to me that in a special clause of his will my uncle bequeathed his library."

"It's too bad he did not at the same time bequeath you some of his culture so you could use it with the library!" Mariana exclaimed mockingly.

And while her husband looked at her severely, Daniel's anger was rising.

"I'm a simple man, a man from the country, that's true, my dear! But even though I do not have one-fourth of the culture you have had the opportunity to acquire—thanks to Uncle Manuel—yet I never made the mistake of calling his house bric-a-brac!"

"But if you have so much appreciation of works of art, why don't you take care of them as you should? House, library, and everything else are crumbling away under spider webs since the death of Uncle Manuel," Mariana caustically said to her brother, obviously furious at being humiliated by him in front of her husband.

"Oh, Mariana," I put in timidly, "you know that even if Daniel and I devoted our entire life to the house, still the mist would somehow get the best of everything."

"Yes," Daniel explained to the Count, giving me a pleasant smile, "my wife means that the dampness there is so frightful that it is actually spoiling everything—paintings, books, tapestries. . . . Especial care would be necessary to preserve . . ."

"Poor Uncle Manuel!" Mariana interrupted. "What a punishment for his avarice to have to see from the next world all his precious treasures crumbling to dust."

"You should be the last person in the world to talk about his avarice, Maria!" Daniel retorted with indignation.

"Well, let's say I speak of it through spite," she answered frivolously.

"Through spite?"

"Yes, you must admit it was not very flattering to me to have him leave to you, who are very nice but decidedly not an artist, all the things my husband and I would have been better able to appreciate and to take care of than yourself."

"But, Maria, really! You forget he's left you very valuable lands, the best of woodlands . . ."

"Which I would readily exchange for the tapestries, the books and, in particular, for the Murillo and the two Corots he left you."

There was a silence, then:

"But, Maria!" Daniel insinuated in a low, honeyed voice which made me fearful for her, "you know there is still time to arrange for such an exchange . . ."

"What do you mean?"

"We might prepare a contract of sale on an exchange basis . . . in which I would transfer to you the works of art left me by Uncle Manuel against your lodge and its woods. . . . Don't you agree that these I'm better able to appreciate and to take care of than yourself?"

Daniel sarcastically queried in turn.

"That sounds very interesting!" the Count exclaimed.

"You might come to the hacienda and make an estimate yourself of all the things there," Daniel continued, addressing himself to his brother-in-law, "and in the meantime . . ."

"In the meantime, we'll have our coffee in the pink drawing room," Mariana interrupted, getting up from the table. And a few moments later in the drawing room, I noticed that her hands were shaking as she took hold of the lovely silver tongs to pass the sugar.

"No coffee for me, thank you, Mariana," Guy de Nevers said to his wife, then, turning to us: "Will you please excuse me if I leave you so soon, as I have letters for Europe to mail before three o'clock. However, I do hope we can resume this conversation tonight," he added, patting Daniel on the shoulder in a friendly manner as he left.

◆

SIX

No sooner had her husband drawn back the curtains of the pink drawing room behind him than Mariana, dropping the tongs she had been holding gracefully in her hand, literally threw herself at her brother like an enraged kitten.

"I forbid you to speak to Guy again about that exchange!" she cried. "I won't have you steal the lodge from me!"

"Steal? My dear Maria, it seems to me I've heard you say that works of art have great value . . . and, furthermore, I don't see any reason why you should get yourself in such a state. After all, the lodge is your property, and your husband is too much of a gentleman to dispose of it without your consent."

"You're cynical, Daniel. A monster of trickery and deceit! You know perfectly well that if my husband insists on such a deal, I would not wish to oppose him."

"And why not, if you please?"

"Because at this time I would not want, under any circumstances, to oppose him openly in that which he loves above all things. . . . Yes, it is on books, paintings, and works of art that he has spent all of his inheritance . . . and if he still owns his château, it is only because it is classified as an historical monument. Yes, all his money and mostly all that was derived from the sale of my lands has gone into his art collections. I don't blame him, but the lodge. . . . I want to keep it, do you hear, Daniel? Those woods have been in the family for four generations and they're the only title of nobility I possess, so I want to keep them, I want to keep them because . . ."

". . . Because it happens to be a convenient place for you to receive your lovers?" Daniel interrupted brutally.

A silence followed, then:

"What did you say?" Mariana cried, greatly disconcerted.

"Just what you've heard," Daniel answered with the greatest calm.

There was another silence, then:

"Helga, Helga, did you hear what your husband has just been saying to me?" Mariana interposed pleadingly.

"Oh don't worry, not only has she heard it but, what's more, a few weeks ago she saw a certain carriage going around the lagoon in the general direction of the lodge."

"And what do you mean by that?"

"You'll find out about it soon enough! Helga, tell her who was in that carriage you saw going by the lagoon a few weeks ago?"

"But, Daniel, you amaze me! You know very well I thought I had seen a carriage under the willows a few weeks ago . . . but you explained and proved to me later beyond question that the willows being a foot under water, it was quite impossible for me to have seen a carriage there."

"Oh, that's another mean trick I played on you in the course of our discussion, Helga! The truth is that it was quite possible for a carriage to have been under the willows at the time you saw one there."

"I don't understand . . ."

"Listen, Helga, there was a difference of several hours between the time you saw the carriage and the time when I made you observe that the trees were under water . . . isn't that so?"

"Yes."

"Well, it was during those few hours that the waters of the lagoon happened to rise, until they came up to the willows. That's all."

"But how did it happen and why?"

"Because just at that time I ordered the locks of a little canal going from the river across the woods down to the lagoon to be opened. A canal I had planned and constructed for the very purpose of bringing under water that piece of land on which your dear willows are standing."

"But what was the purpose of this canal . . . and of all this labor?"

"If I explain to you in detail that I wanted to make out of that piece of land a site for raising beavers, would that mean anything to you? But please don't look so upset, and now that you can see plainly that after all you didn't have a vision, tell the lady right here once for all who it was you had the privilege of seeing in that carriage near the lagoon. Now, Helga, speak! please . . ."

"But . . . you know as well as I do . . . that it was . . . Landa!" I said, articulating with the greatest difficulty.

"Did you hear that?" Daniel cried to Mariana. "Landa, your lover, behind whom you were hiding, while on your way with him to a honeymoon at the lodge! It's the chief steward, whom you asked to keep your visit secret, who took it upon himself to let it be known everywhere, until finally it reached my ears. And now you're cynical enough to pretend that you are attached to that land because of your family feelings! You should in the first place have shown some respect for a house in which your father and mother lived and . . . right now, I don't know what's holding me back from slapping you in the face instead of helping you by my presence here to keep a husband you do not deserve!" Daniel concluded, walking up to his sister with a terrifying look on his face.

"It's not true! It's not true!" Mariana cried vehemently.

"Are you now going to deny the fact that . . ."

"I have no intention of denying I went to the lodge, Daniel, but it was for the purpose of closing the house that I went there and I stayed only a few hours. And if I asked the chief steward not to tell I was there it's because I was afraid you would bother me again with your much-talked-about contract."

"And Mr. Landa, can you tell me what he went to the lodge for?"

"At the time, Landa and I were guests at the hacienda of your neighbors the Mendez. And even though you have managed to break off relations with them, still you must admit they are quite incapable of getting involved in anything that might be considered at all improper . . ."

"I don't care about the Mendez! But can you tell me what Mr. Landa was doing at the lodge with you?"

"Listen, Daniel," Mariana exclaimed in a frenzy, "Landa is not my lover, do you hear? Landa . . ."

". . . Made that long trip in the carriage from the Mendez' hacienda to the lodge just to help you close the shutters and pull up the rugs in the house, is that what you mean?"

There was a brief silence, then:

"Life is very strange!" Mariana sighed and, having suddenly recovered her good humor, she looked at her brother, her eyes sparkling with mischief. "If I told you the reason why Landa wanted to make that journey with me to the lodge, you would be surprised indeed!"

"Well, tell us about it anyway, and if it does surprise me, I will consider it most extraordinary," Daniel answered in a cold, sarcastic tone.

"Well then, my dear, just imagine Landa, whom you're accusing of being my lover, went to the lodge only with the secret hope of seeing, even if from far off . . . your wife."

"My wife!"

"Now come, there's no use taking it so tragically!" Mariana said laughingly. "David Landa is too well known an admirer of beautiful women. His devotion to Helga should in no way be considered compromising or dangerous. . . . But what's happening to you? Why do you both look at me like that?"

"David . . . did you say, David Landa?" Daniel was asking.

"Why certainly, Landa's name is David! Do you mean to say you didn't know it?"

"Landa's name is David!" I repeated like an echo.

Again there was a brief silence, then:

"My God! Of course, I had entirely forgotten!" Mariana exclaimed, looking as though she had suddenly remembered something extraordinarily amusing. "Yes, how odd, Daniel! I had entirely forgotten that Landa also had been a passionate admirer of your first wife, of that beautiful Teresa who is still talked about in society. They even say he was very much in love with her and that the only reason he did not marry her was because . . . marriage is not his hobby!" she concluded with a heavy laugh.

"Stop laughing!" Daniel mumbled in a hollow voice.

"How can I help it? You and David Landa rivals! That's so unexpected, so absurd!"

"Don't laugh!" Daniel cried, grabbing his sister violently by the shoulder. "When I think that you, my own sister, brought to the hacienda and introduced to my wife this man, the only man of whom I cannot even bear the thought that he spoke to her or touched her hand!"

"But, Daniel, I don't see why you. . . . Oh, my God, Helga! What's the matter with her!"

"Helga!"

And now Daniel and Mariana were rushing to my aid, for—and even after so many years I hate to tell about it because I think it so very ridiculous!—I had just fainted!

If my reader will, however, consider all I had gone through since my arrival at Mariana's house, perhaps he will forgive me for acting in such a silly way . . .

One by one, all the elements which I had believed made up no more than a guilty dream, had reappeared clothed in an inescapable reality. And gathered together in what seemed to me implacable logic, there they were now confronting me in the shape of a truth that could no longer be denied:

My running away with Landa had not been a dream. Landa unquestionably had been my lover.

And furthermore, oh height of misfortune! it turned out that Landa was David.

David Landa! The man who was responsible for Daniel's losing his youth and his faith . . . the one man with whom, even if he wished to, Daniel could never forgive me my fault!

David Landa! The shame of my having belonged to him was hurting Daniel so cruelly through me that I never would dare look him in the face. So all was now lost for me. Happiness indeed was gone forever!

◆

SEVEN

If I had ever dared to present this simple account of a woman's experience in the form of a novel, I would have called the chapter that is to come: "The Ball in Reverse."

Although it records an extraordinary and complete turn in events, it begins nevertheless in such a simple manner that it might easily be considered a quite unnecessary sequence to the scene which had just unfolded itself in the pink drawing room.

It was on that much-talked-about sofa facing the French windows that I found myself lying down when I regained consciousness. My fainting spell must have been neither very long nor very terrible, considering that my eyes were not yet reopened when already Mariana was resuming her discussion with Daniel.

"Really you two, for people who profess to be so simple, I find you both entirely too complicated. And anyway, Daniel, I don't see why you should be so outraged because Helga shakes hands with a man whose only crime is to have been in love with Teresa before she was even engaged to you."

"Oh, Mariana, please, not another word! . . . You don't know!" I murmured.

"And as for you, my dear," she continued, turning to me, "you're acting as if you were the adulterous woman in the Gospels! For, after all, I don't see any crime in having made yourself attractive to a man as fascinating as Landa, in having smiled at him and shown him you liked to dance with him . . ."

"As for you," quickly put in Daniel, "you wouldn't even think it a crime if she had gone away with him, stayed out all night, and returned only in the early morning."

"Why do you say that to me?" Mariana inquired nervously.

"Because it's exactly what I saw you do on the night of the ball," Daniel replied very calmly.

"It's not true!" Mariana cried, a terrified look on her face.

"My dear Maria," Daniel retorted, "when a woman does what you did on the night of the ball, she should not go about talking so loudly under her brother's windows and she should not choose to run away in a dress spangled with thousands of stars that seemed to cry out in the night: Here we are! Here we are now going through the garden! Here we are, now going through the little iron gate!"

A silence followed, then:

"Well, all right, it's true! It's true, I went out with Landa that evening!" Mariana admitted at last in a low, trembling voice.

"Do you understand now, Helga, why I felt so sure that what you were telling me could not be anything but a dream?" Daniel said to me then, coming back to the sofa where I was lying dumfounded, unable to utter a single word.

"You saw me go out with Landa, that's true, Daniel!" Mariana exclaimed. "But would you be good enough to tell me if it's your intention to go on shouting it on the housetops?"

Poor Mariana, she was still trying to bluff, yet she looked so pale and seemed so unhappy that Daniel took pity on her.

"No, Maria, I won't. Unless you again drive me crazy with your impertinence."

"Oh Daniel, Daniel, if you only knew . . ." she suddenly moaned.

"Well, I guess I know quite enough as it is," he growled.

"Very well, Daniel," I spoke out at last. "But I would like you to explain to me . . . in fact you must explain to me how and when you saw Mariana go out with Landa for a walk on the evening of the ball?" I added forcefully, notwithstanding the pity I felt for Mariana who was now seated curled up in one of the armchairs sobbing heavily, just like the little red-haired girl I had seen crying in the carriage.

"Well, after all, Helga, it would seem I owe you this explanation and your sister-in-law should not be any the worse for it. A little while ago I told you that as I was leaning over the banister on the stairway, after I had noticed that you had fallen asleep on that same sofa where you're lying down now, I went back to our room . . ."

"Yes, I know, you intended to get dressed and come down for me, but . . ."

"But, as I was starting to dress, the terribly indiscreet grating sound of the little iron gate, together with the well-known voice of my dear sister almost shouting: '*Landa, are you leaving?*' brought me to the window—which, unfortunately for everybody concerned, opened on the garden—just in time to hear our dear Mr. Landa's answer:

"*No, I'm not leaving, I'm running away.*"

I gave a start. Mariana abruptly stopped crying and kept staring at her brother, who holding her gaze, continued in a strange voice:

"*Does it mean I shall never see you again?*"

A breathless silence followed, then Mariana spoke:

"*You're the one who wished it that way, so goodbye.*"

"Did you also hear that other answer of Landa's," she said at last weighing on each word . . . "and do you know what it meant, my dear brother?"

"Yes. It meant that up to that point, anyway, you had retained some semblance of decency, though it was quickly lost, it would seem, judging from the little dialogue that followed:—

"*No, no, stay, Landa. I want you to stay.*"

"*But why?*"

"*Because I love you!*"

Daniel recited with emphasis.

"I could not possibly have said it to him with so much feeling, considering that what he actually answered was:—

"*You mean to say you love me this evening?*"

Mariana in a pitiful voice was attempting to jest.

"At any rate, you made up later for your indifference and he for his caution," Daniel retorted, and then:

"*Yes, that's it only this evening. But this evening, however, I do love you passionately!*"

"*Why? Is it because your husband has forsaken you?*" he recited again while Mariana sobbed out.

"But it's true, my husband had hurt my feelings terribly when he left so suddenly for Europe and insisted on going away all by himself."

"Did that give you an excuse on account of spite to become the plaything of a worthless man?" Daniel interrupted harshly.

"The plaything? That's too much!"

"My poor Maria, it seems to me I can still hear him saying to you:

"*Then prove to me that you love me.*"

and you as meek as a lamb answering:

"*But how? . . .*"

. . . Oh, dear reader! I know, in fact I'm sure, that at this point in my story the light which gradually had come to my understanding as the brother and sister were thus battling with words, had also at the same time entered your mind.

All through their discussion and sentence by sentence I had recognized every word of the same intimate conversation I thought I had had with Landa prior to my presumed departure with him on the night of the ball.

And I realized now that the same grating sound of the iron gate, which had brought Daniel to the window, had at the same time partly awakened me as I was lying on the sofa, and that, in my semi-conscious state, I had appropriated to myself the dialogue which Mariana, unaware of my presence, had so recklessly carried on with Landa.

By the same token I understood clearly that it was quite understandable that it should have been so, considering that every single word of that dialogue could just as well have been spoken between Landa and myself. For Mariana was speaking the thoughts that were actually in my mind, and Landa was proposing to her what in my madness of the moment I secretly desired to hear . . .

"*Come with me tonight.*"

"*What are you saying?*"

"*I will bring you back before dawn. Nobody will notice your absence. Certainly not your husband!*"

"*But that's sheer madness!*"

"*Come. Then you will hold the memory of what real love is. It will help you to bear life at the side of a man who doesn't love you.*"

"*He will love me.*"

Daniel was actually continuing to recite in that same somber, sarcastic voice:

"He will love me! was your answer, Maria, to that wretch, admitting that your husband does not love you and giving that blackguard enough encouragement to speak once more insolently:

"*He will never love you!*" he said to you. "*Besides, he's not worthy of you . . . and everybody knows the reason why he married you.*" And you, you usually so proud did not even rebel but remained there sighing: "*Oh you're cruel!*"

"Everybody seems to think," Mariana protested, "and you among the first, that Guy never would have married me if it had not been for the millions of Uncle Manuel, and as he has been so indifferent to me, I've often come to think the same thing myself."

"Maria, the whole world and I too might well be wrong, you know!" Daniel said. "And as for you, who know so much about flirting, I'm surprised you didn't hide from that fellow a thought so humiliating to you."

"I was far too unhappy at the time to think of being a flirt, you may be sure!"

"That was not Mr. Landa's opinion. Do you remember the reproaches he made to you then?"

"*You've been more cruel to me, many times. You made me lose my head, you lied to me.*"

"And even though you protested, he gave himself the satisfaction of speaking the truth to your face. I can still hear him:

"*Yes, with your eyes and in your manner you lied to me . . . ever since that first day. And still, you believe yourself honest!*"

"Stop it!" Mariana cried.

"Yes, it's with the same conviction that you cried *stop it* to that dear Landa. And yet when he hastened to obey you:

"*Very well then, not another word . . . I'm going . . .*" you rushed behind him crying with no less conviction:

"*No, no, I'm going with you . . . until daybreak . . . my love!*"

Daniel concluded, giving his sister a terrifying look. She lowered her head.

"My God, Daniel, you certainly have a wonderful memory," Mariana murmured caught halfway between tears and laughter.

"That may be, but I can assure you I didn't require wonderful eyesight to see you shooting fireworks across the garden in that dress scintillating with stars and to see you going off on the arm of that despicable fellow through the iron gate . . ."

"Yet I love my husband, Daniel. I can't imagine what happened to me that night!" and for the hundredth time Mariana broke out decisively in a flood of tears.

. . . And so, dear reader, that was the way it all had happened. And now I could understand how, as soon as Mariana had run away with Landa, I had immediately dropped back into sleep and gone away with him too . . . but in my dream. I mean, it was in my dream that I had carried on that mad adventure, a burning desire for which his kiss had aroused in my flesh one hour earlier in the ballroom.

Daniel went on relentlessly:

"You went away and there I stood, like an idiot . . . and that is what I'll never forgive you, Maria . . . that ridiculous night you made me go through . . . for what was I to do? Run after you and beat up the fellow? Or else beat you up yourself? Start a scandal? If ever I had made up my mind to go downstairs, that's just what I would have done. But to start a scandal would have made your shame irretrievable . . . public! . . . And so I stayed there, worrying myself sick, walking up and down, even sleeping at times . . . until once again the grating sound of the damn gate announced your return . . . Pitiful! Ridiculous! That's the way I felt. Yet I don't see what else I could have done under the circumstances."

And so, on Mariana's return, it was again the little gate with its grating sound that had so logically brought my dream to an end. And while she was taking leave of her guests, just as if nothing had happened, I, believing that I had just come back from my lover's house, had gotten up from the sofa, walked up the main stairway and returned to my room where Daniel . . .

"I was pretending to be asleep when you came in, Helga, but I can assure you that from the moment you closed your eyes a new torture was added to all those I had suffered that night. Had you from your sofa heard and seen all I had seen and heard myself? You did not act as if you had. But perhaps it was because you had decided to keep silent and protect Maria. Only one month later, when you told me that Landa had been your lover, I realized at last that all the going back and forth of that unfortunate creature had not awakened you completely and that in some way you had managed from her woeful adventure to build for yourself a new kind of dream to add to your collection."

"What's that? What do you mean? What are you talking about?" suddenly inquired Mariana, her curiosity having gotten the better of her tears.

"About a lot of things you'll never know," Daniel retorted. "And besides, I think it's high time I should be permitted to get a little rest from the pleasure of your company, Maria. So, Helga, please tear yourself away from that miserable sofa and come along with me . . ."

Just then my right hand, which had slipped between the cushions and the back of the sofa, as it might have done when I was lying there on the evening of the ball, struck against an object which my fingers took hold of, raised.

And behold, I got up, holding in my hands a small heavy fan which I instantly opened.

"My embroidered fan!" Mariana exclaimed.

"Yes, that fan embroidered with pearls which I must have dropped while I was asleep on the sofa the night of the ball!" I cried in a transport of joy.

For—Heaven be praised!—this dreadful reality I had seen slowly rising out of the mist of my dreams was now crumbling piece by piece, and going back forever into the mist.

For if it was unquestionably true that I had not spent the night alongside of Daniel on the evening of the ball, yet thank God it was Mariana not I who had run away with Landa!

And I had actually seen the carriage on the bank of the lagoon, but it didn't matter in the least now whether I had seen it or not, or whether Landa had been in the carriage—considering that he had never been my lover!

As for the fan, it had slipped off my wrist and buried itself between the cushions and the back of the sofa while I was sleeping there on the night of the ball . . . no, I had not forgotten it next to that little clock on the mantelpiece of that house in which . . .

I gave a start, a horrible vision having brutally come to cut short the effervescent course of my joy.

"Helga! . . . Where are you going?"

"Helga! . . . What's happening to her? Where is she running?"

"Helga! Helga! Wait for me! . . ."

But already I was gone. I had slipped down into the garden, passed the fountain and opened the little iron gate.

◆

EIGHT

And now going up the little alley, with Daniel running close behind me, I already had reached the square, gone across it, and was there pressing once more against the bars of that gate only too well known.

In order that my flight with Landa should have been only a dream, this old house I could see behind the birch trees, this house so charming and so very real under the weight of the honeysuckle, should disappear, vanish in the spring air like a house of mist.

"Helga, what are you trying to do? Why did you come here?"

"Daniel, that house . . . for there is a house there behind those birches, isn't there?"

"Why, of course!"

"Well then, that house, I know it. I have been inside of it, Daniel!"

"Yes, I know you have, Helga. But why are you crying? Come, come!" he said, suddenly pushing open the gate. "Let's go in!"

"No!"

"But you must, Helga! You shouldn't be afraid of memories."

And taking me by the hand, Daniel dragged me across the lawn, and through the birch trees, up to the very door of the house where I stopped, faltering.

Then, under the pressure of my body, the old door gave way and opened.

I can still hear the frightened cry I uttered as I fell back.

"My poor Helga, don't be afraid. I'm the one who left the door open when I came here a little while ago."

"You?"

"Yes, and it's on account of this door that I arrived late, almost in the middle of lunch, notwithstanding Maria's instructions. The poor lawyer and I had to put in so much time and energy to force it open! But do go in, Helga, go into your house."

"No, no!" I cried. "I don't know what kind of a trick you're trying to play on me this time, Daniel, but I can assure you that if you don't explain everything clearly I will go mad, right here and now!"

"Helga! My Lord, what's happening to you? Control yourself, I beg of you! I had no idea of hurting you, you may be sure! I only thought that since you had recognized the house, you were going, little by little, to guess everything else."

"What? To guess what?"

"Well, that this house in which you were born and where you lived the first five years of your life, this house in which your parents died and which is the only thing in the world they could have left you, was generously bequeathed to you in her will by your most conscientious Aunt Adelaida!"

"This house . . . ?"

"Yes. Are you still afraid to go in now?"

I shook my head and taking hold nervously of the arm Daniel was gently offering me, I stepped across the threshold.

So sure was I that I was about to enter the shadow of a closed house that I remained speechless with astonishment as Daniel proceeded to explain to me, in the manner of a discontented owner:

"Yes . . . it seems that the roof crumbled about ten years ago at the time of the great earthquake . . . the walls and the foundations, however, have stood up very well."

Yes, it had the sky for a roof, my house! A celestial and radiant roof that suddenly seemed to pour out all of its light into the most rudimentary, the darkest recess of my memory . . .

The garden, that garden through which I had just come, turning around to look at it from the threshold, I suddenly discovered it again in my memory, but full of tall trees, sparkling with fountains, and interspersed with wistaria laden arbors . . . I was seeing it again as the big park it had been before the expanding city with its tall waves of masonry, had closed in on it reducing it to this miserable grass plot strewn with a few lean birch trees.

And that is how I could see, resting there under the blue shade of the mauve-colored wistaria a young woman working at her embroidery with a little girl standing by her side.

"You were calling me, Mummy?"

"Yes, Helga darling, my thimble has just fallen to the ground."

And the little girl is kneeling down, is looking around, searching in the grass a long while.

"Oh Mummy, I don't see it; I can't find that pretty little gold thimble of yours!"

"Well now, Helga, perhaps Thumbelina has seen it first and picked it up . . ."

"Thumbelina!"

"You know, that tiny little girl born in a tulip, whose story is told in one of the books I gave you . . . Do you recall? That little girl so small that she uses a walnut shell as a cradle, blue violet leaves as a mattress, and rose leaves for her coverlet. Don't you remember?"

"Oh yes, yes, Thumbelina! She lives in a garden, feeds on the honey from the flowers like the bees and . . . but tell me, Mummy, why should she have stolen your pretty thimble, that little Thumbelina?"

". . . Oh Helga . . . who knows . . . perhaps she wanted to have a lovely little bathtub made of gold! . . . That's it! . . . Two or three dewdrops in my thimble and . . ."

The grating sound of a distant gate interrupts this talk, and the little girl runs towards the young man who has just appeared out there at the end of the path.

That young man is the same one whose portrait I have—my father.

He is tall, elegant, and slender. He has blue eyes and, notwithstanding his extreme youth, his hair is gray. Yes, his hair of a bluish gray bringing out his youth and fine features is a real miracle such as could hardly be discerned in his portrait.

Enrique del Rio, I could see him now, lifting up high in his arms and kissing that little girl, who was I! I could see him putting her down and coming forward with a smile to the perfumed shade of the arbor.

And his beloved, so appealing, I could see her raising herself up on the settee, her heavy locks falling half-undone on the frail nape of her neck, her pale complexion suddenly alight like a rose, all pink, two small golden flames dancing suddenly in the depths of her dark pupils.

The handsome young man, I could clearly hear his voice as he addresses her, tenderly bending down to meet her lips. His was a deep voice, trembling just a little, and it seemed to caress that forehead raised up to him, as softly as would the wings of one of those butterflies fluttering among the flowers of the wistaria.

"It's already cool here under the arbor. That's not the best thing for you, Ebba. Let's go inside."

And I could see myself proudly carrying my mother's scarf and her workbag; following behind the lovers up to this threshold where I was now back again after so many years standing at Daniel's side . . .

For, this garden was in fact the garden of my earliest childhood, it was the park of Ebba Hansen's villa. The park only a few steps away from Mariana's house, that Landa had told me about during the ball, and the walls of which he climbed to look at my mother through the trees.

And now I understood that it was because his words had unconsciously driven my mind to look for that park in my memory that while I was asleep on the sofa in the pink drawing room, it was to this very park that I had come in my dream.

And behold, I could see myself again a very little girl running through that same suite of rooms through which I had passed with Landa in my dream and through which I was now walking followed by Daniel.

This large room with cracked walls along which frolicsome little lizards were now sliding, I could see it all, decorated with dark garnet-colored brocade. And once more I could see Ebba Hansen sitting at the far end of the room behind a long piano. And I could hear her singing.

Oh that small gentle voice, high-pitched, melodious, and tender; the dim sound of velvet notes with which at the piano she accompanies her soft crystalline sighing wherein the words Spring and Love, Nostalgia and Farewell keep coming back over and over again . . . ! I understood at last after so many years that this had been the source of that melancholy yet peaceful chant which so often came up within me whenever I found myself alone or in a pensive mood.

Two rooms, a corridor, and then another room . . .

Ebba Hansen—I was finding her once more kneeling on the carpet of that other room now laid bare.

And behold, I was again seeing her pale little hand, for so many years now motionless and cold, busily engaged putting together the pieces of a large puzzle, my last toy.

And from the depth of my childhood was coming up to my ear her lovely birdlike voice describing that scenery which she was in the act of recreating as much for her own pleasure as for that of her child:

". . . There . . . there . . . this piece here shaped like a clover leaf and this beautiful pine tree all covered with frost is now complete . . . And then . . . let's see . . . this piece is surely a part of that bridge over that frozen river all white with snow . . . and . . . Oh, Enrique, what a good idea you had to bring this present to the little one . . . for this snow scene is a true picture of winter in my country . . . Look, Helga, in your mother's country the snow does not only fall on mountain tops . . . it also falls as it does in this picture over the woods, over the roofs of houses, and over everything, over everything until it forms the beautiful white carpet that you see there."

"Oh tell me, Mummy, the snow is it very cold?"

"Yes, Helga, very, very cold."

"But is it hard, tell me, Mummy? And how does it taste? If I should take a bite out of one of those snowballs the little boys are fighting each other with, what would happen to me? Oh Mummy, and that pretty little animal there, what is it?"

"It's a squirrel."

"A squirrel . . . And what does it do?"

"It plays. It enjoys itself running here and there in the snow."

"Is that all?"

"Yes, God has made it only for that purpose, you see. Only that it might play and enjoy all that is beautiful in the forest, everything that men do not understand or do not want to see—the iridescent reflection of the morning on each dewdrop, mushrooms of unexpected colors that come up under the wet shadow of the ferns . . . and also that it might enjoy each one of the seasons and in each season every incident of the marching day—a brief spell of mist, a sudden burst of sun, a gentle breath of wind, and the strong deep perfume that comes out of flowers when rain is about to fall . . ."

"But at night, Mummy, at night, what does it do the little squirrel?"

"It climbs to the very top of the pine tree where it nestles and keeps still, enjoying every second of moonlight, following the phosphorescent track of every shooting star . . . Oh, Helga, don't you see it is because of this little squirrel that so many lovely things are not lost, have not been given out in vain by God . . ."

"But, Mummy, are there not people also who live only to see all those lovely little things?"

"There are some, Helga . . . they are the poets, the artists . . . the true ones . . . those who with sounds, words, or colors love to create worlds, where it is pleasant for the human mind to descend and to dwell . . . Isn't that so, Enrique?"

And once again I could see my father looking at Ebba Hansen, making no answer, looking at her a long time, fixedly, deeply, as if he had never seen her before or as if he was endeavoring to reach through her one of those worlds she had just described to us.

"Now, Helga, come back! Come back!"

It was Daniel's voice calling me back into the present, and somewhat impatiently warning me that it was high time for us to continue our landlords' tour of inspection.

One last door, and we find ourselves in a large room absolutely bare, its walls badly battered by the years and the storms. In the background a high mantelpiece falling apart. And behold as my memory went back to my recovered childhood, I could see that same room entirely done in lovely chintz of faded colors, illumined by the pink light of a big fire dancing in the high chimney . . . in the middle of the room, a large bed with tulle curtains and in the bed a young woman asleep.

Her beautiful dark hair was spread out on the pillows. And her long eyelashes were resting very still on her pale cheekbones. While sitting at her bedside and holding her hand a young man was watching over her sleep.

All seemed so peaceful, and both looked beautiful, young, earnest, and unhappy! Ebba Hansen and my father!

And even to the little girl I was then, they appeared as the very image of Love . . .

For thirteen years later, it was in this room, their own room, that I had come back in my dream to live with Landa what I had thought at the time the biggest love moment in my entire life . . .

And behold, in my memory, there I was suddenly living again the moment so long ago in my childhood when after having watched the beautiful, silent couple, the very little girl I was then walked across the room to take a look at the clock on the mantelpiece. And I could see myself there on tiptoe, staring in joyful amazement at the arrow-shaped pendulum moving back and forth.

And it was at the side of that clock so much admired by me as a child that I had laid down thirteen years later in a dream that other plaything of my first ball: Mariana's beautiful fan . . .

◆

NINE

Yes, my flight with Landa was nothing more than a dream! And that other house built by my subconscious self in a night of madness out of memories, desires, and mist was now going back, and crumbling down again into the mist.

Happiness! I did not dare yet give myself over into the joy of having at last recovered it, when:

"Helga! Helga!" Daniel was calling to me from outside.

As he had at last succeeded in opening the door at the other end of the room, he must be calling me now from that classical inner patio upon which all the rooms in our colonial houses converge.

"Come, Helga, come quickly!" his voice was insisting.

And as I walked towards the door, on my way to him, a breath of perfume and a sort of musical humming came forth to meet me.

"Look, Helga, isn't this the tree of your dreams?"

I raised my eyes and remained speechless, overwhelmed.

For, oh miracle! it was my tree! this gigantic mimosa, standing there in the midst of crumbling walls, still shedding its perfume on this spring day in Ebba Hansen's patio!

Yes, it was the Tree of Happiness, this blossoming golden tree, swarming with bees, under which Daniel was now enticing me with a tender mocking smile while whispering to me, as is usual at the end of all old-time love stories:

"I LOVE YOU."

Captain's Cottage,
Rockport, Maine.

The Shrouded Woman

ONE

As night was beginning to fall, slowly her eyes opened. Oh, a little, just a little. It was as if, hidden behind her long lashes, she was trying to see.

And in the glow of the tall candles, those who were keeping watch leaned forward to observe the clarity and transparency in that narrow fringe of pupil death had failed to dim. With wonder and reverence, they leaned forward, unaware that she could see them.

For she was seeing, she was feeling.

◆

TWO

And thus, she sees herself lying motionless face upward in the spacious bed, presently made up with the embroidered sheets perfumed with lavender, those usually kept under lock and key. And she sees herself dressed in that robe of white satin which made her look so slender.

Lightly crossed over her breast and pressing a crucifix, she notices her hands, her hands that seem to have acquired the frivolous delicacy of two peaceful doves.

Under the nape of her neck, the thick coil of hair which during her illness was becoming minute by minute more heavy and moist, no longer bothers her. For they had at last succeeded in disentangling it, smoothing it, parting it over her forehead. It is true, they had neglected to gather it together, but she knows that a dark mass of displayed hair lends to any woman reclining or asleep, a touch of mystery, a disturbing charm.

And all at once, she sees herself without a single wrinkle, pale and beautiful as never before.

A very great happiness comes over her in being thus admired by those who could only remember her as a woman tormented by futile anxieties, worn down by many sorrows, and withered by the sharp air of the hacienda.

For now that they know she is dead, here they are, all of them, gathered around her.

Here is her daughter, that golden resilient girl so proud of her twenty years, who would smile mockingly when, while showing old portraits to her, she would shyly remark how elegant and graceful she once had been too. Here and her two sons who seemed unwilling to grant her any longer the right to enjoy life; her sons, who seemed annoyed by her whims, ashamed when they found her running around the sunny garden; her sons, always reluctant to pay her the slightest compliment, even though secretly flattered when their young friends pretended to mistake her for their elder sister.

Here is Zoila, who saw her born and in whose care her mother entrusted her from that moment on, old Zoila, whose arms rocked away her sorrow each time her mother, leaving in her carriage for the city, would forcefully disengage her from her skirts to which she clung screaming. Zoila! the confidant of bad moments, the sweet and timid one, usually forgotten on happy days. Here she is, gray-haired but still hardy and of indiscernible age, as if the drop of Araucanian blood running through her veins had had the power of petrifying her arrogant profile.

Here are some friends, old friends, who also seemed to have forgotten that she had once been slender and happy.

And for a long time, though conscious of her own childish vanity, she takes delight in submitting herself to the gaze of all, so perfectly still, serene and beautiful.

◆

THREE

The murmur of the rain falling over the woods and on the roof of the house very soon makes her surrender herself, body and soul, to that sensation of well-being and melancholy into which she was always plunged by the sighing of the waters on the interminable nights of Autumn.

The rain falls, finely, obstinately, quietly. And she listens to it falling. Falling on the rooftops, falling until it bends the high heads of the pine trees and the broad arms of the blue cedars, falling. Falling until it drowns the clover and obliterates the paths, falling.

The rain stops and she hears clearly the rusty flat note that the wind is rhythmically tearing out of the old windmill. And each wrench of the tin paddles seems to pluck a particular string in her shrouded breast. And for a long time, completely absorbed, she listens to that grave, sonorous note vibrating within herself, a note she never knew was there in her.

Then the rain starts again. And it falls, obstinately, quietly. And she listens to it falling. Falling and sliding like tears down the windowpanes; falling and expanding the lagoons to the far end of the horizon, falling. Falling on her heart and drenching it, dissolving it into sadness and languor.

Now once more the rain stops, and the mill wheel resumes its heavy regular turning, but within her, it no longer finds the musical string to prolong its monotonous rusty note. The sound now plunges down from a very great height, like something tremendous that envelops and overwhelms her. Each wrench of the paddle now seems to her like the tick-tock of a gigantic clock, marking time beneath the clouds and over the fields . . . She does not remember ever having enjoyed, ever having drained an emotion so completely.

So many people, so many worries and small physical annoyances had always come between her and the secret of a night. Now, however, no unwelcome thoughts appear to disturb her. A circle of silence has been drawn around her and even the throbbing of the invisible artery that so often beat violently at her temple, seems to have definitely stopped.

At dawn, the rain finally subsides. A ray of light outlines the window frames. In the tall candelabra, the flame of the candle is dying out, flickering in a clot of wax. Someone is sleeping with head sunk on shoulder, and the diligent rosaries hang down, motionless.

In the meantime, far off, way off, a rhythmic sound rises.

She alone perceives it and recognizes in it the clatter of horses' hoofs, the clatter of eight hoofs that approach, resounding.

They sound, now spongy and light, now loud and near, suddenly uneven, hushed, as if scattered by the wind. Now coupled together again, they draw near, keep on drawing nearer, yet seem as if they would never arrive.

A deafening rumble of wheels finally engulfs the gallop of the horses. Only then does everyone wake up, and all at once start bustling around. She hears them at the other end of the house drawing open the complicated latch and lifting the two bars from the front door.

She watches them now, setting the room in order, coming close to the bed, replacing the burned-out candles, sweeping away a night butterfly from her forehead.

◆

FOUR

It is he, he.

Here he is, standing, looking at her. And his presence suddenly obliterates the long empty years, the hours, the days that destiny slowly, obscurely, tenaciously had interposed between them.

I remember you. I remember you as a youth. I remember your clear eyes, your ruddy complexion tanned by the sun of the hacienda, your body then wiry and nervous.

Over your five sisters, over my sister Alicia and me, whom you considered cousins (we were not, but our haciendas were adjoining and in turn we called your parents uncle and aunt), you reigned by terror.

I see you running after us to lash our bare legs with your whip.

I swear that we hated you from the bottom of our hearts when you set our birds free or hung our dolls by the hair from the high branches of the plantain tree.

One of your favorite jokes was to shriek a savage "Hu! Hu!" into our ears at the most unexpected moment. Neither our fits of nerves nor our tears could move you. You never tired of scaring us by slipping down our backs whatever strange insects you caught in the woods.

You were a cruel torturer. And yet you exerted over us a strange fascination. I think we admired you.

At night you lured us and held us terrified with stories about a gentleman half-wizard, half-lawyer, all dressed in black, who lived in the garret. He was somehow like the Governor of everything that was hostile to us in the forest. He had pockets full of bats and had command of hairy spiders, centipedes and caterpillars. It was he who infused life into those dry twigs which writhed in a frenzy the moment we touched them, unawares, and became the frightful insects known as "devil-horses." It was he who lighted up the eyes of the owls at night, he who ordered the rats and mice to come out.

Besides, he kept in a special account book an exact census of all the subjects in his loathsome domain. And in this book, the pages of which were made of nettle, he posted his entries with the tail of a live lizard, smeared in the slime of bottomless swamps. For several years we could hardly sleep, in dread of the visits of this sinister little man.

Harvest time brought us days of joy, days spent playing at climbing the enormous mountains of hay piled up beyond the harvest field, and jumping from one haystack to another, oblivious of danger, as if intoxicated by sunshine.

It was during one of those mad afternoons that my sister, catching me unawares, hurled me from the top of a stack onto a passing cart overflowing with sheaves of wheat upon which you lay outstretched.

I had already resigned myself to the worst possible treatment or to the cruelest mockery, according to your whim of the moment, when I became aware that you were asleep. You were sleeping and so, with unheard-of-courage, I stretched myself alongside of you in the hay, while the oxen, guided by Anibal the peon, slowly pursued their course. Very soon the harsh panting of the threshing machine was left behind, very soon the shrill chirping of the crickets rose above the creaking of the heavy wheels of the cart.

Pressing against your hip, I was holding my breath, trying to make my presence light. You were asleep and under the spell of an intense emotion, almost doubting my eyes, I kept watching you, our cruel tyrant, lying defenseless at my side!

Rendered childish, disarmed by sleep, all of a sudden did you seem to me infinitely fragile? The truth is that not even a single idea of revenge entered my mind.

You tossed about, sighing, and under the hay one of your bare feet became entangled with mine.

And I did not understand why the surrender in that gesture awakened such tenderness in me, nor why the warm touch of your skin seemed so sweet to me.

A wide open porch stretched out, all around your house.

It was there you started, late one morning, a really original game.

While two peons prodded the rafters with long sticks, one by one, you riddled with bullets the bats forced out of their hiding places.

I can still hear the screams of the cook; I recall the absurd fainting fit of Aunt Isabel, and my terror at your father's sudden appearance.

A curt order from him instantly dispersed your bodyguard and compelled you to surrender your shotgun while with his narrow, clear, cold eyes, so much like yours, he kept staring hard at you. Whereupon, raising the whip he always carried with him, he laid it across your face, once, twice, three times . . .

Facing him, stunned by the unexpectedness of the punishment, you remained at first motionless. Then all at once, you turned red and putting your fists to your mouth, started to shake from head to foot.

"Get out!" your father uttered low between clenched teeth.

And as if that command had been the final blow, suddenly, you gave vent to your rage in a scream, a heart-rending, atrocious scream which you sustained, and prolonged while running to hide yourself in the woods.

At lunchtime you had not reappeared.

"He is ashamed," we girls told one another, somewhat impressed yet perversely pleased. And Alicia and I had to leave, annoyed and spiteful that we should miss your return.

Next morning, however, as we rushed over, eager for news, we found out that you had not come back the entire night.

"He has lost himself in the woods purposely or thrown himself into the river. I know my son . . ." Aunt Isabel sobbed.

"Enough," shouted her husband. "He is trying to worry us, that's all. I know him too."

No one ate lunch that day. Your father, the overseer, the farm manager, all the men, scoured the hacienda, the neighboring haciendas.

"He may have climbed into the cart of some peon and be in the village," they said.

For us and also for the servants—all of whom the event had liberated from their usual tasks—it seemed every moment that we were hearing a carriage arrive, that we were hearing the trot of many horses. In our imagination, we could see you being brought in, sometimes bound like a criminal, sometimes laid out on a stretcher, naked and white—drowned.

Meanwhile, in the distance, the alarm bell of the sawmill kept giving out constantly a repetition of abrupt, sharp beats.

Toward the end of the afternoon, you suddenly entered the dining room in a rush.

I was there alone, sitting on the divan; that horrible divan of dark leather that wobbled, remember?

You came in with torso half-naked, hair wild, your cheekbones burning with two red spots.

"Water," you ordered. I could do no more than stare at you, terrified.

Then, contemptuously you walked over to the sideboard and tipped the pitcher of water roughly without bothering to look for a glass. I drew close to you. Your whole body released heat, was like burning coal.

Moved by a strange desire, I placed my usually cold finger tips on your arm. You suddenly stopped drinking, and seizing my two hands, made me press them to your chest. Your flesh was on fire.

I remember an interval during which I heard the buzzing of a bee lost on the ceiling of the room.

A sound of footsteps made you let go of me so violently that we stumbled. I can still see your hands clutching at the pitcher of water which you had picked up again, quickly.

Afterwards . . .

Years afterwards came between us that sweet and terrible gesture, the nostalgia of which may bind forever.

It happened one Autumn during which it rained almost continuously.

One afternoon, the leaden veil that covered the sky was torn to shreds, and from north to south ran streaks of livid light.

I remember. I was standing at the foot of the outer staircase, shaking the branches of a fir tree clustered with rain drops. I barely had time to hear the splash of a horse's hoofs when I felt myself seized around the waist, carried off the ground.

It was you, Ricardo, who just arrived from the city where you had spent the entire Summer preparing your examinations, had taken me by surprise and lifted me onto the front of your saddle.

The chestnut horse bit the bridle, turned angrily—and suddenly I felt around my waist the pressure of a strong arm, of an unknown arm.

The animal started to go. An unexpected sense of well-being took possession of me and I did not know whether to ascribe it to the measured sway which pushed me against you, or to the pressure of that arm still holding me tightly.

The wind twisted the trees, whipped furiously against the horse's skin. And we struggled against the wind, we pushed forward against the wind. I turned my face to look at you. Your head was strangely outlined against a background of sky where great clouds galloped, they too, as if gone mad. I noticed that your hair and your eyelashes had grown darker; you looked like the older brother of that Ricardo who had left us the year before.

The wind. My tresses were flying undone, entwined around your neck.

All at once we sank into shadow and silence, the eternal silence and shadow of the forest.

The horse shortened its step. Cautiously and noiselessly it went over obstacles: prickly rose bushes, fallen trees with damp, moss-corroded trunks; it trod on beds of pale, scentless violets, and spongy mushrooms which gave forth when crushed a poisonous fragrance.

But I was aware only of that arm of yours which imprisoned me relentlessly.

And you might have carried me off to the depth of the woods, even to that cave you once had imagined to terrorize us, that dark cavern where slept coiled the hideous, bellowing thing whose cries we used to hear rising and receding on long stormy nights.

Yes, you might have done it. I would not have been afraid, as long as that arm supported me.

Mysterious clappings as of frightened wings rustled as we passed through the foliage. From the depth of a ravine came a gentle murmur.

Descending, we skirted a narrow stream half-hidden through ferns. Suddenly, at our back, a rustle of branches and the cautious drop of a body into the waters. We turned our heads. It was a deer in flight.

Tongues of blue vapor rose from the dry leaves. The approaching night was suggesting to us to retrace our steps.

Slowly, we started on our way back.

Oh, what an absurd temptation took possession of me then! So great a desire to sigh, to implore, to kiss!

I looked at you. Your face was the same as it had been every day; taciturn, it remained something apart from your strong embrace.

My cheek suddenly pressed against your chest.

And it was not toward the brother, nor toward the companion, that went this impulse; it was toward the strong, gentle man that was trembling in your arm. The wind from the plains came upon us again. And we struggled against it, pushed forward against it. My tresses flew back undone, they entwined themselves around your neck.

Seconds later, while you were holding me by the waist to help me get off the horse, I realized that from the moment you had put your arm around me, I had been assailed by the fear which I was now experiencing, the fear that your arm would cease to press against me.

And then, remember? I clung to you desperately, murmuring, "Come," sighing: "Don't leave me," and the words "Always" and "Never." That night I surrendered to you, for no other reason than to feel your arm encircling my waist.

During three vacations, I was yours.

You found me cold because you never succeeded in making me share your passion; because I had no desire beyond the taste of dark wild flower in your kisses.

That sudden, cowardly desertion of me, did it result from a peremptory order of your parents or from some rebelliousness in your own impetuous nature? I did not know. I never knew.

"You know Father wants to send me to Europe!" you told me one day.

"What for?"

"To study scientific farming."

There was a silence. "And I, what am I going to do?" I exclaimed, all at once.

Without looking at me you began to unnerve me by a series of remarks totally foreign to your nature:

"It is highly important for the hacienda and for my profession that I learn the rudiments of what is being done in other countries, and besides with regard to the future . . ."

"Do you know whom you remind me of at this moment?" I interrupted.

"Of whom?" you asked ingenuously.

"Of your mother, when she begins to talk seriously and everybody yawns. She is the one who has put those ideas into your head in order to separate you from me."

"You're crazy. What can my mother know about what's going on between us!"

"She's afraid that you will marry me, considering that we've lost all our money and besides, she thinks I'm not well brought up. Why, Zoila told me so. Even in the kitchen they know it, they know that she gets very angry because she thinks you're in love with me. And you, you're just repeating to me, like an idiot, the nonsense she puts into your head."

"I . . . Do you think by any chance that I have no mind of my own?"

"How could you! You've always been a good-for-nothing! . . . No, Ricardo, don't go. Ricardo, if you go, I'll never speak to you again, not as long as I live."

"I'll go and what's more I'll never come back."

You returned the next day and I threw myself into your arms, mad with joy.

"Marry me, Ricardo, and take me to Europe."

"I can't, I can't. I love you and I'm sorry, but I can't. I must think of my future. Didn't you, yourself, scream at me yesterday that I was a good-for-nothing? Well, perhaps you're right. Now is the time for me to be doing something."

Without any dignity—I've never learned to be dignified in love—for several months, obstinately, I persisted in linking my life to yours, not understanding why love should be incompatible with your career.

But now, now that I am dead, it occurs to me that possibly all men once in their lifetime long to make some great renunciation; to sacrifice regretfully something vital; to tear to pieces a butterfly, in order to feel themselves masters of their own destiny.

I remember our last lover's meeting.

We went fishing in the river. The water ran lazily, barely moving the twigs that the willows indolently dropped upon it.

We did not speak. "So as not to scare away the fish," you said.

It was a gray, sultry day, as silent as we were. It seemed as though all in nature was waiting for something undefinable.

What is the matter with me? Why should I be so anguished? I wondered and yet did not tell you of it so as not to spoil your favorite sport.

"I am despondent," you said suddenly to me, and your voice sounded strange in the silence, as if it were the echo of my own thought.

And then, I swear to you, I understood. I knew that you had decided not to see me again.

"Will you come back tomorrow?" I inquired, as we said goodbye.

"Naturally, what makes you ask me that?"

"No reason at all. Look into my eyes."

You looked at me. Your glance for an instant squirmed like a captured eel; then reassured, it held me almost tenderly.

"It's curious," you said, "you have curly pupils."

"Curly!"

"Yes, the design is all rolled up. How pretty!"

"Everyone's are like that."

"No, yours are more so."

"Now, let me see, let me see yours. Yours are full of spirals. Like those crystal marbles we used to play with when we were children."

And like two children, Ricardo, we forgot our pressing sorrow to look into each other's eyes, in a silly way, forehead against forehead.

That sudden, cowardly desertion of me, did it result from a peremptory order of your parents or from some rebelliousness in your own impetuous nature? I do not know.

I never knew. I only know that the period following your departure was the most disordered and tragic in my entire life.

Oh, the torture of first love, of the first disillusion! When one struggles with the past instead of forgetting it! And so I persisted in laying bare my soft breast to the same memories, the same anger, the same agonies.

I remember the enormous revolver I stole and kept hidden in my closet, its muzzle sunk in a tiny satin shoe. One winter afternoon, I went out into the forest. The dead leaves were packed down on the ground, rotten. The foliage hung drenched and lifeless, like a rag.

Far away from the house, I stopped at last and took the weapon out from the sleeve of my overcoat, feeling it suspiciously like a giddy little beast that could twist and bite.

With infinite care, I held it against my temple, against my heart.

Then, abruptly, I fired at a tree.

There was a crack, an insignificant crack, such as that made by a sheet whipped by the wind. But, oh, Ricardo, there in the trunk of the tree what a hideous gap, jagged and black from gunpowder!

My breast torn thus, my flesh, my veins scattered . . . No, I never would have the courage!

Exhausted, I lay down full length, moaning and beating the earth with clenched fists. No, I never would have the courage!

And yet I wanted to die, I swear to you, I wanted to die.

What day was it? I could not tell at what moment that pleasant weariness began.

It seemed to me at first as if Spring was taking pleasure in making me feel lazy. A Spring still hidden under the Winter soil, but occasionally breathing, damp and fragrant, through the half-closed pores of the earth.

I remember. I felt listless, indifferent in body and spirit, as if satiated with passion and grief.

Believing it to be a respite, I abandoned myself to that unexpected calm. For would not the torment come more bitter again tomorrow?

No longer did I stir or move about.

And that languor, that drowsiness, kept increasing, enveloping me stealthily, day by day.

One morning when I opened the blinds in my room, I noticed that a thousand small buds no bigger than the head of a pin dotted the tops of all the ash-colored twigs in the garden.

Behind me, Zoila was folding the mosquito netting and inviting me to drink my daily glass of milk. Pensively and without answering, I kept on staring at that miracle.

It was curious, my two small breasts also were budding, seemingly wanting to blossom with the Spring.

And suddenly, it was as if someone had whispered it in my ear.

"I am . . . oh! . . ." I sighed, lifting my hands to my breasts, blushing to the roots of my hair.

For many days, I lived stunned with happiness. You had marked me forever. Even though you repudiated it, you continued to possess my humiliated flesh, caressing it with your absent hand, altering it.

Not for a moment did I think of the consequences of all this. I thought of nothing but the enjoyment of your presence in my body. And I listened to your kiss, let it grow in me.

When Spring arrived at last, I had my hammock suspended between two hazelnut trees and there I lay down for hours.

I did not understand why the landscape, why all things had now become to me a source of diversion, a placidly sensuous enjoyment: the dark undulating mass of the forest poised on the horizon like a monstrous wave ready to hurl itself forward; a flight of doves with their coming and going streaking with fleeting shadows the book opened on my knees; the intermittent chant of the sawmill—that sharp, sustained, soft note, like the humming of a beehive—cutting through the air as far as the houses when the afternoon was very clear.

Unreasonable, frivolous desires suddenly besieged me so furiously, they became almost an agonizing necessity. First of all I wanted for breakfast a bunch of pink grapes. I pictured the stem bursting with fruit, the crystalline pulp.

Very soon, when they convinced me it was a desire impossible to gratify—we had neither grape arbors nor vineyards and the village was two miles away from the hacienda—I longed for strawberries.

I did not, however, like those the gardener picked for me in the woods. I wanted them cold, very cold, red, very red; and tasting a little of raspberries.

Where had I eaten berries like that?

". . . Then the girl went out into the garden and started to sweep the snow. And little by little the broom began to uncover a great quantity of ripe, perfumed strawberries which she joyfully carried to her stepmother . . ."

Those! Those were the strawberries I wanted! The magic strawberries in the fairy tale!

One whim followed another. Now I yearned to knit with yellow wool, I longed for a field of sunflowers, that I might look at them hours on end.

Oh, to sink my eyes in something yellow!

Thus I lived on, craving smells, colors, tastes . . .

The voice of reality came one day to disturb my childish thoughtlessness.

I can still see Zoila with arms akimbo standing before me. I see her with a hard look on her face as if preparing to meet with possible resistance from me.

"Something is the matter with you! You're sick!"

"Sick, me! You're crazy," I answered insolently, trying to lie to her, more from shame than out of desire to deceive.

"I say sick because I don't know how to say it another way. But you know what I mean."

Faced with her firmness, I suddenly felt an infinite weariness come over me.

"Yes, I'm sick," I confessed brutally. "But what difference does it make to you?"

"What difference does it make to me? What difference does it make to me? I, who am like your own mother! To know what you have done, to know that you are a shameless . . ."

"I! Get out! Get out!" I shouted, infuriated by the name with which she had insulted my love.

"All right, I'll go . . . but to tell all to your father." And she left, slamming the door.

My heart beat violently. A horrible fear grew in me every second, and with it came the realization of the greatness of my crime. "Zoila, Zoila!" I called.

What would my father say? He was so good. I would have preferred to see him hot-tempered, inflexible. I remember how I dreaded his sorrow as the worst of all punishments. So I would just as soon not have seen Zoila coming back, her eyes full of tears.

"I cannot tell on you, poor child! I am the one who's responsible, I didn't know how to take care of you."

I threw myself into her arms, choking with unspeakable anguish and gratitude.

"No, not you, Zoila."

"Yes, you were good. I am to blame, and also that cursed Amanda who bewitched us all with her guitar. It was high time

I chased her out! To think that while I listened to her you went astray with that Judas of a don Ricardo! Ah, but he'll have to deal with me, Zoila. He'll marry you, I tell you!"

"But since he doesn't love me any more," I sighed weakly.

And it was Zoila who cried bitterly while I kept repeating in a colorless voice, "Since he doesn't love me any more, Zoila, since he doesn't love me any more!"

I think Zoila wrote you. Only now, can I picture her poor letter. Now that I am dead and can no longer weep, I am moved to pity by her queer handwriting, made up of ignorance and love.

I think she even threatened your parents. I think so. I never knew quite what she did; I had surrendered myself to her will.

I remember when she began to awaken me in the morning with a potion of bitter herbs.

"What is this awful stuff?"

"Drink it and ask no questions."

And so I would drink, asking no more questions.

"Don't you feel anything?" she used to ask me occasionally.

"No, nothing."

"My God, Blessed Jesus, what are we going to do! We must make some decision before it's too late."

"Bah, tomorrow, Zoila, tomorrow . . ."

I remember. I felt as though I were quite secure in that web of laziness, of indifference; I felt invulnerable, calm toward everything outside the small tasks of everyday:—existing, sleeping, eating.

Tomorrow, tomorrow, I would say, and so the first month of Spring went by.

The first week of the second month filled me with an unaccountable anguish which seemed to wax with the moon.

On the seventh night, unable to sleep, I arose, went down to the parlor and opened the door leading into the garden.

The cypresses stood out motionless against a sky of deep blue; the pond was like a sheet of metal all blue; the house extended its shadow, velvety and blue.

Absolutely still, the woods seemed hushed as if petrified under the spell of the night, that blue night of the full moon.

For a long time I remained standing on the threshold not daring to enter into that new, unrecognizable world.

Suddenly, from one of the turrets of the house, something like a narrow ribbon of feathers unfolded itself and floated by.

It was a flock of white owls.

They flew by. Their flight was smooth and heavy, silent as the night.

And it was so harmonious that suddenly I burst into tears.

Afterwards I felt complete relief from all pain. It was as if the anguish which had been torturing me had found its way out of my being through the channel of tears.

That anguish, however, I again felt weighing on my heart the following morning; minute by minute its weight increased, oppressed me. And then, after many hours of struggle, it escaped from me in the same way as the day before and again was gone but without revealing to me the secret reason for its being.

The identical thing happened to me the next day, and the day after that.

From then on, I lived in wait of tears. I waited for them as one waits for a storm on the hottest days of Summer. And it happened that a harsh word, a gentle glance, would open the floodgate of those tears. And thus I lived, confined to my physical world.

Now as Spring was drawing into Summer, mottled storms of bluish lightning would at times suddenly explode, like the last burst of some skyrocket.

One afternoon, as I was venturing on the path that led to your hacienda, my heart suddenly began to beat faster.

From out the horizon, an unknown force seemed to be drawing my steps, from out there where the dense black sky was lit up, stabbed by electric discharges—hallucinating signals sent out to meet me.

"Come, come, come," the storm seemed to be shrieking frantically at me.

"Come," it murmured again, as it flashed lower and paler.

As I moved forward, a soft, glowing warmth stimulated me; and I kept going forward just to feel myself more and more filled with life.

Almost running, I followed the path that descends toward the glen where your house lay burdened with honeysuckle, while the dogs, barking gaily, were coming up to meet me.

I remember throwing myself exhausted on a chair the caretaker's wife had offered me in the kitchen. A torrent of words poured forth from the good woman . . . "What weather! What humidity! Don Ricardo arrived this afternoon. He's resting. He asked not to be called until dinner time. Perhaps it would be better if the señorita would return to her house before the shower bursts . . ."

I sipped the maté and lowered my head meekly.

"Don Ricardo arrived this afternoon!" Were we then so closely bound to each other that my senses had made known to me your arrival?

I did not send for you, no, for I knew your ill-tempered awakenings. I returned home hastily, as the first drops of rain were beginning to fall.

But as I left you behind, sleeping, half-dressed, in a room with a musty, closed-up smell, I felt subsiding within me the sweet fever which had been pounding at my temples.

My hands felt like ice as I sat down at the table opposite my irate father, and I was shivering with cold. "You always manage to keep everyone waiting. The gong has rung three times. While Alicia and you do no more than loll around, your brothers and I are working side by side with the peons . . . and we must have our meals on time. Oh! if your mother were only living! . . ."

All the following day I spent waiting for you. For I was simple enough to think that you would come to me.

It was dusk and I was lying in the hammock when again I felt the warning throb. I got up and began to walk. And once more the same surge of life welled up in me, and when I paused, the physical enjoyment stopped also, paused within me, pulsating violently again each time I hastened my step.

And so it was, that my heart—my heart of flesh—guided me toward the north fence.

Far off, at the edge of a field of clover, beneath a vast sky made crimson with blood-red clouds and outlined against the disk of the setting sun, I caught sight of a rider driving a pack of horses.

It was you. I recognized you instantly. And while leaning against the wire fence, with my eyes I could follow you for an instant as brief as a sigh. For suddenly, with the sun, you disappeared from the horizon.

How strange! I never bore you any malice for the meeting that was to separate our destinies.

And, yet, and yet, on account of things infinitely less important, I have suffered, I have hated and avenged myself more than once on others. I was very young at the time, Ricardo. And when we are young, feeling a wide road full of possibilities ahead of us, we forgive rather easily, as easily as later on we obstinately cling to a sterile love or to a miserable chance for retaliation, even if it is to bring us torment day after day.

No, strangely enough, I never bore you any malice for the most brutal attitude a man can take toward a woman.

"And if I don't love you any more, what am I going to do about it?" you said to me. "Love affairs are not eternal."

"And is this all you have come here to tell me?" I answered, knowing only too well that if you had not come, I would have been the one to go looking for you, in search of that irretrievable wound.

"Yes, and also to tell you that Zoila's advice to you is not of any use. The thing she's talking about is not true. And if it were true . . . *I'm* not the one to blame."

Oh, Ricardo, now I know what it must have cost you to tell me that monstrous, filthy lie. But how could I, so young, so impulsive, interpret your paleness and that form of dizziness which made you stammer. I could only hear your words: "I'm not the one to blame."

Because of those words, I threw myself at you with that blind fury which has caused me to lose every battle in life. I began to beat and abuse you. For violence has always been my argument at critical moments when the injustice of others makes the words choke in my throat. Always, always, even when I understood that it was the last argument, the argument of the defeated.

To wrest yourself away from me as I assaulted you like an enraged spider, you had to do violence to me and to yourself. For a long time we fought like two children.

And we were in reality two children appalled by the consequences nature had imposed upon certain acts which we had considered nothing more than a marvelous and forbidden game.

Finally, taking advantage of my utter weariness, in the midst of the battle you escaped from me and ran downstairs.

And then, I had to see you leave or rather flee. Yes, flee.

The same night long before dawn, I dreamed . . . an endless corridor along which you and I were flying, closely bound together.

The lightning was pursuing us, striking one by one the poplars, unreal columns holding up a stone vaulting, and that vaulting was continually crashing down behind us without ever catching us in its fall.

A sudden burst of thunder flung me out of bed, and I found myself awake and trembling in the middle of the room.

Then at that moment, I heard the sustained howling, the horrible clamor of an angry wind.

Blinds shook, doors creaked, the whirl of invisible curtains whipped me. I felt as if borne away, lost in the very center of a gigantic waterspout struggling to tear the house from its foundations and drag it yoked to its own wild course.

"Zoila!" I cried; but the crash of the hurricane made my voice scatter.

Even my thoughts seemed to waver, small, flickering, like the flame of a candle.

I wanted . . . what? Even to this moment, I do not know.

I ran to the door and opened it. Painfully, in the darkness, I moved forward with arms outstretched like a sleepwalker, when suddenly the floor sank beneath my feet in an unexpected void.

Zoila picked me up at the foot of the stairs.

Silent and tearful, she spent the rest of the night mopping up the flow of blood in which your flesh joined with mine was slowly disintegrating.

The next day found me once more stretching myself out on the veranda, displaying the same girlish innocent eyes, under the same innocently arched eyebrows. And there I was, knitting, knitting furiously, as if my life depended on it.

◆

FIVE

Did her lover's sudden cowardly desertion of her result from a peremptory order of his parents, or from some rebelliousness in his own impetuous nature?

She does not know, nor does she want to again find grief in the attempt to unravel the enigma which had tortured her so much throughout her early youth.

The truth is that either unconsciously or through fear, both of them followed separate paths. And all through their lives they carefully avoided each other, as if by mutual accord.

But now, now that he is standing there, silent and pale; now that at last he dares again look at her, face to face, with that curious blinking of the eyes he always displayed as a boy when under the stress of real emotion, now she understands.

She understands that within her the love that she thought was dead had slept hidden. She understands that this man had never remained entirely apart from her.

And it was as if some of her blood had always been feeding a vital center within her of which she herself was unaware, and that this hidden core had thus grown secretly, aside from her own life, yet always part of it.

And at last, she understands that although she was never aware of it, she had in fact been waiting eagerly, longingly, for this moment.

Must we die in order to know certain things? For now she understands also that in the heart and in the senses of that man she too had planted her roots; that never, though she often might have believed it, was she ever altogether alone; that never, though she often might have thought so, could she ever have been really forgotten by him.

Had she been aware of all this before, she would not on so many sleepless nights have turned on the lights to read some book or other, endeavoring to stop a flood of memories. Neither would she have avoided certain corners of the park, certain solitudes, certain strains of music, nor feared the first breath of some overwarm Spring.

Oh God, dear God! Must we die in order to know?

◆

SIX

"Arise, come!"

"Where?"

Someone, something takes her by the hand, makes her rise.

And as if entering suddenly into a tangle of conflicting winds, she finds herself whirling on a fixed point, as light as a snowflake.

"Come!"

"Where?"

"Farther on."

She goes down the slope of a damp and shadowy garden.

She now perceives the murmurings of hidden waters, and hears the falling of frozen rose leaves all around the bushes.

And she descends, slides down moss-covered lanes, brushed by the wet wings of invisible birds . . .

What is this force enveloping her, carrying her up? All of a sudden, abruptly, she feels herself flowing toward a surface.

And now, she finds herself again, lying face upward in the spacious bed.

At the head of the bed, the sputtering of the two wax candles.

Only now does she notice that a bandage is supporting her chin. Yet she has the curious sensation that she does not feel it.

◆

SEVEN

The day burns hours, minutes, seconds.

An old man comes and sits beside her bed. For a long time he looks at her sadly, then strokes her hair without fear and says that she looks pretty.

Only the woman in the shroud remains unimpressed by his despondent calm. She knows her father well. No, no sudden blow is going to strike him down. He has already seen too many people thus stretched out, pale, and invested with that same implacable stillness, while everything around them breathes and stirs.

"Ana Maria, do you remember your mother?" he would ask her, when she was still a little girl.

And in order to please him, each time she would close her eyes and, concentrating intently, succeed in capturing for an instant the fleeting image of two other very black eyes looking at her playfully from behind a light, transparent veil tied to a small hat. Something like a perfume floated around that tender evocation.

"Of course, I remember her, Papa."

"She was very pretty, wasn't she? Did you love her?"

"Yes, I loved her very much."

"And why did you love her?" he had insisted one day.

She had answered candidly:

"Because she always wore such a lovely veil tied around her hat and smelled so sweet."

"You are a silly girl," he had said, his eyes suddenly full of tears, and hastily slipped out of the room.

But since that time, all her life, she had suspected that he too had loved her mother for the same reason as she, the silly girl. Yes, he had loved her for her fleeting perfume, her treacherous veils and her premature death, as disconcerting as the frivolous mystery of her eyes.

Now he lifts his hand, traces the sign of the cross on his daughter's forehead. Did he not always bid her good night just in that same tender manner?

No, no sudden blow is going to strike him down. She knows her father well.

Later on, after having closed all the doors, he will stretch himself on his bed, turn his face to the wall, and then, only then, give himself up to suffering. And he will suffer in solitude, rebellious against any reference to his affliction, against the slightest display of sympathy, as if his grief were not within reach of anyone.

And for days, for months, perhaps for years, he will go on mute and resigned, fulfilling that part of sorrow destiny has assigned to him.

◆

EIGHT

Ever since the beginning of the night, and almost without rest, someone has been keeping vigil over the dead body.

Yet the woman in the shroud notices her for the first time, so accustomed is she to see her thus, grave and solicitous, at the bedside of the sick.

Alicia, my poor sister, it is you! You are praying!

Where do you think I am? Rendering account to that terrifying God to whom you offer up day after day in your prayers the brutality of your husband, the burning of your sawmills, and even the loss of your only son, that disobedient, smiling boy, dragged down in the fall of a tree and whose young body was pitifully dislocated when they lifted it from out the mud and the dead leaves?

No, Alicia, I am here, just beginning to disintegrate quite close to the earth. And I am wondering if I shall ever see the face of your God.

Already at the convent where we were educated, after Sister Marta had turned off the lights in the large dormitory and while with your forehead sunk on the pillow you were tirelessly completing the last two decades of your rosary, I would slip out on tip-toe to the window in the bathroom to spy on the young couple in the house next door.

On the ground floor a lighted balcony and two servants spreading the tablecloth and lighting the silver candelabra on the table. On the second floor another lighted balcony. Seen through the shifting curtain of a willow tree, this was the balcony that attracted my most eager looks. The husband stretching himself on the divan. She, seated before the mirror, absorbed in the contemplation of her own image and from time to time carefully lifting her hand to her cheek, as if to smooth some imaginary wrinkle. She, combing her thick brown hair, flinging it like a banner, perfuming it!

It required some real effort on my part to go back and lie down in my narrow bed under the oil lamp with its flickering flame, distorting and bringing into play on the naked walls the shadow of a big crucifix.

I never liked to look at a crucifix, you know that, Alicia. And if I spent all my money buying holy images, it was only because the white, frothy angels' wings delighted me and because the angels frequently resembled our older cousins, those who had become engaged, went to dances, and wore diamonds in their hair.

Everyone was grieved at my indifference when I made my First Communion.

Neither a sermon nor a retreat ever affected me. God seemed to me so remote, and so severe!

Or perhaps it might be, Alicia, that I have no soul!

Those must have a soul who feel it within themselves stirring and demanding. Or maybe after all, men are like plants, for not all plants have a second crop and there are some that live in the sand dunes without thirst or need of water.

Or it might be also that all deaths are not the same and even that after death each one of us follows a different path.

But pray, Alicia, pray. You know I like to see you pray.

What would I not give though, my poor Alicia, that you might be granted here on earth a particle of that happiness you think is reserved for you in your heaven. Your paleness, your sadness, grieve me. Sorrows seem even to have faded your hair.

Do you remember the golden hair you had as a child? And do you remember how our cousins and I envied it? Because you were so blond, we admired you and we thought you the most beautiful. Do you remember?

◆

NINE

Luis, my dear brother, now that I see you coming close to me and watching me intently, I remember that it was you who assisted me at my death.

Yes, now I remember that I died clutching at your hand.

Your hand! How many years is it since I felt it between mine? Not since the nights in that far-off Winter, do you remember? Then it happened that your hand often searched for mine at the dinner table beneath the folds of the tablecloth, as if to ask me to hold back the sharp phrases bursting forth from the lips of Elena, my intimate friend and your great love.

Luis, what have you done with yourself during all those years; where did you bury your past and your soul? For a long time, I was looking at you without seeing you, because long since, you had lost all importance and meaning in my eyes. What do our brothers matter to us anyway? They are like extensions of ourselves, prickly extensions falling back on us in the great moments of our lives, wounding us even though they are trying to protect us.

And yet, oh Luis, now that I see you close to my deathbed, watching me intently, I remember there was a time when we loved each other very much; a time you may have dared to deny, a time you had forgotten but which my death reawakened in you, I am sure.

What joy! For this one night at least you have lost that vacant look, that very correct manner that separated you from me; you have become again the anxious boy who used to take refuge in his sister.

Elena, divorced, scandalous, pure and haughty! If my death finally succeeds in making you remember her, I am glad to have died, Luis.

You never knew how grieved I was by the cruelty with which you tore yourself away from her in order to give your life immediately afterwards:—that life for which she craved longingly and tenderly, to that charming fool whom you made your wife, to that Luz-Margarita, model of honesty and of conventional kindheartedness.

Elena would become wild whenever you treated her like a child or when you reproached her for her imprudent and much talked-of passions.

"What does it matter losing one's reputation, the support of a husband or the respect of a stupid family. The one really important thing is to save one's heart," she used to say to me.

And proudly she would shake her splendid head, curly and dark. Her hair was chestnut-brown, but when she came near a window it lighted up all over making her appear redheaded.

And at dinner time, she would relate and enlarge upon her love affairs, insulting you with veiled words. And you, Luis, groping beneath the tablecloth, would search with your trembling hand for mine and press it as if to beg me to make her stop talking.

"Why don't you marry Elena?" I asked you one day. "Then she would stop insulting you and you would no longer suffer needlessly."

"Marry Elena! You haven't thought of her past! I adore her, but . . ."

"I am not judging her, but what guarantees can a woman like Elena offer?" the blond and delicate Luz-Margarita would say to you at the time, wisely instructed by her parents in the way to get you to marry her.

And she was right. What guarantee of mediocrity and of stability could someone like Elena have offered you; someone pure, fanciful and passionate, whom fate had compelled in her heart and in her flesh, to live every second intensely as the drop of dew is compelled to catch eagerly every reflection of the morning. What guarantee! Luz-Margarita, on the other hand, with her sweet name, her concealed energy and her post-card goodness, offered you all that security which gradually has made of you a commonplace man.

Oh Luis, Luis—it isn't that I blame you!—All men are cowards and it is natural that you too should have looked for an easy quiet life. But if you knew how much I was shocked, always, by your inertia in defending Elena whenever some abusive or sarcastic anecdote would come forth out of her restless life, ever in search of love.

"I am a vagabond. I have a foreboding that I am going to die on a train," she used to say. And until now, no one knows just how or where she is. Yet slander will always pursue her. That is the tribute women like Elena must ever pay for their liberty.

All I know is that she loved you very much, Luis, and that you were the man with whom she could finally have found appeasement by concentrating on you her passion.

But men like you are unconcerned about making vagabonds. And when Christmas calls at your selfish windows you quickly drive away with a glass of champagne the sad vision of a woman, straight, very pale, alone in the bustle of a large house covered with snow, in some foreign land. You drive away from your mind the idea of her loneliness and of your own loneliness. You drive away the idea of all that loneliness you might possibly have prevented.

In what part of the Bible can be found that sentence which says: "The sin God punishes most sternly is the sin against life"? Did I imagine it or is it really there? I don't know, Luis, but I have the conviction you will have to pay later for those moments of real life your lack of moral courage caused you to elude.

Luz-Margarita? No, nothing will ever make her suffer. There are people so small that life and death will always pass them over without reaching them. And there she will remain, repeating over and over:

"What a scandal! One has no right to have so much bad luck! What guarantees can so much unhappiness offer. God should punish girls who are not born like me—pretty, sweet, rich, and destined to marry the man they love."

◆

TEN

Someone, something, takes her by the hand.

"Arise, come!"

"Where?"

"Come!"

And she goes. Someone, something, drags her along, leads her through an abandoned city covered with a slight layer of dust of ashes, as if some evil breeze had delicately blown over it.

She walks. Night falls. She walks on.

A lawn. In the very heart of that accursed city, a lawn recently watered and phosphorescent with insects.

She takes a step. She crosses the double ring of mist surrounding it, and enters shoulder high into the fireflies, as in a floating golden dust.

Oh! What is this force enveloping her, carrying her up?

Now, she finds herself again lying motionless, face upward in the spacious bed.

Light, she feels light. She tries to move but cannot. It seems as if the most secret, the deepest layer of her body were revolving, imprisoned within some heavier layers which she cannot lift and which hold her there, fastened, between the waxy sputtering of the two candles.

◆

ELEVEN

Now, only Maria Griselda's husband remains near her.

How is it possible that she too calls her son "Maria Griselda's husband"!

Why? Is it because he watches so jealously over his beautiful wife, because he keeps her isolated, far away down South, in that house lost in the heart of the forest?

Somehow, all through the long night, she has missed the presence of her daughter-in-law and has been annoyed by Alberto's attitude; this son who has done nothing but move about and cast uneasy glances around the room.

Now that he is resting, lying on a chair, sleeping perhaps, what does she notice about him that is new, strange . . . terrible?

His eyelids! It is his eyelids that change him, that frighten her. Those eyelids, rough and dry! It was as if, closed night after night on some taciturn passion, they had withered, burned from within.

It is strange that she should notice them for the first time. Or could it be only natural that the perception of everything that is a sign of death should be sharpened in the dead?

Suddenly those lowered eyelids begin to stare at her fixedly, with that inscrutable fixity with which the insane stare.

Oh! Alberto, open your eyes!

As if in compliance with her request, he actually opens them . . . only to cast another suspicious look around.

And now he approaches her, his shrouded mother, and touches her on the forehead as if to make sure that she is really dead.

Then reassured, he steps resolutely toward the back of the room.

She hears him moving about in the dark, feeling the furniture as if he were looking for something.

And now he is coming back with a picture in his hand, the picture of Maria Griselda. Now he is holding it over the flame of one of the candles concentrating on burning it thoroughly, and as the lovely image vanishes, breaks into ashes, his features distend, pacified . . .

Except for the dead woman, no one knows or will ever know how much those numerous effigies of his wife have made him suffer—channels through which she escapes him in spite of his vigilance.

Does she not give away a little of her beauty in each one of those pictures? Does not every one of them open to her some possible means of communication?

Yes, but now that the last one has been destroyed by fire, there remains only one Maria Griselda, she whom he keeps in seclusion, far down South, in that shabby old house lost in the heart of the forest.

◆

TWELVE

That house! She remembers clearly the day she had sworn never to set foot in it again.

It happened one afternoon when with the help of Anita, her daughter—and that of Anita's intimate friend, Beatriz, she had undertaken to embroider on the long tablecloth the garlands which were fated to remain unfinished . . .

"It sounds like Alberto! I hear the tinkle of his spurs . . ." Beatriz had suddenly exclaimed, her needle still in the air, and her sweet face getting red as the silvery jingle of Alberto's heavy silver spurs was heard coming up the long corridors of the house.

"That fellow! he might as well stay in his forest!" she can still hear her daughter grumbling. "Since Father has given over the management of the hacienda in the South to him, he is getting more and more unsociable. Imagine, Mummy, he has refused to be Beatriz's partner at the ball of . . ."

"But Anita, he's quite right!" Beatriz had protested, with a desperate look toward the door, then turning to her, she had hurriedly concluded: "He wrote me he could not make the journey from the far end of the hacienda to go to a ball just when he has the new mills to get going . . ."

"Yet, he has actually made the trip, and I'm sure it's only on account of some trifling thing!" Anita retorted cruelly.

Poor Beatriz, so much in love with Alberto who had never deigned even to look at her! But who did the handsome, taciturn Alberto ever deign to look at anyway? Young girls would seldom hear the sound of his voice, and nobody ever spoke of his having a mistress. His only interest, his only love, seemed to be for his horses, his dogs, the land, the trees, and lately the new mills on that fabulous hacienda for which the gossips still insisted his mother had married his father . . .

"I would like to have a talk with you, Mother," he had said, kissing her on the forehead.

"That means we must get out, so come along Beatriz." And with a sarcastic laugh, Anita had pulled her friend out of the room behind her.

No sooner was the door closed, when she had dropped her needle and looking at her son: "What a strange face, what's the matter?" she had smilingly inquired.

He had muttered a few meaningless words, then like someone deciding suddenly to throw himself in the water: "I got married a week ago," he brutally let out, "I wanted you to know and tell Father."

She remembers how at first she failed to understand and remained there motionless, staring at him. It was only gradually and through all those words he was now pouring out while taking advantage of her silence, that the truth finally dawned on her:

Alberto had married . . . an unknown girl he had met in that town down South from where he made his lumber shipments . . . She was good, and so pretty! Yes, there never was a girl prettier than Maria Griselda! Maria Griselda was her name. Her father was not native born though well known in the entire region, and an excellent contractor; really very good people, even if not of the same social class . . .

That was where she blew up. She still can hear her own shrill cry: "Good people! Good! . . . A girl who would get married secretly! People who . . ."

Alberto had interrupted her energetically:

"It's not they, not she! I'm the one who insisted on getting married that way . . ."

"But why? why??" It seems to her she can still feel in her throat choking her that hard knot of distracted words she could not manage to untie.

"I'll admit, it's hard on you, Mother, what I've done . . . but I didn't want a large wedding . . . and I was afraid you'd force me to wait . . . and you know how I am . . . my fiancée, I didn't want all those friends of Anita's, I didn't want anyone to see her, I . . ."

"Well, you'll have your wish. Nobody will see her. Certainly not I. No, I will never see her! I will never, never accept as a daughter that stranger, that little nobody, that adventuress . . ."

The knot of words seemed to have got untied in her throat, and she recalls how, now she could at last pour out all she had on her heart, she wanted to stop but could not.

. . . No, she would never accept that stranger! that adventuress! who had married him for his name, for his money, for the hacienda in the South! He could keep her there hidden in the old house; and she would see to it that his father and all the family would not accept her either; besides, he too, she would disown him; he was no longer her son, he had taken the most serious decision in life without consulting his mother; yes, he could go away, she didn't wish to see him any more, he was no longer her son! . . .

She remembers that she was still talking while the rattle of Alberto's spurs was slowly getting more and more distant down the corridors of the house . . .

Yet, how strangely ironical life can be!

It was not the news of that horrible marriage of Alberto's that had caused her first heart attack. It had come a year later, as she was returning from the ball where Fred had so nicely consulted her about his own marriage. She can still see him walking across the dance floor, holding the hand of the most popular debutante of the season. She can see them standing in front of her, such a lovely couple! so full of fun and smiles.

"Mummy, this is Silvia. I would like to know if you think her pretty enough to become your daughter-in-law . . ."

That shabby old house lost in the heart of the forest, where she had sworn she would never set foot again! . . . Now in her shroud, she recalls how once again, nevertheless, on that day a year ago she stopped in front of the gate in her carriage, after a long exhausting journey . . .

"It looks as if that gate hasn't been used for centuries!" the old coachman was grumbling, as he struggled with the chain all covered with rust.

"Never mind, Juan de Dios, take your time . . ." she had answered, stepping out of the carriage. "I can go on from here on foot."

She remembers, as she was walking toward the house across the park—that park with its bushy paths, its badly kept lawns, and scant flower beds of wild carnations—a flash of lightning had ripped the sky and shivered livid for the space of a second. Next had come a clap of thunder. And quickly again all was silence.

A clap of thunder! A single brief clap of thunder, like the stroke of a gong, like a signal! Thus from the top of the Cordillera, Autumn was giving warning that it had begun to rustle the sleeping winds, to urge on the waters and to prepare the snowfalls . . . And she recalls, as she was ascending the stone staircase outside the house, how the echo of that brief thundering had reverberated unpleasantly within her as if it was warning her that something evil was about to enter her life . . .

On the top step of the staircase, a toad was lifting up to her its tremulous little head when at last Fred, her younger son, opened the door of the house to her.

"Oh, Mother, I wouldn't have thought . . . I heard a carriage at the gate . . . but I never would have thought it could have been you . . ."

"Where is Alberto?" she had asked as she entered the hall, taking in at a glance the disorder, the untidiness of the room; a curtain dropping down, withered flowers in the vases, the fireplace dead and filled with charred papers.

"At the village . . . I suppose," Fred murmured. A world of veiled allusions trembled in his voice as he stood in the middle of the hall, obstinately avoiding her inquiring look.

"Light the fire, Fred, I feel cold. Isn't there any firewood around? What is Alberto's wife doing? Does she think, perhaps, housework might be harmful to that famed beauty of hers?"

"On no, no, this untidiness is no fault of hers. Alberto hardly allows her to leave her room. He is so jealous of her and there are so many of us here all the time," he concluded with a nervous laugh.

"Then why . . ." she started to say when Fred whispered: "Mother!" just as he used to do when as a little boy he would run to her when he had hurt himself or was afraid. Yet now instead of clinging to her as he used to do then, he drew away as if ashamed and let himself drop down on the sofa.

She came over to him and placing both hands on his shoulders:

"What's the matter, Fred?" she asked gently. "What's happening to all of you? Why don't you leave this house which is not yours anyway, since Alberto is the one who . . ."

"Oh, Mother, it's Silvia who doesn't want to leave. I most certainly do and if you will remember, Mother, it was Silvia who insisted on coming here . . ."

Yes, she remembered the absurd plan the girl had confided in her a few days before the wedding, out in the big city.

"We want to spend our honeymoon at the hacienda in the South!"

"Silvia!"

"Señora, please don't feel badly. I know that you have never been willing to meet her or accept her, but I do want so much to meet Maria Griselda. They all say she is the most beautiful woman in the world. I want Fred to see her too and to say: 'No, it isn't true. It isn't true. Silvia is the most beautiful!'"

Yes, she remembered all those things while Fred went on excitedly:

". . . Oh, Mother, I'm so glad you've come! Perhaps you will be able to persuade her that we must leave. She's now got it into her head that I'm in love with Maria Griselda because I think she is so beautiful. And she insists on remaining here to give me a chance to think things over, so that I can compare them, so that I can choose . . . and I don't know what else! She's simply mad! And I want to leave. I must leave. My studies . . ."

His voice! His quivering like a cornered animal sensing imminent danger!

Indeed, as a woman, she understood Silvia's frenzy, her desire to measure herself against Maria Griselda. She understood and pitied the stupid pride of that vain girl in love, ready to risk even her own happiness provided she could make herself supreme in every way in her husband's eyes.

"Fred, you know Silvia is capricious. She will never go if you ask her that way, as if you were afraid."

"Afraid! Well, Mother, maybe I am. If you could only see her! If you had seen her this morning! She was dressed in white and wore a yellow dahlia at her breast."

"Who?"

Fred had suddenly thrown his arms around his mother's waist, laid his forehead against the fragile hip and closed his eyes.

"Maria Griselda!" he sighed at last. "Oh, Mother, if only you could have seen her! With her pale face and her black hair! With her little head just like a swan's; with her regal and melancholy carriage, all dressed in white with a yellow dahlia at her breast!"

She gave a start. From her memory of the picture Alberto had once sent to arouse her interest, she could see the delicate, haughty creature moving.

"Oh, Mother, every day it's a new image, every day some new admiration I have to fight against. No, no, I must not stay here another day . . . because I can't help admiring her more than I do Silvia, every day more. And Silvia who adores me and hates me, who avoids me and doesn't want to leave. You speak to her, Mother, right now, please! Maria Griselda has not yet returned from her horseback ride . . . this is the time . . ."

"I will speak to Silvia, Fred, but not now, later; I must first see Anita and Zoila . . . Where is Zoila?"

As if it were the very heart of the house, the tick-tock of a clock, now light, now heavy, was sounding relentlessly down the corridors . . . while she was going up the stairs looking for her daughter Anita, and turning over in her mind the letter from Zoila, that strange, disturbing note brought to her secretly by a little peon.

Señora, come immediately! . . . said the note. *Very strange things are happening here. I will not say anything about what is taking place between Fred and his wife; that is none of my business. But although you have sworn never again to set foot in this house, you'd better come for the sake of your daughter.*

Anita has always had her own way, but this time it looks as though things were not going her way. It seems to me she made a big mistake when she came here chasing after don Rodolfo.

Since he stopped writing to her it must have been for some good reason, and in my opinion, she should have had enough pride to forget him. That's what I told her when she made up her mind to come out here. But no one listens to me. And you ordered me to come with her.

Well now, getting down to facts, my guess is that although don Rodolfo has been Anita's sweetheart since her first long dress, he doesn't love her any more and maybe even without knowing it himself (and may God forgive me if I'm wrong) he's in love with Señora Maria Griselda.

To me, it has never made sense that don Alberto should have given don Rodolfo employment at the hacienda just when don Rodolfo's own irate father dismissed him, calling him a good-for-nothing. But no one pays any attention to me . . .

Alone, flung on her bed still fully dressed, her face sunk in the pillows, that was the way she had found Anita.

She waited a few seconds before calling to her.

Oh the shyness that would always come over her when she had to face Anita!

For with Fred, although he usually kept himself on the defensive, she always felt sure he would end by giving in to her. And even with the taciturn Alberto, she knew that although somewhat ashamed of it, he would eventually show an impulse of confidence and tenderness toward her.

But Anita, the arrogant Anita, never deigned to let her into her intimate life. Ever since she was a small child, she had called her "Ana Maria," delighted when she answered without heeding the lack of respect which was implied in such a young daughter calling her mother by her first name. And later, with what pious haughtiness she had looked down on her from the height of her studies! "She has an exceptional mind, that girl!" that was the phrase with which everyone had praised Anita ever since her adolescence. And she, her mother, had always felt proud and at the same time intimidated by that extraordinary daughter . . .

She had waited a few seconds before calling to her, but to her amazement, when she did finally call, Anita lifted to her a face half-incredulous, half-delighted. And she had already started a gesture of endearment toward her, when encouraged by that unexpected reception, she had blurted out quickly, stupidly:—

"Anita, I came to get you. We're going away tomorrow."

Then, immediately, Anita had repressed her impulse and become herself again.

"You forget that I'm no longer of an age to be fetched and carried like an object."

She remembers how already discouraged by this first retort, and foreseeing a struggle too harsh for her sensitiveness to bear, she had then begun to plead, to try to persuade.

"Anita, for that insignificant boy, that good-for-nothing, you're making yourself cheap! You who have your life before you, you who can choose the husband you want, you so proud, so intelligent."

"I don't want to be intelligent, I don't want to be proud, and I don't want any other husband. I love Rodolfo and it doesn't matter to me if he is a good-for-nothing. I love him."

"But since *he* doesn't love you any more . . ."

"And what do I care if he doesn't love me. *I* love him, that's enough and I will marry him even if he comes to hate me later on!"

"Anita, Anita, you spoiled child . . . Do you think your own wishes are all that matter in such a case? Believe me, you will never get anywhere with a man who doesn't love you any more. Anita, come home with me. Don't expose yourself to worse things."

"To what things?"

"Since you will not release Rodolfo from his promise, he may one of these days ask you to release him from his."

"No! Now he can't."

"Why not?" she had asked ingenuously.

"Because now he can't; not if he is a man and a gentleman."

"Anita!" She had looked at her daughter, a surge of blood burning her face. "What are you trying to tell me?"

"Just that. That thing you just thought."

"No!" she had shouted, and the bourgeois feeling in her, in all touching her children, had rebelled with the ancestral rebellion of all the bourgeois women in the world.

". . . Oh, he has dared! Your father! . . . and me! . . . Oh, the infamous wretch . . . !"

"Calm yourself, Mother. It was I who wanted it. He didn't want to . . . he didn't want to . . ."

Her voice had broken into a sob, and again dropping her head on her pillow, the proud Anita had started to cry like a child.

"He didn't want to. I kept after him and after him, until . . . It was the only way to prevent him from leaving me. Now he is mine, now you have to help me . . . you'll have to tell him that you know everything, that he must marry me immediately. Because he wants to wait. And I don't want to wait. I don't want to wait . . . I adore him . . ."

Anita was crying. And she had covered her face with her hands but actually could not cry.

How long did she remain thus, mute and overwhelmed? She does not remember. She only remembers that suddenly, that clock she had first heard when she went upstairs began to sound once more its noisy tick-tock as if it had, along with her, just emerged out of the frozen waters of a long painful stupor. Only then did she get up and walk out of the room, without even looking at her daughter.

Now on the ground floor again, she had opened the door of Alberto's room and walked in mechanically. A very faint odor of perfume floating about made her very quickly remember that this was also Maria Griselda's room.

She heard footsteps in the corridor. It's "she," she thought, suddenly moved in spite of herself.

But it was not she, it was Zoila arriving breathless.

"My goodness, Señora, they just told me you had arrived. I was in the laundry. And no one to receive you! How pale you look! Don't you feel well?"

"I am tired. And that? What is that? . . . those faces glued to the windowpane? Now, they're gone! Who was it trying to look in?"

"Those are the caretaker's children. They come every day to leave flowers on the window sill for the Señora Griselda. When she happens to be in, they even climb the hazelnut tree to be able to see better inside the room. They say that the Señora Maria Griselda is even prettier than the Holy Virgin herself."

"And where is Alberto?" she had asked, deliberately cutting short Zoila's evident enthusiasm.

"Well, he must be . . ." Zoila hesitated one moment, then brutally like one making a radical decision: "He must be in the village drinking somewhere. For I prefer to tell you, once for all, don Alberto spends his time drinking now . . . he who never even used to taste wine at dinner. It's not even possible to keep servants in this house any more. They're afraid of him . . ."

"Marriage's good influence!" she had sneered, cheaply, and with bitterness.

"You always judge recklessly, Señora. Nothing whatever can be said against doña Griselda. She is very good and has to spend most of her time in her room, when she is not out walking by herself, poor child. I have often found her crying. It looks as if don Alberto has come to hate her only because he loves her too much. Dear God, I'm beginning to think that to be so beautiful is a misfortune, like any other."

As she entered Silvia's room, she found her seated in front of her mirror, wrapped in a loose chiffon negligée.

Her unexpected appearance did not seem to surprise the girl. She scarcely greeted her, so absorbed was she in the contemplation of her own image.

"How lovely you look, Silvia!" she had said, as much from habit as to escape from this disconcerting situation:—Silvia looking at herself in the mirror intently, obstinately, as if she had never seen herself before, and she standing, looking at Silvia.

"Lovely! Do you really think so?" the girl had cried in a harsh voice. "Lovely! No, I thought I was lovely until I met Maria Griselda. You haven't seen her? Maria Griselda is a hundred times more lovely than I!" Silvia's voice broke.

Against the evening darkness, the windowpanes were reflecting the many lighted lamps on her dressing table. From the nearest tree, a chuncho owl was screeching repeatedly its brief, mysterious, soft cry.

"Fred has just told me he is very unhappy and that he adores you, Silvia."

But the girl gave way to bitter laughter.

"What do you think Fred answers when I ask him: 'Who is the loveliest, Maria Griselda or I?'

"He says, 'You are the loveliest,' of course. I know what Fred thinks."

"No, no, that's not what he says, he answers: 'Both of you are so different.' And then I know, I am sure, he thinks Maria Griselda is the most beautiful."

"But it's you he loves, Silvia!"

"Perhaps, maybe, I don't know. I really don't know what's happening to me. Oh, Señora, I am so unhappy."

And the girl had begun to explain her wretched torment:

Why did Maria Griselda's presence always give her a feeling of inferiority? It was strange. Both were the same age and yet Maria Griselda made her feel shy. It was not that she was proud, no, on the contrary, she was sweet and considerate and very often came and knocked at the door of her room to chat with her. Why then did she bring out that shyness in her? Because of her gestures, perhaps. Those gestures always so harmonious and sure. None of them ever seemed out of place like her own. They never remained in suspense . . . No, she didn't really envy her! Didn't Fred use to say to her: You are blonder than wheat; your skin is as golden and smooth as a ripe peach; you are as tiny and graceful as a squirrel; and many other similar things. But why then, she wanted to know why it was that when she saw Maria Griselda, when she met her narrow eyes of turbid green, why she no longer liked her own blue eyes, as limpid and wide open as stars? And why did it seem so futile to her to have prepared herself for hours in front of her mirror, and why did that so much praised smile in which she delighted to show her small white teeth, why did it now seem so ridiculous to her?

Thus Silvia was talking while from the nearest tree, the chuncho owl continued to screech its brief, mysterious cry, regularly and insidiously.

She still can remember and feel, as if it were yesterday, that sensation of mental and physical suffocation that had pushed her toward the door of the house and made her go out on the terrace looking for a breath of air free from that latent anguish weighing so heavily inside the house.

On the last step of the outer staircase, the toad was still there, lifting to her once again its tremulous little head.

"It is waiting for Maria Griselda. It always climbs up to wait for her when she goes out horseback riding in the afternoon. Sometimes it huddles up in the folds of her riding skirt," Rodolfo quietly explained to her, pushing it delicately with his boot as he went by and up the steps to meet her while apparently on his way back from work.

Rodolfo! she had seen him grow up almost entirely with her own children, frivolous, good-natured and at times even more affectionate toward her than her own sons.

Rodolfo! he kissed her gently, with his usual tact, finding immediately the words that could put her at ease:

"At last you've come, Godmother, it was about time, you know. Maria Griselda will be so delighted to meet you. I wonder why she should have taken such a long walk this afternoon . . . there may be a big storm on the way . . . let's go . . ." he had finally concluded, taking her firmly by the hand with his usual abruptness, ". . . let's go and find her, come along."

And that was how like pursuers of a gazelle in flight, they had started to follow through the forest the tracks of Maria Griselda.

They had first entered on the narrow path leading to the river, a path, Rodolfo had explained to her, traced by Maria Griselda's horse patiently day after day. They had separated the shrubs and leaned over the crevice opening at their feet.

Close, orderly, implacable, like soldiers in line, the trees went down the slope of ferns, until their first row plunged in the mist banked between the steep walls of the canyon below. And from the depth of that sinister ravine rose a strong wet smell, the smell of a forestal beast, the smell of the great river, tossing untiringly its tumultuous back.

And they had begun to walk downhill. Heavy branches of hazelnut trees and frozen copihue-flowers brushed their faces as they passed, while Rodolfo was telling her that with the point of the whiplash she always carried in her hand, Maria Griselda frequently amused herself lifting the bark of certain tree trunks to dislodge the creatures hiding under it: crickets that fled carrying a drop of dew, earth-colored night butterflies, a pair of mating frogs.

And they went down and down the steep winding slope from

where the sound of the river mounted louder and louder; down until they sank into the mist stagnant in the depth of the ravine; there, where birds did not venture, where the light condensed itself, livid and sinister, where the crash of the water roared like a sustained, permanent thunder.

Still another step and they had found themselves at the bottom of the canyon and face to face with the monster.

The vegetation stopped at the edge of a narrow beach of pebbles, as dark and hard as coal. Malcontent in its bed, the river gushed out, dashing furiously its waters filled with whirlpools and black bubbles . . .

The great river!

Rodolfo explained to her that Maria Griselda had no dread of it. He showed her the big rock standing in the middle of the stream on which she was wont to stretch out at full length, the tail of her riding skirt and her long tresses adrift on the water. And he told her how no sooner had her head become alive with tickling and caresses, she would laughingly search her dripping hair to extract from it like a forgotten hairpin some silvery fish, a living gift of the great river.

For the great river was in love with Maria Griselda.

"Maria Griselda, Maria Griselda! . . ." They called her, searched for her, until Rodolfo suggested that they go up again following the path he knew Maria Griselda always took on her way back. And so it was they started to climb the slope, faltering in the shadows now rapidly filling the bottom of the canyon. And the silence of the forest once more came out to meet them.

The first firefly floated before them.

"The first firefly! it always alights on Maria Griselda's shoulder, as if it wanted to guide her!" Rodolfo had explained with sudden tenderness.

And she, finally overcoming all that shyness and weariness which had been oppressing her:

"Rodolfo," she had said, "I've come to find out what is going on between you and Anita. Is it true that you don't love her any more?"

She had asked this cautiously, expecting a noncommittal or evasive answer. But he, with what shamelessness, with what vehemence, he immediately had acknowledged his guilt!

Yes, it was true he no longer loved Anita. And it was true what they were saying, that he was in love with Maria Griselda. But he was not ashamed of it, no, he was not to blame, nor was Maria Griselda, nor anyone else. Only God, assuming that there is a God, was to blame . . . for having created a being so prodigiously beautiful, a being such that when one has known her, one must go on seeing her every day, in order to be able to live.

Oh, to see her! Yet, he would avoid looking at her all at once afraid that the shock might make his heart stop abruptly.

Like one entering cautiously into glacial waters, little by little, he would meet the gaze of her green eyes, the sight of her luminous pallor. And, he would never get tired of seeing her, his desire for her would never be exhausted because that woman's beauty could never be wholly familiar to him. For she changed imperceptibly according to the hour, the light and the mood; and she was ever new, like the foliage of the trees, like the face of the sky, like all that is alive in nature . . . Anita was beautiful too and he really loved her, but . . .

The name of her daughter thus brought into such a confession, offended her in an unexpected way.

Her mind torn between indignation, sorrow and anger made her feel destitute for the time being of all capacity to act wisely and justly. And fearful of betraying herself and losing her daughter's case:

"It's late, let's hurry," she had interrupted dryly.

He did not speak again, as he guided her on the way back through the darkness of the forest.

Only when once again inside the park, the report of a gunshot followed by an immense flurry of frightened wings had come to brush their foreheads:

"They are Maria Griselda's doves! Somebody is killing Maria Griselda's doves!" he had exclaimed, letting go of her hand in order to rush forward.

She had followed him without difficulty through the avenues now illumined by a constant quiver of lightning.

No, Zoila had not lied, or Fred been alarmed in vain; there, on the lawn in front of the house, she saw Alberto, pistol in hand, pursuing Maria Griselda's doves, as if out of his mind.

She saw him bring one down, then another; she saw him rush on their fluffy bodies but only succeed in imprisoning between his eager palms miserable little remains to which a few feathers soaked in blood were adhering.

"Alberto!" she cried.

"There is always something that escapes out of everything!" he was moaning, as he threw himself in her arms.

"It's just like Maria Griselda!" he suddenly shouted, shaking himself loose. "What's the use of her telling me: I am yours, I am yours! As soon as she moves, I feel her already distant; as soon as she gets dressed, it seems to me she never was mine. Why does she light the lamp just that way? She has a way of lighting the lamp immediately afterwards that makes it seem as if everything that happened had been planned by her long before, frivolously, elaborately."

And Alberto, possessed like all, possessed even more than all the inhabitants of this house, had begun to explain his torment:

Yes, it was in vain that in order to feel secure, he recalled and reminded himself of the many and intimate embraces by which Maria Griselda was bound to him. In vain. No sooner out of his arms, she seemed to live a life of her own, a life that seemed detached and apart from his own physical life. And it was obviously in vain that he would force himself on her, trying once again to impress on her his warmth and his scent. From his desperate embraces, Maria Griselda would emerge once more distant and as if untouched.

"Alberto, Alberto, my son . . ." scandalized and grieved, she was trying to quiet his frenzy, reminding him that she was his mother, while with the help of Fred who had rushed out on hearing the shots, she was pushing him into the house.

But he went on talking and pacing the hall wildly.

Jealousy? Yes, it might be. A strange jealousy! Jealousy of that something in her that always escaped him in every embrace.

Oh, the incomprehensible anguish that tortured him! How to capture, understand and exhaust every one of this woman's gestures! If he could only surround her with a tight net of patience and memory, perhaps he might succeed in understanding and capturing the source of her beauty and of his own anguish. But he cannot, because no sooner does his passionate ardor begin to soften in the contemplation of her round knees, ingenuously placed one behind the other, her arms begin to stretch harmoniously, and he has not yet apprehended the thousand undulations that this gesture imparts to her slender waist, when . . . No, no, what was the use of having her as his own if . . .

He could not go on. Silvia was coming down the stairs, pale, entangling herself at each step in her loose chiffon negligée.

"Silvia! What's the matter?" Fred barely had time to stammer, when a horribly shrill voice began to issue from that frail body.

"All of them, all, all the same!" cried the strange voice, "All in love with Maria Griselda: Alberto, Rodolfo, and Fred, too! Yes, you too, you too, Fred. You even write poetry to her. Yes, Alberto, now you know it; your brother writes love poems to your wife. He writes them in hiding from me. He thinks I don't know where he keeps them. Señora, I can show them to you, if you don't believe me."

She had not answered, afraid of that disordered and feverish creature, whom one unfortunate word could have thrown into insanity.

"No, Silvia, I am not in love with Maria Griselda," she suddenly heard Fred declare with astonishing serenity. "It is true, however, my whole life has changed since I first met her. Yes, Alberto, it is true, I have written poems to your wife, for because of her, I have at last found my true vocation."

And Fred had begun to recount his first meeting with Maria Griselda:

When, newly married, Silvia and he had arrived unexpectedly at the hacienda, Maria Griselda was not in the house. Eager to meet her at once, they had gone out in search of her, accompanied by Alberto. And that was how one time, in the middle of the forest, he had stayed behind, silent, quite still, almost hearing within his heart the echo of some very light steps. Turning out of the path then, he had parted the foliage haphazardly and . . .

Slender, melancholy and childlike, the end of her riding skirt trailing behind her, he had seen her pass. She was carrying emphatically a yellow flower in her hand as one would carry a golden sceptre, and her horse followed her at a short distance without having to be led by her.

Her narrow eyes, green as the foliage, her serene bearing, her small pale hand! Maria Griselda! He saw her pass.

And through her, through her pure beauty, all at once, he seemed to touch an infinite and wondrous beyond: algae, waters, warm sands often visited by the moon, roots that decay silently growing deeper into the slime, and his own grief-stricken heart.

From the very depth of his being began to issue ecstatic exclamations, music never heard before; phrases and notes until then sleeping his blood and which were now rising and falling triumphantly with his breathing and with the regularity of his breathing.

And he knew of a joy at once solemn and light, without name, without origin; and of a quiet madness, rich in conflicting sensations.

And he understood what the soul is and felt it within himself . . . timid, vacillating and anxious; and he accepted human life for what it is: ephemeral, mysterious, useless, with at the end its magical death that leads perhaps to nothing.

And he sighed, for he knew at last what it was to sigh, and he had to raise his two hands to his breast, take a few steps and throw himself on the ground between the tall roots.

And meanwhile, in the growing darkness they were calling for him, searching for him a long time—did they remember?—he, with his forehead buried in the grass, was writing his first poetry.

Thus Fred was speaking while Silvia was slowly retreating, without a word, growing paler and paler every second.

Then, oh my God, who could have foreseen that gesture in such a spoiled child, at once so pretty and foolish?

Quickly taking possession of the pistol which Alberto a moment before had carelessly laid on the table, she had pressed the barrel to her temple, and without even closing her eyes, courageously, as men do, she had pulled the trigger . . .

Once convinced that all was over, Fred had closed her eyes which remained wide open as if scared, then Rodolfo had picked her up and carried her to that same sofa in front of the fireplace where she used to lie down every evening at that same hour. Zoila had washed her forehead soaked with blood, Anita had thrown over her that ermine cloak, a wedding gift of her rich godmother, laying there always ready to cover up the knees of her indolent, pretty goddaughter . . . And later, oh what a ghastly thing! as a frightened little servant was lighting as usual the fire it was her duty to light every evening at the same hour, Fred had come to sit by the side of his dead wife, had sought her hand which he had picked up and was holding in his own . . . as he had been in the habit of doing every evening at that same place, at that same hour.

And while a great silence had fallen over this beginning of a tragic vigil, she, Ana Maria, had all of a sudden become conscious of the responsibilities it was now time for her to assume. She left the room, went out to meet the peons gathered in front of the house awaiting news, spoke of an "accident," sent to the village for the doctor and the mayor, thank God, honest men and old friends.

Only after she had written several telegrams and dictated them herself over the telephone, did she remember Maria Griselda's existence, Alberto's monstrous attitude . . .

For to what extent that tragic death would harm his wife was the only thing which had concerned Alberto from the very first moment; it was the impulse that made him rush not toward the stricken Silvia but toward the door of his own bedroom in order to shield Maria Griselda from all contact with the tragedy she had so unwittingly provoked.

She remembers as if it were yesterday the pent-up hate that was in her heart as she went up to knock at the door of that room where was that woman she wanted above all to curse. Alberto had opened to her, pale and undone. The humble outburst of gratitude he had shown, seeing her there on the threshold of his room!

"Mother, how good of you to have come! Maria Griselda! she fainted . . . for such a long time . . . I didn't know what to do . . . She's better now, I think. She's resting, sleeping, I don't know, come . . ."

She had entered the room, and approached stealthily toward the edge of the big bed.

Maria Griselda! From the pillows her face emerged serene.

Never, oh never, had she seen eyebrows so perfectly arched! It was as if some slim dark swallow had opened its wings over the eyes of her daughter-in-law and had remained there very still in the center of her white forehead.

The eyelashes! Black, dense, lustrous eyelashes!—in what generous and pure blood they must have plunged their roots to grow with such violence!

And the nose, the small proud nose, its nostrils so delicately open. And the compressed arch of her enchanting mouth. And the frail slender neck. And the shoulders rounded like ripe fruit. And . . .

In order to help her out of her fainting spell, Alberto had just taken off her blouse, her riding skirt.

Oh, her small firm breasts! so close to her body, with that fine sky-blue vein winding between them. And her round smooth hips. And her long, long legs!

"She's opening her eyes!" Alberto had announced suddenly.

Maria Griselda's eyes! Of how many colors was composed the uniform color of her eyes, of how many different greens their dark green? There is nothing more minute, more complicated than a pupil, than the pupil of Maria Griselda!

A circle of gold, one of clear green, another of turbid green, another very black, and again a circle of gold, and another clear green, and . . . together: Maria Griselda's eyes; those eyes of a green, like the moss that sticks to the tree trunks dampened by Winter; those eyes in the depths of which twinkled and multiplied the flame of the candles. All that resplendent water held there, as if by a miracle! With a pinpoint, to prick those pupils! It would have been like the splitting of a star. She was sure that some kind of a golden mercury would have instantly gushed out, like lightning, to burn the fingers of the criminal who would have dared . . .

"Maria Griselda, this is my mother," Alberto had explained to his wife, helping her now to raise herself on her pillows.

The green glance had caught hers and quivered, clearing up by seconds . . . And then, all at once, she had felt a weight on her heart.

It was Maria Griselda laying her head on her breast.

Amazed, she had remained very still. Very still, yet held by some strange, disconcerting, overwhelming emotion.

"Forgive me," a grave voice had suddenly said.

Yes, "forgive me" had been Maria Griselda's first words.

And a cry, out of the very depth of her innermost tenderness, instantly had escaped from her:

"Forgive what? Are you to blame for being so beautiful?"

"Oh Señora, if you only knew! . . ."

She does not remember very well in what terms Maria Griselda had then begun to complain of her beauty as of a sickness, as of a curse.

Always, always it has been like this, she said. Ever since she was a small child, she had had to suffer on account of her beauty. Her sister did not love her and her parents as if to make up to her sister for all the beauty they had given her, had always kept for the other child all their affection, all their devotion. As for her, no one had ever petted her. And no one could ever be happy with her:

Neither Anita who could have been like a sister to her, nor Rodolfo, nor Fred and Silvia, oh poor Silvia! . . . and Alberto who loved her with that tormented, insatiable love that seemed to search for something through her, beyond her, and left her so lonely!

If she only could have had a son! That would have made Alberto feel sure of her. But no, she was chosen, she seemed predestined to a solitary beauty which nature for some unknown reason would not allow her to prolong. And in its cruelty, destiny did not even grant her the small privileges always given everyone else. For her parents did not resemble her at all, or her grandparents; and in the old family portraits, she could never find any common feature, any expression that could have made her recognize herself as a link in a human chain. Oh what loneliness was hers! Such loneliness!

She remembers, she once more remembers that experience, the strangest in her life . . . Yes, she remembers how all her hatred for Maria Griselda, that hatred she had thought invincible and final, had faded away while she was there talking to her. She remembers the warmth, the involuntary gratitude she had felt rising in her at each one of the gestures with which Maria Griselda enveloped her, at each one of the words she spoke to her. It was a kind of mellowness, a kind of intimate satisfaction, very much like that awakened in us by the spontaneous and unreasoning confidence given us by a shy animal or an unknown child.

For how could one possibly resist the pure beauty of Maria Griselda? She recalls having at that moment compared it in thought with the daring, healthy beauty of her daughter Anita, with the blond beauty of poor Silvia . . . Both girls were indeed beautiful but their beauty was like a partly conscious means of expression they might possibly have changed to another, while Maria Griselda's beauty, that beauty seemingly ignorant of itself was never a weapon but a rising tide, something inherent in her and inseparably bound to her being.

Maria Griselda! She can still see her wearing her beauty discreetly and modestly, like a soft hidden lamp that lights with a secret charm her glance, her walk, her slightest gesture, the gesture of sinking her hand into a crystal box and taking out the comb with which she dresses her black hair . . . the gesture of winding that clock she had heard resounding in the corridors as if it were the very heart of the house; that clock that had marked with its relentless tick-tock every second of that disconcerting, far-off tragedy!

◆

THIRTEEN

And you, Anita, proud girl, here you are by my bedside, with this man who does not love you and whom you coerced and won! This man who may betray you some day and confide in some other woman: "I married her because I had to."

To tremble for the past, for the present, for all they might possibly be telling you about Rodolfo, for the slightest change in his attitude which might threaten the happiness you should be building up for yourself, day after day; to pretend, to smile, to struggle for the conquest of a little bit of soul every day . . . Such will be your life.

Rodolfo! Here he is at your side, helping you with the candles and with the flowers, holding your hand as you wish him to.

To go through an endless number of acts foreign to his desire, pouring into them a false enthusiasm while a thirst he knows to be insatiable consumes him from within . . . Such will be his life.

Oh, my poor Anita, such is perhaps the fate of all of us: this evasion, this losing of that real self we cover up with an infinity of trifles having the appearance of vital things!

◆

FOURTEEN

The day burns, hours, minutes, seconds.

"Arise, come!"

"No."

Tired, she longs nevertheless to rid herself of that last particle of consciousness which keeps her bound to life, she longs to let herself be borne backwards, down into the deep and soft abyss she feels there below.

But an unsatisfied anxiety prevents her from ridding herself entirely of that last bond.

Meanwhile the day burns, hours, minutes, seconds.

◆

FIFTEEN

This lean, swarthy man whose lips are trembling as if he were speaking. Make him go away! She does not want to hear him.

"Ana Maria, come back!

"Come back to forbid me once more the entrance of your room. Come back to shun me or wound me, to take life and happiness away from me day after day. But come back, come back!

"You! dead!

"You, in a brief second incorporated into that implacable race, disdainful and motionless, ever watching us exerting ourselves!

"You, minute by minute, drawn down a little deeper into the past. And the live substances of which you were made, separating, slipping away through different channels, like rivers that can never again turn back in their course. Never!

"Ana Maria, if you only knew how much, how much I have loved you!" . . .

This man! Why does he still want to impose his love on her even now that she is in the shroud!

Isn't it strange a love can humiliate, can do nothing but humiliate.

Fernando's love always humiliated her. It made her feel poorer. It was not the sickness which blighted his skin and embittered his character or even his disagreeable intelligence, positive and haughty, that disturbed her as it did others, no, she despised him because he was unhappy, because he had no luck.

In what way, however, did he succeed in impressing himself on her life until he became to her a necessary evil? He knows it very well; by making himself her confidant.

Her confidences! What remorse always overwhelmed her, afterwards!

She felt obscurely that Fernando thrived on her anger, on her sadness; that while she was speaking, he was analyzing, calculating, enjoying her disappointments, believing that they might perhaps drive her on until eventually she would fall in his arms. She felt that with her grievances and her complaints she was feeding the secret envy that man harbored against her husband. For he pretended to despise her husband, yet he envied him; he envied precisely the faults he found in him.

Fernando! All through those long years, so many nights, while facing the terror of a lonely evening, she had called him to her side in front of the fire as the heavy logs in the fireplace were beginning to burn. In vain she had wanted to talk about trivial things. With the flame and with the night the venom mounted, went past her throat, up to her lips; and she would begin to speak.

She spoke and he listened. He never gave her a word of solace, offered a solution or allayed a doubt, never. But he listened, listened attentively to what her children used to call her jealousies, her whims.

After the first confidence, the second, the third would flow naturally, and also the next ones, but then almost against her will.

Afterwards it was impossible for her to control her intemperance. She had admitted him into the intimacy of her life and she was not strong enough to cast him out.

But she did not know that she could hate him until that night when he in turn had confided in her.

The coldness with which he told her of his awakening next to the already inert body of his wife, the coldness with which he spoke of the tube of veronal found empty on her bedside table!

For several hours he had slept beside a dead woman and her contact had not marked his flesh with the slightest tremor.

"Poor Inés," he said, "I still cannot explain the reason for her decision. She did not seem sad or depressed. There was nothing about her that seemed unusual either. Yet from time to time, I remember having noticed her staring at me as if she were seeing me for the first time. She left me. What does it matter to me if it wasn't to go off with a lover! She left me. Love has always eluded me, trickled away from me like water trickling through closed hands. Yes, Ana Maria, neither of us was born under a star propitious to love . . ."

He spoke, and she blushed as if he had treacherously slapped her full in the face.

What right did he have to consider himself her equal?

As in a sudden flash, she had then seen him and seen herself, both sitting together by the fireplace. Two beings outside the realm of love, outside the realm of life, holding hands and sighing, remembering, envying. Two miserable wretches, and because misery is always drawn to itself, perhaps, some day, these two . . . Oh no! Not that! Never, never that!

After that night, many times it happened that she hated him. Yet, she could never escape him.

She tried, yes, many times. But Fernando would smile indulgently at the sudden coolness in her attitude and would accept calmly her vexations, well realizing that she was struggling in vain against the strange feeling that impelled her toward him, knowing that she would very soon again fall on his breast, intoxicated by the need of new confidences.

Her confidences! How often he too wanted to avoid them! Antonio and the children; the children and Antonio. They alone occupied the thoughts of that woman, alone could lay claim to her tenderness, to her sorrow.

How much, how much indeed, he must have loved her to have listened for so many years to her insidious words, to have allowed her thus gently and laboriously to lacerate his heart.

And yet he could not remain weak and humble to the end.

"Ana Maria, your lies! I should also have pretended to believe them. Your husband, jealous of you, of our friendship!

"Why not have accepted this innocent invention of yours if it flattered your vanity? No, I preferred to lose ground in your affection rather than appear credulous in your eyes.

"It was not so much my bad luck as it was my tactlessness that kept you from loving me.

"I see you bending over the edge of the fireplace, throwing ashes on the dying embers, I see you gathering up your knitting, closing the piano, folding up the newspapers scattered about the room. I see you coming to me, disheveled and plaintive:

"'Good night, Fernando. I am sorry to have spoken to you again about all this. The truth is that Antonio never loved me. Then, why protest? Why struggle? Good night.' And your hand would clutch mine in an interminable farewell and, in spite of yourself, your eyes would question me, begging for a denial of your last words.

"And I, envious, petty and selfish, would go away without moving my lips, except to murmur 'Good night.'

"However, much should be forgiven me, for my love forgave you much.

"Until I met you, whenever my pride was wounded, I instantly ceased being in love and never forgave. My wife could have told you that, she who received from me neither a reproach, nor a remembrance, nor a flower on her grave.

"For you, only for you, Ana Maria, have I known the love that humbles itself, the love that is able to resist offense and can forgive offense.

"For you, only for you!

"Perhaps the hour of pity had sounded at last for me, that hour in which we commune even with our enemies, knowing that sooner or later they will be called upon to experience a fate as miserable as our own.

"Perhaps did I love in you that pathetic beginning of decline. Never did any beauty move me as much as yours on its wane.

"I loved your fading complexion which brought out the freshness of your lips and the splendor of your girlish eyebrows as smooth and glossy as a fringe of new velvet. I loved your mature body in which the slenderness of the neck and the ankles acquired by contrast a twofold and touching seduction. But I do not wish to deny you any of your merits. I was charmed also by your intelligence because it was the voice of your sensitiveness and of your intuition.

"How often did I ask you to define more exactly some exclamation or comment?

"You remained silent, angered, assuming that I was making fun of you.

"But no, Ana Maria, you always thought me stronger than I really was. I admired you. I admired your calm intelligence the roots of which went deep down into the concealed parts of your being.

"'Do you know what makes this room so pleasant and intimate? The reflection and the shadow of that tree so close to the window. Houses should never be higher than trees,' you would say.

"Or again: 'Quiet, Fernando, what silence! The air is like crystal. On afternoons like this, I am almost afraid to move. Who knows how far a gesture might lead? Perhaps, if I should lift my hand, I might bring about in some other world the shattering of a star.'

"Yes, I admired you and I understood you.

"Oh, Ana Maria, if you only had wanted to, out of your sorrow and of my misfortune we might have built a friendliness, a life; and many would have enviously gathered around our union as they gather around true love, around happiness.

"If you had wanted to! But you did not even take notice of my patience. You never even thanked me for my kindness. Never.

"You felt resentment against me because I appreciated you and knew you better than anyone else, I, the man you did not love."

Poor Fernando, how he trembles! He can hardly stand. He is going to faint.

A boy shares the fear of the shrouded woman. Fred approaches and puts his hand on the sick man's shoulder, and speaks to him in a low voice. But Fernando shakes his head and somehow refuses to leave the room.

Then she observes how Fred leads him toward an easy chair and bends down solicitously. And the tender past that the boy's presence pours into her heart flows over from this picture of Fernando in the arms of Fred, the favorite son.

She remembers that as a boy Fred was afraid of mirrors and that in his dreams he used to speak an unknown language.

She remembers the summer of the great drought and the afternoon, about three o'clock, when Fernando had said, "Shall we go out to see the land I bought yesterday?"

The children climbed into the carriage without waiting a moment.

Antonio, as usual, declared that it was unpleasant to go out at that hour.

But she, because she did not wish to disappoint Fernando and also in order to make sure that the children would not expose their heads to the sun, had accepted the unwelcome invitation.

"We'll be back long before dinner," she called to her husband as the coach drew away. But Antonio who was leaning back in the rocking chair, smoking, did not even deign to wave his hand.

And thus, silent and hurt, she had had to endure the first ten minutes of dusty plain.

Fred's dogs, that pack composed of all the stray dogs on the hacienda, followed the carriage for a while, then lagged behind, lapping the muddy water of a ditch.

The children moved about incessantly, shouting, singing, asking questions. Oppressed by the heat, she smiled without answering them. And the carriage continued on its way, between a double row of owls gravely poised on the fence posts, watching them go by.

"Uncle Fernando, I want an owl. Here, take your gun and kill an owl for me. Why not? Why not, Uncle Fernando? I want an owl. That one. No, not that one, this one . . ."

And Fernando gave in as he always did when Anita would hang on his sleeve and look into his eyes. For fear of falling into disfavor with the girl, he never failed to gratify her evil desires. He called her "Princess," and used to join her in stoning the little lizards that ran horizontally on the garden walls.

Now he stopped the horses, pressed the gun to his shoulder and took aim at the owl standing on top of a post, watching them confidently.

A sharp report suddenly stopped the immense throbbing of the crickets, and the bird dropped, instantly dead, at the foot of the post. Anita ran to pick it up. The song of the crickets rose again like a scream. And they resumed their way.

On the little girl's knees, the owl kept its eyes open; round eyes, yellow and wet, fixed like a threat. But, undaunted, the child returned the stare:

"It's not quite dead. It's looking at me. Look, it's closing its eyes, little by little . . . Mama, Mama, its eyelids close from the bottom!"

But she was scarcely listening, her attention drawn to a somber violet mass which from the far end of the horizon was advancing toward the carriage.

"Children, put down the hood! A storm is coming!"

It was only a matter of a moment, and a dark wind was sweeping over them dry twigs, pebbles and dead insects.

Once they had successfully passed through it, the old framework of the carriage was trembling all over and the sky was spread out all gray. The silence was so complete that one felt a desire to stir it, as one would stir some very dense water.

Abruptly, they felt as if they had been dropped down to another climate, another time, another region.

The horses were now racing, terrified, across a plain that none of them remembered ever having seen before. And as they dashed forth, they dragged the carriage up to a farmhouse in ruins.

Standing on a threshold without doors, a man seemed to be waiting for them.

"The road to San Roberto, please?"

The peon—was he a peon?—he had boots on and a whip in his hand—looked at them queerly, waited a second, then answered:

"Keep to the right. You'll find a bridge. Then turn to the left."

"Thanks."

The horses again resumed their disquieting run. And then Fred cautiously leaning towards her had spoken in a very low tone:

"Mama, did you notice the man's eyes? They were just like those of the . . ."

Appalled, she had turned to her daughter and shouted:

"Throw away that owl; throw it away I said, it will spot your dress."

The bridge? How many hours did they wander in search of it? She does not know.

She only remembers that at some point, she had ordered: "Let's go back."

Silently Fernando obeyed, and then began that unending return journey during which night closed in on them.

The plain, then a hill, the plain again, and then another hill.

And still again the plain.

"I'm hungry," mumbled Alberto, timidly.

Anita was sleeping, leaning against Fernando, and Fernando's delight was so evident that she tried not to look at him, suddenly overcome by a strange shyness.

Abruptly, one of the horses slipped and fell.

There was a brief silence, then, as if they had suddenly come to life, the children threw themselves out of the carriage, bursting forth with shouts and cries of joy.

At last Fernando spoke. "Ana Maria, I lost my way hours ago," he said.

The children went scampering about in the darkness of the field. "It must have rained here," yelled Alberto sunk knee-deep in a quagmire.

Urged by Fernando the horse straightened itself up, staggered, fell down, and rose again, neighing low.

"Ana Maria, we'd better not attempt to go on. The horses are worn out. The carriage hasn't any lanterns. Let's wait until morning."

"Antonio!" she had moaned, feeling suddenly very weak.

Instantly Fernando clapped his hands to bring the scattered children together.

"We're leaving! We're leaving! And Fred? Where's Fred? Fred! Fred!"

"Here, here," shouted a voice, while at a distance a point of light shone and went out.

"He has taken the flashlight and is playing 'fire-fly,'" his brother explained.

She remembers how she stepped down and rushed angrily into the brambles, stumbling in her high heels.

"Fred, we're leaving. What are you doing there?"

Standing still, facing a shrub and holding up its branches, Fred, as his only answer, had mysteriously made a signal to her. And as if letting her in on a secret, he focused the circle of light on the muddy ground.

Then she saw, close to the earth, an enormous cineraria, a cineraria of a dark, intense, dark-blue color, trembling slightly.

For the space of a second the boy and she stood with their eyes fixed on the flower, which seemed to be breathing.

Then all at once Fred turned off the light and the ghastly thing sank back into the shadows.

Why did that cold-blue image remain with her? Why did her flesh tighten and shiver as she walked back to the carriage leaning on Fred's shoulder? Why did she say softly to Fernando: "You're right. It's dangerous to go on. Let's wait till morning."

As if they had heard an order, the children spread out the blankets. She then, as in a dream, saw her son Alberto drawing close to her, giving Fred a bump on the head so that he could sleep next to her all by himself under the same covering.

Never, no never, did she forget the terror which gripped them when they woke up in the morning.

One more step and all of them that night would have been swept away. The carriage was standing on the brink of a cliff. And down below, enclosed between two slopes, they could glimpse, running black and deep . . . a river.

After that memorable day she had watched over Fred uneasily, without knowing why. But the child seemed unconscious of this sixth sense which linked him to the earth and to that which is secret.

And even when he grew up into an insolent and robust boy she continued to take care of him as if he were a very delicate creature. Only because suddenly and at the most unexpected moment he would look at her with the childish, grave eyes of the mysterious boy of yesterday.

"Don't deny it," Antonio often said to her, "he is your favorite, you forgive him everything." And she smiled. It was true she forgave him everything, even the rudeness with which he freed himself when she would bend down to kiss him.

And how could she forget that little hand which for three days and three nights in a room at the hospital had clutched hers without relaxation. For three days, she had not eaten and for three nights she had only dozed seated beside the bed, tormented by this avid hand of Fred's transmitting to her his suffering, forcing her to sink with him into nightmare and suffocation.

Little by little, without realizing it, she had become accustomed to Fernando's vexatious presence.

She loathed the desire burning in his eyes, yet that spontaneous daily homage in a sense flattered her.

Now she remembers Beatriz, her daughter's most intimate friend. She remembers her pathetic contralto voice. The girl scarcely knew how to sing, but there was in her throat a certain velvety note, at once grave and tender, which when she accompanied her at the piano she could make her prolong at will, amplify, extinguish softly.

She remembers the past Autumn with its moonless nights, strident and clear.

We had barely risen from the table when you, Fernando, hurried out with a cigarette to your lips, hoping that I would follow you and lean by your side against the balustrade on the terrace. But instead I ran to settle myself at the piano. And Beatriz began to sing.

For one, two, three *lieder* you stood waiting for me, then sat down on the iron bench, your back against the vines on the wall.

Far into the drawing room floated the smoke of the cigarettes you kept lighting one from the end of the other without regard for your health.

But your nervousness did not matter to me, no, not at all, nor the dampness the honeysuckle breathed on your shoulders. Tomorrow you would be sick, of course, but was I to blame because you stubbornly insisted on waiting for me in the cold; was I to blame because the music thrilled me a hundred times more than your company?

Many times, immediately after the last chord, I would slip up to my room without waiting for you, denying you even the kindness of a good night.

It never occurred to me to think that this was unnecessary cruelty. I believed your presence or your absence left me totally indifferent.

One night, however, between one song and the next, I peered out on the terrace.

I found no one on the iron bench.

Why had you gone away without telling us? And at what moment? Not even in the distance could be heard the gallop of your horses.

I remember my annoyance. I took a few steps, breathed heavily and lifted my eyes. There was in the sky such a swarming of stars that I lowered them again almost immediately, feeling dizzy. Then I saw the garden, the pastures crudely flooded in a direct, uniform light and I felt cold.

Facing the piano again, a great discouragement came over me.

No longer did the music and Beatriz' singing hold any interest for me. No longer did I find any meaning in anything I was doing.

Oh, Fernando, you had caught me in your snares. From that time on, in order to feel myself alive, I needed your constant suffering by my side.

And how many times during my illness did I not raise myself in bed, for the pleasure of hearing you hovering behind that door I had forbidden to you.

◆

SIXTEEN

Poor Fernando! Now he comes near to her and touches her hair timidly; that long hair of a dead woman, grown longer even that night.

The blinds are suddenly opened. Gray light of daybreak or twilight?

Not a shadow is now possible in the room in that ugly light. Things stand out harshly. Something flutters about heavily among the flowers and alights on the sheet, something abject . . . a fly.

Fernando has lifted his head. At last he will attain what he has so long desired.

But why does he look at her fixedly and not kiss her? Why?

Just then she sees her own feet. She sees them unattractively stretched out and placed there at the end of the bedspread like two things alien to her body.

And because in life she had herself many times attended the dead, the woman in the shroud understands. She understands that in the space of one fleeting moment her nature has changed. She understands that on raising his eyes, Fernando had found a wax statue in the place where the coveted woman was lying.

Those who enter the room now move quietly about, indifferent to this woman's body, livid and remote, whose flesh seems made of a substance different from theirs.

Only Fernando holds his gaze fixed on her; and his trembling lips seem almost to articulate his thoughts.

"Ana Maria, can it be possible! Your death brings me some kind of peace.

"Your death seems to have uprooted in me that restlessness which kept me, a man of fifty, by day and by night, running after your smile, answering your many calls as a woman of leisure.

"No longer on cold winter nights will my poor horses drag between your hacienda and mine that sulky with a sick man inside of it, shivering with cold and bad humor. I will not have to bear any longer the anguish into which a phrase, a reproach of yours, a petty attitude of mine plunged me.

"I needed rest so much, Ana Maria. Your death gives me rest!

"From today on I shall no longer be concerned with your problems but with the work of my farm, with my political interests. Free from your sarcasms and from my own thoughts, I shall lie down to rest several hours a day, as my health requires. I shall find interest in reading a book, in conversing with friends; I shall enjoy my pipe and a new brand of tobacco.

"Yes, I shall again enjoy the humble pleasures that life has not yet taken away from me and that my love for you managed to poison at their source.

"I shall sleep again, Ana Maria, sleep until morning is well along, as those sleep who are not hurried by anyone, or anything. For me, no more will there be any joy but no bitterness either.

"Yes, I am glad. I need no longer defend myself against some new sorrow every day.

"You knew I was selfish, didn't you? But you did not know how far my selfishness could go. Perhaps I desired your death, Ana Maria."

◆

SEVENTEEN

"Arise, come!"

"Where?"

"Come!"

This sudden cold. This sudden silence! A bridge white and heavy with snow through which something, someone, drags her.

And there she is now entering into this other secret corridor through which death draws her to its center.

A gentle rustle. The rustle of the snow that falls and falls, down from the sky, fluttering through the crystalline air with a buzzing of phantom bees.

And now a forest.

She penetrates into a petrified thicket, its trees bristling with water drops, pierced by stars and white frost. Now and again, beneath the gust of a cold eerie breeze, their branches clash with a sound of shattering crystals. Now and again, their trunks creak as if bored from inside their skeleton by icy worms of glass.

And now another bridge that leads to a vast plain covered with snow.

Oh! the sad blue magic of snow! Here the earth seems to have swallowed up the moon, and the immense lighted space sheds a kind of eternal silence.

And she understands that on the stairway leading down to earth, one of the last steps is the step of silence . . .

Oh! to cross that bridge and to stretch out full length on the snow on the other side, so that seconds, minutes, hours, days and years of silence might fall and fall on her face, on her limbs, on her tired heart!

But no, within her heart an earthly image endures intact; a sorrowful longing rebellion against eternity, which impels her to return to the surface of life, to reintegrate herself once more in her shrouded body, stretched out between the two wavering tapers.

Meanwhile, the day burns hours, minutes, seconds.

◆

EIGHTEEN

Quite late in the afternoon, the man she has been waiting for, finally arrives.

As everyone moves away from around her bed, she realizes he is in the house and perhaps in the adjoining room.

For a time, which seems unending to her, nothing disturbs the silence.

Then suddenly, she knows her husband is there, leaning heavily against the side of the door.

They have left him all by himself, lord and master of this death. And there he stands, motionless, gathering strength to face it with dignity.

She then begins to stir the ashes of her memory, and through them recedes to a very far-off time, to an immense, silent, sad city, to a house where she had arrived on a certain night.

At what time? She could not say.

Already, on the train, tired out by the long journey, she had rested her head on Antonio's shoulder. The bouquet of orange blossoms pinned to her muff exhaled a sugary fragrance which made her slightly dizzy and kept her from paying attention to the things her young husband was whispering to her.

But, did it matter? Was he not merely repeating things he had already told her once, twice, and many times?

. . . that she was knitting, doing nothing but her knitting on the glass porch of her house opening out on the garden . . . and that fate had willed that his property, that black, wild forest adjoining her hacienda, did not have a single open path, and as he was going through on a road her father permitted him to use, he had had occasion to admire her, evening after evening, for a year . . . that a heavy knot of black tresses was binding back her head, her little pale forehead . . . that in the Spring, as if to touch her cheek, a tree had reached into the veranda, its branches laden with flowers and bees . . . that it was then easy for him to spy on her; that he did not even need to get off his horse . . . that scarcely had Winter shortened the days, he had gathered up courage and dared to lean his forehead against the windowpanes and, for a long time, out of the darkness of night, he would lose himself in the contemplation of the lamp, of the flames in the fireplace and of that silent girl who was knitting there, stretched out on a long straw rocking chair. Frequently, as if she had felt him there hiding in the darkness, she had lifted her eyes and smiled absent-mindedly. Her pupils were the color of honey and always cast the same lazy, gentle glance. The snow once fluttered over his intruder's shoulders; in vain did it weigh down the brim of his hat and stick to his eyelashes; already hopelessly in love, he had stayed on in spite of everything, taking delight in that smile that was not directed at him . . .

The bouquet of orange blossoms pinned to her muff! Its sickly aroma that made her drowsy was depriving her of the strength to react and cry out to him: "You are mistaken. That sweetness, that laziness of mine was deceptive. If you had only pulled out the thread of my knitting, if you had only undone it, stitch by stitch . . . in each one was entangled a tempestuous thought and a name I shall never forget."

In that cold bridal chamber, when coming out of her first sleep, how many times had she tried to pierce the thick veil of darkness which clung to her eyes?

Her heart throbbed fearfully. The darkness was so black! Could it be she had gone blind?

She stretched out her arms, groping nervously around, ready to jump out of bed, choking, when a fiery hand placed at her breast would draw her back again. And as if it had touched an open wound, the gesture of that imperious hand made her feel weak and plaintive each time.

She remembers how she had lain motionless, hoping at first to avert, then to discourage by her impassivity the amorous assault and how she had kept still, even to the last final kiss.

But on a certain night something happened, something she had never known before.

It was as if from the very depth of her flesh a seething shiver was born which with each caress would begin to rise, to grow, to envelop her in rings up to the roots of her hair, until it clutched her by the throat, cut short her breathing and shook her, casting her finally, exhausted and sobered, upon the disordered bed.

Pleasure! So then, this was pleasure! This quivering, this immense flap of wings and this falling back joined in the same shame!

Poor Antonio, how great was his shock at her almost immediate repulse! Never, never did he know to what extent she hated him every night at that moment.

Never did he know how night after night the frantic girl he held in his arms clenched her teeth with rage trying to ward off the urgent shiver. Never did he know that she was struggling not only against his embraces but against the tremor which night after night those embraces made inexorably rise in her flesh.

It's dawn, she thought, after the maid had opened the blinds on the first morning of her marriage, so scant was the light that penetrated into the cold room.

Nevertheless she heard her husband calling her from outside "Get up."

She recalls, as if it were today, the narrow flowerless garden, carpeted with somber moss and the inky water pool on the surface of which was outlined her own image wrapped in a long white dressing gown.

Poor Antonio, what was he saying? "It's a mirror, a big mirror for you to comb your hair in from the balcony."

Alas, to be forever combing her hair in that desolate dawning light!

Distressed, she looked at the landscape reflected upside down at her feet. Some very high walls. A house of greenish stone. She and her husband as if suspended between two chasms: the sky, and the sky in the water.

"Lovely, isn't it? Look, break it and it comes together again . . ."

Always laughing, Antonio had swung his arm and violently hurled a pebble which hit there below, striking his bride right on the forehead.

Thousands of phosphorescent snakes burst in the pool and the landscape within twisted and broke.

She remembers. Clutching at the wrought-iron balustrade she had closed her eyes, shaken by a childish fear.

"The end of the world. It must be like that. I have seen it."

Her new house.

That uncomfortable, sumptuous house where Antonio's parents had died and where he himself was born, her new home; she remembers having hated it from the very moment she went through the front door.

How different from the pavilion of fragrant wood with its lighted interior inviting one to spy through the windowpanes!

Perhaps it bore some resemblance to her grandmother's old house in the provincial city where she had passed her early childhood, where she had lived in the Winter, where she had come out socially.

But where could be found the billiard room, the sewing room, the garden fragrant with mint?

Not even a single fireplace here. And horror! the mirror in the hall cracked from top to bottom! Large drawing rooms with furniture since always buried in slip covers.

She remembers how she wandered from room to room searching in vain for some corner where she would like to stay; and she would lose herself in the corridors; on the splendidly carpeted stairways, her foot would strike against the brass rim of each step.

She could not find her way, she could not adapt herself.

Invariably, as the evening was beginning to fall, Antonio would settle his wife in the back of the coupé, would draw a fur rug over her knees and lean back at her side.

But never did they reach the house of the paralyzed godmother dozing by the silver brazier. And every afternoon the old survivor of that almost extinguished family waited for them in vain beside the tea already served—and she went down to rest with her people without having known the woman who was to continue her race.

"Let's go tomorrow," the enamored husband would sigh when the coach had scarcely cleared the gate. "Today let me look at you, let me make love to you." And they would drive about at random.

Thus, newly married, she had become acquainted with that immense, silent, sad city.

At the end of its narrow streets, one could always see the steep, craggy mountains. The city was ringed in granite as if sunk in a depression of the high Cordillera, isolated even from the wind.

And she, accustomed to the eternal rustle of the wheat and of the woods, to the clatter of the river striking the stones set up against the stream, was beginning to feel afraid of this absolute and total silence which was causing her to wake up suddenly in the middle of the night.

She was haunted by the image of the world she had seen shattered in the pool on the first day. That silence seemed to her a presage of catastrophe.

Perhaps unknown to all, a volcano was there close by, waiting, watching for the moment of explosion and destruction.

She tried then to seek refuge in something familiar to her, in some gesture, in some memory.

She could no longer recognize her body now dressed in new clothes, her hair badly done. That Zoila, why had she brought her up to be so helpless? Why hadn't she even taught her how to do her own hair?

Day by day, she postponed the desire to open her bags, to look for photographs, for personal objects, for some kind of friendly belonging. The cold, an unprecedented cold, was making her cowardly and without any initiative; her benumbed fingers were not even capable of tying a ribbon.

She would try to remember everything she had left behind, only a few months ago. She would close her eyes trying to evoke her warm room but could only see it in the disorder in which it had been left by her sudden departure; the great reception hall where the crystal drops trembled in the chandeliers and where, with her tresses gathered together for the first time, she had danced madly all one night until dawn, but she could only recall it in that gray afternoon when her father had said to her: "Child, kiss your fiancé." She had then obediently approached this man so handsome . . . and so rich; had stood on tiptoe to kiss his cheek.

She remembered that as she drew away, she had been impressed by the serious face of her grandmother, and by her father's trembling hands. She remembered having thought of Zoila and of her cousins whom she suspected of eavesdropping at the door. She also remembered having suddenly felt the solicitude with which they had surrounded her for so many years.

And now, already, she was incapable of evoking anything but the fear which had come over her from that moment on, the anguish which grew with the days and with Ricardo's obstinate silence.

But how can one undo a lie? How could she say she had married out of spite?

If Antonio . . . But Antonio was neither a tyrant nor the spiritless man she would have desired for a husband. He was a man in love yet sensitive and strong, a man she could not despise.

One day, at last, as if suddenly coming out of his passionate frenzy, her husband had looked at her for a long time—an inquiring, affectionate look.

"Ana Maria, tell me, will you ever come to love me as I love you?"

Oh God, such dignified humility! It had brought tears to her eyes.

"I love you Antonio, but I feel sad."

Then he had continued in the same reasonable, mild tone.

"What can I do that you may not feel sad any more? If you don't like the house, I will change it to suit your taste. If you are bored here alone with me, from tomorrow on we shall see people. We shall give a party. I have many friends here."

But she shook her head from side to side murmuring:

"No, no . . ."

Now, Antonio's tone was odious to her; now, a silent affliction was rising in her. What was he suggesting to her? To organize her whole existence there in that place, as desolate as the bottom of the sea, away from relatives, among new friends and unknown servants?

"Perhaps you miss some kind of entertainment? I will have a pair of saddle horses sent from the hacienda and we will go out in the Park every morning. Ana Maria, speak, tell me: what is it you want?"

She had seized her husband's arm, wishing to speak, to explain, and it was then that a sudden fit of rebellious panic had overridden all argument.

"I want to leave."

He had looked at her intently. Never had she seen anyone turn pale. From that day she knew what it was: an unusual whiteness sharpening up the cheekbone, a motionless face in which only the eyes remained alive, brilliant and fixed.

And so it was that Antonio had come to send her back to her father, for a while.

Alas, one does not sleep with impunity so many nights by the side of a man, young and in love!

She remembered the depression that had come over her as soon as she resumed her former existence. It seemed as if she were repeating gestures which had been drained beforehand of all interest.

She was wandering from the woods to the house, from the house to the sawmill, perplexed to find that there no longer was any purpose in a life she had once thought so complete.

Is it possible that in a few weeks all our dreams and all our habits, everything that seemed to be so much a part of ourselves, could have become foreign to us? Beneath the tulle of the mosquito netting, her bed now appeared to her narrow and cold; and stupid and in a bad taste which humiliated her, seemed the wall paper sprinkled with forget-me-nots that decorated the room. How could she have lived there so long without loathing it?

Then one night she dreamed she loved her husband, with a love that was a strangely, desperately, sweet feeling, a heart-rending tenderness, that filled her breast with sighs and into which she surrendered herself languidly and ardently.

She awoke crying. Against the pillow, in the darkness, she then called very gently: "Antonio!"

If at that moment she had had the courage not to speak that name, her life possibly would have been different.

But she did call: "Antonio," and within her had come the strange revelation:

"One does not sleep with impunity so many nights beside a man, young and in love!" She needed his warmth, his embrace, all the encumbering love she had repudiated.

And she had remembered a wide bed, disorderly and warm.

She had longed for that moment when grasping her tresses as if to retain her, Antonio would prepare himself for sleep. A few light jolts against her hip would then tell her that her husband was detaching himself little by little from life, was slipping into unconsciousness. Whereupon, that temple abandoned by him upon her ungrateful shoulder would begin to beat fiercely as if all the feeling in his body flowed into it and was concentrated there.

A great emotion, a deep respect, was stirring in her as she recalled with what limitless generosity he used to give up his sleep to her.

And she was longing to kiss that trusting temple of Antonio, which was at night the most vulnerable part of his being.

Month after month, his absence—he delayed answering the persistent summons of the family, demanded time to heal his wound—increased her repentance, her thirst for love.

It was early Fall. In her grandmother's house, the first braziers were already lighted when Antonio deigned to come.

She remembers. She arrived exhausted from the hacienda and did not even think to rearrange her tousled hair, her tired face. She went directly into the library where her husband was waiting for her, smoking.

"Antonio!"

"How are you?" answered a calm, unknown voice.

Very little she can recall of that interview which she now knows was decisive.

Now that she is in the shroud, she realizes how very often in one's memory only the inflection of a voice or the gesture of a hand remains as a sign of identification of those events which have weighed most heavily on one's destiny.

How absurd, how remote must have seemed to Antonio at that moment, the passion he had felt for that girl, disheveled and thin, now sobbing at his feet and encircling his waist with her arms.

With her face buried in the shortcoat of a man now indifferent, she was searching in vain for the scent, for the warmth of that fervent husband of yesterday.

She remembers, she can still feel, on the nape of her neck a forgiving hand which nevertheless was holding her off gently . . .

And so it was then, later on and always, always.

They lived where she wished. Antonio built for her a house on the small parcel of land her father had assigned to her as a dowry, but he retained his own hacienda, that dark forest the limits of which extend far down to the extreme South.

With her, his manner was easy, affable, but never did he make any allusion or gesture that could have given her occasion to rehabilitate herself in his eyes. Without any effort, he had released himself from a past to which she had become enslaved. And at night, his embrace was still strong, tender, yes, but distant.

And then she came to know the worst of solitudes; that which in a wide bed seizes the flesh intimately joined with another flesh adored and aloof.

Her first child did not bring back to her either Antonio's love nor his spirit.

Neither sickness nor death ever created between them the bond usually created by sorrow.

But she learned to find a refuge in family, in sorrow; she learned to overcome anxiety by surrounding herself with children, and with small duties.

And perhaps this saved her from new and disastrous passions. This? No.

It was because in spite of everything, throughout her entire youth, she never exhausted the jealousy, the love, and the sadness of the passion Antonio had inspired in her.

He, on the other hand, deceived her so many times!

His life of gallantry came upon her in a wave of anonymous letters and denunciations. For a time, although actually hurt, she remained disdainful, refusing to listen to rumors, shielded in her position as legitimate wife, sure that in it was a choice, a definite place of honor in her husband's distant heart.

Until that day . . .

It was one morning. Delayed while braiding her long hair, she was taking a look from the bathroom through the partly open door at the disorder in the bedroom, when she saw Antonio, back from an early shooting party, come in unexpectedly. Thinking himself alone, he was keeping his hat on his head, tipped over one ear and chewing a twig of boxwood. As he approached the bedside table to lay down his cartridge belt, his boot struck against one of her blue leather slippers.

Then, oh then—she saw and she never could forget it—brutally, almost with fury, he flung it away with a kick.

And in a second, in that brief second, she was rudely awakened to a truth, a truth which might have been concealed in her mind for a long time but that she had avoided facing squarely until now: she realized she was, she had always been, only one of Antonio's many passions, a passion circumstances had shackled to his life. He tolerated her, that was all; he accepted her, champing at the bit, as a consequence of an act without recall.

She remembers. She drew back very gently, trying hard to remain unnoticed. She heard a sigh, then the creaking of the bed under the weight of Antonio's body.

It was a sunny morning and the day gave promise of being radiantly beautiful. Against the stained glass of the windowpanes dragonflies beat in great numbers. From the garden rose the cries of the children running after each other with the sprinkling hose.

A long sultry day ahead. To have to fix her hair, to speak, to give orders and to smile. "Is the Señora sad on such a beautiful day?" . . . "Mama, come and play with us." . . . "What's the matter with you? Why are you always in a bad mood, Ana Maria?"

To have to do her hair, to speak, to give orders, to smile. To have to go through the horror of a long Summer, bearing that kick in the middle of her heart!

She leaned against the wall, feeling all at once very tired.

Her eyes filled with tears which she dried immediately, but already silently others were flowing, then others . . . She does not remember ever having cried so much.

Years passed, years in which she withdrew within herself and became, day by day, more narrow and petty.

Why, oh why must a woman's nature be such that a man has always to be the pivot of her life?

Men succeed in directing their passion to other things. But the fate of so many women seems to be to turn over and over in their heart some love sorrow while sitting in a neatly ordered house, facing an unfinished tapestry . . .

In vain did she exhaust all the instinctive ways of passion to reconquer Antonio: tenderness, violence, reproaches, silence, amorous pursuit. He either avoided her affectionately and dreadingly, or pretended to ignore her gloomy attitudes.

But sometimes when worn out emotionally, it would happen that a momentary indifference made her act naturally, her husband's sympathy and confidence would be drawn back to her spontaneously. He would then invite her to the city, escort her to the theater and to the stores and chat with her about herself, about himself, about the children, about life "which is so sad after all." "You are the most charming woman I have ever known, it's too bad you are my wife, Ana Maria," he used to say to her then.

His very white teeth gleamed in his splendid mouth which seemed so frank, his prodigiously brown eyes enveloped her caressingly. And in order not to stay the course of that distant caress, she would suppress that ardent desire in her to throw her arms around his neck and to kiss his handsome forehead.

It is strange that she always had had to behave that way with all those whom she loved: with Ricardo, with her husband, with her sons.

"One must be wise in matters of love," she would say to herself.

And she had indeed succeeded quite often in being wise. She had quite often found herself able to adjust her own passionate feeling to the moderate and restricted love of others. Trembling with tenderness and truth, she had so many times been able to smile frivolously in order not to frighten away the small measure of love coming toward her . . .

For it would seem that not to love too much might be the best proof of love which can be given to certain people.

Are all those born to love compelled to live as she did, compelled to drift toward self-destruction, to smother minute after minute within themselves all that is most vital in their own being?

"Because of you I suffer, I suffer as from a wound continually reopening."

For years, in an undertone, she had repeated that sentence which had the mysterious power to make her burst into tears. Only in that way did she manage to stop for a few moments the action of that ardent needle lacerating her heart without respite. For many years, to the point of exhaustion, to the point of weariness.

"I suffer, I suffer, because of you . . ." she was beginning to sigh one day when suddenly tightening her lips she remained silent, ashamed. Why should she continue to hide from herself the fact that, for a long time, she had had to force herself to cry?

It was true she was suffering but she no longer felt hurt by her husband's lack of love. The thought of her own misfortune no longer made her feel sorry for herself. A certain antagonism, a mute rancor, was withering and perverting her suffering.

Then the passing years lashed up this antagonism into wrath, converted her timid rancor into a fixed determination for revenge.

And hatred came to prolong the tie that bound her to Antonio.

Hatred, yes, a silent hatred which instead of consuming her, fortified her. A hatred that made her conceive grandiose schemes, almost always ending in petty retaliation.

She still remembers that absurd nightmare of a trip and sees herself pacing up and down the aisles on that train racing through the night less rapidly than her thoughts, toward the city where she expected to catch Antonio by surprise.

Anything, she was ready to do anything, to show no pity or indulgence of any kind. Waves of fury rushed in on her at times with such violence that her throat contracted in a spasm of pain.

She sees herself arriving at dawn at a lonely railroad station. Then comes that humiliating waiting room at the private house of the lawyer whom she had been bold enough to cause to be awakened.

She remembers as if it were yesterday his reproving silence as he listened to her, and the care, the deliberateness with which he measured his conventional reply.

"That is not possible, Ana Maria. Consider that Antonio is the father of your children; that there are steps a lady cannot take without lowering herself. Perhaps your own children would criticize you later. Besides, what difference can this unfortunate woman make to you, this woman who is surely going to regret very soon the indiscretion she is committing . . . Just a moment," he said suddenly. "Wait for me a moment," and he left the room.

No, even though for the rest of her life she never wanted to see him again, no, deep in her heart she has no feeling of bitterness toward the poor man who having known her since childhood had betrayed her plans as kindheartedly and clumsily as her own father would have done.

The fact is that when the door opened again it was Antonio who entered the room, severe and pale.

Accustomed as he always was to win his battles over a woman afraid of the wound that with a single word he had the power to inflict on her, he had already begun to assume a haughty attitude when, trembling with rage, she started to insult him for the first time in their long married life. The abuses poured out of her mouth, first intelligent and sagacious, then so infamous and unfair that suddenly she stopped talking, ashamed and ready to submit to the reprisals of the violent Antonio.

But no, all through a long period of silence he had been watching her attentively.

"How you love me!" he said finally, in an affectionate and aggrieved voice.

And then she had fallen into his arms weeping and calling out his name. Yes, how much, how very much she loved him! . . .

That semblance of a reconciliation was to last only a short time. Quite soon he relapsed into his former indifference and she went back to her hatred as strong as the love which once again she had given him for the space of a few weeks.

Hatred, yes, hatred, and beneath its somber wing she breathed, she slept, she laughed; hatred, now her main purpose, her primary concern. A hatred that victories did not lessen but made fiercer, as if the fact of meeting so little resistance could only increase its fury.

◆

NINETEEN

And that hatred grips her even now as she hears her husband approaching and sees him kneeling down close to her bed.

He has not looked at her. Almost immediately, he buries his face in his hands, half-collapses on the bed.

A long time thus motionless, he seems far away from his dead wife, to be thinking of some painful yesterday, of an infinite world of things.

She feels with repugnance his abhorred head weighing on her hip, weighing there where her children grew and weighed so sweetly. Angrily, she begins to examine for the last time that carefully groomed chestnut hair, that neck, those shoulders.

And suddenly, an unexpected detail strikes her. Very close to his ear she notices a wrinkle, only one, very fine, as fine as a cobweb thread, but a wrinkle, a real wrinkle, the first one.

My God, is it possible? Antonio not immune!

No, Antonio is not immune. That single, imperceptible wrinkle will not be long in sliding down his cheek, where it will very soon divide in two, in four, and finally mark his whole face. Slowly it will begin to corrode that beauty nothing succeeded in altering, and together with it will go crumbling the arrogance, the charm, the opportunities of that cruel, fortunate man.

Like a spring that snaps, like a force that has lost its aim, the impulse which had kept her implacable and venomous, ever ready to lash out, all of a sudden has died in her. She now feels her hatred as something passive, almost indulgent.

As he lifts his head, she notices with amazement that he is crying. His tears, the first she has ever seen him shed, slip down his cheeks without his giving thought to wiping them, taken unaware by the sudden burst of his own crying.

He is crying, crying at last! Or perhaps is he only crying for his youth he feels gone with this dead woman; perhaps is he only crying for those failures the memory of which he was able until now to escape and which are now rising, unavoidable, before this first assault. But she knows that the first tear stands as an open channel for all the others; she knows that sorrow and perhaps also remorse have at last made a breach in that stony heart, a breach through which in time they will infiltrate with the regularity of a tide that mysterious laws impel to strike, to corrode, to destroy.

From today on, at least, he will know what it means to carry a death in one's own past. Nevermore, nevermore will he enjoy anything completely. In each joy, even the simplest—a Winter moon, a festive night—will come a certain emptiness, a certain strange sensation of loneliness.

And as his tears appear, slip and fall, she feels her hatred abating, evaporating. No, she no longer hates. How could she hate a poor being, destined as she herself had been to old age and sadness.

No. She does not hate him. But neither does she love him. And as she no longer loves him and no longer hates him, she feels the last vital bond of her physical structure being released. Now nothing matters to her any more. It is as though neither she nor her past have any longer a reason for being. A great weariness encompasses her, she feels herself stumbling backwards.

Oh, that sudden rebelliousness! That desire which now goads her to rise up sobbing: "I want to live! Give me back, oh give me back my hatred!"

◆

TWENTY

"Arise! Come!"

From far down a road, burning under the sun, huge whirlwinds of dust come to meet her. There she is, wrapped in impalpable sheets of fire.

"Come, come."

"Where?"

"Farther on."

Resigned, she lays her cheek against the hollow shoulder of death.

And someone, something, pushes her down a watery channel to a region of damp woods. That little light in the distance, what is it? That tranquil little light? It is Maria Griselda getting ready for dinner. At the approach of twilight, she has called for a lamp and has had the table set outside on the terrace. At the approach of twilight, the peons have opened the sluicegates for the watering of the lawn and of the three beds of wild carnations. And from the sunken garden a wave of fragrance rises up to the lonely woman.

The night butterflies flutter against the lighted lampshade, brush half-singed the white tablecloth.

Oh, Maria Griselda! Do not be afraid, as on the stone steps the dogs are standing with hair bristling, it is I.

Sequestered, melancholy, thus I see you, my sweet daughter-in-law. I see that admirable, wondrous, graceful body of yours and those long slender legs. I see your jet-black hair, your pale skin, your proud profile. And I see your eyes, those narrow eyes of the same somber green as the moss floating on the surface of forestal waters.

Oh, Maria Griselda! I am the only one who really understood how to love you. For I, and no one else, it seems, was able to forgive you for so great, so unbelievable a beauty.

Now I am about to blow out the lamp. Don't be afraid. I only want to caress your shoulder as I go by.

Why did you jump out of your seat? Do not tremble so, I am going, Maria Griselda, I am going . . .

And a current pushes her once more down the watery channel . . . as far as a gray beach on which she alights and where for an indeterminate length of time she moves about blinded, lost in a heavy fog. Two by two, the high cypress trees of a long avenue then begin to appear and to take shape in front of her as she edges forward . . .

That endless avenue of dark cypresses and those spacious lawns and ponds where the lotus flowers spread their heavy wax petals on the still waters, it seemed to her she has seen them before! It seemed to her that some time in her life, a very long time ago, in that same smooth, golden twilight she had walked by those same bushes of giant azaleas and under this arbor with its pink marble colonnades around which the red vine entwines itself . . .

Sofia! Sofia! Yes, this silent and royal park must be the park where Sofia so often told her she came in her dreams.

". . . Last night again, I had the same dream I told you about, do you remember? that dream of the beautiful park . . . and there I was walking again around the lawns until that silly shower in the early morning woke me up . . . Ana Maria, tell me, does it ever happen to you to have the same dream, over and over again?" it seems to her she is still hearing Sofia pensively asking her on the terrace one of those beautiful moonlit evenings of that Summer already so long past.

Sofia, Ricardo's wife! that elegant, foreign-born girl whom Ricardo preferred to her and eventually married; that girl who in turn treated him with contempt and left him, graciously conceding to him at the time the guardianship of their son, as if everything that came from him meant absolutely nothing to her.

A strange thing, the human heart! She recalls how, though already married herself, the news of Ricardo's wedding in Europe where Aunt Isabel had sent him so as to get him away from her, had distressed her . . . and how one year later though already deeply in love and miserably unhappy with Antonio, the news of their separation had filled her with an unseemly joy. She remembers vividly how nevertheless that morbid curiosity she felt about Ricardo's wife, that kind of painful attraction, had remained with her, making her still linger dreamily before those numerous pictures of her displayed so prominently in their house by Ricardo's sisters.

For what a strange thing indeed the human heart! Those girls who with Aunt Isabel had once worked underhandedly to prevent their brother from marrying her, their childhood friend who adored him, now seemed to be mad about that elegant, frivolous foreigner whom they had never seen and who had brazenly humiliated and forsaken him. They had felt that she, Ana Maria, would not have brought enough money to him, in fact only that small piece of land from her father's hacienda; yet they did not hesitate to sell part of their own lands every time they had to send Sofia the large sums she insisted she must have to resist the temptation to take her son back to Europe with her. Ricardo's son, that big blue-eyed child they called Ricky, whom they entertained and petted in the most ridiculous manner! "Isn't he adorable, it seems he has his mother's eyes, although Ricardo says her eyes are even prettier. He says Sofia's eyes are the color of forget-me-nots . . ."

Poor girls, foolishly they had for years prepared the house every Summer for the visit that brilliant and so much admired sister-in-law promised each year to make. And anxiously, year after year, they had waited for her in vain . . . until that Summer.

Sofia! her friendship with Sofia had lasted only that one Summer! And yet before slipping forever into infinity, it is her sleep, not that of any of the many friends, companions of almost all moments of her life, that in her light shadow this night she is coming to haunt.

Sofia, here she is, here she is! coming toward her out of the depth of that park in which she is walking in her dream! Here she is, coming to her in that same dress and with that same airy step with which she came, at the hacienda, down the avenue of cherry trees that afternoon so long ago . . .

"Here comes Mummy," little Ricky, perched high up in a cherry tree, had called out.

"I hope she's not coming for you so soon!" Fred sitting astride a few branches lower down had protested.

"We only have half this tree to finish," Alberto added, throwing down a handful of cherries into the oilcloth in which Anita and herself were catching on the wing that tempting, perfumed harvest the three little boys were sending down to them from above.

"You see, Mummy, I was right, it was her carriage I heard a little while ago," her daughter was explaining to her, as she stood motionless, under the stress of the strangest emotion, watching that woman moving gracefully toward them along the avenue.

This young woman, so blond, tall and slender, dressed all in white and holding over her shoulder the prettiest little mauve umbrella of gauze in the world; surely, it was the last person she would have expected to see calling for her child as would any other country neighbor.

"Ricardo says Sofia's eyes are the color of forget-me-nots." She had always thought that description stupid and in bad taste and yet now that Sofia herself was there at last, standing before her and holding out her hand smilingly, she had to admit the comparison made by Ricardo was altogether exact and charming.

Yes, Sofia, your eyes encased in those long, blond eyelashes seemed to me of the same timid, tender blue as the celestial forget-me-nots!

I admired your hair of a very pale, almost white gold and your complexion of that delicate rose color that can be seen only in roses. Then I heard your voice so mysteriously soft, the voice of a bee.

"How do you do, Ana Maria. Excuse me for having come in that way and also for calling you Ana Maria but it seems to me I have known you always. Ricardo spoke so often about you in the old days and then Ricky also did continuously in his letters. It seems there is nothing he enjoys as much as coming here . . ."

I could not believe my eyes, my ears. You, Sofia, the elegant one, the bewitching one, the triumphant one, the distant one, you knew of my existence, of my dull little self, and . . .

"I hope you would not mind becoming my friend?" you were asking me now, almost timidly.

That was indeed the last stroke. Would I mind? I literally threw myself in your arms, realizing suddenly that behind the curiosity I had always felt for you was concealed a feeling of real admiration, and in that painful attraction which for so many years had made me linger in front of your pictures was hidden an unconscious desire to know you and to make myself be known to you and be loved by you. Of course, of course, I was your friend; I had always been your friend!

"She looks like the Angel! She looks like the Angel!" Alberto, Anita, and Fred were now yelling, as they surrounded and jostled us in great excitement.

"The Angel! . . . What Angel? . . . they are nice, those children . . ." you laughingly observed, made dizzy in the turmoil.

"The Angel in the picture Mummy has on her bedside table . . ."

"But it's true, it's true!" I myself had in turn cried out to you. "Come, come and see . . ."

And suddenly, as childish as my own children, with them I led you on a run down the avenue of cherry trees toward the house as far as my own room and the bedside table on which stood the naïve Annunciation Zoila had given me on the day of my First Communion. Unbelievable, extraordinary as it seemed, that tall Angel, blondishly pale, standing there very straight with its wings to its sides before a small, frightened Virgin was indeed your very image, Sofia!

And I remember how surprised I was I had never noticed it from your pictures before, and I remember how I told you then the fascination your pictures had always had for me and the curiosity I had about you for so many years and many, many other things . . . Yes, I see ourselves once more in the garden talking, while arm in arm we walked exactly as we are doing now, down the cypress avenue of this beautiful park of your dream.

"Oh, Ana Maria, blessed be my dream, blessed be my dream, if because of it I see you again and can now tell you everything I was not able to tell you that afternoon so many years ago when we were walking together in the garden at the hacienda! . . . No, I was not able to confess to you then the passionate curiosity I too had felt about you ever since that day when two or three months after we were married, Ricardo had begun to speak to me about his childhood and about you. I remember how he was describing to me in a half-nostalgic, half-amused manner, your games and those gay sunny holidays you spent together. I realized with amazement how dull and solitary my own childhood had been in that sumptuous, cold apartment, in that gray building in the middle of a misty city, with no brothers or sisters to quarrel with and parents so very distant from me and so terribly polite to each other . . . And as he told me of your love and of your fault, of your kisses intermingled with laughter and fear even at your first ball, where you had the courage to disappear between two dances and kiss him behind the ferns in the winter garden, I understood that my adolescence in fashionable schools had been without color, without warmth and that, if it had not been for the looks of admiration I had awakened all around me while dancing and for Ricardo's thundering marriage proposal, my first ball would have had no place in my memory . . . And when at last lowering his voice and turning pensive, Ricardo related to me how he had forsaken you, told me of your grief, of your anger and of your recent marriage with someone else whom, according to his sisters, you loved as passionately as you had loved him! the most overwhelming revelation flashed through my mind: I did not love Ricardo! What I had thought to be love was nothing more than the thrill of the success I had achieved over him, mixed with an ardent desire to escape as quickly as possible from the tyrannical indifference of my mother. And all at once I felt in amazement that some day not far distant, I would leave him to go seeking with someone else the same disordered, unselfish love you had lived with him . . . unless perhaps, the son I was already expecting . . .

"Alas, poor Ricky! He did not succeed in waking up my heart! But neither did anyone else ever succeed in awakening it. Yes, Ana Maria, I left Ricardo, I had lovers, I lived dangerously, but nothing came of it, nothing was changed in me. I seemed only to be going through the motions that usually accompany the passionate feelings I was trying to experience. 'How then and why that Ana Maria,' I would ask myself, after each one of my failures, 'could she . . .' Ricardo's description of a very young girl, a little too thin, with chestnut braids carelessly undone, with a childish mouth and somber sulky eyes, coming back to my memory.

"However, Ana Maria, on that day of our first meeting, I did not confess to you the curiosity mixed with envy I too had felt for you or the admiration you inspired in me at that very moment.

"But now, I must tell you . . . that afternoon, I would willingly have given up my jewels, my smart life, my travels, to be able to feel the coming of a storm or enjoy the blossoming of a creeping rosebush, as I could see you do. Or to be able to love and hate with that same intensity which brought tears to your eyes, while you were talking to me! or to be capable of feeling jealousy for a woman to the point of going to some village sorceress to render ineffective through witchcraft the dark beauty of the notorious Marta, Antonio's latest passion."

Antonio! I recall, Sofia, how at the end of the afternoon he had just appeared at the bottom of the outer staircase when, after taking leave of me, you were going down the stairs. In a gay voice from the top of the stairs, I introduced you to each other and watched you exchanging formal greetings while the horses impatiently stamped their feet and little Ricky pulled you by the hand saying it was getting late. Antonio! I can still see him helping you into your carriage with that same pleasant manner he always had with women, even with those who did not interest him. I can still see him, as soon as the carriage had pulled away, coming up to me with a shrug of the shoulder.

"Really! that much talked about Sofia is quite a disappointment after all!"

"Now, you're going to tell me you think she's not pretty!" I protested indignantly.

"Well, just because that princess has deigned to call on you to escape for a few hours from her boring sisters-in-law, you're not going to tell me she's an angel of beauty!"

"An angel! Oh Daddy, of course, she's an angel!" the children at that moment exclaimed, greeting their father. "She's just like the Angel on Mummy's bedside table."

"Not really!" Antonio laughed.

"Why, certainly," I affirmed defiantly, "if you'll only take the trouble to go to our room and . . ."

He interrupted me with a broad carefree gesture which seemed to throw me as well as you, Sofia, far outside the circle of interest that bound his life.

"Well, anyhow, angels with or without wings are not at all my style!"

"Indeed! We all know too well angels are not your style!" I retorted perversely, the image of the dark Marta having suddenly flashed across my mind.

He pretended not to hear and turning to the children:

"Now, hurry up, children! We're going to clear up that grove over there, so we can put in our bowling alley. And we're going to have lots of fun this Summer, you can be sure of that!"

"And they did, Ana Maria, they certainly did! They amused themselves royally that Summer, your children and Ricky too bowling with Antonio in a great uproar of catcalls and laughter . . . while you and I would remain lazily stretched out in the hammocks in the shade of the casuarina trees.

"Those casuarina trees, I remember. You made me notice that the constant murmuring in their high branches was like a far distant echo of the incessant whispering of the waves in the ocean . . . So many things you made me notice that Summer, so many enchanting little things you made me discover.

"For instance, the joy of getting up early in the morning and going to your hacienda across the countryside still covered with dew, steaming under the morning sun, the fun of putting up at a moment's notice a long table under the linden trees to take our lunch there with the children, the excitement of helping them to get their kites going, and basking in the sunshine on the big lawn looking for four-leaf clovers. But above all, above all—you made me discover the thrilling, sorrowful delight it could be to have a husband one might adore, detest, be jealous of . . . a husband with whom one could spend the entire day, go riding with to the mills or wait for him until at last he would come home late, carrying some unexpected present and bringing some of his most odious friends to dinner.

" 'Well, I'm sorry but this evening you won't be able to have your little whispering conferences on the terrace after dinner' . . . I still can hear Antonio declaring to us in a menacing tone . . ."

And yet, Sofia, I can see us again that same evening as on every other evening leaning over the balustrade of the terrace, bathed in the blue light of the summer moon.

We, leaning over into the murmuring night overshadowing the garden behind us in the library, the men smoking and talking politics and from time to time breaking into heavy laughter. And you, whispering in my ear the soft verses of the French poet:—"*Mon enfant, ma soeur, songe à la douceur* . . ." or listening to me, endlessly relating the story of my heart and of my small life!

And there by my side on the terrace in the moonlight night, you so blond, so slender and light, more than ever reminded me at that moment of the Angel of Zoila's Annunciation . . .

For you actually were an angel, the angel sent by God to reveal to me that sentiment called friendship. Friendship, a sentiment in which one never knows solitude as one does in love. Friendship, the sweetness of being able to love without passion, the joy of being able to give without fear!

" 'Well, well, when will you two be through telling secrets to each other? You're worse than schoolgirls, you know?' Antonio toward the end of the evening, suddenly bursting in on the terrace would invariably complain. And we would make fun of him, do you remember, Ana Maria? And he would object because all evening I paid no attention to him even though almost every night he was to see me home at the most impossible hours.

"For you will recall that my sisters-in-law, so jealous of our friendship, would take back their carriage early in the afternoon, trying in that way to discourage me from staying with you so very late.

"But you would arrange to send me back in your own carriage, insisting that Antonio see me home every evening, seemingly because Juan de Dios, the coachman, was afraid of a hold-up though actually more on account of all the things I managed to get out of Antonio concerning his relations with the seductive, dangerous Marta.

" 'How childish the most wicked of men are, after all! Imagine, Antonio not having the slightest suspicion that anything he might say to you would be repeated to me the moment you got up next morning,' you would say to me, half-amused, half-disdainful.

"And I can still see you, Ana Maria, on the terrace waving goodbye to me while the carriage was taking me away with your husband on the dusty road white in the moonlight . . . in that moonlight, one of those moonlit nights that were to separate us forever!"

Forever, yes, Sofia, oh what sadness! How can I explain what it did to me when I happened to learn . . . It was the beginning of Winter, you had just gone back to Europe. Zoila awakened me one morning with the news that Juan de Dios' wife, although she had stubbornly and passionately prepared baby clothes all Summer for a boy, had just had a little girl. "If you would be the child's godmother, perhaps it would make her feel better."

"Surely, surely, Zoila, and besides I can look after the poor little baby. Tell Juan de Dios for me and also tell him I would like him to name her Sofia."

"That, I feel sure, he will never do!"

"And why not?"

"Because he doesn't like that woman!"

"That woman! Zoila, would you mind not talking that way of my best friend!"

"Your best friend, don't make me laugh, Señora, and besides that comedy has been going on long enough! It makes me mad to see you make a fool of yourself on account of that Sofia. All the time saying she's an angel . . . an angel! the worst friend you've ever had, that's what she is!"

"But Zoila, really, have you gone out of your mind? What's . . ."

"What's making me say that? Well, ask Juan de Dios, he'll tell you. He'll tell you how, seemingly, because the tremor in the old bridge made her afraid, your best friend would step out of the carriage every night with your husband and would go across the river on foot where the big stones lay. He will also no doubt tell you of the good long hour he had to spend jumping up and down on his seat, waiting for them on the other side of the river. Yes, more than one hour they would stay at the bottom of the ravine, cooing and kissing in the shadow of the weeping willows. And he is not the only one who saw them. I must tell you doña Carmelita, the washerwoman, coming back to pick up some linen she had left to soak near that point, saw them quite often too and . . ."

"Oh, enough, Zoila, shut up!" . . . I murmured, with throat tight, throwing myself back on the pillows. And I closed my eyes, for the first time in my life, feeling sick, physically sick, from disgust, humiliation, deception . . .

"And yet, yet, Ana Maria, however strange, however absurd and impossible it may seem to you, I swear I never betrayed you!

"Everything Zoila had related to you was actually true: my stepping out of the carriage every evening with Antonio, our long conversations under the willows and our kisses . . . yet, I swear to you, I never betrayed you.

"I can even now see myself leaving the carriage, nervously, as it was about to enter the bridge that first night.

"'Antonio, this time it's going to crumble down. I feel sure!'

"'Nonsense, for years it has been threatening us with falling down!' I hear Antonio protesting laughingly, 'but, if you're afraid, we'll find down below some large stone stretching across the stream! . . .' saying which he was drawing me by the hand down the embankment.

"That little stream you all so pretentiously called a river was shining in the moonlight like liquid silver murmuring mysteriously as it went by, and a sort of phosphorescent moondust seemed to float under the willows.

"'What a lovely night!' I recall having exclaimed as we reached the water's edge. At that moment, Antonio dropped my hand and took hold of my waist. One second later, he had pulled me up to the first of the big stones which formed across the peaceful stream that sort of natural bridge children and young rams sometimes used in their escapades, do you remember? And, in the meantime, we found ourselves stepping across the river, jumping carelessly from stone to stone as would have done the children and the young rams.

"Each stone was different; some were large and ragged and on them it was easy to set down and grip the foot; others were flat and there the water splashed mercilessly; some were round and too smooth, putting one in danger of slipping headlong into the stream. Antonio kept jumping ahead of me on each stone and with much care and good advice helping me to join him afterwards.

"'What an adventure!' I lamented, suddenly discouraged, between two stones, as he was stretching out his hand to help me jump to him.

"'A fine adventure!' was his answer. And before I had a chance to realize what was happening, he had made me fall to his breast and was pressing his lips hard against mine.

"I uttered a cry and freeing myself from his hold, raised my hand. But all of a sudden, seesawing on the extreme edge of the rock, I had to throw my arms around his neck instead of slapping his face. He held me close to him for a moment then when into a burst of laughter. And his laugh was so friendly and free from malice, that I couldn't help starting to laugh too.

"I think the comradeship between him and me started from that moment. At any rate, it was that evening he began to tell me about that part of his life he kept hidden from you.

"Poor Antonio, he never suspected that I was the one responsible for the amazing knowledge of his sayings and doings you unexpectedly disclosed.

"'Those sisters-in-law of yours do a lot of dirty work every time they poke their noses in my house! It seems that Ana Maria now knows I meet Marta "accidentally" at the pastry shop in the village every Saturday' . . . he complained bitterly one evening under the willows.

"'But Antonio,' I answered, trying hard to hide my embarrassment, 'you are very foolish to let yourself be seen in the village with a woman who could never pass unnoticed . . .'

"'Right you are about that! With that figure and those eyes! I often ask her if they were slit with a gypsy dagger at the time she was born . . .'

"'Bah!' I pouted disdainfully, 'I much prefer Ana Maria's eyes!'

" 'Yes, I do too, I do too . . . only, you see, when Marta looks at me with those terrific slanting eyes of hers, I am seized with a frantic desire to beat her up. As a matter of fact, I'm keeping up this affair with her only with the hope that she will give me some day an excuse to beat her up. Yes, frankly, if Ana Maria only knew how much I hate this woman, she would stop worrying about her.'

"I pretended to laugh and allowed him to take my arm and hold me close while he went on talking.

" 'Yes, angel, it seems you're the only one who understands that it's possible to be in love with one's own wife and yet at the same time be crazy about a lot of other women. Really, there are too many beautiful women running around in the world!'

" 'But then it must be you're still in love with your wife?' I inquired ingenuously, having in mind the instructions you had given me that afternoon.

"Antonio remained silent. A light breeze laden with the scent of heliotrope out of some distant garden drifted under the willows. He inhaled it deeply and it sounded like a sigh.

" 'Answer me!' I insisted sternly.

"For another few second he kept silent, then:

" 'I believe Ana Maria is the only woman I've ever loved,' he at last confessed pensively.

" 'But are you still in love with her?'

" 'Well! You seem pretty inquisitive, for an angel . . .' he grumbled abruptly, now himself once again. 'And what's more, you're going to pay for this!' he concluded, bending down to my lips . . . which I let him take for an instant before drawing away and jumping over to the first of the large stones.

" 'Now come, Antonio, we've got to get across. Poor old Juan de Dios by this time must be about ready to become petrified in his seat.'

" 'Here, angel, take hold of my hand, of my shoulder . . . be careful, that second stone is the most difficult of all on account of the moss growing on it . . . and by the way, angel, while we're attempting to get across this river, couldn't you make use of your wings? . . . I've never seen anything quite as clumsy as you are, never . . .'

"And so, Ana Maria, that was all that happened during those moonlight nights which were to separate us forever!

"No, not even the shadow of a guilty desire was in me as I stepped out of the carriage every night with Antonio when came the time to cross the river . . . only the pleasure of feeling inexpressibly young and foolish and proud to be able to draw out of a man such as Antonio his most intimate secrets.

"And I must also tell you an absurd thing: I never felt as close to you as when that tall handsome young man who was your husband held me in his arms making fun of me, as I had seen him do with you . . . And those kisses he gave me and forced me to return under threat of leaving me standing between two stones in the middle of the river or of not telling me his latest prank, those kisses as of a college boy on a holiday which in my youth I had never known, seemed to me to belong to the moonlight night, to that unforgettable Summer and to our own friendship. Yes, Ana Maria, however absurd it may seem to you, those escapades with Antonio were to me like an extension of my day with you, like some kind of a game, almost as innocent as the ones we played with the children . . . 'Don't be afraid,' Antonio would say whenever I lost my temper, as he became more pressing than usual: 'As a matter of fact, you're not my type. I don't like blondes.' And he would draw away somewhat vexed but not in the least spiteful. All women liked him. To be finally spurned by one must have been for him too like some kind of a new game . . .

"Oh, Ana Maria, so many times a desire to tell you everything came over me as I felt sure it would amuse you as much as it did me . . . but the words would choke in my throat whenever I made up my mind to speak to you about it and I could not make myself do it or yet know how to do it. Once, much later on, it seems to me I almost did . . . but it was in a letter, in one of those letters you implacably sent back to me unopened until I had to understand that I must stop writing you, that our friendship had become to you nothing more than a memory, forever sullied . . .

"Oh, perhaps I was reckless, selfish, foolish, Ana Maria! But you made me pay bitterly for it. No, not the slightest opportunity did you ever give me to vindicate myself. Without a word of explanation, you even returned to me the little diamond brooch I had offered you as a gift just before leaving . . ."

Yes, Sofia, I returned to you that lovely little diamond star which had brought me so much joy in the midst of my tears the day you went away. I returned to you also the poems of Baudelaire bound in red leather you had autographed for me and finally all those letters you wrote without getting discouraged for an entire year! I found a way to remove discreetly from my bedside table the little image of the Annunciation for every time my eyes fell upon it, the sight of the Angel would throw me in the same state of uneasiness as had Zoila's revelation of your betrayal.

I tried bravely, as you see, to erase your passage across my life as one erases a bad dream from memory. And circumstances seemed to favor me. Very soon the children stopped talking about you and Antonio no longer "casually" asked for news of you. Ricky whom you had finally taken to Europe for the Winter never came back to your sisters-in-law and they in revolt against what they termed your disloyalty banished your memory forever from their house. And so the years went by . . .

Yes, all seemed to be definitely at an end between you and my heart when, one afternoon in search of a paper which he had misplaced, Antonio got it into his head to go through the drawers of the old writing desk, at the other end of the bedroom.

"Well! here is Sofia!" he exclaimed, suddenly straightening up the little Annunciation which had finally drifted there behind a pile of books. Then: "By the way, do you ever hear from her any more?" he added in the most casual manner, as he pulled up a chair seating himself down in front of the desk.

"No," was my tart reply from the other end of the room.

"Strange," he murmured, opening one of the drawers, "strange how life always ends up by separating us from our friends."

"Friends!" I almost screamed, indignation having made me break in an instant the silence full of bitter dignity I had maintained for so many years in regard to your despicable betrayal. "Friends! I don't believe Sofia was my friend when she left the carriage 'to chat' with you under the willows, every evening you took her home that Summer" . . . My voice broke suddenly, foolishly. A silence followed during which Antonio shook his head sadly, looking through a lot of old papers without seeing them.

"Zoila . . . doña Carmelita, everyone at the hacienda saw you there kissing . . . They told me everything!" I added, angry with myself once I had succeeded in swallowing my tears.

"Yes . . . of course . . . that was to be expected" . . . Antonio muttered, putting aside the papers he held in his hand in order to open another drawer . . . "poor Sofia!"

"Poor Sofia?" I could not help protesting while I moved up to him, "did you say poor Sofia?"

"Why, yes! I said poor Sofia!" he grumbled, looking very much annoyed. "For a few kisses I took from her, she is now treated like nothing at all and you even ignore the great affection she had for you."

"Affection! You don't even know the meaning of the word!"

"All right, all right! you're the only one who knows what affection is" . . . he sneered, pulling out a pile of papers made yellow by time.

"Yes, you're right, I'm the only one!" I asserted defiantly.

"In that case, why don't you get rid of all this!" he almost shouted, throwing violently at my feet the papers he held in his hand. Dazed, I leaned over and before I could even pick them up, I recognized the love notes Ricardo had written me long ago during the brief, stormy idyl of our youth.

". . . and this, and this . . ." Antonio went on, still throwing on the floor with the most complete lack of self-control I had ever seen in him in all my life, papers and more papers . . . letters of Ricardo's and photographs of Ricardo and those drawings of Ricardo's he used to make on the slightest pretext: a horse, a rodeo, our old well, Alicia and me disguised as butterflies, Aunt Isabel with her knitting, the windmill, their first motor car . . .

"But Antonio, I don't understand why those . . ."

"No, you don't understand, you the woman who knows what affection is, you never have understood how much having that individual all the time around me, in my house, in my life, could . . ."

"But I never see Ricardo, never, never . . ." I interrupted vehemently, "and he has never set foot in our house, never! . . ."

"Maybe, but you spend your life hanging around his sisters, around his house. All your life you have done nothing but run around everything that belongs to him, his wife, his child! . . . And there is not a move, not a word from that man you haven't brought in here to poison my life through all these years . . ."

"Oh, Antonio, Antonio . . ." I moaned, completely overwhelmed . . . "you're crazy, absolutely crazy!"

"All right, I'm crazy. You're the only one who can be hurt, be offended by other people's tactless behavior, you're the only one who has the right to be . . ."

At that point he stopped abruptly, as if afraid of a word that could burn him. Then lowering his head over another set of papers, he pushed them away almost immediately with exasperation:

"Besides, I'm getting tired of all this, it's like looking for a needle in a haystack . . ." he concluded, and, pushing back the drawers of the writing desk, he quickly left the room slamming the door rudely behind him.

You're the only one who can be hurt, you're the only one who has the right to be . . . jealous. Yes, jealousy, that was the word pride had prevented Antonio from speaking.

Overcome, dumfounded, suddenly in a flash of intuition I saw how notwithstanding my great love for him, I had never ceased doing many things that could hurt him. "Oh God, oh God! how difficult, how difficult everything is!" I wailed, kneeling down on the carpet. And while I was picking up and destroying one by one all those papers Antonio's anger had thrown in my face like a mighty reproach from the depth of his past and of his soul, the disturbing thought was taking shape in my mind that love is a virtue hard to practice, that one does not love as one wants to, but only as one is able to . . .

Just then, my eyes fell upon the little Annunciation. For the first time in all those years, my glance did not draw away from the Angel. I even dared to look at it face to face, carefully. And while I was looking at your image, Sofia, I could feel my former uneasiness dissipating, vanishing, and some kind of sweetness, of very timid hope, awakening in its place in my heart . . . "Sofia! the great affection she had for you," Antonio had said . . . Yes, after all, why not, even after your betrayal. Had he not proved to me that I had offended him for so many years, he, whom I adored.

It was from that Spring on, Sofia, that little by little I began to allow myself to think of you again as I was taking my walk in the avenue of cherry trees or after dinner on the terrace while relating to Fernando those other conversations I used to have there with you so many years ago . . . "Oh, Fernando, I don't know, I'm not sure, but it seems to me that perhaps I should not have sent back all those letters or broken with her without giving her an opportunity to explain! Perhaps Antonio is right . . . perhaps, for the sake of the great affection she had for me I should have forgiven her silly, insignificant betrayal . . . Don't you think so, Fernando?"

"No, really, Ana Maria, I cannot follow the way you women

talk; you use the big word 'betrayal' and then choose to qualify it with the words 'silly,' 'insignificant.'"

"But Fernando, why not? You can betray, and yet . . . well, anyhow, it is so difficult to love as one should, so difficult . . ."

"Not to betray those we love! you were going to say?"

"That's it, that's it, Fernando . . . If you only knew, the other day I was thinking that perhaps, after all one does not love as one wants to but only as one is able to! . . ."

"Not really!"

"Stop your sarcasm, won't you. What I've just said, I can prove to you. Look at me, for instance, with Antonio. . . ."

"Now listen, Ana Maria, let's not talk about Antonio again this evening! The night is so peaceful, so warm, it is years since we have had a Summer with such a glorious moonlight night!"

"Yes, not since the year Sofia was here . . . listen, Fernando, suppose I write to her now. What would you think of that?"

"I think you should leave the whole episode buried where it is. Why return to what is past," Fernando answered, at the same time trying to suppress a yawn . . . "Besides, I don't want to make you feel badly but . . . I don't believe those kisses or a friendship of six weeks could possibly mean anything in the life of a woman like Sofia. Possibly, by now, she might even have forgotten your name . . ."

"No, not that, not that!" I protested, outraged.

Yet, Sofia, that ironical, impatient statement poisoned my soul with a doubt that paralyzed my heart's outburst toward you . . .

Because, actually, it was on account of that statement that I delayed for years the moment of sending you that letter I wrote in my heart over and over again, right up to the moment of my death . . .

Death! Death! Death! The word she never should have spoken in that fragile world of a dream!

For there is Sofia's beautiful park vacillating, breaking up . . . its avenues falling apart . . . the cypresses going back one by one into nothing.

"Ana Maria, Ana Maria!" Sofia still has time to shout while standing in the midst of the disaster and battling to delay coming up again to the surface of consciousness.

"I must go now, Sofia, farewell!"

And someone, something, is drawing her again into that watery channel down which she had found the way to come to a living woman in order to tell her the things she could not say to her before she died.

Feeling light, she starts once again to slide down into infinity, knowing now that the dead cannot entirely depart until altogether free from terrestrial anxieties and that is why so often they return, giving out signs and messages through things, sounds, or magnetic fluids . . . poor signs, desperate messages, that the living most of the time do not see.

But Sofia, when someone will say to her: "Ana Maria is dead," she will turn pale and ask on what day, at which hour? Then she will remain pensive, realizing that her dream was true, that an almost forgotten friend had come to her in death to tell her she was forgiven . . . And from that day on, with a shiver, she will vaguely begin to believe in God, and in the existence of an invisible, disturbing world stirring there, very close to her own pleasant, frivolous world.

"Let's go! Let's go!"

Down the watery channel, the current pushes and pushes her through a tropical region where the vegetation fades in color as the earth parts into thousands and thousands of serried islands. Beneath the pale transparent foliage nothing but fields of begonias. Oh, the begonias, with their watery pulp! All nature absorbs water, subsists here on nothing but water. And the stream still pushes her slowly on, and with her it drags along enormous tangles of plants on the roots of which travel entwined gentle water snakes.

And over this entire world through which she is gliding in death, lingers and hovers persistently a livid streak of lightning.

The sky, however, is dense with stars. Every star she looks upon, as if responding to her call, whirls swiftly and falls.

◆

TWENTY-ONE

"Don't go, don't, don't . . ."

What cry is this? What lips are searching and feeling for her hands, her throat, her forehead?

The living ought to be forbidden to touch the mysterious flesh of the dead.

For the lips of her daughter caressing her body have interrupted within it that light tingling in its deepest cells, making her again as lucid, and attached to all around her, as if she had never been dead.

My poor child, I have known you having fits of anger, capricious tears, but never would I have imagined such a wild outpouring of grief as now compels you to sob, clinging to me with hysterical strength. "She is cold, hard, even with her mother," everyone used to say. Yet, you were not cold, you were young, only young. Your tenderness toward me was like a seed borne within you which my death has forced, has compelled to mature in a single night.

No gesture of mine ever brought out what my death achieves at last. You see, you see how death can also be an act of life.

But don't cry, don't cry! If you only knew! I shall continue to breathe within you and to evolve in you and to change as if I were alive; you will love me, you will reject me and you will love me again. And perhaps you will yourself die before I become exhausted and die in you. Don't cry . . .

◆

TWENTY-TWO

Now they come, and with infinite solicitude they lift her out of the bed and place her carefully in a large wooden coffin. A spray of white roses falls down on the carpet. They pick it up and lay it at her feet. Then they heap the rest of the flowers on her as one spreads a sheet.

How well does the body mold itself to the casket!

She does not feel the least desire to rise again. She never knew she could have felt so tired . . .

And now, one by one, silent and light, they lean down to her forehead and rest their lips on it, briefly, in a last farewell. Farewell Antonio! Alberto, Alicia, Luis, farewell! Farewell Zoila, and you my father, suffering to see me go before you do! . . . And farewell to you, Fred, who I know would like to kiss me longer. I love you! All is well, farewell!

And now she sees the ceiling sway, slide; her eyes partly open almost immediately perceive another ceiling whitened not long ago; it is that of her dressing room.

An enormous crack caused by the last earthquake makes her

aware later on that she is in the guest room. And thus long rows of rooms go by, showing her familiar angles, moldings, beams. Before each door with mathematical regularity comes a brief pause, and she realizes that it is the extreme narrowness of each threshold that is hindering the progress of those who are carrying her.

Now, sacrilege, they are treading on the blue carpet. Who dared bring it into the hall? And what for? The polished floors suit the style of the house a thousand times better.

There, exposed to the sun and to constant wear, will fade that which not so long ago was her refuge on winter days. For it was only by keeping it spread out in some far-off room, almost always closed, that she had been able to keep the blue carpet intact and blue.

When the storm wind raged outside, her children used to extend to her a strange invitation, one that always aroused the curiosity of strangers.

They would say: "Let's go to the beach." The beach was that square of spongy carpet. There as children they would run to lie down with their toys and later on with their books.

And it really seemed as though cold and bad weather stopped at the edge of that square piece of wool, the violent and joyful color of which brightened the eyes and the mood, so that the hours flew by warmer, more intimate, in the closed room.

Never would she have allowed the blue rug to be taken into the hall. Who dared to take advantage of her illness?

Oh Lord, the waters have not yet closed over her head and things are already changing; life is pursuing its course in spite of her, without her.

All at once, she sees the sky above her.

She realizes at that moment that she is on the landing of the stone staircase leading down to the garden. Here the pause is more prolonged. Perhaps they are gathering strength to go on.

The sky! A leaden sky and the birds are flying low. Within a few hours it will rain again.

What a beautiful end of day, so restless and wet! She had never liked it like that and yet for once she appreciates its harsh beauty; she even delights in the light gust of air that seems to reach out and touch her through the joints of the coffin.

And now she feels herself shaken, lowered, now she is resting on the last step.

Here, it was here, that she used to huddle up to get some sun. For a long time she would remain reclining with her cheek upon the last step, as if to rob it of a little warmth. When her children were little, they also used to press their ear to it insisting that they heard something moving inside, that the stone was ticking like a clock, or beating like a heart. And when it was watered it gave off the peculiar smell that slate blackboards emit when the lessons written on them have been rubbed off.

Once again the sky moves overhead.

Farewell, farewell, my stone! I did not know that objects could occupy such a place in our affection.

The procession has started to move over the lawn. She feels herself jolted in an unexpected sway; it seems as though the coffin is being rocked gently. And suddenly she senses, she recognizes, the strong arms of her two sons supporting it from behind and she guesses that at her feet the left side sags slightly because it is held by her father. Endeavoring to compensate for this weakness, Ricardo zealously lends his support to the right; she knows it.

And she is quite sure that there are many around her and that many others are following her. And it is infinitely sweet to her to feel herself carried thus, with her hands upon her breast like something very fragile, very dear.

For the first time, she feels herself entering majestically into the broad avenue of trees. No longer is she exasperated by the haughty bearing of the poplars; for the first time she notices their foliage undulates and glistens like moving water.

Then come to meet her the massive eucalyptus trees. Along their trunks, narrow slices of bark hang loosely, uncovering stripes of milky, sky-blue nakedness.

With emotion, she thinks: It is curious. I had never noticed this before either. They shed their bark just like snakes their skin in springtime . . .

The wind raises up whirls of dry leaves that hit the coffin as violently as would pebbles. For a moment the sky clears and they can faintly see the still, pale disk of the crescent moon.

Now the procession enters the wood.

And she is beset by a desire to trample down, to crackle beneath her feet, the heavy layer of pine needles that carpets it in a rust iron color, by a desire to lean over, to gaze down for the last time on that great silvery web, nocturnal track knitted patiently on the pine needles by the snails.

Now she is enveloped as in a third shroud by the vapors that rise from the ground, by all the acrid perfume of the plants that live in the shadows.

They have passed the limits of the park. Now they are carrying her across open country.

Over beyond the field of stubble extends the marshy land. A heavy fog floats almost level with the ground, clustering among the rushes.

The pace of the procession becomes slow, difficult, and finally assumes the cadence of a funeral march.

Someone sinks in the mire up to his knees; then the casket lurches violently and one of its sides touches the ground.

Unknown longings stir within her. Oh! if they would only deposit her here, out in the open! She yearns to be left in the heart of the swamp so she could listen until daybreak to the song the frogs make in their throats out of water and moonlight; so she could hear the velvety bursting of the thousand bubbles of the slime. And straining her ears, detect even the sinister humming on the distant road of the electric wires' wail, and perceive the first flapping of wings of the flamingoes among the reeds before sunrise. Oh, if that were possible!

But no, it is not possible. They have already righted her, they are already moving on again.

All of a sudden a wall limiting the horizon reminds her of the village cemetery and of the wide, clear family vault.

And toward it their march is directed.

A great calmness pervades her.

There are unfortunate women buried, lost in cemeteries as big as cities—and horror—even with asphalt streets. And in the beds of certain rivers with black waters there are suicides whom the current incessantly beats over, gnaws, disfigures and beats over again. And there are girls, recently buried, whose relatives impatient to find for themselves free space in the narrow family crypt will reduce and reduce as if willing to erase them completely even from the world of bones. And there are also young adulteresses whom incautious appointments had attracted to lonely places where they were discovered and shot down on their lover's breast and whose bodies were profaned by autopsies, and abandoned for days and days to the infamy of the morgue.

Oh God, there are insensate people who say that once we are dead, we should no longer have any concern for our bodies! She feels an infinite happiness in being able to rest among orderly cypresses, in the same chapel where her mother and several brothers are sleeping side by side; happy that her body should disintegrate there, serenely, honorably, under a gravestone with her name,

TERESA–ANA MARIA–CECILIA . . .

Her name, all her names, even those she discarded in life. And beneath, two dates separated by a hyphen.

As the procession finally reaches its destination, a last gust of wind suddenly breaks off the warble of a fountain. Within the vault, night is about to dim the gems in the stained-glass windows. Facing the altar, Father Carlos, robed in alb and stole, moves his lips, sprinkles unctuously with the aspergill.

◆

TWENTY-THREE

Father Carlos!

A flood of memories overcomes him, as he faces her for the last time.

Peace be with you, peace be with you, Ana Maria; you, mad, capricious, good child! And may God have mercy on you! That same God, apart from Whom you so stubbornly tried to live!

"I have no soul, Padre, I have no soul!" I can still hear you repeating, with a smile, striving not to listen when I said I well knew you had a soul, a tender, pure soul which you did not want to see or acknowledge for fear of having to give up, because of it, all the passions and sadness of this life.

I can still see you a playful, boisterous little girl, ever absent-minded at church, always first in Bible Class. I can still hear you describing vividly the stairway of angels God sent down to Jacob during his sleep, the fiery bush in which he revealed His Presence to Moses, the Red Sea compelled to rise and part in twain in order to open the way for the Chosen People, and the mysterious hand appearing at Balthasar's banquet, tracing on the wall the three words through which the ruin and destruction of Babylon were predicted.

"Oh she's well versed in Bible History because Bible History amuses her," was the complaint made to me then, "but she doesn't know the first thing about her catechism. And in her religious practice she only takes an interest in what she can turn into a game: helping to tidy up the sacristy, blowing out or lighting the candles in the chapel, or collecting images and rosaries . . ."

"Let her be, let her be," I would answer, "all roads lead to God."

I remember the day when at your father's request, I went to the convent, "You will understand better than I do what happened, Father, it appears that Ana Maria said something that . . ."

"I said, when we came out of the sewing class where Sister Carmela had explained to us what heaven is like, I said I did not care to go there because it sounds like such a boring place."

I could not help smiling, as I looked upon the candid, distracted face of very young Sister Carmela, almost a child herself, and putting off telling her not to touch upon such delicate subjects in the sewing class, I leaned over to you:

"Now then, tell me, how would you like heaven to be?"

For a moment, you gave thought, then:

"I would like it to be exactly as it is down here. I would like it to be like the hacienda in summertime when the rosebushes are in blossom, when it is green everywhere, and there are all sorts of birds around and raspberries in the woods . . . I would like also little gazelles in heaven coming to eat out of my hand and also my cousin Ricardo always with me, and we be allowed sometimes to sleep on the moss in the evening, near the spring . . ."

"But, don't you know, it's the Garden of Eden you're talking about, child!" I exclaimed, suddenly pensive.

"Yes, the Garden of Eden, lost by Adam and Eve because of their disobedience!" the Mother Superior who presided at the inquiry, quickly interposed. "And I owe it to myself to tell you that in addition to everything else this child is the acme of disobedience. She is the worst example to others we have had since the two little Rodriguez girls were dismissed a few years ago, as you will recall . . ."

The Garden of Eden! Poor Ana Maria! Your whole life was nothing but a passionate search for that Garden of Eden, lost irretrievably, however, by man! I can still see you as a very young girl, violent and rebellious, giving yourself over to the demons of the flesh and of anger. I can still remember the start you gave that day I drew close to you in the darkness of our little country church where your soul sometimes guided your steps in spite of yourself whenever you felt too unhappy . . . "No, Father, I don't want to go to confession. Don't talk to me about novenas or prayers. I'm here only because it's nice to be here, that's all. And nobody stares at me as they do at home, trying to find out what's happening to me and what I'm thinking about or not thinking . . . No, Father, no, I have no intention of doing my Easter duty this year. Why not? Because I'm angry with God, that's why!"

"And why, may one inquire, are you angry with God?" I asked, edging you in the direction of the parish house, greatly relieved to find that after all you had not yet reached the point of no longer believing in Him.

"He never gives me any of the things I want."

"Perhaps it's because you want things that are not good for you."

"Good for me, good for me! . . ." you grumbled.

Oh, the mean, sad eyes you had that entire year! You had them still that morning before the altar, under your beautiful veil of white tulle, when you were married by me, those eyes! . . But your soul, that poor soul you always denied, it found a way, somehow, to make you run to the cloister looking for me before leaving in your carriage. "Goodbye, Father, pray for me," you whispered in my ear, kissing me nervously.

And I did pray for you. All my life, I prayed for you, calling to God to inspire me with the words that would bring you back to Him.

"Ana Maria, I'm gravely concerned, greatly disappointed, with your attitude."

"But, Father, what attitude? I go to Mass every Sunday. I take the children to Holy Communion myself every Friday. And if I did not attend Anita's Confirmation last Thursday, it was because I was ill, I assure you . . ."

"Those are not the things I happen to be concerned about and you know it very well. You gave me your solemn promise to go on a retreat this Summer . . ."

"But Father, it's not possible. I have entirely too much to do. You don't realize all the work that has to be done in this house with

Alicia and Luis, with Luz-Margarita and the children, all visiting me and now Zoila who's got it into her head to take a vacation, and Antonio who . . . If you only knew how much he is making me suffer at this moment. Oh Father, really, I'm suffering too much, I can't pray, I can't concentrate, I . . ."

"You can concentrate and you can take trouble only for the things of this world. Your heart is brimming with love but only for this sad world."

"After all, wasn't it God who created it? You're not going to tell me now that I should not love His works!"

"Ana Maria, Ana Maria . . ." I bewailed, suddenly overcome. "I don't know really what to do with you!"

"Oh, but I know!" you quickly answered, moving up to sit on the arm of my chair and leaning over me with a teasing smile on your lips. "All you've got to do is to ask God to perform a great miracle; that is, send me His Grace."

"Indeed! what vanity! what colossal vanity! You want God to come to you but you will not take a single step to go out to Him . . ."

"Exactly!"

"Well, frankly, your lack of consideration is most distressing; and besides what do you mean leaning so casually on the arm of a chair in which is seated a vicar of the Church!" I added smilingly when little Anita appeared outside the French windows.

"Daddy sends word to you that we are ready for the bowling match and waiting for you, Father Carlos. Fred and I are going to play on his side. Alberto will be on yours . . ."

"And so will I!" I can still hear you impetuously interpose, "but this time, I warn you, my dear Anita, neither you nor your father will be allowed to cheat as you did so brazenly last time . . ."

"Oh Mummy! when she doesn't win, she thinks it's because she's being cheated . . ." the child quietly explained to me as we went out on the terrace.

How different from that turbulent young woman who could not accept being a loser at games, this woman whom I visited a few days ago on her sickbed!

"Wouldn't you like me to bring here to you the Holy Eucharist, some morning soon? It will help you get well . . ." I insinuated discreetly.

"Yes, why not?" you answered, much to my surprise. "Why not, if it can make you happy!"

"In that case, wouldn't you like to go to confession now?" I added quickly, pretending not to have heard your last remark.

"I would prefer tomorrow . . . the doctor is going to be here in half an hour . . ."

"Half an hour would be plenty of time."

"I don't think so, Father. I must warn you, you have never dealt with a sinner with such a long and important list of sins as I have."

"I see already that bringing vanity even into sin might well be your most important sin," I snapped back.

You attempted to laugh but instead uttered a groan of pain, and dropped back very pale on your pillows. And suddenly I saw you so exhausted, so undone, so unlike yourself that I recall remaining a moment transfixed at the foot of the bed, overcome by an overwhelming sense of doom.

"Don't look at me with eyes like that, Father!" From the depth of your crisis, you still found courage to banter with me while they were rushing to give you an injection and some medicine. "I'm still far from being dead you know . . . so do come back tomorrow will you please, Father, do come back tomorrow . . ."

"She is in pain but the doctor says there is nothing to fear at the moment; he even says she is showing improvement . . ." Alicia was telling me as she escorted me to the front door . . . "But you must come to hear her confession tomorrow, won't you, Father? It's so wonderful she's agreed to do it . . . If you only knew how much I've prayed this day might come! . . . Did you notice the lovely smile with which she said to you: come back tomorrow?"

Yes, indeed, my poor child, indeed I had noticed the lovely smile with which you were at last saying: "Come!" to God, through His humble servant!

The last smile I was ever to see from you!

For your doctor was mistaken and the sinister feeling which had come over me as I looked upon your tired face was in fact a warning from heaven. The carriage from the hacienda was sent for me the following day much earlier than had been anticipated. You had just had a stroke, it was even feared you might not recover consciousness . . . Juan de Dios all out of breath had explained to me.

Yes, indeed, Ana Maria, you were already far out on the great journey when I bent forward over your absent eyes that seemed to be staring at something within yourself! . . . I gave you absolution.

"She had already made her act of contrition yesterday, don't you think, Father, when she agreed to go to confession today . . ." Alicia with a smile full of bliss in the midst of her tears, was saying.

I administered Extreme Unction.

I remained there praying by your side all those long weary hours your struggle lasted, the struggle of your soul. For in that sustained, sinister rattle of death tearing the throat of those in agony, I always can see the determined march of the soul on its hard journey through the body, in its struggle to reach the door behind which You are ever to be found, dear God, waiting in Your Mercy, with Life everlasting . . .

In the name of the Father, and of the Son, and of the Holy Ghost! Peace be with you, Ana Maria, my child, farewell . . .

And to you, my Father, my friend, I say farewell too and also thank you . . . thank you once more, and if I should ever know another death beyond this one, so sweet, so earthly, I'm going through now, I pray that your blessing remain with me to sustain me before God's infinite Justice, Light and Love.

And now she finds herself submerged in utter darkness.

And she feels herself precipitated downwards, precipitated dizzily downwards for what seems to her endless time, as if they had dug out the bottom of the crypt and tried to bury her in the very bowels of the earth.

◆

TWENTY-FOUR

And someone, something, was attracting the shrouded woman into the autumnal ground. And so it was she began to descend down in the mire among the tangled roots of trees, beneath the burrows where little timid animals breathe huddled up; falling at times into deep wells filled with dense silvery dew.

Slowly, slowly, she was falling, avoiding flowers of bone and strange beings with viscous bodies that looked through two narrow clefts; knocking against human skeletons marvelously intact and clean with knees bent up as if once again in their mothers' womb.

She sets foot on the bed of an ancient sea and rests there a long time among nuggets of gold and millenarian shells.

Subterranean waterfalls drag her in their course beneath huge domes of petrified forests.

Certain emanations attract her to a specific center, others repel her violently toward zones of climate more in harmony with her own substance.

Ah, if men only knew what stretches out beneath them, they would not find it so simple to drink the waters of springs! For everything sleeps in the earth and everything rises out of the earth.

◆

TWENTY-FIVE

Once more the shrouded woman flows back to the surface of life.

In the darkness of the crypt, she had the feeling that she could move at last. And she could actually have pushed up the lid of the coffin, arisen and returned, erect and cold, over the paths to the threshold of her house.

But, born of her body, she was feeling an infinity of roots sink and spread into the earth like an expanding cobweb through which was rising, trembling up to her, the constant throbbing of the universe.

And now she desires nothing more than to remain there crucified to the earth, suffering and enjoying in her flesh the ebb and flow of distant, far distant tides; feeling the grass grow, new islands emerge, and on some other continent, the unknown flower bursting open that blooms only on a day of eclipse. And she even feels huge suns boiling and exploding and gigantic mountains of sand tumbling down, no one knows where.

◆

TWENTY-SIX

I swear it. The woman in the shroud did not feel the slightest desire to rise again. Alone, she would at last be able to rest, to die.

For she had suffered the death of the living. And now she longed for total immersion, for the second death, the death of the dead.

◆